C NUNDRUM

CONUNDRUM

A Novel by

Tom Bleakley
Marcia Lange

ABSOLUTELY AMAZING eBOOKS

ABSOLUTELY AMAZING eBOOKS

In Honor and Memory of Paul Lynch

Acknowledgements

Very special thanks to Anne Lynch , Paul Lynch, Marilyn Creavy, and Kyle Ann Robertson who traveled every step of the way with us on the writing of Conundrum. Without their thoughtful efforts this work would not exist. Special thanks to Bob Diforio, our literary agent, whose confidence and patience in our writing efforts has been inspiring and gratifying.

Finally, a very special thank you to Mary Ellen Bleakley and Ronald Legere whose understanding and valuable advice always provides a solid foundation for our writing efforts.

Tom Bleakley
Marcia Lange

CHAPTER 1

June 2018

"It's about sex, but it's not about sex."

Katie Hornsby woke up with this brainteaser on her mind. On a phone call yesterday, a potential client had made the puzzling statement, and its meaning intrigued her. And why would someone travel all the way from New York to Detroit to meet with her? She was still clueless as she looked at Sylvia Anderson, the attractive woman seated across the desk from her.

"You wanted to see me because it's about sex?"

Sylvia nodded. "I need legal advice regarding a colleague of mine, Dr. Arnold Pittsburgh. While we worked together, he forced me to have sex with him for more than two years. He used his power to manipulate and abuse me, and he threatened to prevent me from furthering my career. When a younger graduate student came along, he took up with her and tossed me aside like a piece of trash. He ruined my career and stopped me from becoming successful in my field. Everything in my life that I worked so hard to achieve was destroyed by what he's done."

Sylvia placed a thick file on Katie's desk, and Katie noticed a bulging brown paper grocery bag at her feet. Sylvia's furrowed brow, bloodshot eyes, and meager attempt to frame that lovely face with a smile told Katie she needed to proceed gently. This was a troubled woman sitting across from her.

Katie leaned forward. "Okay, but you also said it's not about sex."

An awkward silence hung in the air before Sylvia nodded and continued. "Dr. Pittsburgh heads the department of biochemistry at Filmore University in New York. My friend told me I should stay away from New York lawyers and that a woman lawyer would give me the best representation. He said, 'Go see Katie Hornsby in Detroit. She's the best lawyer in America.' That's why I'm here."

1

Katie blushed. Who in the hell in New York would be saying that about her? She gestured for Sylvia to continue.

Sylvia hesitated as tears appeared in the corners of her eyes. "This is so difficult to talk about."

Katie kept a box of Kleenex on hand for times like this. She slid it across the desk, next to Sylvia's thick file. "Take your time and tell me what happened. And I want to assure you that anything you tell me is one hundred percent confidential."

Sylvia took a Kleenex and wiped her eyes. "That's what Eric said."

"Eric?"

"My friend who told me about you. Eric Ohmert. That's why I'm here."

Katie knew Dr. Ohmert from a case she'd had last year involving a drug allegedly used in a murder. He'd been extremely helpful but couldn't appear as an expert witness in that case due to a conflict of interest. She had added him to her list of drug experts for future consultation. She smiled at Sylvia. "Any friend of Eric's is a friend of mine." She was stretching the truth a bit, but she wanted to help her client feel at ease.

Sylvia took a deep breath and shrugged. "I was a doctoral candidate in biochemistry at Filmore University, and Dr. Pittsburgh was my mentor and boss." She slumped in her chair. "I feel so guilty, bringing this whole thing up now. I have been condemning myself, thinking that I must have deserved it. For years, I have been going over it in my mind, and I can't help thinking that it must be my fault. He made me confused about my role in the relationship. But I am not confused about what he did to me."

Katie studied Sylvia's face. It was difficult to guess her age, but stress had taken its toll. "You've mentioned the sex, but why do you also say it's not about sex?"

Sylvia took another deep breath. "It all started when he first announced his claim about HIV and AIDS."

"Claim?"

"He claimed that he was the first to discover that HIV causes AIDS. He was so proud of this discovery."

"How long ago was that?"

"I forget the exact date, but sometime in 1985."

Damn, Katie thought. She hadn't even been born yet but remembered reading about Dr. Pittsburgh in school. He was the Jonas Salk of the AIDS crisis in America and, therefore, world-famous. She asked, "Didn't he receive a Nobel Prize?"

Sylvia nodded. "Yes, in the early nineties." Another awkward pause. "From the first day I began working with him, I tried to be the best doctoral candidate he'd ever had. Dr. Pittsburgh was well known in the program for being difficult, if not impossible. Most of his doctoral students quit before completing their studies. I was thrilled to have the opportunity to study with him, and I worked hard to show him that I was different than all the others."

Katie did the math in her head. Sylvia was at least thirty years older than her, and she looked pretty damn good. She hid her body under a cheap, oversized top and coordinating slacks with orthopedic-type black shoes. Dress her up in a Ralph Lauren silk suit and a pair of pumps, Katie thought, and she would turn men's heads no matter their age, no matter who they were. Katie hoped she looked that good when she was her age.

Katie asked, "Why is his claim regarding HIV important?"

"He jumped the gun on making the claim that the virus causes AIDS. His ego got in the way, and he didn't wait until I had finished the laboratory research to verify our original findings. Other research labs in the world were looking at AIDS at the same time, and he wanted to make sure his claim would be first. Without consulting me, he submitted the unfinished work for publication and listed me as co-author. When my research didn't confirm the original results, I immediately brought it to his attention. He ignored my warning. It's always necessary to repeat a study, sometimes several times, to confirm original findings. If the results are the same, it's more likely to be valid." Sylvia held up the index fingers of each hand as she said the word "valid." "I must sound like I'm giving a classroom lecture, but you need to know what happened."

Katie nodded and gestured for her to continue.

3

Sylvia took a deep breath. "As cumbersome as it may seem, this is how science advances. Dr. Pittsburgh reported the results of our original findings as though we had confirmed them. My subsequent research did not do that. Do you understand?"

"I do understand." Katie had faced the same issue in several of her recent trials. She knew how important it was for scientists to repeat and verify their research. It was a basic scientific requirement. In a trial, research that has not been verified by subsequent research cannot be admitted into evidence. Verification was a big deal.

Sylvia hesitated again. "At the time, I was shocked. I didn't know what to do. When I asked him how we were going to handle the new findings, he gave me an ultimatum. He told me that if I wanted to have a career, I needed to keep my mouth shut, that he was not going to be publicly humiliated by my stupidity. I started to argue back, and he became angry. He jumped out of his chair and moved toward me with a look of disgust on his face that I had never seen before. He grabbed my arm, pushed me up against the door, rubbed my breasts roughly with his hands, and pressed his body to mine. I begged him to stop and told him he was hurting me."

She reached for another tissue, dabbed her eyes, took a deep breath, and continued.

"I was so scared. I thought he was going to hurt me. He put his hands on my shoulders and pushed me to my knees. I struggled to break away from his grip, but he had me pinned against the door so I couldn't move. I pleaded with him to let me go, but that just seemed to fuel his anger. He forced me into giving him oral sex. When he was done with me, he said he owned me and the only way for me to get ahead was to do whatever he wanted whenever he wanted. He then told me to get out of his sight and not come back until I could validate the original study. He said that there were others who would gladly take my place in his program and I should be grateful for the opportunity to continue to work with him."

She stopped and blew her nose. "From then on, he made me do whatever he wanted. He constantly threatened to ruin me if I ever mentioned to anyone that the original research had not been validated. This went on for more than two years until a new student entered his program, a girl younger and prettier than me. He turned his attention to her but warned me all the time that I was indebted to him and needed to make myself available whenever the fresh young replacement wasn't around. He constantly warned me to keep my stupid mouth shut about the lack of validation and not discuss our private relationship with anyone or he'd see to it that my career was over. What choice did I have but to do what he wanted?"

The man was an obnoxious piece of trash. Katie couldn't imagine working in such a hostile environment. Regardless, this was a classic "she said, he said" situation, unless there was any way to confirm Sylvia's accusations. If it was going to be only her word against his, there was probably nothing Katie could do for her legally. But she would love the opportunity to kick this scumbag in the balls.

She asked, "Did you ever tell anyone about this? A good friend? A minister or priest? Unless you have some way of proving that this happened, it makes it very difficult to pursue litigation."

Sylvia nodded. "I have proof, but I'd rather show you than tell you." She reached down, picked up the bulging brown grocery bag, and then stood and emptied its contents on the desk. She gestured at the pile, a shameful look on her face. "These are Hallmark day-at-a-time monthly calendars. I knew that what he was doing to me was wrong, so I kept meticulous details on the sex stuff."

She picked up one of the calendars and handed it to Katie. "Scan through, and you'll see what I mean. On each date that he forced me to have sex, I taped a pubic hair."

Was she freaking kidding? Katie tried her best to keep a professional expression on her face as she riffled through the calendar. Sure enough, many of the dates had curly black snippets of hair fastened with Scotch tape. Her first thought was to remember to wash her hands as soon as Sylvia was gone. She asked, "Whose hairs are these?"

"His, of course – Dr. Pittsburgh's. I needed proof of what he was doing to me. Why would I use my pubic hairs? That would be insane. There are twenty-six monthly calendars in there. We had sex fifteen to twenty times each month, 442 times altogether."

Control yourself, Katie. Don't laugh, she silently urged herself. This was funny as hell.

Sylvia said, "I can see by the look on your face that you think I'm weird. But remember, I'm a research scientist. I write things down when they happen. I make notes and keep anything that documents my research. That's who I am and what I do, so keeping these calendars was natural for me."

She sat down, and her eyes welled up with tears again. She cried for several moments.

Katie waited until Sylvia regained her composure. Then she asked, "Why now, Sylvia? After all these years?"

"When I heard the news about Weinstein and Epstein and all the brave women who have come forward with their stories, I knew I had to do something. No one should have to endure the shame and humiliation I have my whole adult life. He needs to be stopped. That's why I'm here. Not only about the sex, but about Dr. Pittsburgh and his research. He needs to be exposed for the fraud that he is, and I want to be the one who takes him down." She sat up straighter and squared her shoulders. "I want to fuck him over so badly that he never hurts anyone else like he's hurt me. I want them to take away his Nobel Prize."

Wow, Katie thought. She was right. It was not just about sex. It was about power: men feeling empowered to use women as their personal slaves. She'd had a couple of similar experiences and knew how Sylvia felt. She had recently finished the trial of a murder case, and the judge had made sexual advances towards her. When she'd rejected him, he'd started calling her in the middle of the night, wanting to talk about sex. When she'd refused to engage in sex-talk with the jerk, he'd gotten so mad that he'd made some decisions in the case that had sent her client to prison for life. Many men were like that, stuck in the past, with Woody Allen, Bill Cosby, and Harvey Weinstein as role models: powerful, dirty old men with an assumed sense of entitlement.

However, Katie knew she had to look at Sylvia's situation from a legal standpoint, and her initial thought was that the passage of time was a big problem. Someone could have the best case in the world, and if too much time had elapsed, if the statute of limitations had run out, nothing could be done. She had to explain that potential right away.

"Sylvia, you're a brave woman. I do understand what you've gone through, and I'm glad that you came here to see me. However, there is a legal issue that might make it impossible for me to help you. The time for you to bring a lawsuit may have run out. Any lawsuit would have to be filed in New York because that's where this all happened. Right now, I don't know what the law on the statute of limitations is in New York. Because of the current Me Too movement, some states have extended their statute of limitations in cases involving coerced sexual abuse, and New York may be one of them. If it is, I'll certainly try to help you."

Sylvia looked at Katie. "Anything you can do for me would be greatly appreciated, and I understand there may be some problems. Would the statute of limitations also apply to telling the world that Dr. Pittsburgh is a fraud? His claim about HIV and AIDS overshadowed the role of endocrine disruption as the real probable cause of AIDS. Awareness of endocrine disruption as a major health problem was set back for years, all because of his lies."

Katie sat back. "Endocrine disruption? What is that?"

"It's a simple concept, complicated but simple."

"Like a potential lawsuit about sex but not about sex? Sylvia, you are an enigma."

Sylvia smiled at Katie for the first time in the interview. "Endocrine disruption simply means that some outside agent, like a drug, chemical, or virus, can damage various endocrine systems in the body. It becomes complicated because there are several endocrine glands. For example, the thymus, thyroid, adrenals, sex organs, and pituitary are all endocrine glands, and they all secrete hormones of different types that help maintain normal bodily functions. It's now well known that hundreds of chemicals can cause endocrine disruption. It wasn't so well known back when all this was happening, but a

7

study that came out about the same time as Dr. Pittsburgh's showed that endocrine disruption was a more significant factor in causing AIDS than a virus."

Katie had a lot to learn, she thought. "I don't know the answer to your questions, but I'll certainly research your legal options." Rule number one for a trial lawyer was to never promise a client that you could do something when you didn't know whether you could or not – a rule most lawyers violated all the time.

Sylvia gestured at the thick file she had placed on the desk. "This is a copy of all the pertinent research. It includes my bench notes and the paper that Dr. Pittsburgh published that made him famous. You will see that he included me as co-author of the published paper. He used this against me by warning me that he would say I was the one who falsified the data if I ever tried to claim the original results hadn't been validated."

"I'll need some time to review these documents and think about how I can help you."

Sylvia nodded. "If you need anything more, you can call me anytime, day or night."

They stood and shook hands, and Sylvia left the office. Katie headed to the restroom to wash her hands. She wished she could take a shower instead – she felt dirty all over.

She walked down the hall to the office of Gary Newton, her senior partner, and said, "Got a minute? You won't believe the interview I just had with a prospective client."

Gary was a doctor and a lawyer. Five years ago, he'd hired Katie on the spot after she'd passed the Michigan bar exam with the highest score anyone had ever made. Since she'd started with the law firm, she'd had some successes in a couple of big pharmaceutical cases and made a lot of money for the firm, the lifeblood of young lawyers seeking to enhance their legal reputations. Last year Gary had made her his partner and renamed the firm "Newton and Hornsby." Katie often thought about how proud her father would have been of her.

She told him the details of her interview with Sylvia. He asked a few questions and took notes. "This is a fascinating story, Katie. I think you should talk to Alex." Doctor Alex

Hartley was one of the leading toxicologists in the country and the founder of one of the largest poison centers in the US, located at Detroit City Hospital. He was Gary's best friend and testified quite frequently as an expert witness in the firm's cases involving claims against the pharmaceutical industry.

Gary continued. "Alex did some research in that same area of science a long time ago and knows a lot about the subject of endocrine disruption. He took a lot of heat for it at the time, and our firm helped him out of a jam. It was my first year with the firm, and I worked on his case. After you finish with Alex, I can fill you in on any details he may have forgotten. You did know that he and I were medical school classmates, didn't you?"

Katie laughed. "How could I forget? As I remember, you were number one in his class, and he was number one in your class. I'm still trying to figure that out."

Gary laughed back. "We old guys do tend to exaggerate."

"I'll call Alex right now."

As Katie stood and turned to leave, Gary said, "Don't throw those calendars out. Maybe the client is a little strange, but she's right. They could turn out to be helpful."

Katie went back to her office, called Alex, and filled him in on Sylvia's visit. When she finished, he said, "C'mon over. I've got a story to tell you, and it will take quite a while. I'm on call today, and the odds are good I'll have enough time to fill you in."

Forty-five minutes later, Katie was seated across from Alex in his office at Detroit City Hospital.

He scratched his chin. "Let me see. Where should I start?"

She smirked, "Why not at the beginning?"

He smiled at her. "So that's why lawyers get the big bucks. You get right to the point."

They laughed.

Katie took a legal pad out of her briefcase and nodded. "I'm ready when you are. Fire away."

"What I'm about to tell you may seem radical, but it's my humble opinion that AIDS is not caused by HIV, a virus, but by endocrine disruption, a force we knew little about at the time your client was working with Dr. Pittsburgh. We now

9

know that the effects of endocrine disruption are more widespread than we ever imagined back then."

Endocrine disruption? Second time today. "Hold on. I'm writing as fast as I can. You say this widespread force is endocrine disruption? My client talked about it and explained what it was, but I'm still a bit confused. Can you explain it again for me?"

"That's what I'm going to tell you right now. I'm going to cover a lot of ground, so maybe you should forget about taking notes and just sit and listen instead."

"Sounds good to me. I was starting to get writer's cramp." She put her pen down and wrung out her hand.

"It all began in July 1984. I was in the third year of my internal medicine residency at Detroit City Hospital."

CHAPTER 2

July 1984

It was a steamy summer day in Detroit. Alan Gosten said to his partner, Paul, "It's hot as hell in here. This place stinks like a bar with your constant smoking. Why do you have to smoke so much?"

Alan could feel the clammy wetness of his shirt sticking to his skin. He went to the refrigerator, grabbed the milk carton, and gulped down the cold, comforting drink. He wiped his mouth with the back of his hand as Paul approached and pressed up against him.

"I'm sorry. I can't. I really don't feel well," Alan said as he pulled away. He sat down at the kitchen table and continued drinking from the milk carton.

"You're acting like my fucking ex-wife. She complained about feeling sick all the time, too. What the hell is going on with you?"

Alan looked at Paul, a pained expression on his face. "It's this feeling I have that I can't seem to shake no matter how hard I try. I feel terrible most of the time."

Paul sat down at the table and searched his pockets for another cigarette. He lit it and blew his first exhalation into Alan's face.

Alan was stung by the action. "Please don't smoke. You know it makes me nauseous. I can't believe you said those things to me about your ex. Do you really think I'm making this up?"

~ ~ ~

A week later, Alan was admitted to Detroit City Hospital, which served the city's poor and uninsured and also served as the main teaching facility for the local medical school. The next morning, Alex Hartley stood at his bedside with an entourage of residents, interns, and medical students during morning rounds. Dr. Hartley was in his third year of an internal medicine residency and the chief resident of the Department of Medicine at the hospital. Half of the four

11

hundred beds were set aside for medical cases; the rest were for surgical patients. As chief resident, he was responsible for overseeing the treatment of all of the patients in the medical wards. Additionally, he supervised the medical students, interns, and other medical residents on their rotations through the medical service. He nodded at the medical student who had performed the physical examination of Alan on his arrival. "Tell us about Mr. Gosten."

The medical student checked his notes and cleared his throat. "This young man presents with a complicated medical picture. He has lost a great deal of weight, thirty pounds, over the past six months. He came in yesterday evening with the clinical picture of pneumonia, but we haven't been able to identify any bacteria in his cultures. So far, he's shown no response to aggressive antibiotic therapy, although it's too early to tell if that will help. His breathing has become progressively worse since his arrival. Dr. Hartley had me order a complete battery of blood studies on his arrival, and this has been repeated every day. We received the first results of the tests this morning."

Dr. Hartley hesitated. Was it wise to discuss the next topic in front of the patient? He turned and looked at the group. "Mr. Gosten's white blood cell count, given his clinical status, is exactly the opposite of what I expected. His lymphocyte count is low, and his T-cell lymphocytes are practically non-existent."

He pointed at one of the interns. "Can you tell us what the significance of T-cell depletion is?"

The intern blushed and stammered in accented English, "T-T-lymphocytes are the k-killer cells of the immune system. They seek out and destroy bacteria, viruses, and malignant cells that may be present in the bloodstream. No T-cells means no ability to fight infection."

Dr. Hartley was surprised and pleased that the young man, who had arrived from India less than a month ago, knew about T-lymphocytes.

"That's right." Dr. Hartley looked at Alan and chose his words carefully. A couple of nurses on the ward had mentioned that he had a boyfriend who visited him. They'd described the boyfriend as a flamboyantly obvious homosexual. Dr. Hartley had recently read a brief report in a medical journal about a small group of homosexual men in the San Francisco area who had died from a rare form of cancer, Kaposi's sarcoma, and he had to take this into consideration with this patient.

He looked at the group huddled around the bed. "I strongly suspect an underlying oncogenic process, but we haven't been able to identify anything specific. We'll keep him loaded with antibiotics until his immune system takes over. And we'll continue to monitor his blood picture daily."

He patted Alan on the shoulder and said directly to him, "When we finish rounds, I'll come back and talk with you."

The group moved on to the next patient.

~ ~ ~

At the end of rounds, Alex retrieved Alan's chart from the nursing station and walked back into the young man's room. He sat down in the chair next to the bed.

"Let's see if we can find out what's going on. I'm ordering some additional tests." He scanned through the chart. "Your white blood count and T-lymphocytes did not improve this morning. They haven't changed since you were admitted, but that was only yesterday, so I'm not surprised."

"What does oncogenic mean?" Alan looked at Alex. A glaze of perspiration coated his skin.

Alex hesitated. He couldn't mince words with the young man. "I thought you might ask me that. It means that your body is acting like it has some type of cancer."

"I was afraid of that." Alan closed his eyes.

"There's always a reason for results like these. We'll find out why with additional testing."

"Thank you, doctor." Alan smiled, turned toward the window, and attempted to hide the tears that streamed down his face.

Alex looked at him for a long moment, closed the chart, and left the room. This was the worst part of being a doctor, not being able to help someone and not knowing why.

~ ~ ~

"I wish I knew what in the hell to do for him," Alex muttered to Ted Wallace later that afternoon while they took a short break in the doctors' lounge. Ted and Alex had been friends for a long time, since elementary school. At thirteen, Ted's family had moved away, and he'd gone to a different high school, but the two of them had stayed in touch for quite a while. They'd lost contact again when they'd gone to different colleges but had renewed the friendship in medical school. Ted had been one year behind Alex in school and was a second-year internal medicine resident at Detroit City.

Alex continued. "Funny thing. This really nice kid is sicker than hell. I'm afraid he's in deep trouble. His boyfriend, however, is a faggot. The nurses say he's the worst they've ever seen. He swings his ass when he walks, can't pass a mirror without checking himself out, and is impeccably dressed in the latest fashion."

Ted stared at his coffee cup. "You do realize they are born that way, don't you? They really can't help it."

"Oh, come on, Ted. I can't agree with you on this one." Alex shook his head. When had Ted become such a bleeding heart?

~ ~ ~

On rounds the next morning, Alex was back with the group of medical students and interns in Alan's room. After a medical student brought the group up to date on Alan's condition, they left the room while he hung back.

"Any answers yet?" Alan looked pathetic. His hospital gown was soaked with perspiration, and his skin color was not good.

Alex reached out and put his hand on Alan's shoulder. "I can't tell you anything new yet because we still don't know what's causing your problem."

"I appreciate everything you're doing." Alan reached up and placed his hand on top of Alex's, who quickly removed his, reached for the intravenous bottle, and pretended to study the label.

Alan hesitated. "Does it bother you that I'm gay?"

"Not at all. I'm a doctor. I can't let something like that influence the way I treat my patients."

"I thought you'd say that." Alan smiled. "At least someone around here treats me like a human being."

Alex shrugged and walked to the doorway. "Is there anything I can do for you? Can I get you anything?"

"My partner, Paul, takes care of everything, but thanks."

"What about your family? Do they know where you are?"

"They don't know." Alan looked ready to cry.

"Would you like me to speak with them?"

Alan blinked, and a tear rolled down his cheek. "That would really upset Paul. He's in charge of my medical decisions and needs."

"Regardless, I'm certain they would like to know where you are and how you're doing."

Alan took a deep breath. "My dad threw me out of the house years ago and refuses to speak to me."

Alex sat down in the chair at Alan's bedside. "I'm sorry to hear that. Even if your father is mad at you, I'm sure your mother would want to know how you're doing."

Alan's face brightened. "Do you think so?"

"I see it happen all the time." Alex told the lie with greater conviction than he felt.

Paul pranced into the room and glared at Alex. "Am I interrupting something?"

Alex stood, and ignoring Paul, he looked at Alan. "I'll see you tomorrow." He walked out of the room.

Paul glared at Alan. "That son of a bitch was making a move on you."

"Don't be silly. He's my doctor. I really like him. He's very professional and caring, and he's easy to talk to."

"Bullshit. I could see the way the two of you looked at each other."

~ ~ ~

Alex walked into Alan's room early the next morning. It was empty. The bed was freshly made, no sign of Alan's presence. He went to the nursing station to retrieve his chart, and the head nurse looked up. "I'm sorry, Dr. Hartley. He died early this morning."

Alex was stunned. He'd seen many people die during his brief medical career, but it bothered him more when it was a young person. It didn't make him feel any better that he didn't know what had killed Alan and that he'd not been able to help. "Has anyone notified the family?" he asked the ward clerk.

She shook her head and handed him Alan's chart. He sat down and reached for the phone to make the call.

A man with a gruff voice answered, "Who's this?"

"This is Dr. Hartley at Detroit City Hospital, calling about Alan Gosten."

"No one lives here by that name," the man barked into the phone and hung up.

Alex dialed again, and the line was busy. He wrote the phone number down on a piece of paper and put it in his pocket to try again later. Maybe someone else would answer the phone next time.

When he tried the number again later in the afternoon, a pleasant-sounding woman answered.

"Is this Alan Gosten's mother?"

"Yes. Who is this?"

"I'm Dr. Hartley from Detroit City Hospital. I have some bad news about your son." He heard the sudden, sharp intake of her breath.

"He's dead, isn't he?" She started moaning.

"Yes, ma'am, he is." Alex's eyes moistened as he listened to the gut-wrenching sounds that could only come from a grieving mother.

"I knew something was seriously wrong with him. I've worried about him his whole life. The last time I saw him, he'd lost so much weight. I knew that he was very sick, or worse, had a terminal illness."

"Why's that, ma'am?" Alex was intrigued by her response, especially her comment about being worried about her son his whole life.

"A mother knows her child even before he is born. Alan was very special to me." She paused to stifle a sob. "When I was pregnant with him, I almost lost him. The doctor had me flat on my back for six weeks and put me on special hormone medicine so I wouldn't lose him. He was so different from my other children. He always seemed so vulnerable. I know this doesn't make any sense, but it was a feeling I had. He knew

16

exactly how I felt about everything. He always knew the right things to say, even when the other kids would laugh at him for saying it. And now my special boy is gone. You knew that he was gay, didn't you?"

"Yes, I did."

She wept gently. "My doctor told me I'm taking the same medicine now for my menopause that he prescribed for me then, a female hormone. I've always thought that medicine made my son gay. I don't know why, but I've always thought it did. I didn't take the drug with my other pregnancies, only Alan, and my other children are not gay."

~ ~ ~

The conversation with the young man's mother intrigued Alex. He'd learned over the years to honor red flags whenever they surfaced during the treatment of patients, particularly if drugs of any type might be involved, and the mother's comment fits into that category. Hell, it was more than a flag. It was a big red banner waving back and forth that basically yelled, "Pay attention." During his pediatric rotation in medical school, one of the legends in pediatrics, Dr. Paul Woolley, had presented a lecture to his class and emphasized how important it was to listen to the mother when treating a child. Dr. Wooley had been emphatic that no one would know a child better than the mother of that child. Alex had carried that piece of wisdom in his thinking ever since. Alan's mother's comment was a clue, a potential piece of a puzzle that might help him understand what had caused the young man's death.

There had recently been a buzz in the medical literature about an increasing number of deaths in the gay community of San Francisco, but there was nothing but conjecture about the causes of what was happening. The men were dying from pneumonia or of a fairly rare type of cancer, Kaposi's sarcoma. Both conditions were rarely seen, so it was assumed that the diseases were limited to gays. Inflammatory reports in the press and nasty statements by politicians had started an anti-gay reaction in the public based on fear. In the last year, reports of gay men being attacked simply for being gay frequently appeared in newspapers.

It was Alex's responsibility to complete the chart in Alan's file, and he sat at the nursing station and finished his notes on Alan. He thought for a moment about whether he should include Alan's homosexuality but decided against it. Other than what was already in the chart, there wasn't much to add, but he did include the mother's comment regarding the hormone medication during her pregnancy, and he placed the file in the basket where it would be sent to medical records.

Alex made a mental note to go to the medical library and brush up on information regarding the use of hormones in pregnant women. In 1971, problems had been reported in young women whose mothers had taken hormones during pregnancy years before. He wondered if there was any literature on what this estrogen did to male offspring. If there was, he hadn't heard about it.

Since starting his internal medicine residency, one of his main interests had been the effect of drugs on the immune system. The body's immune system produced antibodies, blood proteins, to attack molecules the body recognized as foreign, usually from cancer cells, viruses, and bacteria. But the immune system could also produce antibodies against drugs given to patients. Antibodies directed against a particular drug could attach to the drug and completely neutralize its effects. Unfortunately, there was no way to know in advance which drug was likely to trigger such a reaction in patients. The problem seemed almost intractable, but new information was coming out every week.

Alex sat in the medical library and looked for articles about hormones taken during pregnancy and the impact on the immune system of users or their male offspring. The literature on the subject was limited to the impact on female offspring. Daughters of mothers who had taken diethylstilbestrol – DES – during pregnancy had developed a rare form of vaginal cancer in their late teens that had previously been reported only in women in their sixties. These cases and their connection to DES had been first reported in 1971, and hundreds of lawsuits had been brought against the DES manufacturer. Several trials of these cases had resulted in a lot of publicity.

Alex left the library, intrigued by the possibility that the estrogen taken by Alan's mother during pregnancy might be involved in the cause of the disease that killed the young man. It didn't make any sense to him that only female offspring would be affected.

CHAPTER 3

During hospital rounds, Alex recognized the thin, pale man in the next bed while a medical student told the group about a patient in the adjoining bed. It was Paul, Alan Gosten's boyfriend. Several months had gone by since Alan Gosten's death. The time had treated Paul badly. He'd lost a great deal of weight, and his face had a mask-like rigidity.

Paul noticed Alex looking at him and waved. "I remember you." He coughed convulsively and strained to turn on his side. After the failed attempt, he stared blankly at the ceiling.

Paul was suffering from the same problem that had killed Alan, Alex thought. Something strange was going on. He thought back to his conversation with Alan's mother and felt a pang of guilt as he recalled his commitment to look further into her son's death. Other than his cursory look at the medical literature, he hadn't done a damn thing.

After rounds ended, Alex went back to the nursing station and pulled Paul's chart. The course of his illness was identical to Alan's – same symptoms, same lab results, same prognosis. Paul was going to die soon. Most interesting was the result of Paul's bone marrow test. His bone marrow was virtually devoid of T-lymphocytes. Like Alan, his body had no ability to fight infections. Alex had a thought. He called and spoke to Paul's mother, who confirmed that she had taken hormones during her pregnancy with Paul, just as Alan's mother had done. He decided to consult with Dr. Abe Slotkin, the hospital's chief of pathology.

He went to Dr. Slotkin's office in the basement of the hospital. The doctor was well known around the hospital as an interesting character. There was a joke that anyone could identify his last two or three meals just by looking at his shirt. Dr. Slotkin claimed to others that his preoccupation with his work relieved him of any obligation to concern himself with such a trivial thing as personal appearance. True or not, when

Alex walked into his office, he saw that the front of the man's shirt was a smorgasbord of stains.

Dr. Slotkin sat at his desk. "Hartley, what brings you here?" He gestured for Alex to sit.

Alex moved a pile of papers and medical journals from the only available chair in the tiny cubicle and sat down. The small space reeked of garlic. The huge man must have eaten spaghetti recently, as his wrinkled white shirt was spattered with tomato sauce, as well as other indecipherable stains. Dr. Slotkin fiddled with a nail clipper and chewed compulsively at a pesky cuticle. Gray locks of hair curled over his ears.

"I've seen two unusual cases in the past year, and I thought I'd ask for your advice." Alex told him about Alan and Paul.

"Let's go grab a cup of coffee," Dr. Slotkin said, jerking his bulky frame out of the chair and heading for the door. Alex hurried to keep up.

As they stepped into the crowded elevator, Dr. Slotkin turned to him. "Hartley, I think something strange is going on. I've autopsied four other cases like yours within the past six months. I'll pull the materials, and we'll take a look at them. These findings are highly unusual for someone in this age range." Everyone on the elevator listened quietly.

As they stepped away from the elevator, a young woman in a white lab coat trailed several steps behind them. When Alex noticed her, she said, "Excuse me. I couldn't help but overhear your conversation. My name is Ingrid Kubilus. I'm an epidemiologist."

Dr. Slotkin stopped and turned to her. His eyes sparkled through his squint as he leered at her, inspecting her from head to toe. "An epidemiologist? You can treat my epididymitis any time." He broke into a raucous laugh.

Ingrid shuffled her feet and kept her eyes on the ground. Alex reached past Abe to shake her hand. "I'm Alex Hartley."

She smiled. "Pleased to meet you, Alex. I attended your presentation on viral pneumonia a few weeks ago. It was excellent." She ignored Dr. Slotkin.

"Come on, you two. Let's sit and talk." Abe pushed between them with the backs of his hands and strode through the cafeteria door.

Alex looked at the young woman. Abe's lewd comment had upset her, and her discomfort was obvious. She set her jaw and followed him to a table in the corner of the large room. Once seated, she said, "What you were discussing in the elevator about these unusual cases interests me very much."

Dr. Slotkin peered at her over the top of his bifocals. "What does epidemiology have to do with our conversation?"

She looked at Alex. "This cluster of cases would make a good study."

"Tell us more, little lady," Dr. Slotkin leaned forward and gestured for her to continue.

Ingrid stiffened and refused to look at him. She again turned to Alex. "Since the early 1960s, statistical and mathematical principles have been applied to study groups of people. It was in this way, for example, that cigarette smoking was shown to be a cause of lung cancer."

"Assuming you accept that cigarettes cause cancer is true," Abe interjected.

Ingrid hesitated and frowned at him. She didn't back down, though. "Our group in Ann Arbor found a highly statistically significant relationship between smoking and lung cancer. I do not know of anyone who has looked at all the available studies who would conclude otherwise." She glared at Abe.

Alex admired her tenacity.

Abe broke eye contact first, and she continued. "What we do is compare a group of people who have a disease with a group of people who do not have it. We look at all kinds of parameters, and it's amazing sometimes what can be determined. It's particularly useful, like here, when the disease is rare. Two groups are compared using statistical methods. So, the whole significance of doing an epidemiological study – especially in a situation such as this – is to use carefully constructed data to trace possible causes of a disease that might take much longer using traditional methods."

This interested Alex. He trusted numbers. Not all numbers, but some. Elections were a good example of what he didn't trust. It seemed as if every election was decided before people even voted. The public was told in advance who was going to win because some pollsters had talked to ten or twenty people on the phone and projected those few numbers into a prediction of the winner. Half of the damn time, they were wrong.

Then there were the studies that proved young women developed blood clots because they were taking birth control pills. Alex had thought it was nonsense when he'd first heard about it. Women had had problems with blood clots long before the pill had come on the market. But now, fifteen years later, he knew the causal proof was substantial and accepted by every responsible scientist because of epidemiology.

Ingrid continued. "This kind of information can provide valuable clues as to what is causing something to happen. It is most helpful when the cause is not clear. Over one hundred years ago, an English doctor traced an epidemic of cholera back to a contaminated well in London. By careful questioning, he determined that those who used the well became sick. It was the first classic epidemiologic study and served to show how valuable this kind of information can be."

"Excuse me for interrupting, doctor," Abe said, "but this cigarette-smoking business is complete and utter bullshit. Hell! Lots of people who smoke never get lung cancer, and lots of people who don't smoke do get lung cancer. I think it's a bunch of malarkey."

"I understand your skepticism, doctor," Ingrid replied icily, "but the statement that smoking causes lung cancer is what we call a probabilistic statement. All it means is that smoking increases the risk that cancer will develop. No one is suggesting that smoking causes all lung cancer or that smokers will always develop a problem. Smoking is a definite risk factor that increases the risk of lung cancer in men by seven times. In women, the risk is increased twenty-two times."

As Dr. Slotkin leaned forward to say something, but Ingrid cut him off. "It's like when you're driving down the street. If you travel forty-five miles per hour, your chances of having an accident are far less than if you are traveling at a hundred miles per hour. The risk is less the slower you go, and it's greater if you drive faster."

"My old Volvo won't go a hundred miles an hour." Dr. Slotkin leaned back in his chair and rested his coffee cup on his protruding belly. "But what do I know? Shit happens. Time marches on. Maybe there's something to all this. Hell, I'm such a skeptic I still believe CBS faked all those pictures of guys walking on the moon."

He laughed at his own joke. Alex was grateful for the eased tension between the two. It gave him time to think. Maybe this was a way to approach the problem that Alan's and Paul's deaths had presented. It certainly wouldn't hurt to try. Besides, Ingrid was sexy as hell. He wasn't the only one to think so. He noticed that two interns had checked her out as they'd passed by the table.

He looked at Dr. Slotkin. "What could it hurt, Abe? Why don't we have her set up an outline about how to look at this?"

Dr. Slotkin shrugged, giving a non-verbal okay.

Ingrid smiled and lowered her eyes. "I'll get on it right away and contact you shortly with a study design for the two of you to think about."

She stood and walked away.

"Great ass, Alex, my boy," Abe whispered as they watched her move away from the table. On that point, Alex couldn't disagree with the old fart.

CHAPTER 4

2018

The day after Katie saw Sylvia, she placed a call to Dr. Eric Ohmert. Despite her claim about their friendship, she had met him only once. She thought he looked like Mark Twain, and she'd kidded him about it at the time. They'd gone back and forth, trying to outdo each other with silly jokes.

When he answered the phone, she said, "Is Mark Twain there?"

"Hello, Katie. This is Mark Twain. You're calling about Sylvia, right?"

"How did you guess?"

"I know these kinds of things. It's in my DNA, but enough chitchat. What do you need from me?"

Katie hesitated. "I assume you sent her to me because you think she has a legitimate complaint, not about the sex stuff but about Dr. Pittsburgh's research, such as it is."

"She didn't tell me about any sex stuff. Sounds juicy, though. Maybe you can fill me in some time. But what we talked about was the validity of the HIV and AIDS research the two of them did."

"Tell me your thoughts on that issue."

"I've always thought the evidence on HIV causing AIDS was a bit shaky. There are some basic principles that, in my opinion, still haven't been met to satisfy the issue of causation. But when Dr. Pittsburgh's report first came out, we didn't know enough to guard against overly hasty application of preliminary science reports." He hesitated and then said, "Of course, you know all that stuff. That case last year you consulted me on had this issue in spades."

Eric was referring to the criminal case Katie had handled in which a forensic toxicologist claimed he had identified the presence of the drug succinylcholine in embalmed body tissues eleven months after the death of a young woman. Her client, the dead woman's husband, was charged with murder. For more than forty years, scientific research had irrefutably shown the drug disappeared from the body within minutes after being administered. Her client was found guilty by a jury after the judge allowed the questionable evidence to be admitted after she'd rejected his sexual demands. So, Katie did know "all that stuff."

"So, Mark Twain. Can you help me with Sylvia's case? She thinks highly of you."

"I'll do whatever I can to help. I've known her for a long time, ever since I finished writing *Huckleberry Finn*. Sylvia's a good person."

Katie laughed. "As you already know, that other book you wrote, *Tom Sawyer*, was my favorite as a kid. Back to the topic at hand, Sylvia mentioned endocrine disruption. Are you familiar with that?"

"You'll need to study up on the thymus gland. It's an endocrine gland that makes T-cell lymphocytes, which are important in understanding AIDS. T-cells help keep the body free of bacteria and cancer cells. The diagnosis of AIDS is made on the basis of T-cell levels – actually, specific types of T-cells, CD-4 cells. A healthy immune system normally has a CD-4 count ranging from five hundred to sixteen hundred cells per cubic millimeter of blood. When the CD-4 count is lower than two hundred, a person is diagnosed as having AIDS. AIDS patients die of either overwhelming bacterial infections or cancer because they do not have enough CD-4 cells to destroy the bacteria or cancer cells."

Katie laughed. "I guess you are familiar with endocrine disruption. But I'm confused about why this has anything to do with Sylvia's case. Maybe I have to go back and read Tom Sawyer again. The answer is probably right there in the book."

Eric chuckled. "HIV isn't the only thing that damages these cells. Drugs, like DES, can do the same. Today we know a lot more about endocrine disruption than we did back then."

"As soon as I decide if I'm going to take the case, I'll get back to you. I've got some preliminary digging to do first. By the way, thanks for the compliment. Sylvia told me what you said about me."

"I meant it. Call me anytime, Katie."

"Why should I call you Any Time? I thought your name was Mark Twain."

He laughed. "You don't give up, do you? There's a lot of comedians out of work. Don't give up your day job."

CHAPTER 5

Early April 1985

Dr. Bruce Olmstead was the chief of staff at Detroit City Hospital. Alex reported directly to him. Evelyn, Dr. Olmstead's secretary, had mentioned several times to Alex that Dr. Olmstead had been watching him for a long time. According to her, Dr. Olmstead liked what he saw, and he had started giving Alex teaching assignments usually reserved for attending staff. Alex relished these opportunities and did his best not to disappoint the man.

"You have the potential to become a great teacher, Alex," Dr. Olmstead said after Alex had made a particularly complicated presentation during a weekly staff meeting. A surgical patient had become jaundiced for no apparent reason, and Alex had been the only one to recognize that the surgeon had inadvertently sutured the common bile duct closed.

Dr. Olmstead took him by the arm. "Let's go back to my office."

He escorted Alex to the suite of administrative offices on the main floor of the hospital. Evelyn waved a handful of messages at Dr. Olmstead and gave Alex a wink and huge smile as they passed her desk. Dr. Olmstead took the messages, gave them a cursory glance, and tossed them on his desk. He gestured for Alex to sit in one of the chairs facing him.

Dr. Olmstead ran his hand through his stylish gray hair. "Hartley, I want to make you an offer I trust you're smart enough not to refuse. I want you to stay on as a permanent staff member at the end of this year. You can spend next year working on your pharmacology studies, and after that, you can set up a poison center for us inside the emergency room."

Alex was speechless. The man was a giant in the field of pharmacology, the study of drugs. He and Dr. Robert Ratner, another staff doctor, were the co-authors of the standard

31

textbook of pharmacology used in medical schools and hospitals throughout the US.

Alex opened his mouth to speak, but Dr. Olmstead cut him off with a wave of his hand.

"We offer many opportunities for research, teaching, and private practice, Alex. Our teaching program is second to none, and I want you to be part of it."

The phone rang. Dr. Olmstead answered, listened, and then placed his hand over the mouthpiece and said to Alex, "My secretary has all the paperwork ready for you. See her on your way out."

He dismissed Alex with a wave of his hand.

As Alex left the room, he glanced at the wall covered with memorabilia. The various awards and framed photos of Dr. Olmstead with three US presidents impressed the hell out of him. As he walked to Evelyn's desk, she looked up and handed him a sheaf of papers. "Doctor wants you to fill these out." Another huge smile. "I told you he liked you. Congratulations, Dr. Hartley."

Alex glanced down and saw the words "Staff Application" in bold letters on the top page.

Evelyn continued. "He wants you at his house for a cocktail party tomorrow evening. The invitation is there with the papers. Be there at eight o'clock and make sure you get that application back to me as quickly as you can."

~ ~ ~

The next evening, Alex put on his best suit – his only suit, truth be known. He laughed to himself as he thought about how his life circumstances had changed so dramatically in the past two days. He drove out to Birmingham, an upper-class suburb of Detroit, and into an opulent neighborhood, and he found the doctor's house after making several wrong turns on the winding streets. He was nervous. The palms of his hands were damp, and his mouth dry as he walked to the Olmstead's front door.

A servant in a tuxedo, holding a tray of champagne flutes, opened the door, ushered him in, and offered him one of the flutes.

Alex looked around and spotted Dr. Olmstead standing with an attractive woman in the center of the packed room, and he walked over.

"This is the young man I've been talking about." Dr. Olmstead shook his hand vigorously and nodded at the woman. "Alex, my wife, Mary Elizabeth."

She smiled. "Alex, make yourself comfortable. The bar's over there, and I'm sure you will find someone you know."

The couple turned as one and disappeared into the crowd. Alex stood in the center of the room, awkward and uncomfortable. He wasn't used to fancy parties like this. He went to the bar, got a drink, and worked his way into a corner where he could safely watch the crowd.

"Hi, I'm Rachel."

He turned toward the voice and nearly dropped his drink. A young woman had moved so close to him that his first response was to back away. The wall behind him stopped him in place. She was one of the prettiest girls he'd ever seen.

"I'm Dr. ... uh, Alex. Alex Hartley."

"Daddy's been talking non-stop about you. I'm glad to put a face to the person worthy of the high praise he has been giving you."

Alex shifted his drink to his left hand and wiped his right hand on his coat pocket. He shook her extended hand. "You're Dr. Olmstead's daughter?" he murmured. He felt awkward and stupid, like a babbling fool.

"Last time I checked." She grinned. "Your cold hand feels good. It's so hot in here." She smiled, squeezed his hand, and studied his face. "Daddy's very excited about you joining his staff."

"It's really a great opportunity." Alex couldn't take his eyes off her. He felt his face redden when she returned his stare. She had the bluest eyes he'd ever seen. Her ivory skin and jet-black hair had him mesmerized. Sweat trickled down his chest and under his arms, and his heart was beating as if he'd just run a road race. She was right. It was getting very hot in the room.

33

"Buy me a drink?" Rachel handed him her empty glass and gave him a smile that made her eyes twinkle. "I'll wait here. Tell the bartender it's for me. He knows what I want."

And Alex certainly knew what he wanted. Geez, he'd almost said that out loud. He turned and threaded his way through the crowd to the bar, glad for the opportunity to regain his composure and do some deep breathing. Her impact on him was overwhelming.

He looked back at her, and she was talking with an older couple, giving him an opportunity to observe her entire body. His thoughts were racing. Damn, her legs were endless. Who has legs like that? Why is it so hot in here! Must be because she's smoking hot! He needed to find a way to get her alone and explore that gorgeous body of hers. Keep on dreaming, Alex. He laughed to himself. He extended the empty glass in the direction of the bartender without taking his eyes off her. "One for Rachel Olmstead, and I'll have the same."

The bartender nodded. "Two double bourbons, coming right up."

~ ~ ~

Alex's reaction had amused Rachel. Why did men act like that around her? She knew the answer, but it was still fun to think about. She made small talk with the couple but kept an eye on Alex. She could see that he was checking her out. Good. He came back with the drinks and hovered at the edge of the conversation she was having with the couple. She turned toward him and took the offered drink as the couple walked away.

"I'm curious. Do you have this effect on all men?" Alex was shocked that he'd said that.

"I bet you say that to all the girls." She smiled at him and winked, leaning her body a little closer to his.

He felt the flush from the top of his head down to his toes.

She continued. "I watched you while you were at the bar."

As she spoke, she pressed further forward until their bodies came into contact, and Alex flinched. He couldn't move away. Not that he wanted to. She had him pinned against the wall. He felt like a gangly teenager on a first date, afraid that he was going to say something stupid, or worse yet, do

34

something stupid. He took a deep breath, and whatever perfume it was that she was wearing excited another of his senses.

"Don't you hate cocktail parties?" she whispered.

Alex moved his head closer to hear her above the background noise. He was actually enjoying the party at this moment, but he nodded without saying a word.

"Let's go out on the back porch, where it's cooler and quieter." Rachel took his hand and shepherded him through the kitchen to an enclosed porch. They were finally alone.

She sat down, crossed her very long legs, and searched her purse for a cigarette. The distraction allowed him to examine her more closely. Her long black hair framed a perfect face. She wore a simple black dress with a hemline well above her knees. The dress did little to hide her magnificent figure. It was going to be difficult, he thought, to carry on a meaningful conversation with so much of her leg showing.

She handed Alex her matches, and he lit her cigarette. "Daddy likes you a lot. He says you are one of the best he's ever seen."

"Really?"

"He doesn't say much about people at the hospital, and when he does, it's usually negative."

"He's a great man and a highly respected physician."

Rachel emptied her glass, turned it upside down, and examined it. "He's a shit. He knows nothing about people. I know more about goddamn quantum mechanics than he knows about people ... and I don't know fuck about quantum mechanics."

"Another drink?" Alex felt uncomfortable. This was not a topic he wanted to get into with her.

"Let me get it."

She stood and walked back into the house, returning with a full bottle of champagne and two flutes. "Let's get down to some serious drinking."

Alex had thought that the double bourbons they'd just had were some pretty serious drinking, but he kept the thought to himself.

She sat down, and her dress rose even higher up her thighs than before. Alex nearly poured the champagne on the floor as he filled the flutes. She raised hers and gestured for him to do the same.

"Here's to you."

"And you."

She drained the entire flute and held the empty glass towards Alex. "Did I tell you why my father's a complete shit?"

Alex shook his head and stayed silent while he refilled her glass.

She took a sip and looked at him. "You are lucky you're not a girl. If you were, you wouldn't be here right now."

What the hell did she mean by that? Alex was nervous about where this was headed. He needed to change the topic fast, lighten the conversation. "You are right! If I was a girl, I wouldn't be here alone with you, drinking champagne."

"You men are all alike. Try to talk seriously, and you change the subject."

She drank deeply and gestured for another refill. "Let me tell you about my brothers, my two asshole brothers." Her speech was slurred. "I can buy and sell both of them. My father nearly had to buy their fucking way into medical school."

Alex was unsure of how to react. He had met one of Dr. Olmstead's sons at a medical meeting in the hospital last year and had been surprised by the dumb question he'd asked the guest speaker. Regardless, he was uncomfortable about where she was going with this. She was getting drunk, and they were treading on dangerous ground. He needed to change the dynamics quickly.

"Why don't we go for a walk?"

"Fuck the walk. I'm trying to tell you something here." She finished her drink and glared at him. She snatched the bottle of champagne from him, took a long drink from the bottle, and wiped her mouth with the back of her hand. "My father has never forgiven me for being a girl." Another long swig. "My whole life, I've had to do whatever he wants. Regardless of what I do to try and please him, it's never enough. He refuses to see any value in me."

Alex stood. "We should get back to the party."

36

"Stay here, please. I'll stop bitching, I promise." The look on her face, a mixture of anguish and anger, increased his discomfort. He sat back down with the thought that she was a very complicated person.

"I'm sorry for ranting," she said and reached out to place her hand on his arm. "I'm ready for that walk." As she stood, Alex jumped up and steadied her to prevent her from falling.

"Where's your car?" she asked.

"Not that far. It's at the bottom of the driveway."

"Bring the champagne." She took his hand and led him out the back door of the porch. It was a clear, crisp night, and the cold air felt good. It didn't take long to arrive at his rusty old MG.

"I bet this baby has seen some fun times," Rachel said. She opened the passenger door and leaned in to look around. "This is a classic."

She climbed into the car, and Alex sat behind the wheel. Her hemline was almost at the top of her thighs. Her legs were amazing, and he found it difficult to take his eyes off them.

"Daddy's parties are so boring," she said, curling into the seat and placing the champagne bottle between her knees. "Let's make a toast." She took a long pull at the bottle and then handed it to Alex.

He took a swallow. How could this night get any better?

She leaned over and kissed him squarely on the lips.

He was sitting in his car, outside the boss's house, making out with his daughter, who was hot to trot. Not the smartest thing he'd ever done, he thought, but it sure as hell was exciting. Risky but exciting. He broke away from the kiss. "What about our toast? Who and what are we going to toast?"

"We were kissing. Don't you like to kiss?"

A couple of thoughts flashed through Alex's mind. Sure, he loved kissing the boss's daughter in plain view in the driveway of his house while a hundred people were within shouting distance, and sure, he loved kissing the boss's daughter within ten minutes of meeting her for the first time, and he sure wished she'd keep her tongue to herself because it was definitely turning up the heat in him when she jammed it down his throat. Instead, he nodded.

She kissed him again. Apparently, she hadn't read his mind about the tongue. She broke away and took another long drink from the champagne bottle.

He sat up straight and cracked a car window so the steam could escape. Maybe things might cool down if he changed the subject. "Tell me about you. What kind of work do you do?"

"What is this? Twenty questions?"

"No. I'd like to get to know who you are, that's all."

"I'm Dr. Ratner's girl Friday. I do everything for him. Wind him up, point him in the right direction, and send him on his way. I buy his clothes, pick out his ties, write his speeches, edit his research papers. You name it, and I do it." She took a long drink of champagne. "Why are we talking? Kiss me."

She leaned toward him and kissed him hungrily, her tongue darting into his mouth again. He couldn't help but notice that her skirt rode even further up her thighs.

The windows were seriously fogged, and he waited until the kiss was over before continuing his efforts to distract her.

"You mean Dr. Ratner as in Olmstead and Ratner?"

"Who in the hell else would I be talking about?"

"Your father and Dr. Ratner are the authors of the most widely read and famous pharmacology textbook in the world."

"Tell me something I don't know. Are we going to make out, or are you going to sit there and talk about my damn father?"

Alex looked around. Despite the slightly cracked window, the windows of the car were completely fogged over. If he couldn't see out, no one could see in, either. He leaned toward Rachel and put his arms around her. "I vote for making out."

~ ~ ~

The next day, Alex and Ted Wallace went to the Detroit Tigers' opening game of the season. The Tigers won the game with a ninth-inning home run, and the two walked to Nemo's, the legendary Michigan Avenue tavern one block from Tiger Stadium.

Alex held up his mug of beer and touched Ted's glass. "Thanks for coming with me. I've heard a lot about Tigers' opening day, but this was my first time. I was at the game last

September when they clinched the pennant, and it was amazing. I sure hope they repeat this year."

Ted looked at the crowd milling around inside the tavern. The two had found space at the crowded bar. He leaned closer to Alex and said quietly, "I've wanted to talk to you about something for quite a while, and right now seems like a good time."

Alex nodded. "Go ahead. What is it?"

"Alex, we've been good friends for a long time. Generally, you are a kind and sensitive person. You've spoken disparagingly this last year about gay men quite a few times in front of me. You've called them queers or faggots. When you use those derogatory names about gay men, it puzzles me as to why you're so nasty. We treat gays all the time at the hospital, and I really think you need to adjust your attitude about them. A while back, when you complained about them, I told you that they were born that way and suggested you treat them with more respect. You took issue with my comment then and implied that you believe that they choose to be gay, like what they do is by choice simply because they want to be gay."

Alex nodded. "I remember. I do think that most of them choose to act and be the way they are."

Ted shook his head. "I suggest you get some reading material about homosexuality and give some thought to what you're saying. I think you'll find out you're wrong."

Alex looked at Ted. "Why is this such a big deal to you?"

"I have friends who are gay. They are some of the nicest and smartest people I know. And you and I see them all the time in medical situations. As I understand it, about four percent of the population is gay. So, it isn't just limited to us being doctors, but to having friends, close friends, who are gay and treating them with respect."

Alex shook his head and said, "I don't have friends who are gay, and I stay away from those people because I disagree with the way they choose to live."

"Alex, do me a favor and just think about what I've said."

"I will do that."

39

But Ted was right, Alex thought. He did need to adjust his attitude. He'd give it some thought and talk to Ted more about it some other time. But at the moment, he had other things on his mind. "This is the place to see and be seen." He gestured toward a group of attractive young women whose eyes were collectively dancing around the throng of celebrating fans. "That babe in the bleachers was really something."

Smiling, Ted said, "She shows up every year on opening day, takes her top off during the seventh-inning stretch, and dances topless until she gets thrown out." He gestured toward the other end of the bar. "She's in here right now, surrounded by a pack of guys who are salivating as if she were a rare piece of meat."

Alex nodded. "I guarantee you every guy in this place would try to hit on her, given a chance."

Ted looked at him, a serious expression on his face. "Not me. She's not my type."

"From what I hear, Ted, they're all your type."

"That shows how little you know about me." Ted nearly shouted to be heard above the din.

"Well, then what is your type, Ted?" Alex laughed. "Look around. Take your pick. It's a smorgasbord here."

Ted shrugged and mumbled something.

Alex strained to hear him. "I missed what you said."

Ted looked at him and hesitated. "Never mind. Ready for another beer?" He leaned over the bar, caught the eye of the bartender, and held up two fingers.

Alex turned and spoke to the attractive girl who had worked her way next to him at the edge of the bar. Ted handed him the fresh mug of beer, and Alex whispered in his ear, "A guy would have to be deaf, dumb, and blind not to score in this place." He grinned at Ted. "I'm headed out with this gal. I hope you don't mind."

Ted had a stunned look on his face. "I thought we were going to Greek Town for dinner."

"Hey, Ted, lighten up. This is me, and this is the old American pastime here – baseball, booze, and broads. If the Tigers can score, I can, too. We can do dinner some other night." He punched Ted lightly on the arm, took the girl by the hand, and ushered her through the crowd.

As they reached the door, He turned to wave at Ted and saw that two girls had already moved into the spaces next to him. Ted stood at the bar and looked at Alex with a hurt look on his face. Alex wondered why he was so upset.

CHAPTER 6

April 1985

To Ingrid, the chance meeting with Drs. Slotkin and Hartley presented a great opportunity to prove her worth. It had not been easy. She was a woman in a man's world. As an epidemiologist, she was in a profession that dealt with an area of science few physicians knew or cared about. Most physicians were skeptical of the information her science provided. An additional factor was her looks, and the run-in with Dr. Slotkin was typical.

Her beauty had always made it difficult for her to function effectively and professionally in her chosen field. She'd had to develop a defensive posture toward men who came on to her and treated her as a purely physical object. Men often thought that because she was blonde and beautiful, she was also dumb and would therefore fall for any line that happened to come to their sleazy minds. The notions were reinforced by the fact that while she held a doctorate degree in epidemiology, she was not a medical doctor.

She jotted down a few notes about an idea she had for the study and then closed her notepad and sat back, closing her eyes. Her thoughts drifted back to when she had been a teenager.

~ ~ ~

"Honey, you look beautiful."

"I don't feel beautiful, Mama. I feel ugly. Why can't I wear my jeans and a sweatshirt?"

"Because it's a dance and you don't wear jeans and a sweatshirt to a dance."

Ingrid turned and looked at herself in the mirror. She stood there with her arms folded across her chest and glowered at her reflection. "I hate the way I look. All the kids are going to make fun of me."

Her mother looked at her astonishingly beautiful fifteen-year-old daughter. "No one is going to do that. You're beautiful and very interesting to talk to. You just wait and see how much fun you will have tonight."

"I really don't feel like going, Mom. Please don't make me go."

The woman put her arms around her daughter. "New experiences can be scary. You're growing up, and sometimes it isn't easy. But you are not alone. Every girl in your class is going through the same thing you are right now."

"Really?" The girl blinked back a tear as she looked at her mother. She trusted her. At least, she wanted to trust her. But she couldn't help feeling ugly. She was all skinny arms and legs, except for her boobs. Her boobs were much larger than those of the other girls in her class. The boys always stared at her as she passed and then huddled together and laughed. She hated being the source of their jokes. To make things worse, the dress her mother had picked out for her to wear to this dance accentuated both her boobs and her knobby knees. Everything stuck out as if she had walked into an electric pencil sharpener.

"Can I at least wear my sweater?"

Her mother hugged her again. "Of course you can. Let me get it for you."

Ingrid slipped the sweater over her head and examined herself in the mirror.

"Honey, I worry about how serious you are about everything. You're a kid, and a dance is supposed to be fun. Go and enjoy yourself. Make new friends and invite them over for popcorn and some pop."

Ingrid turned and looked thoughtfully at her mother before speaking. "There are things that happen that you don't know about."

A look of alarm spread across her mother's face. "What kind of things?"

"You don't see the way boys look at me. You don't hear the things they say. Men, too. Grown-up men. It makes me feel awful when they look at me like that when they say things to me as I pass by, like 'Ooh-la-la' and 'Baby, baby.'" She burst out crying.

Her mother put her arms around her and waited for her sobbing to subside.

Ingrid sniffled. "The girls are just as bad. All they talk about is boys, and they think I'm stuck up because I don't want to participate in their silly get-togethers." She blew her nose into the hankie her mother offered her. "They make fun of me because they say I act like I'm better than any of them. And all I want is to be left alone, not bothered by silly talk of making out or going all the way."

Her mother held her tighter and wondered what she could say to this beautiful woman-child who was in so much pain. How could she help her understand the changes in her body that had transformed her from a gawky, skinny thirteen-year-old to a stunningly beautiful fifteen-year-old? Ingrid was, she thought, the most beautiful person she'd ever seen. Her maternal instinct screamed out to protect her child from the torrent of abuse that had already started and that would only grow worse with the passage of time, something she knew because she'd gone through the same thing. At thirty-six years of age, she was still beautiful in her own right.

She gently rocked her daughter back and forth. "I understand what you're going through. I do understand."

Ingrid broke free from her mother's grasp. "You don't understand. If you did, you wouldn't make me go to this dance."

"Oh, but I do understand. I was young once and faced the same problems. Listen to me. You are the way you are, and nothing is going to change that. It's important that you think about your beauty in the context of being grateful that you aren't ugly or blind or physically deformed."

Once again, Ingrid folded her arms across her chest. "Mother, I know all that. It's the way others look at me that makes me feel so uncomfortable ... so dirty ... like there's something wrong with me." She burst out crying again and flung herself across her bed.

Her mother stood at the doorway and looked at her. "I wish there was something I could say or do to make you feel better."

~ ~ ~

Ingrid had wanted to be a doctor as far back as she could remember. She refused to accept the stereotype that doctors were men and nurses were women. However, she was double-crossed in her ambitions and dreams by her good looks. She repeatedly tried to get into medical school, and despite excellent college grades, not a single one was willing to accept her. There was always a doctor on the interviewing panel who would make an offensive remark about one or another of her physical attributes. It was like high school all over again. On several occasions, a male interviewer would suggest that having dinner with him would increase her chances of admission. On each such occasion, she was denied admission because she'd refused to go along with the suggestion. She attempted to conceal her beauty by wearing no makeup and dressing in frumpy, plain dresses to hide her outstanding figure. It did little good. The more she attempted to disguise her physical appearance, the more her sensuality emerged.

Frustrated by her inability to convince these schools that she would make an excellent physician, she looked elsewhere. Her fallback choice was not going to be dictated by her gender. She had no intention of becoming a nurse to serve as a handmaiden to doctors. Instead, she enrolled in the School of Public Health at the University of Michigan in Ann Arbor when the head of the program assured her that everyone in the program was treated equally, without regard to their sex. In short order, she found what she wanted in that program. The growing science of epidemiology fascinated her, and she knew that it would give her opportunities, intellectually speaking, which were not available to her in medicine, particularly for women. She obtained a PhD under the tutelage of the best-known epidemiologists in America.

CHAPTER 7

July 2018

Leslie Gibbons, Katie's paralegal assistant and best friend, walked into her office and sat down. The two had first met when Katie was job-hunting the day after she was sworn in as a member of the Michigan Bar. Leslie was standing outside the front door of the Newton law firm, removing the nameplate of a lawyer who had left the firm that day to move to California. After some polite chit-chat, Leslie asked Katie what she was doing in the building. When Katie told her, Leslie marched her into the office, called back to Gary Newton, and told him there was a new attorney in the waiting room looking for a job. Within thirty minutes, Katie was hired.

With Leslie as her best friend, Katie had experienced the best five years of her life, professionally and personally.

Leslie was, in Katie's opinion, one of the most beautiful creatures that walked the planet, bar none. As usual, Leslie was impeccably dressed. Today the earrings she wore were round gold hoops, big enough to encircle her tiny waist. Katie was crazy about Leslie, but there was no romance between the two. They had fun together.

Katie had been in enough social situations with Leslie since she'd joined the firm to observe and appreciate the impact the young black woman had on men, all men. When she walked into a bar, all conversations ceased. To say she was hot wouldn't do her justice; she was torrid. To be honest, Katie was a little envious. But Leslie's physical beauty was a distant second to her intellect. She was both book-smart and street savvy, a necessary combination for an attractive black girl to survive growing up in Detroit's inner city.

Katie asked her to meet to discuss Sylvia's case. Leslie was in her final year of law school, and she also worked full time for the firm. The firm was paying for her education, and the mutual understanding was that she would become an associate upon graduation. Her full-time commitment to the firm meant that she worked a lot of evenings and weekends.

She was in school the morning that Sylvia came in for her initial interview, and Katie needed to brief her on the facts so she could determine whether the New York statute of limitations would permit the filing of a lawsuit, since the acts had occurred back in the 1980s.

"You look exhausted," Katie said.

"I am. I been up all night studying for an exam this afternoon. Do you know anything about wills and trusts? Don't know why I got to learn that shit when I'm never going to use it when I get out of school."

Katie laughed. She got a huge kick out of Leslie. Every time she got upset about something, she started her street talk, and Katie gave it right back to her. "The only Will I ever knowed was that guy I dated a couple of years ago. I done wiped my brain clean of him."

They both laughed.

Leslie said, "Honey, you're the wrong color. If you're ever out in the hood, you better not be talking like that. So, tell me about this Sylvia person."

Katie told her about Sylvia's situation, and they discussed Leslie's assignment regarding the statute of limitations. Katie said, "I don't need the information today. Go take your exam and get to it when it's convenient." Then she grinned. "I 'trust' you 'will' do well on the exam."

Leslie stood. "Katie, girl, that isn't 'punny.'"

As Katie continued to grin, she decided to claim the joke she'd just heard from Eric Ohmert as her own. "There's a lot of comedians out of work, so don't give up your day job."

Leslie rolled her eyes and walked out of Katie's office.

Two days later, Leslie came back with the answer. "We're good to go on this Sylvia chick's case. Just last year, the New York legislature revised the statute of limitations law. Time limits have been removed on sex assault claims. I also read up on Dr. Pittsburgh. He's big-time. Really big-time. A Nobel Prize winner. I'm excited about this. I have never been to the Big Apple before and can't wait to strut my stuff down Broadway! We'll schedule all your depositions when I'm out of school for the summer. You want me to draft the complaint?"

Katie nodded and grinned. "I 'trust' that you 'will.'"

Leslie turned as she left Katie's office. "That wasn't funny last time, and it's still not."

~ ~ ~

Gary Newton had a lawyer friend who practiced in Manhattan, Bill Canady, who agreed to act as local counsel, a requirement that would permit Katie to appear pro hac vice, the Latin phrase that meant her admission was limited in New York to Sylvia's case only. Once that was arranged, Katie filed Sylvia's Me Too complaint and demand for jury trial against Dr. Pittsburgh and Filmore University.

Two weeks later, Lamar Luxton, the senior partner in the law firm of Cotton and Wisner, filed an answer on behalf of both Dr. Pittsburgh and the university. Katie called Bill Canady and asked him about Luxton.

"He's a good trial lawyer, and his firm is one of the biggest in the city. I've had a couple of cases against him, and he's been fair. Tough but fair."

"Good. I'll be setting up a few depositions."

"Why don't you plan on using our conference room. Just make the arrangements with my secretary. She'll get a court reporter and do anything else for you that needs to be done. I look forward to meeting you. Gary brags about you all the time."

"Gary's said nice things about you, too," Katie replied.

# # #

Quite often after work, Katie and Leslie would head to Gordie's, a downtown Detroit bar off the lobby in the office building next to theirs. The place was Detroit's answer to Boston's Cheers. When they went there, they had two options: if Leslie had classes later in the evening, they'd both drink soda water, but on other occasions, they'd let loose and have a few real drinks. At those times, men would often approach their table, largely because Leslie was a good-looking girl and, as she put it, "They want some of this." She was a master at handling situations that occurred, especially when a guy who'd had a few too many drinks would insist on taking her home or, failing that, would ask Katie instead. Katie felt invisible around her but never jealous and would listen with envy of her ability to reject drunks so nicely and forthrightly without offending anyone. She admitted to Leslie that she could never be as nice when handling such situations.

Katie's favorite response was to tell a guy, "Stop being a dickhead and go home to your wife," while Leslie's was a simple, "Nice try, but no." When Leslie told guys no, they knew she meant it without offense, no hurt feelings, no slut-shaming comments. Katie told her that she should write a book entitled *How to Tell a Guy to Fuck off without Hurting his Tender Feelings*, while Katie's would be entitled *Just Fuck Off*.

When Katie took Sylvia's case, she explained to Leslie that her intention was to have her come to New York with her for the trial. Two days later, Leslie sent her a memo with a list of the top twenty places to never miss when in New York. For the past two months, she had updated the list to include fourteen other places. She added a postscript: "Hey, girl, we ain't gonna have time to try a case. Jus' make sure you pack your 'come fuck me' shoes."

Katie blushed when she read the memo, but to be honest, she was as excited as Leslie to spend some time in the Big Apple.

CHAPTER 8

May 1985

Ingrid designed the study as thoroughly as possible. She read the research that doctors in Boston had conducted on the young women with a rare form of vaginal cancer. They determined that the only feature the women had in common was their mother's synthetic estrogen use during their pregnancies. Ingrid modeled her study protocol after the Boston research. She selected the six patients who had been discussed in the first meeting with Alex and Dr. Slotkin, the four patients that Dr. Slotkin had autopsied, and Alex's two patients, Alan and Paul. Each of the six young men had suffered and died from the same unknown disorder. She developed a questionnaire for determining anything of significance that this group of six patients shared in common. The same questionnaire would include another group of twenty-four young men who had been chosen because they had been born in the same hospital in the same months as the six patients. This group would be called the control group.

She met with Alex several times while she was setting up the study design, and they arranged to meet in the hospital cafeteria to discuss the current status of the plan over coffee.

Ingrid looked over at Alex and smiled. "This is a unique experience for me."

He smiled back. Man, she was gorgeous in a wholesome way. "Why is that?"

"You're going to think this is a strange thing to say, but you're different from most men I have worked with."

"Different how?"

"You treat me like a real person."

Based on what Alex had seen happen between her and Dr. Slotkin, he had an idea where she was going with this conversation. He decided to keep it light. "As opposed to a robot?"

51

Ingrid laughed. "No. You're silly. I'm trying to compliment you, but you're making it difficult. I think you know what I'm talking about."

Alex grinned. "I do know what you're saying. You drive most men crazy because you are so damn good-looking." May as well tell it like it is.

Ingrid said, "That's part of it. I don't know about the 'crazy,' but it's more about what most men say or try to do to me. I don't get that vibe from you at all."

"Thank you." Alex thought about his recent encounter with Rachel. "That is a compliment, and I can see how it would be a problem for you, a problem that men don't have to deal with."

Ingrid was quiet for a moment. "I don't think I have ever had a guy who could be my friend without thinking about getting into some funny business."

"I can't imagine what that must be like for you," Alex said, thinking about how much he'd love to explore some funny business with her.

"Thank you again for saying that. And I appreciate you treating me the way you do. I try hard to be a serious scientist but find that most times, I have to fight my way through a lot of crap."

Chuckling, he said, "Let's get the crap out of the way between us, then. I think you are beautiful and smart as hell, but I respect you for who and what you are, a bright and ambitious scientist. I like your brain better than your body." Well, that was a bunch of bullshit. "There. I've said it. Let's get back to work."

Ingrid blushed and sat for a moment. Wow. A dream come true, she thought. She'd waited her whole life to hear some guy tell her something like this. Not knowing how to react or respond to the compliment, she decided to stick to her serious side.

"There are published studies of young women with cancer whose mothers took the drug DES during pregnancy, where a cause and effect was established without question. The first study regarding young women whose mothers took DES during pregnancy confirmed a cause and effect by itself. I've designed our protocol based on that study. I think we will find that it won't be any different with the male offspring in our study."

Interesting. Alex had thought the same thing when he'd first encountered Alan Gosten's issue. "There is a prominent doctor, Dr. DC Hines, on the medical faculty in Ann Arbor, who achieved national recognition some twenty years ago. He took a stand against the approval of a drug in this country that caused major birth defects in children throughout the rest of the world. The drug was thalidomide. Have you heard of it? I think we should talk with him. He could give us some insight. If you agree, I'll set it up, and we can go see him together."

Ingrid nodded. "Oh, that would be fabulous! I have heard a lot about thalidomide, and I had the opportunity to hear Dr. Hines speak at a seminar during my training at the University of Michigan. I'd love to meet him."

Alex made an appointment, and a week later, the two of them went to Dr. Hine's office. He was eager to speak about his achievements. After filling a pipe with tobacco and lighting it, he sat back in his chair and told the history of prescription drugs that cause problems when given to pregnant women. He spoke with relish, a twinkle in his eyes.

"Cultural tradition has always considered that the life of a human being begins at the time of birth. For this reason, clinicians of the 1940s and '50s virtually ignored the unique history and biology of mankind between conception and birth. The prevailing belief, then, was that the infant in the womb was protected from harm."

Ingrid was shocked to hear what Dr. Hines was saying. "How could that be?"

"Within the uterus of the pregnant woman, the connection between the fetus and the mother is made through the placenta. It was believed at that time, without any scientific evidence, that the placenta formed a barrier throughout the entire pregnancy to protect the developing infant. The concept of the placental barrier emerged shortly after World War II and was enthusiastically embraced by the pharmaceutical industry. They saw the opportunity to create a vast market of products for pregnant women as thousands of soldiers returned home to begin families. Of course, the use of these products would be enhanced if physicians could be convinced that there was no potential danger to unborn children. Almost without challenge, the medical profession began to prescribe all sorts of medications indiscriminately to pregnant women."

Alex could barely believe what he was saying. "Was it really as primitive as that?"

Dr. Hines nodded. "Yes, it was. There was no data whatsoever to support the concept of the placental barrier. Basic scientific principles were ignored. In retrospect, the concept itself could only have developed because of naive, wishful thinking on the part of physicians untrained in the subject of pharmacology. This ignorance was exploited by the drug industry, which was willing to put its profits before safety. The result was a gold mine for the drug industry during the post-war baby boom."

Ingrid excitedly interrupted. "I heard you speak when I was a student here. I was fascinated by your story then, and I'd love to hear it again."

Dr. Hines smiled and took a long puff on his pipe. "In the early 1960s, a drug named thalidomide sold heavily in Europe. It caused grotesque deformities in young children whose mothers took the drug while pregnant. The American drug company that had distribution rights to the drug gave it to several thousand physicians free of charge while trying to obtain FDA approval in the US. I raised hell because I was on the FDA committee to oversee the approval of all drugs. Several hundred American children were born with these striking malformations, and the drug was never approved for sale."

Dr. Hines paused. "Some people think I'm a hero for being such a stubborn cuss, but I do admit it does give me a tremendous sense of satisfaction to know that I probably helped save a lot of children from living a life of deformity."

He took a puff of his pipe. "And of course, you know the story of DES and what it does to the girls whose mothers took that drug while pregnant. Early life, especially for the fetus and infant, is a period of vulnerability. Any disruption to natural processes may change, sometimes irreversibly, the structure or function of a physiological system. It stands to reason, then, that because some chemicals and drugs interfere with hormone actions, their exposure during a sensitive developmental period can have immediate and later consequences. The timing of exposure is key to understanding which organ or tissue may be affected, as the development of different parts of the body occurs at different rates. Thus, an organ that is developing during the harmful exposure is more likely to be affected than an organ that has already completed development. The outcomes of exposures during vulnerable periods may be physical malformations, functional defects, or both. Consider again the example of DES given to pregnant women. Their female offspring often had structural malformations of the reproductive tract, along with an increased propensity for rare vagino-cervical carcinomas later in their teens or twenties. DES causes damage to the endocrine system. The thymus is an endocrine gland that makes T-cells, whose function in the body is to fight against infectious agents and cancer cells. If the T-cells are damaged or destroyed, it is not surprising to see what happened in the DES daughters. They developed cancer."

Both Alex and Ingrid nodded. Ingrid said, "I have planned our study on male DES offspring based on the original study that identified DES as the problem in the daughters."

She briefly sketched the research protocol for Dr. Hines.

He nodded his approval. "You must include a history of the drugs taken by the mother. That was the way the thalidomide disaster was discovered. Without such a history, the drug would have caused far greater damage than it did."

Alex said, "Because two of my patients were gay and their mothers took DES during their pregnancies, I think it is necessary to find out if their sexual orientation played any part in their deaths. What do you think?"

"By all means. You must go where the science takes you. But be careful about what you say and do about homosexuality. It's a touchy subject because a hell of a lot of people think it's a sin."

~ ~ ~

The question about whether the study would ask for information about subjects' sexual preferences became particularly touchy. Alex argued with Dr. Slotkin at length on this subject, while Ingrid listened patiently and said nothing. Dr. Slotkin's argument was political. Alex's was scientific.

Alex had thought a great deal about the conversation he'd had with Ted about gay men. He'd opened his mind to the possibility that there was no choice in becoming gay and maybe they had just been born that way. It was an intriguing thought.

"Alex, you can't go around asking people if they're queer," Abe argued forcefully, slamming his fist on the table.

"But Abe, it's a factor we can't ignore. It may be one of the keys."

Ingrid tried to mediate. "I agree with Alex, Dr. Slotkin. We think that there is good reason to believe our results might show that the use of DES in pregnancy has caused the male offspring's disease in our study, like the Boston research showed on females. But it may turn out that the only difference between the two groups is that these men were gay. The fact that the men are gay is a variable that must be looked at independently of a history of drug exposure. If we don't look at that variable, it may distort our study results."

Dr. Slotkin stood and folded his arms across his chest.

"If I were queer, I wouldn't answer these questions, and if I did answer them, I wouldn't answer them honestly. No one in their right mind would."

The three of them took a straw vote, and the inclusion of the issue in the study won two votes to one. The questionnaire would include a request for information regarding sexual preferences.

Four second-year medical students were provided modest grants from Dr. Slotkin's research budget to conduct the interviews. They would spend the summer collecting information and interviewing mothers and their sons. The information would be collated on computer punch cards and placed into a central registry.

Alex challenged Ingrid as to why they needed a control group. She patiently replied, "Using such a control group for each subject will allow the study to see if something happened during the lives of the deceased men that did not happen in the control group. Alex, you should read the Boston study. It provides an excellent discussion as to why controls are necessary."

After reading the study, he saw Ingrid's point. If their research was going to have any validity whatsoever, a control group was absolutely necessary as a basis for comparison.

The four medical students gathered the necessary information. The family members of both the subject and control groups were interviewed in depth, and releases were signed so that medical records could be obtained. Under Alex's supervision, the students summarized the data and completed the questionnaires.

As the subject men who had died had all been in their early twenties, there were a few problems obtaining information from old medical records. Memories were also vague. Due to the passage of time, some mothers simply could not remember what drugs they might have taken during pregnancy. Others provided detailed accounts and backed up their memories with entries in baby books kept in storage over the years. Nevertheless, the work went forward. For the most part, the information, some sketchy, proved to be readily available.

A huge mound of paperwork piled up until the data collection was completed and painstakingly entered on individual cards.

"Somewhere in that pile lies the clue," Ingrid said to Alex as they looked at the large stack of materials.

For now, Alex's part of the task was over, and he turned the individual cards, medical records, and other materials over to Ingrid for transferring the information into the computer.

~ ~ ~

Thirty sets of medical records take up a lot of space, Ingrid thought, as she looked at the stacks of documents. She felt a sense of gratitude that she didn't have to sit down and read through all that stuff. Alex and the four medical students had spent hours poring over these materials, extracting bits of information that had been transferred to the computer cards.

What made her anxious was that the medical records were all original copies, giving her an additional sense of responsibility for safekeeping. What if there was a fire? What if she somehow lost them? She thought about the words of one of her instructors on statistical research during her graduate school program: "Always back up your research. Never put yourself in the position of being unable to document your research results." What had seemed like common sense then now seemed so vital. Rather than worry about protecting these originals, she'd make copies to store in a safe place. The originals could then be returned, providing her some assurance that the data would be protected from a disaster. And as long as she was making one set, why not make two? That way, she wouldn't have to carry these massive files back and forth between home and work.

Ingrid grinned as she thought about her college roommate, a psychology major, who had diagnosed her with "anal-retentive obsessive-compulsive personality disorder" when she'd seen how neat and orderly Ingrid kept her half of the dormitory room. If she only could see me now, she'd really have something to crow about.

CHAPTER 9

September 1985

The entire fifth floor of Detroit City Hospital had been a psychiatric ward. With the advent of psychopharmacologic drugs, the number of in-patient hospitalizations of patients with mental disorders had been sharply reduced. Now the floor had been renovated into many small cubicles, each containing a locker, desk, chair, and single bed for use by residents and interns during their twenty-four-hour workdays.

Alex sat in the chair of his cubicle, which served as an escape from the seemingly never-ending problems that waited for him elsewhere in the hospital. It was early Saturday morning. He'd been on duty since midnight and looked forward to a quick catnap before morning rounds began. He figured that if he sat in the chair rather than on the bed, he'd be less likely to oversleep and miss rounds. He closed his eyes and settled back. The sound of approaching footsteps interrupted his thoughts.

"Alex?" It was Ingrid.

"What are you doing here so early?' he asked.

"I know you've been up all night, but I couldn't wait to talk with you." She smiled brightly at him.

"What's up?"

She dropped a thick computer printout on the desk. "Something outstanding. We've made an amazing discovery." She pointed to the printout. "You know DES and the problems in the young women whose mothers took the drug?"

"Of course. We discussed it."

"Our study shows the exact same thing: a relationship between DES and the deaths of these young men that's so strong it couldn't be due to chance."

"What are you saying?"

"DES caused these deaths, Alex. These young men died because of the drug that their mothers took. It's one of the strongest statistical results I've ever seen."

Alex thumbed through the printout. "That's a pretty strong statement."

"If you think that's strong, listen to this. DES also caused these men to be gay. The strength of the statistical association for them being gay is as strong as for DES causing their deaths. Neither result could occur by chance."

"Wait a minute. You said epidemiology doesn't claim to prove cause and effect. Are you joking?" He grinned. She was pulling his leg.

"I'm not joking." Ingrid stared directly at him, her eyes unblinking.

Alex's distrust of epidemiology clouded his thinking. He wanted to avoid saying something that might offend Ingrid. Walking to the window, he studied the deserted street below for a few moments while thinking about what to say to her. "Let's go get some coffee."

They walked side by side to the elevator.

"Seriously, Alex, this really is a major scientific discovery," she said.

"Let's sit down before we talk about this. I've been up all night, and my mind is still fuzzy."

The hospital cafeteria was empty except for a couple sitting at a table in a far corner. Ingrid and Alex took a table in another corner and sat down across from each other.

Alex looked at her, thinking, Tread gently, Alex. "Honestly, Ingrid, I'm having difficulty understanding such sweeping conclusions from such a small study." The intensity of her facial expression made him uncomfortable as he met her eyes.

"Yes. The study is small, but its design permits these conclusions with statistical certainty." She spoke in a professional tone, like she was reading the words.

"For all we know, this so-called relationship may be a chance occurrence," he said.

"I don't get you, Alex. The study was designed to determine if what we were thinking occurred by chance. The statistical result ruled out chance, just as the 1971 study on female offspring did with the young women who had cancer. You know DES has been confirmed time and time again as causing all of the reproductive tract problems seen in young women. Why would this be any different for men? After I compiled all the results, 1 personally contacted the four mothers of the cases that Dr. Slotkin provided to confirm that three of their sons were gay as well. So, five of the six men in our study were gay and had been exposed to DES during their mothers' pregnancies."

Alex shrugged. "I really don't know enough about statistics to respond."

Ingrid handed him a folder. "You've got to get up to speed on DES. I've made you a copy of the key articles on the problems with DES daughters. The original study done in Boston was done on only seven girls. That study is considered a classic in epidemiology. The size of the study doesn't matter as long as the statistical results can be analyzed. Our study was modeled after that one."

"OK. I'll go through these papers after morning rounds."

She smiled. "That would be great. It's important that we get this research published as quickly as possible."

"Published?"

"Of course. Why wouldn't we publish it?" Her smile disappeared as she stared at him.

"Because we'll look like a couple of fruitcakes, claiming that DES causes homosexuality."

A flash of anger passed across her face. "We wouldn't say it that way ... but it's a damn accurate statement."

"I think there is a lot for us to talk about, Ingrid." He gave her a nervous smile.

"Remember that this study was your idea, too." She sat back and folded her arms.

"I know, but I didn't expect anything like this."

~ ~ ~

The medical library was one of Alex's favorite places. He felt comfortable there as it had been his second home during his four years of medical school. He'd spent countless hours hidden away in secluded carousels among the stacks, dreaming of the day he would become a successful doctor – maybe even making his mother proud of his accomplishments.

61

Ingrid had given him copies of seven journal articles, which he read thoroughly, taking notes. She was going to have to explain the statistical techniques to him, but he also needed to know more about the basics of the drug DES.

He knew exactly where to start his research. He went to the shelves where annual copies of the *Physicians Desk Reference (PDR)* were kept. It was a publication in which most of the commonly used prescription drugs were described in detail. Nothing was listed for DES in the current book. He searched previous years and finally found a reference to DES back in the 1966 edition. He read the DES monograph of that year and learned that in the 1930s, the drug had been isolated from coal tar by cancer researchers and inadvertently discovered to possess certain pharmacologic properties that resembled the female hormone estrogen. In 1941, after approval by the Food and Drug Administration, it had begun to be widely used for the treatment of menopause. In 1947, doctors had begun prescribing the drug to pregnant women, hoping that miscarriages might be prevented.

The *PDR* information said nothing about the effects of DES on the offspring of pregnant women.

Alex became concerned about the credibility of the results shown by his and Ingrid's research. His skepticism was fueled because, unlike the papers Ingrid had given him about the effects of DES on female offspring, he found no study describing its effects on male offspring. He spent hours searching and came up empty. Not a single reference was found.

The next morning, he made an appointment with Dr. Oleg Lindstrom, chairman of the Department of Pharmacology.

"I've looked very hard to see if there is any literature on the subject and have found absolutely nothing."

Dr. Lindstrom asked, "What does the animal literature say?"

"Animal literature?"

"Yes. Some questions can be answered only by animal research."

"I didn't even think about animal research."

Dr. Lindstrom went into lecture mode. "Almost every advance in medical science has taken place because of animal research. It's the starting point for most information that becomes known about drugs. If I were you, I'd begin looking for information about your drug in the animal literature."

Alex grimaced. "I have to admit, Dr. Lindstrom, that I'm skeptical about animal studies having any application to people."

Dr. Lindstrom smiled. "That's no surprise, Alex. Most doctors are skeptical because they haven't been taught in medical school about the importance of the basic similarities between various animals and the human being. I've been fighting a battle for years for an extra semester of medical school training on this subject to be added to our core curriculum. Do you know what the average life expectancy in America was in 1900?"

Alex shook his head.

"In 1900, it was forty-six years. Now, eighty-five years later, information obtained from researching animals and then applied to humans has added another thirty years to life expectancy here in the US. I can give you a strong argument on how most of that increase would not have happened if there was no animal research. Go back to the library and start your research again by looking for animal studies done with DES. I expect you'll find something."

Alex returned to the library and searched for animal studies on DES and pregnant animals. There was nothing to be found. He was puzzled that a drug could be on the market for decades for use in pregnancy with nothing in the medical literature about effects on pregnant animals of their offspring. He found several hundred scientific articles on the subject of DES causing tumors and malignancies in all kinds of animals; rats, mice, rabbits, dogs, and many others. These studies were about the effect of DES directly on the animal; none of the articles dealt with the offspring of those animals.

Alex sat back and reflected about the implications of giving DES for years to human beings, knowing that the drug caused all types of cancers in virtually every animal species. He also thought about the implication of giving female hormones to males. He knew from his reading that DES was prescribed in the treatment of prostate cancer. Men treated with estrogen would develop enlarged breasts and diminished facial hair. In his first year of medical school, he also learned that the fetus was always more sensitive to the effects of drugs than adults. It didn't seem too much of a stretch to speculate that DES administered to a pregnant woman carrying a male fetus might have some long-lasting effects. At first, what had seemed ridiculous to him – the notion that DES could have any relationship with homosexuality – now didn't seem so far-fetched. If estrogen grew breasts in men, it seemed logical that it could also make a male fetus more effeminate.

The simplicity of the relationship was convincing. He didn't need to be a Rhodes scholar to understand that a female hormone given to a male would produce a feminizing effect. There was obviously a relationship. Did these results justify saying that DES caused the problems seen in the six patients in their study? Was it scientifically plausible? If so, he agreed with Ingrid. They had to publish the study. It was too important to ignore.

Dr. Slotkin was going to give them a hard time because, for some reason, he'd been opposed to including homosexuality as a factor in the outcome of the study. Ever since that discussion, he had avoided Alex and wouldn't return any of his calls. Alex decided to track him down, and he cornered the big man just as he was starting an autopsy.

Abe rumbled about the morgue, pulling on his plastic apron and rubber gloves, peering over the top of his glasses, first at Alex and then at the body lying on the slab. The expression on his face never changed.

Alex hesitated and looked around at the cold, gray walls, the slop sinks, and the instrument cases filled with scalpels, hammers, and saws.

"So, talk," Abe said as he slit the body open in a Y-shaped incision with a couple of deft strokes.

Alex stared at the wall behind Abe and took a deep breath. He never liked autopsies, watching bodies being cut up, or the smell of formaldehyde.

64

"Abe, I'm getting a mixed message from you concerning this research. We need to know where you stand."

"Let's talk about the facts of life." Dr. Slotkin looked up from the corpse and pointed his scalpel at Alex.

"I don't understand."

"Alex, my friend, it's an interesting piece of research. But you're entering into dangerous territory by including the homosexual discussion in this paper."

Alex felt his face redden.

"Damn it, Abe. How can we not do this?"

"You don't need to shout, Alex. Calm down." Dr. Slotkin pointed the scalpel at Alex again. "There are some things you don't understand. Life is give and take. We give a little. We take a little. The system goes on."

Alex persisted. "What am I missing here? This is an important discovery, and you're as much a part of it as we are. But for some reason, you don't share our enthusiasm. Why is that?"

Dr. Slotkin stood straight and backed away from the table. His apron was covered in blood, and he held the dead man's liver in one hand. He placed it on the overhead scale, dictated a description of the organ into the microphone, and turned to Alex.

"I don't want to be involved in this discovery in any way, and I advise you not to go any further with this study. If you do go ahead, it will be without me. And you may not use my name on the paper. Do you understand?"

Dr. Slotkin turned his attention to the body on the table. A trickle of sweat rolled down his forehead. He wiped it away with the back of his sleeve as he peered over the top of his glasses at Alex.

"Why?"

"It's nothing personal, Alex. It's just that there are only so many battles one can wage in a lifetime. Go back and find something else to do, as this one is a certain loser and it's going to be trouble for you if you push this any further."

Alex stood and waited, wondering what the hell Abe was saying.

65

Abe continued. "By the way, I've seen the way you look at Kubilus. I think your penis is controlling your brain."

"That's a cheap shot." Alex couldn't believe Abe was saying this. He was so off base.

"Maybe yes, maybe no. Do whatever you want, Alex. But do it without me. I have read the draft of the paper. My name is on it, and I want it taken off. Do you hear me?"

"I'll take your name off, Abe. No problem."

Over the next week, Alex wrote another draft of the research findings. He gave a copy to Ingrid and kept one for himself. She added the statistics and a description of the study's design to her copy, and the two of them sat down and went over the revised draft. They made sure to take Abe's name off as a co-author.

Alex thought long and hard about Abe's resistance to the study and the concerns he'd shared with him. "Ingrid, we should think about not including the information regarding homosexuality. Dr. Slotkin did make a good point. Dr. Hines said the same thing. We might be opening a can of worms here."

They argued until Ingrid reluctantly agreed to limit the report's findings to the DES–T-cell association and omit the results and conclusion that DES had anything to do with homosexuality.

It took Alex another week to remove the data on homosexuality and complete the research's final draft. After describing the study design and results, he carefully rewrote the conclusion.

Differences were found in immunodeficient men when comparing those whose mothers had a history of DES usage and those in the control group. These results suggested that DES usage contributed to, or acted as a trigger factor in producing, the immunodeficient status in each case. The effects of DES on secondary sexual characteristics when used for the treatment of prostate cancer were well known. The statistical association of maternal use of hormones and the presence of immunodeficient status in male offspring implicated a previously unreported impact on T-cell-producing tissues of the thymus gland. The association was strong enough to be considered causal in nature by the authors.

Alex sat back and reread the conclusion. He smiled to himself. There was no question in his mind now that this was the right thing to do.

He showed the draft to Ingrid the next day. The day after that, after Ingrid suggested a few minor changes, he carefully packaged the manuscript and mailed it to the editor of the *American Scientific Journal*. They had selected this journal at Dr. Hines's suggestion because, as he'd explained, it was considered the most prestigious medical journal in the world.

CHAPTER 10

Katie walked into Gary's office. "Sylvia's deposition is scheduled in New York tomorrow afternoon, and I need to get to the airport. I'm wondering if you have any other thoughts or suggestions."

"It's always good to save a surprise for the defendants until trial," he replied. "If there is any way to avoid disclosing those calendars with pubic hairs during discovery, that would be a good surprise to spring in the middle of trial."

Katie smiled. "I can picture introducing those calendars when I've got Dr. Pittsburgh on the witness stand."

Gary nodded. "Me, too. It would be the highlight of the trial."

Katie flew into LaGuardia airport and took a cab to Sylvia's apartment. The Sylvia that greeted her was a different Sylvia from the first meeting in Katie's office. Her face was less stressed, and her eyes held a glimmer of hope. Her apartment's relaxed atmosphere seemed to give her the security to discuss the demons that haunted her.

"Sylvia. Why don't you start right at the beginning?"

"Okay, but I'm warning you, it's a long story."

Sylvia closed her eyes, took a deep breath, and exhaled slowly before continuing. She spent the next hour relating the details she'd provided Katie during their first meeting in Detroit.

"Do you have anything more to add?" asked Katie.

Sylvia thought for a moment. "For some reason, Dr. Pittsburgh took a liking to me. I knew it because he'd occasionally pat me on the ass when no one else was around or touch me gently on my back or neck. Because I'd never seen him do anything like that to the other girls in the lab, I believed I was special to him. He would go out of his way to talk with me about my dreams and goals for my future, offer me advice when I was struggling to fit in with my peers, and compliment me on my clothes and hair. He told me I was his favorite and that he would make sure I became a world-renowned scientist. It was important to me to gain his respect, and I never wanted to do anything that would cause him embarrassment or be disappointed in me. I loved his reactions to my research. He always told me he was so proud of what I was accomplishing and would always offer me a big smile and fatherly hug. My heart was finally beginning to soften, and I looked forward every day to making Dr. Pittsburgh happy that I was in his life. All that ended the day I finished the repeat T-cell study and told him I couldn't confirm our original findings. I told you before how he reacted.

"For the next few minutes, I did what he told me to do. When he was done, he told me to get out of his sight and not return until I could validate the original study.

"I left his office and stopped outside his door, and a chill ran through my body. I was humiliated, scared, and helpless. I thought about what had just happened and the potential ramifications for my career. How could I protect myself? Thinking about the HIV/AIDS study, I reminded myself that everything I'd done on the project had been under his direction. I'd followed his demands to the T. And now this. What in the hell was I going to do? It's always necessary for research scientists to verify their findings. It's a mandatory step in any research, but the first result couldn't be confirmed. I tried another two times and still couldn't verify the original work. Dr. Pittsburgh had bypassed this essential requirement by announcing and then submitting the research prematurely to beat the competition."

Katie said, "During the deposition, tell it to the lawyer like you just told me. You have nothing to be ashamed of. Nothing whatsoever. I'd prefer that the subject of the Hallmark calendars not come up. Don't volunteer any information about those unless they ask you specifically about them. It would be a nice surprise to spring on them at trial."

Sylvia hesitated. "I wasn't quite finished with what I wanted to tell you."

Katie looked at her watch. "We are running late. Is it something that can wait until after the deposition? We've got to leave now."

~ ~ ~

They took a cab to Lamar Luxton's office, adjacent to Penn Station. He was the attorney defending Dr. Pittsburgh and Filmore University. Luxton was out of town, and a young associate had been assigned to take Sylvia's deposition. Together with a court reporter, the three of them sat in the law firm's huge conference room. It was difficult for Katie to decide who was more nervous about the proceeding, Sylvia or the young attorney, who blushed every time Katie said something to him.

Of course, Katie thought, she would never dream of using her feminine wiles to make the process more difficult for him, but somehow he seemed easily distracted when she flashed him her best smile each time he spoke to her. He looked like a choirboy, probably at least two years younger than her, and she was having fun. When he introduced himself, she didn't quite catch his name. It might be Max or something like that.

The deposition had barely begun when Katie asked him, "How much longer are you going to be?" She looked at her watch.

He blushed. "I'll probably take two hours. Is that all right?"

She smiled. "As long as it doesn't go longer than that. I don't want to miss my flight back home."

"I don't think that will be a problem." He blushed again.

"Aren't you sweet?" She smiled again, a little flirty grin. She had him right where she wanted him.

He looked at Sylvia. "I have just a few questions about what you say happened sexually between you and Dr. Pittsburgh. Okay?"

"Objection," said Katie. "I object to the form of your question as argumentative. It is not what she says that happened. Her testimony is what actually did happen."

Another blush. "Ms. Anderson, please tell me what happened sexually between you and Dr. Pittsburgh."

Katie smiled at him and shook her head. "Objection to the form of the question. Nothing sexually happened between my client and Dr. Pittsburgh. He was perpetrating sexual assaults on her. Your question suggests that there was a mutual interest in having sex. There was nothing mutual about it."

Katie could tell by the look on his face that he didn't have the slightest idea what she was talking about. She glanced over at the court reporter, who was enjoying this as much as Katie was.

The red-faced young lawyer, Max or whoever, looked down at his notes and studied them as though there was something vital in them that the world had yet to discover.

Katie waited politely for at least five seconds. "Did you have any more questions, Max?" she looked at her watch again.

He looked up at her. She flashed the smile.

"It's Mike. I think that's it for today. Thank you – both – for being here today."

Katie wasn't going to cut him any slack. "When you say, 'That's it for today,' that implies to me that you want to continue the deposition at some future date. That's not going to happen. Ms. Anderson is here today to answer your questions. She's not coming back some other day."

"I didn't mean to imply that."

Katie smiled. "Mike, that's good. As long as that is understood. Sorry for calling you Max before."

~ ~ ~

Sylvia and Katie stood on the street in front of the law firm's building and attempted to hail a cab.

Sylvia said, "That went pretty quick. I thought he was going to take a long time."

Katie grinned at her. "Something distracted him."

Sylvia laughed. "I think I know what and who it was. You're good, Katie." A cab pulled up, and Sylvia gave him directions to her apartment building. On the way over, she said to Katie, "Can I tell you now what I wanted to say earlier?"

Katie looked at her and nodded. "Go ahead."

"From the day I started college at Rutgers, I had a clear vision of who I was and how I could serve humanity. Even now, years later, because of what Dr. Pittsburgh did to me, I still question everything about myself, who I am, who other people are, and what life is all about. I've thought a lot about this. My suffering is a moral injury, a transgression of my conscience. My values, beliefs, or ways of being in the world

72

were violated by what Dr. Pittsburgh made me do against my will, things I couldn't stop from happening. I haven't recovered from that, and I don't think I ever will."

"A moral injury? That's profound. I never thought about it that way, but you are right."

When they arrived at the apartment building, Katie gave Sylvia a big hug before she got out of the cab. Katie went on from there to LaGuardia Airport and was back home in Detroit by nine o'clock. All in all, it had been a good day.

But she was tired, so she had a glass of wine and went to bed. Her mind was swirling about the day's events and her conversation with Sylvia. She tossed and turned, but sleep escaped her. What Sylvia had described had brought up events in Katie's life that she'd tried so hard to forget.

A vivid picture of Father Schmidt, the local priest, came to mind. She was thirteen years old, and he was visiting their home. She was still in her school uniform, and his eyes focused on the hem of her short pleated skirt.

He said, "I should like to see you at church some afternoon soon."

She knew it wasn't a request but an order. "Yes, Father." That was all she said.

Two days later, she walked into the church after school, trembling at the thought of the coming punishment for whatever sin she must have committed. She knocked on the door of his office. Father Schmidt beckoned for her to enter and swiftly closed the door behind her. Then, with no warning, he crushed her against him, her cheek so close to his chest that she could hear his heart pounding. She was too shocked to move away, to do anything. What was happening? Was this her punishment? Her body was frozen.

The priest pulled back and appraised her with greedy eyes. She looked away, focused on a nearby portrait of St. Cecilia on the office wall, and mouthed a silent prayer for protection.

He took her chin in his hands and, with a rough jerk, forced her to look at him. She smelled alcohol on his breath. He kissed her and forced his tongue inside her mouth. It nearly gagged her. She didn't, couldn't, move, could only wait

73

for it to be over. She prayed for it to stop. She could hardly breathe. She stood stiff, her arms at her sides.

It was the first kiss of her life.

The memory of the moment haunted her and kept her from sleep even now.

Father Schmidt mumbled something about punishment, and she struggled to understand what she had done to deserve it.

The ritual was repeated three or four times a month throughout high school, as unvarying as the host's consecration at Mass. Father Schmidt would explain the necessity of her "showing God how much she loved him." He reminded her frequently of that duty, especially when she was doing "something she did not feel like doing." And she kept the meetings secret, as he insisted. Others wouldn't understand the nature and extent of her devotion to God, he said.

All she remembered now was the kissing and the horrible stench of his breath. And sometimes the rearranging of clothing. Some vague thought buried deeply in her brain told her that something more than kissing had happened, but she didn't want to think about that possibility. She got out of bed and watched TV until she fell asleep on the couch.

When she woke up the next morning, she realized what had triggered the nightmarish thoughts. She had suffered the same kind of experience that Sylvia had talked about during the cab ride, a moral injury.

CHAPTER 11

September 1985

Everything started after Ingrid and Alex finished their research and submitted it for publication. Once the paper was submitted, both were surprised by the reactions they received.

Alex, armed with the study results, was convinced that when he met with Dr. Olmstead, he would get a positive response to submitting the research for publication. Dr. Olmstead was a stickler for detail, and in his teaching, he had always emphasized the need for careful analysis before accepting anything as accurate. Once he saw how thorough the study was, Alex felt confident that he would do everything he could to see that the paper was accepted for publication in the *American Scientific Journal*.

Still, it was essential to make a good presentation. While waiting nervously outside Dr. Olmstead's office, Alex found it difficult to relax. After Dr. Olmstead invited him in and they had chatted a bit, the man said, "So, Alex, tell me. What can I do for you?"

Alex took a deep breath, hesitated, and began his plea.

"Dr. Olmstead, I've come to you for guidance and support for an important piece of research that's been completed and submitted for publication. Dr. Slotkin, Dr. Kubilus from Ann Arbor, and I have conducted a research project over the last six months, and the results of the research are what I want to discuss with you."

"Don't beat around the bush. Get to it!"

Alex placed a copy of the research draft on the desk in front of him and began to describe the research methods and the essence of the findings. He presented what he regarded as obvious: the common-sense effects of female hormones on the male. He deliberately avoided mentioning the study's conclusions on homosexuality.

As he spoke, Dr. Olmstead's demeanor changed dramatically. His face reddened. He jumped to his feet, leaned across the desk, and jabbed a finger in Alex's direction.

"Why are you wasting my time with this nonsense? I'm disappointed in you, Alex. You should have asked me about this project before you started it. I could've saved you a lot of time. Did you say Abe Slotkin was in on this? And the paper has been submitted?"

"Yes. But Dr. Slotkin didn't participate in writing the paper."

"Abe is far too savvy a professional to go along with this kind of pony ride. It would be professional suicide. I'm sure he's told you the same thing."

Alex was struck dumb. He didn't know what to say or how to respond. He sat silently.

After a few uncomfortable seconds, Dr. Olmstead sat back and smiled thinly. "There are some things you need to know if you're going to be a success as a doctor in this program. One of them is loyalty. I've been chief of this department for twenty-three years now. I've published over three hundred peer-reviewed papers in the scientific literature. The drug industry – the people who would suffer most from the publication of nonsense like this – has sponsored more than two-thirds of my research. The only progress in science and medicine in the last twenty years has occurred because drug companies provide funds for research. Do you think this piece of garbage you've come up with is going to make the industry want to continue our funding? Don't be stupid. Forget about this study. I'm sorry you wasted your time. You should have told me about it before you submitted it."

He leaned forward and tapped his cigar ash into the giant ashtray on his desk. Then he sat back in his leather chair and glared at Alex.

The man's anger so paralyzed Alex that he couldn't respond.

Dr. Olmstead continued with his rant. "Orex, as you probably already know, is the biggest producer of DES. I've conducted research for Orex for many years. Therefore, I am

76

telling you that you will not publish this data. Not now. Not ever."

Alex shuffled in his seat and looked down at his feet. "This is an important health issue, sir. We think we have a responsibility to alert people to our findings."

Dr. Olmstead wagged an index finger in his direction. "Drug companies spend millions of dollars on research. They also spend millions of dollars developing and protecting their reputations. A good doctor understands these things and tries to work within the system so nobody comes out a loser. This kind of study hurts everybody."

He picked up the study copy and crunched it into a ball. Then he pointed at Alex again. "Orex will squash you like a bug if you go public with this. Does that make them bad people? Of course not. They are simply pragmatic. The bottom line is that it takes money to conduct research. Without research, there is no progress in medicine. Anything that gets in the way of progress is bad. It's as simple as that." He threw the crumpled paper at Alex, dismissed him with a flick of his wrist, and turned to pick up his phone.

Alex retrieved the report and attempted to smooth out the papers. Walking out of the office, he closed the door behind him. His hands shook, and his heart pounded in his chest. What had he done?

CHAPTER 12

September 1985

Alex wondered whether he should broach the topic with Rachel. He decided it wouldn't hurt to get her opinion, so he invited her to lunch. "I was surprised by your father's negative reaction to my research."

"Daddy told me about it," she replied. "I'm not surprised. Your research makes a drug look bad, and he does a lot of work for drug companies. He makes them look good, and they take care of him. He doesn't want anyone in his department to jeopardize that relationship. You understand that, don't you?"

Alex thought for a moment. "Maybe I am naive, but I don't think science works that way. If I worked for a drug company, I'd want to know if one of my drugs was hurting users."

She looked at him and smiled. "You are naive. It doesn't work that way."

"I think it does. A prescription drug is not toothpaste or a candy bar or a bottle of dish soap. When I prescribe a drug for a patient, I want to know what the risks are and the potential benefits. I'm in academic medicine, and if I want to have credibility, I must publish any information, good or bad, that my research discovers about a drug. That's the way it should work."

He paused. "You've read my study. Do you think it's important for a doctor to know that a drug he is considering prescribing to a pregnant woman is going to hurt the baby she's carrying?"

She leaned forward and took his hand. "I think you have really stumbled onto something important that will make you famous someday. It's just that today is not your someday."

Alex was miffed. "I don't care about being famous. I want to be a good doctor and respected by my patients and colleagues."

Rachel shook her head. "My father receives a lot of money from drug companies, and there's no way he would jeopardize his position with a company like Orex. So, be warned. Your paper is a threat to that relationship."

Alex thought about his encounter with Dr. Olmstead. All the old man had done was yell at him and make him feel like he had done something outrageously wrong instead of making a fantastic discovery. Alex continued. "First of all, the damn drug is not used on pregnant women anymore, and it hasn't been for a long time. So, no way publishing my study could possibly hurt sales of the drug."

"You should have told him that."

"I was going to make that point with him, but he didn't give me a chance. I also thought he'd recommend that it be sent to the editor of the medical journal."

"Dr. Ratner and my father have written dozens of articles together, all sponsored by the drug industry. They would not want anything to interfere with that gravy train."

"How long have you been working for Dr. Ratner?"

"Ever since I got my nursing degree. More than four years now. Dr. Ratner is a nice man, but he's ambitious as hell, like my father. Nothing will stop those two from getting what they want. So, don't be naive, Alex. Do you honestly think any drug company is going to sponsor research that makes one of their drugs look bad? Or that it would publish any study it sponsored if the results were negative? If so, I've got a bridge for sale." She grinned and punched him gently on the arm.

Alex was shocked. "I think that if a drug company found out something harmful was happening with one of its drugs, they would feel an obligation to let doctors know about it so people wouldn't get hurt. And with this particular research, it doesn't matter, because the drug is no longer marketed."

Rachel squeezed his hand. "That's what I like about you. Your purity, your innocence –"

"I'm not all that innocent." Alex felt defensive. "And I disagree with you. I know the difference between right and wrong, and I believe that drug companies do, too. Their credo is the same as mine, 'First, do no harm.' They want to do things right, make the right decisions, and I think that when problems develop, when the chips are down, they do whatever it takes to correct any issues. Particularly when safety issues are involved. Even if it means affecting their bottom line."

Rachel smiled. "I like your attitude. As long as you stay so sweet and innocent, I'm sure I will always look good to you."

Alex smiled back. "I can't imagine you not looking good to me ... under any conditions. Some guys may be intimidated by you, but I'm not. I like it when you tell me what you're thinking. You aren't afraid to express your thoughts."

She sat back and was quiet for a moment. Finally, she said, "I seem to have a problem with men. A lot of guys are turned off by my willingness to speak my mind. My brothers say it's because I've got a big mouth, but I think my assertive nature threatens them."

"So, what do you expect from your brothers? I'm sure they are jealous of your intelligence and charisma."

Rachel laughed. "You're right! And they should be jealous of me. But I will admit, most of the time, I do speak my mind a little too quickly."

Alex studied her face. She was beautiful and sexy as hell. Her high cheekbones, big blue eyes, and pouty lips contrasted with her dark hair, which was fashionably cut in the new pixie style. She had a face that was fun to look at. When he looked into her eyes, he was a goner. "You're a very strong woman, Rachel."

She broke eye contact and looked down at the table. "Thanks, Alex. That's sweet of you to say. It's so rare that I receive such a compliment."

The waiter approached the table and started clearing dishes. "Dessert?"

Rachel responded immediately. "No thanks. We have dessert at home."

As the waiter walked away, Alex leaned forward. "Dessert at home?"

"You're looking at her." Rachel licked her lips and gave him a seductive smile that nearly brought him to his knees. "I'm taking you to my apartment for the rest of the afternoon."

~ ~ ~

Except for the night clerk, Ingrid was alone in the medical records room. It was nearing seven o'clock in the evening, and

81

she realized she hadn't eaten since breakfast. She was surprised that she hadn't heard from Alex. He'd told her he would present the study to Dr. Olmstead, and she was excited to hear his response. Why hadn't Alex called?

Time and time again, she had reviewed the hospital charts of the six men in the study and meticulously re-calculated her statistics. One thing was clear: there was no chance that the relationship between these illnesses and DES was coincidental. Unless doctors were made aware of this relationship, there would be many similar tragedies in the future.

"Excuse me," she said to the night clerk. "Would you be able to make copies for me?"

"Sure, no problem. I've got time right now," the clerk replied.

"Make two copies, please."

The clerk took the stack of papers and left the room. Ingrid knew it would take some time for her to make the copies. She looked around and, finding herself alone, stood and stretched. Raising her arms high overhead, she leaned forward to touch the floor in an attempt to ease her back pain. Dropping her head down, she took a deep breath and let her long blond hair cascade to the floor. Her eyes closed, she straightened and on stood on tiptoes. As she allowed her head to fall back, she took another deep breath and stretched her arms toward the ceiling.

"What do you call that move?"

She quickly lowered her arms. "Alex. You startled me." She blushed and tried to compose herself.

Alex had enjoyed the brief view. The lab coat she always wore hid far too much. What a fabulous body she had. He thought for a moment about the afternoon with Rachel. Should he be feeling guilty right now for what he was thinking about Ingrid?

"I expected to hear from you earlier. Tell me about your meeting with Dr. Olmstead."

Alex flopped down into the chair across the table from her. "Dr. Olmstead was really angry."

"Angry?"

"Yes. Orex is the biggest producer of DES. He does work for Orex, and he thinks the study will hurt them."

Ingrid sat upright. "So, what is that supposed to mean?"

"His concern is that the report might result in Orex reducing their funding to the hospital."

"I don't understand. How does the report hurt them?"

"The way he put it to me was that if the study was published, it would hurt Orex's business. In turn, Orex would react by withdrawing funding for his research at the hospital. He told me to forget about publishing. He absolutely won't allow it."

"'Allow' us to publish? Allow us? Alex, what the hell are you talking about? It's not his research. It's our research. We've already submitted it. Of course, we'll publish it. Why wouldn't we?"

"I wish you'd been there. You would realize how angry he was that we did this study."

"I get it. To him, money is more important than doing the right thing." She was angry. Her eyes narrowed, and she looked directly at Alex.

"Ingrid, I'm on your side. Don't get mad at me for the way he responded."

"None of this makes sense to me. Frankly, I'm a little surprised at how calm you seem."

"We need some time to think this through."

"What will we be thinking through, Alex? You've already submitted the paper. Meeting with him was a huge mistake."

"He's my boss, Ingrid. There's a lot at stake for me if I rock the boat. He's asked me to stay on after my residency, become a staff member and set up a poison center."

She looked at him hard. "Nothing should prevent the truth from coming out, Alex."

He nodded. "I agree that meeting with Dr. Olmstead was a mistake."

"We can't allow that to stop us, Alex. Young men have already died because their mothers took that drug. It didn't happen by chance. And there are thousands of others at risk. Isn't this what medicine is all about – saving lives?"

"Of course it is. That's what's important here." However, he didn't feel quite as confident as he should have about saying it.

The clerk returned with Ingrid's copies, and the interruption gave Alex a chance to think.

Ingrid scooped up the papers on the table, put them in her pouch, and led the way out of the records room and down the hall.

"Alex, we simply cannot let this work go unpublished."

He held the door open for her as they walked into the hospital cafeteria. They sat in the corner, and he waved to a small group sitting halfway across the room.

"Who's that?" Ingrid whispered. "The one with the dark hair."

"That's Ted. Ted Wallace. He's my best friend."

"Your best friend?" She raised her eyebrows.

"Yes. Why do you ask?"

"I don't like the way he looked at me when we walked in." She glanced warily over at the other table.

Alex smiled. "Oh, don't mind him. He does that to all women. He's got a reputation to uphold."

"That's not what I mean. He looked at me like he hates me, and he doesn't even know me."

"But he does know who you are. I talk about you all the time. Come on. I'll introduce you." Alex started to stand up.

"No thanks. With a friend like that, you don't need any enemies." Ingrid shuddered.

"What's that supposed to mean? You don't even know him, and you're making that kind of judgment?"

"Please don't ask me to meet him. He's not someone I would like to be associated with."

Ted could do that to people, Alex thought. He could be a real pain in the ass.

Ted had spotted them and walked over to their table. He extended his right hand to Ingrid. "Hi, I'm Ted Wallace. You must be Ingrid." Ingrid accepted his hand, and Ted turned to look at Alex. "How'd the meeting with Dr. Olmstead go?"

"I'll tell you about it later."

"Hey, I can take a hint. Sorry for the interruption." Ted turned and walked back to the other table.

"I still don't like him. Did you notice the way he looked at me this time?" Ingrid flushed.

Alex shrugged. "That's Ted. Let's get back to business. We'll give Dr. Olmstead some time to think about the meeting today. Then we can talk some more."

She nodded.

CHAPTER 13

October 1985

Jay Petersmark, MD, the senior editor of the *American Scientific Journal*, enjoyed the power that his position granted. He sat back, removed his bifocals, and polished them on his shirt. He'd finished reading the manuscript that Dr. Alex Hartley had sent, and he knew exactly what he was going to do. Since it was within his control to determine what was printed in the *American Scientific Journal*, the decision was his and his alone. Like all other prestigious medical and science journals, the *American Scientific Journal* used a system of "peer review" to assess newly submitted research articles. When one reads a published scientific paper, it's important to know that the paper has been reviewed and recommended for publication by experts in the particular scientific field. There had been a flood of papers submitted to the *American Scientific Journal* about what was happening in the San Francisco area, and most of them had yet to be peer-reviewed. The majority would never make it into the journal.

He sat and thought for a moment. Then he picked up the phone and made a call.

"Dr. Klimpf, this is Jay Petersmark. My purpose in calling is to let you know about a study sitting on my desk that claims that your drug, DES, caused the deaths of gay men in the San Francisco Bay area. I know what Orex has gone through with the DES daughters over the last fifteen years, and the reasoning of this new research is essentially the same as the original DES study on female offspring, except that it applies to DES sons. I'll send you a copy of the research and sit on the paper until you have time to make a response. Let me know if you will prepare a written response after you've had a chance to review the article."

Dr. Klimpf replied, "Why don't you just toss the damn paper in the wastebasket?"

"I can't do that. Our board of directors controls our intake procedure here at the journal, and everything that comes in is logged into our system and must be accounted for. About the only control I have over an individual paper is to select who the peer reviewers will be and when it should be published, if at all. I've gone over this study carefully, and if we don't publish it, some other journal is likely to do so. It's that good."

"Damn. We're still paying out millions of dollars on the DES daughter cases, and we don't need this aggravation."

"Sorry, I can't do more, other than to give you a heads-up. If anything changes, I'll let you know."

As the chief editor, Dr. Petersmark's power was derived from his selection of which peer reviewers to send submitted papers to. An individual peer reviewer's integrity or bias would affect whether or not a given piece of research ever saw the light of day. The scientists who performed the peer-review work did so under a veil of secrecy. No one other than Dr. Petersmark ever knew who performed the reviews on any given paper. He was accountable to no one in that regard. He smiled. The secrecy of the process served as a perfect foil for him.

If a submitted article was rejected for publication, he could fob off the responsibility on the peer reviewer, whose identity was always protected. If a piece of research was accepted, he could take personal credit. Sometimes the stakes were enormous. A paper describing the beneficial effects of a new drug was worth hundreds of millions of dollars to the pharmaceutical company making the drug. Such companies always managed to express their gratitude to him in a variety of ways. He smiled again at the thought. With such advance knowledge, he'd purchased thousands of shares of stock of various drug companies in his wife's name. They were set for life, and he looked forward to an early and luxurious retirement. Life was good and would only get better.

The flip side of this cozy arrangement occurred when new research came in that disclosed the harmful effects of a drug, like this study on his desk.

There were few ways to limit the amount of negative information that a research paper such as this one in front of him would bring to a company like Orex. He needed a way to block this paper. Fortunately, one man came to mind.

Dr. Petersmark knew that John-Gunnar Fordland of Bergen, Norway, had the highest standards of any reviewer he'd used over the years. Dr. Fordland was an expert in the field of hormones and would, in all likelihood, give the paper the short shrift it deserved. Dr. Petersmark knew that Dr. Fordland's comments on the paper would be scathing when he rejected it. Sharing these comments with Drs. Hartley and Kubilus would enlighten them as to just how bad the research was and lower the likelihood that they'd try to publish it elsewhere. He didn't have to tell the young doctors the source of the disparaging comments, but nothing was preventing him from letting them know exactly what was said. Petersmark's control over the peer-review process fed his soul.

He sent a copy of the work to Dr. Fordland with the standard letter asking for his assistance. He sent another copy of the research paper to Dr. Klimpf.

~ ~ ~

It was nearly midnight when Dr. Fordland finished reading the paper. Sitting back and removing his glasses, he rubbed his eyes. He felt as though he were experiencing a historic scientific moment. One of the prices one pays for living in Norway, he thought, was a certain amount of isolation from the mainstream of commercial medicine in the US. Bergen was a small city on the country's west coast, located at the juncture of the Atlantic Ocean and the beginning of a major fjord that slashes northeast across nearly the country's entire length. Half of the buildings in the city had been in daily use since the fourteenth century.

He often thought about his humble beginning in medicine. Most of the citizens of Bergen were given to quiet introspection. They were taught from early childhood to think before they spoke, a quality, he thought, essential to science and the maritime occupations of most of those living in Bergen. From early childhood, he'd dreamed of becoming a doctor and a scientist. He'd wanted nothing else, and his dreams had paid off. The University of Bergen was a mecca for doctors and scientists, and within that setting, Dr. Fordland had excelled.

Belying its remote isolation from the rest of Europe and the world, the city had a world-class world's greatest authority on the effect of sex hormones in the developing fetus. He had conducted hundreds of experiments in which pregnant animals had been exposed to various hormones. He remembered very well the series of studies he'd done for Orex some twenty years earlier. Every single one had demonstrated some type of abnormal effect on the offspring of pregnant animals to which he'd administered DES. He was disappointed when Orex would not let him submit the papers for publication, and he remembered being chagrined when he'd read the fine print of the contract he'd signed. They had retained exclusive control over the research. If they said no, it meant no publication.

He'd been disturbed to read about the effects on male offspring of the DES mothers in the Hartley paper and was intimately familiar with the findings regarding the impact on female offspring more than ten years earlier. He understood statistics. It was a subject he taught to medical students and his fellow scientists.

He carefully went through the article again. The research design was flawless, and there were no errors whatsoever in the methods used or the conclusions drawn from them. This research was an essential piece of work, and it was essential that it be published.

Dr. Fordland put on his glasses again, reviewed his notes, and dictated a letter to Dr. Petersmark recommending the paper's publication.

~ ~ ~

Dr. Petersmark was shocked when he received Dr. Fordland's reply. It was unexpected. He'd banked on Dr. Fordland rejecting the paper and that being the end of it. Dr. Fordland's standards were high, and he had rejected the last seven papers that he had reviewed. Dr. Petersmark reluctantly called Dr. Klimpf and reported the news.

"I have no choice now but to publish it."

"Why? There is nothing good that will come of it being published."

"The reviewer will raise all kinds of hell if I don't."

"Who is the reviewer? Let me talk to him."

"You know I can't share that information with you. It would make matters a lot worse."

"Well, you damn well better let me know when it's coming out. We'll follow up with something a month later."

Dr. Petersmark found himself staring at the phone. After issuing the order, Dr. Klimpf had hung up without saying goodbye.

At the other end of the disconnected line, Dr. Klimpf sat back in his chair. Then he reached for the phone again to make another call.

"We've got a serious problem here. We'll meet tomorrow morning at eight sharp in the conference room."

~ ~ ~

Ed Herold didn't like getting up early. In fact, he didn't much like anything at all. His torso's thickness reflected a lifetime of sitting behind a desk and a lack of regular exercise. His odd physical appearance, with his spindly arms and legs, mirrored his personal and psychological makeup. Doing and enjoying were separate and distinct entities, not to be confused. He took great pleasure in eliminating joy whenever it appeared in those around him. He was known as a mean, nasty son of a bitch, which was the way he wanted it.

As he got dressed, he thought about his work and the upcoming meeting with Orex. Once again, they needed him to do damage control. He would spin his magic and make their problems disappear. Chuckling at the euphemism, he realized it was what he did, and no one was better at it than him, even though his knowledge of science was limited. His name was not a household word, and it never would be, but no one in the past twenty-five years had had a greater impact than him on what the American public believed about the value of certain drugs.

He laughed. He'd saved countless numbers of pharmaceutical products from being removed from the marketplace due to the harm they were causing. For his efforts, he'd received no medals, but there was something far more significant than awards: money, lots of money. His job was to get results, and no one ever questioned how he made the magic happen.

The meeting with Dr. Klimpf lasted all morning. When it was over, Herold sat alone in the conference room for a few minutes and thought about the discussion. It was a good plan. If he did this right, he'd save Orex millions of dollars, regardless of who got hurt. Fucking lawyers would sue anybody for anything, and it was his job to stop that from happening to Orex.

Time was running out. What needed to be done had better be done quickly.

CHAPTER 14

October 1985

Dr. Pittsburgh looked at the folder on his desk after Sylvia was gone. If what she had said was true, it was a disaster, a fucking disaster. The stakes were too high for him to back down. The research paper had already been sent to the *American Scientific Journal*, which meant he would look like a fool if he withdrew it now. He had to handle this alone. He had no one in whom he could confide.

This was all about dealing with the politicians, he thought. Next to those bastards, science was a model of integrity. Science was no more immune from mistakes or fraud than any other human activity, but compared to the world of politics, it was pure. Facts didn't matter all that much to politicians as a tool of persuasion. Research going back decades confirmed again and again that people have a preference for information that matches what they already believe, and they avoid facts that might disabuse them of their notions. The lesson to him, he thought, was not to rely on the facts alone to make his case – more critical by far was the role of emotion. Everybody in the country hated gays, and he'd put that hatred to use to keep others from asking too many questions about his research. Truth-telling was only a small part of a recipe for success – sometimes. He was in this one to win, and nobody would stop him from reaching his goal.

It was standard operating procedure for the goddamned politicians to avoid any suggestion that something they'd done was wrong. Denial of the obvious was their trademark pattern of behavior. Declaring HIV to be the cause of AIDS was an important milestone in science, he thought. There was a great deal of merit in his work. It would trigger new ideas and research, which was the real process of science. As the leader in this field, his laboratory would also benefit handsomely from increased funding.

He'd tough this out, and Sylvia would be no problem. He held a big carrot over her head. He thought for a few moments about his clever metaphor and then laughed. He'd simply throw her ass out of the department if she raised a fuss. She couldn't do anything to him, wouldn't do anything. If she tried to cause problems, he wouldn't hesitate to use the carrot. Again and again. Who knows? She might even start to enjoy it. He smiled at the thought. He was untouchable.

CHAPTER 15

October 1985

Rachel and Alex stood side by side on the southern tip of Belle Isle, an island in the middle of the Detroit River, slightly north of downtown Detroit. They watched as the sun rose from the east over Windsor's skyline, the Canadian city on the other side of the river. They sipped on coffee and enjoyed the freshening breeze that signaled the onset of a beautiful late summer day. Alex looked at Rachel. Something was on her mind, but she was taking her time before getting around to talking about it. It was unlike her, he thought. Usually, she blurted out whatever popped into her pretty head. She joked that she had no filter about things she'd say, and he realized it was true. If it showed up on the radar of her brain, she'd say it. He also wanted to talk with her about his research paper.

"I'm concerned about my research article. It seems like a long time since I received any communication. Other than a postcard acknowledging receipt of the manuscript, I've had no other word."

He felt uneasy about the delay. He was adept at waiting; delayed gratification was what getting a medical education was all about, but this was more than that. Publication of the paper would assure Ingrid and him of recognition within the medical community. Due to Rachel's father's hostile reaction, Alex had mixed feelings, and his anxiety over the paper made it difficult for him to concentrate on other work. He had to talk this out with Rachel in hopes that she could ease his tension.

She shivered, and he wrapped his arms around her, nestled his face in her hair, and shielded her from the strengthening breeze. He felt the heat of her body as she leaned more heavily against him. Together, they took in the brilliant sparkle of sunlight as the rays glinted unimpeded off the ripples of the water of the Detroit River.

After a long moment, she pulled away from him, walked to the railing, and looked down into the dark, cold river. She was giving something some serious thought, and Alex felt it would be best if he left her alone until she was ready to talk.

~ ~ ~

Rachel reflected on the meeting with her father two days earlier. They met for lunch at his request, and after a few minutes of polite chatter, he got right to the point.

"I want to talk about Dr. Hartley."

Rachel's stomach muscles tightened. She had been wondering for some time when he would get around to this conversation.

"What is it, Daddy?"

"I understand you've been seeing each other."

He fiddled with his coffee spoon and did not make eye contact with her.

"We've been dating, yes."

"Has he mentioned anything about this research project he's been working on?"

"Yes. He's submitted it for publication."

"Really?" His attempt to sound surprised was lame and transparent.

"Why? Is there something wrong?"

He hesitated, uncertain about Rachel and her loyalties. "Yes. There are some major mistakes in the research. Dr. Hartley makes some totally unreliable assumptions. If that paper is published, it will prove to be a major embarrassment, both to him and the department."

"Daddy, I've read the paper. On its face, I don't see anything wrong with it."

Her father sat back and sneered at her. "Who in the hell do you think you are? Do you honestly think that anybody cares what a secretary thinks about a sophisticated piece of medical research?"

Rachel's face reddened. It couldn't have been any worse if he'd slapped her face. She leaned forward and said in a quiet, controlled voice, "That's not fair, and you know it. Why is it that you never show me respect for who I am and what I have accomplished? Your two sons, who pretend to be doctors, hardly know how to read, and they need someone to tell them the difference between their asses and their elbows."

"Don't use that language around me, young lady."

"I'll use any kind of language I want, and you can't stop me. Now, do you have a point you want to make about Alex's research, or are you going to sit there and insult me again?"

"Whether or not you think there's something valid about it, let me assure you that there isn't. And I want you to convince him to withdraw the paper from consideration before it is published."

"I know Alex, Daddy. There's no way he would do that. He's proud and stubborn and ..."

"And stupid, Rachel. He's stupid if he thinks he can do something like this without suffering the consequences. He and that woman who helped him with the research. That blonde who thinks she's so smart. She walks around the hospital like she owns the damn place."

"Yes, I've heard of Dr. Kubilus, Daddy, although I don't know her."

"And I can tell from the expression on your face you don't care for her very much. She's probably sleeping with your boyfriend to get him to do what she wants. People like that are dangerous. I tried to dissuade him. Abe Slotkin also tried. If you want to prove to me that you're better than your brothers, well, here's your chance. Get him to withdraw the paper."

"But I –"

"He must be stopped, Rachel. And it must be withdrawn immediately. There's a lot at stake."

"I'll see what I can do. Maybe Alex will at least agree to talk to the people at Orex and get their perspective. Then he might revise it to reflect a more balanced perspective. Regardless of what you say, I do think the paper has scientific value."

"Yes. That's a good idea. He should talk to Oskar Klimpf at Orex. I'll set it up for him whenever he wants. But don't let this slip, Rachel. There's too much at stake. Do whatever you must to get this done immediately." He stood. "And I could care less about your opinion."

Rachel sat silently and watched her father stalk out of the restaurant. She knew what she had to do. It would be easy, except for her mixed emotions.

Control. It was the only way to get what she wanted. Rachel would take control. She had decided long ago that love was a complication she neither wanted nor needed. Alex had simply come in through the side door of her defenses. He was like an illness, a fever that sapped her will while, at the same time, filling her with longing. She wasn't going to allow anything – this professional hassle, Ingrid Kubilus, or anything else – to come between them. She'd never played second fiddle to anybody, and she sure wasn't going to start now.

It'd been easy to get a copy of Alex's paper. She'd cuddled up to him and asked him for it. He trusted her and respected her opinion. At least somebody did. As Dr. Ratner's assistant, she had the power to manipulate people and events without anybody being aware that she was doing it. She would put those skills to use now. She would finally make Daddy proud.

Her father's words rang in her ears: "Do whatever you must."

~ ~ ~

Alex walked to the railing and stood beside her, staring out across the river. "What is it? You're so quiet."

"Something's going on. I tried to talk to Daddy about it, but I didn't get very far."

"What do you mean?"

"Several days ago, Dr. Ratner asked me about your research. I told him I didn't know much about it but that I would discuss it with you."

"That's strange. Why would he be interested? It has nothing to do with him."

"You know how my father feels about your research. You know how close he and Dr. Ratner are. He wants to be sure it's not an embarrassment to the hospital. I guess that he asked Dr. Ratner to take a look at it."

"I don't get it." Alex crossed his arms and turned away from the railing. "I know your father is against the idea, but I made a choice. This paper has to be published. If it's accepted for publication, he'll see how important it is."

Rachel turned, put her arms around him, and looked up into his eyes. There was a coldness in her eyes he'd never seen before.

"I don't want you to get hurt, Alex. Daddy's offered to arrange a meeting for you with someone from Orex so you can understand their position and perhaps change your mind."

Alex stiffened and pushed her away. "The paper's already been submitted, Rachel. I hope that it'll be published soon.

Following the littered path alongside the water, Rachel slowly walked away and kicked at a beer can.

He approached her from behind, grabbed her arm, and spun her around to face him. She buried her face against his chest and clung to him. She said, "I want things to be good for us. It's important to me that you and my father get along. If you would see his side of this and realize he knows what's best for both you and me, we could begin to focus on other things, like us."

"I thought you were on my side. I thought you believed in me and realized how important this research is to me."

They looked at each other for a long moment.

Alex interrupted the silence. "I've got to get going. I've got an eight o'clock meeting." He turned and walked away.

Rachel ran after him. "Alex, please!"

He ignored her. She stopped and watched him as he got into his car and drove away.

Daddy's little girl, he thought. Why had he thought he could compete with that?

CHAPTER 17

October 1985

Rachel had done what her father wanted. She'd tried to convince Alex to withdraw the paper and meet with Orex. She kept the pressure on him to do so every chance she got.

When she dutifully reported the substance of Alex's non-responsiveness, her father was annoyed.

"Let me try one more time, Daddy. I really think he's beginning to see it my way."

"Time is running out, Rachel. This is serious business. If you can't get him to pull that paper, then I will find someone who can. I should have known you were incapable of doing this one little thing I asked."

"I can get him to do it, Daddy. I know I can."

"Well, stop trying and get it done," he said brusquely, dismissing her with a wave of his hand.

~ ~ ~

It was a warm, sunny, early fall day, and Rachel surprised Alex by showing up at the hospital with a full picnic basket for the two of them. After he signed out for the afternoon, they walked to the park across from the hospital and spread a blanket out on the lawn. The park was packed with other hospital personnel also taking advantage of the beautiful weather.

As soon as lunch was finished, Alex fell backward on the blanket and stared up at the sky. "Makes you feel good all over, doesn't it?"

Rachel slid closer. "They say that in the spring, a young man's fancy turns to love. I wonder what happens in the fall of the year," she quipped.

Alex laughed and pulled her gently down beside him on the blanket. "Let's find out!"

"Alex, you're incorrigible." She laughed, pushing him away.

Alex rolled off the blanket onto the grass, laughing. "And you're irresistible," he said, shading his eyes from the sun and staring at her. He moved back onto the blanket, close to her. "Happy?"

"Yeah ... You?"

"Yes, I am. For the first time in a very long time."

She tickled his cheek with a blade of grass. "Me, too. Alex, could you please do me a favor?"

"Sure –"

"Go talk to the people at Orex."

"Are we back on that again? Come on, Rachel. We have better things to talk about."

"Please, baby. For me."

He sat up and brushed the grass off his pants. "Why is this so important to you?"

"Dr. Ratner has completed his review and says it's well written but the statistics are way off base. He doesn't think it should be published. He ... we all think you should talk to Orex."

"We? Who is we? And when did this become a 'we' thing?" Alex felt anger build up inside him. How dare she share or discuss his work with her boss? He felt his face redden, and he struggled to calm himself.

"I don't want you to get hurt." She smiled at him demurely.

"How could I possibly get hurt? What is going on here, Rachel?" He wondered what kind of game she was playing and who's side she was on.

She hesitated a moment. "It's several things that are at stake: your credibility, reputation, integrity, and more. The world isn't ready to accept the conclusions you've reached. People simply won't believe them."

"I'm beginning to understand what your father's version of science is all about. Somebody comes up with a different viewpoint, and he doesn't like the possibility of losing research money. So you all try to get it buried?"

"If this research won't stand up to scrutiny, you'll be the laughingstock of the medical community. That's not a risk you should take." Rachel reached into her purse, produced a business card, and handed it to him. "Take this, Alex. Call them. Please."

He stared at her and folded his arms, letting the card flutter to the ground from her outstretched hand. They both stared down at it. Neither moved to pick it up.

With quivering lips, she stood and stepped off the blanket. Tears began streaming down her face, and she stifled a sob. She looked down at him. "It's that bitch, isn't it? You can't think straight when it has anything to do with her."

Alex didn't bother to respond. Her ploy was so obvious. He had never given Rachel any reason to question his working relationship with Ingrid. Did she really think he would give in on such an important principle because she was shedding a few tears? She was desperate to have him walk away from publishing the results of his study. But why?

Rachel squared her shoulders, waiting for him to respond. He said nothing, so she walked away.

The afternoon had started beautifully, but sitting alone in the cooling air, Alex began to consider the possibility that Rachel was right. Maybe all of them were right. Damn it.

"Shit."

He picked up the card and placed it in his wallet. Then he stood, folded the blanket, and walked back to the hospital.

The next day, he called Rachel.

"Hello," she answered tentatively, as though expecting the call.

"Rachel, this is Alex —"

"Please tell me you made the call to Orex."

"No, I haven't."

She hung up with a resounding thud.

Alex stared at the phone. What the hell was happening? He needed to talk to someone who could help him understand what the fuck was going on. Or give him some guidance or tell him what in the hell to do. Certainly not Ted, but Ingrid? Yes. He called Ingrid and arranged to meet with her in the cafeteria.

When they met, he explained what was happening. She sat in silence until he finished.

"This doesn't seem right. How would Orex even know about the paper unless it was given to them by someone at the *American Scientific Journal* ... or by Dr. Olmstead?"

"I don't know. Maybe I should talk to Orex. Maybe we should talk to them together."

"All they're going to do is put pressure on you to withdraw the paper. I think it would be a huge mistake, Alex. I do. I won't go with you because I don't trust them."

She reached across the table and placed her hand on top of his. "But I trust you. I'll leave it to you to make the right decision."

Alex felt like his temperature had risen several degrees. Her touch was friendly, very comforting.

At that moment, Rachel walked by. Neither Alex nor Ingrid saw her.

Seeing the two of them together – holding hands, for God's sake – infuriated her. What she'd suspected all along was true. She knew what she had to do to protect Alex from this bitch, and also from himself. He needed to be taught a lesson, and she was the one to do it. It was about time this little boy learned the facts of life. He needed to realize that no man, not even him, would ever treat her this way.

She refused his phone calls for the next week while she mapped out her plan in detail.

~ ~ ~

Finally, Rachel agreed to meet with Alex over coffee. Not wasting any time with small talk, she launched right in. "I understand that you've been seeing Ingrid."

"Yes. We occasionally meet to discuss the paper."

"Sounds to me like she's more than a colleague."

"She's a sensitive, thoughtful person with qualities that I don't find in many people."

"I bet you don't. Tell me, Alex: how many times has that sensitive, thoughtful person slept with you?"

"I won't dignify that with a response," he snapped.

She stood and walked away without saying a word.

~ ~ ~

Rachel's plan wasn't working. Alex hadn't budged an inch, and nothing was resolved. She had attempted to maneuver him into talking to Orex, but she'd succeeded only in driving him closer to Ingrid. Nothing was working out the way she wanted, but she wasn't going to stop until she got her way.

A couple of days later, she came at him from a different angle.

"Alex, I want to talk. I want you to listen to me while I tell you my concerns. I have the hardest time accepting your idea that DES causes homosexuality."

He shook his head. "We don't claim that, Rachel. You're personalizing this. You thought this was a good study until you got it in your head that I had something going with Dr. Kubilus."

"Alex, your conclusions are so farfetched. Gay people were around a long time before pregnant women ever used DES. I don't think hormones have a damn thing to do with it. Every once in a while, I fantasize about having sex with another girl, but my mother didn't take DES. And I'm not a lesbian. One thing has nothing to do with the other. This so-called research you and that bitch put together is bogus."

He was angry. "We've gone through all of this before, Rachel. I'm very aware of your assessment of Dr. Kubilus. We don't claim that DES causes homosexuality. We're simply reporting the results of our research. Believe me, this isn't something we made up."

"Some people think you did, Alex. That bitch is leading you down a path that you'll regret for the rest of your life." She folded her arms across her chest and glared at him.

"Why are you so angry? I don't understand why this is such a big deal to you."

"Because, Alex, you won't listen to reason. You're accusing a prominent drug company of doing something terrible, and you're not willing to meet with them to discuss it. That's irresponsible and unprofessional. You and that conniving bitch are going to hurt a lot of people, including yourselves."

He'd had enough of Rachel's crap and was unwilling to listen to any more of her unreasonable accusations. As he walked away, she yelled at him, "You're making a fool of yourself!"

Alex stopped, returned to the table, and stood over her. "Why do you care, Rachel? Why the hell do you care?"

"Because I care about you, Alex. If I were in the same situation, I'd want you to point out something that I was doing that would hurt my career."

Alex's reluctance to do what she wanted was making her angrier and angrier. She wasn't accustomed to losing control of a situation, especially when the stakes were so high. What made it worse was that her father belittled her at every opportunity. She needed to make Alex do something, anything, to prove that her father was wrong about her.

She gave it one last try, leaving a phone message for him to meet her in the cafeteria.

When Alex walked into the room, he looked around and saw her. He went over, put his hands on the table in front of her, and said quietly, "I am going to talk with Orex, but not because of you. After thinking about it, I agree that it's the right thing to do."

He turned and walked away.

Rachel suppressed a grin until he was out of sight.

CHAPTER 17

October 1985

Alex called the number on the card Rachel had given him and made an appointment for the next day. When he arrived at Orex headquarters, the receptionist directed him to an area outside a glass-walled conference room. A pasty-skinned man in a gray banker's suit came out of the room, took him by the arm, and led him toward a chair next to the head of the table.

"Won't you have a seat, Dr. Hartley?" he said quietly. "Dr. Klimpf is on his way."

Shortly after that, a distinguished-looking, gray-haired man with a tan face strode confidently into the room.

The man walked directly to Alex and extended his hand. "Thank you for coming, Dr. Hartley. I'm Oskar Klimpf."

Alex caught the hint of a German accent. Klimpf gestured for Alex to sit and then took the seat at the head of the table.

Klimpf smiled at Alex. "Let's get right down to business. Why don't you give me a summary of your research?"

No small talk here. Alex liked that. He spent fifteen minutes detailing point by point the history, design, and results of the study. When he finished his presentation, he leaned back in his chair and looked at Dr. Klimpf.

Klimpf smiled. "Very interesting. Our company is always interested in learning about new research regarding our products. I'm sure you understand how much it concerns us when we learn of any potential negative effects that might arise from using one of our drugs. This is why I wanted to have the opportunity to speak with you."

Klimpf checked his watch. "Dr. Hartley, Orex is extremely concerned about this research." He paused as though he expected Alex to respond.

Alex said the first words that came to mind. "How did you find out about my research?"

Dr. Klimpf eyed him. "It's standard practice for journal editors to let us know about articles that concern our products before they are published. This courtesy allows us to provide meaningful input if it is considered necessary."

Fair enough, Alex thought. It made sense that a drug manufacturer was allowed to comment on research affecting its products. "What concerns do you have regarding my research?"

Klimpf thought for a moment. "As you are no doubt aware, DES is no longer being marketed. I can assure you that Orex has no profit motive for the proposition we are about to make. I know you are a hard-working, honest, and bright young doctor. I think you have a great future in medicine. Because we feel the way we do, we are willing to offer you a generous research grant as well as a teaching position at the university."

Alex was wary. "What do I have to do?"

"Withdraw the paper from consideration."

"I can't do that."

"Dr. Hartley, you appear to be fair-minded. Let me tell you why Orex is concerned."

"I'll listen to what you have to say, but I can tell you right now that I'm not going to change my mind."

Dr. Klimpf scowled at Alex. "It's the lawyers. The goddamn lawyers. If this article is published, the goddamn lawyers are going to be filing lawsuits against us on behalf of every queer in the country."

Alex thought about his discussion with Ted regarding degrading comments about gay men. "Ordinary people must accept responsibility for any harm they cause to others. Why should it be any different for a large corporation? Also, at the risk of offending you, calling other people 'queer' offends a lot of people, including me."

He sat quietly and waited for a response.

Dr. Klimpf scowled again. "Those people are queers, and I'll use whatever language I want. If it offends you, I'm sorry, but that's what they are." He put a phony smile on his face before continuing. "There are a lot of perks that come with working with us. We would put you in our speakers' bureau, giving you the privilege of speaking wherever you want in the world, twice yearly. Of course, all expenses paid, for a week at a time. That plus the university affiliation and research grant. Everything, of course, depends on whether you withdraw your research or not."

"And if I don't go along with your offer, what then?"

"I don't think you'll be pleased with the turn of events. We've looked at your research, Dr. Hartley. Has it ever occurred to you that it's odd that no one else has ever made this connection?"

No one else could make the connection if Orex bought off everybody who ever studied the subject. Alex kept the thought to himself. "That's a good question. Dr. Kubilus and I have discussed it many times. As you know, back in the early seventies, Dr. Arthur Herbst and his colleagues discovered how DES damaged DES mothers' daughters. We've always wondered why no one ever asked the same question for the sons of DES mothers as well. We concluded that the reason no one has ever made this connection is that no one ever thought about it or studied it in the same detail we have."

Dr. Klimpf looked at him for a long moment, long enough that Alex began to feel uncomfortable. Sweat pooled under his arms.

Finally, Dr. Klimpf said, "We would rather amicably deal with you, Dr. Hartley. The speakers' bureau is an example. There are many other things we can do for you to make your professional life comfortable and fulfilling."

"Dr. Kubilus and I think this is an important scientific discovery that must be brought to the attention of the medical and scientific communities."

Dr. Klimpf cleared his throat. "You need to understand that there's no reason whatsoever to suspect that we had any idea that this could happen, even if we accepted the idea that your research was valid."

Alex looked at the man coldly and said, "I don't understand your point."

"The goddamn lawyers are ruining our country, and your paper could give them a license to go crazy. It will cost us millions of dollars just to defend ourselves. Not to mention that runaway juries would award many millions more. Surely, you can understand why we're concerned."

"What does the fact that lawyers might file lawsuits have to do with me?"

"It's us versus them. You are either on our side or against us. There is no middle ground here. Some people may believe in your research. However, I can assure you that the vast majority of the scientific community will consider you an outcast."

"That sounds like a threat."

Klimpf shook his head. "I'm not threatening you. It's your choice. Whatever you do, you'll have to live with the consequences. Your research is far off base. We've been interested in immune disorders for a long time. Our research has shown that a virus causes the problems you attribute to DES."

Alex raised his eyebrows. "A virus?"

"Yes. We have research groups working on it at this very moment. I mention this so you'll know that we're serious about getting to the reason why these young men are dying."

"It seems to me that you are talking about something entirely different. This is apples and oranges. I fail to see what a virus has to do with our research."

Dr. Klimpf looked around the room, measuring his words carefully. "This is a plea for fairness. We think it's appropriate for you to delay the publication of your research until our research is completed. At that time, the medical profession will see all the available evidence together instead of one particular slant that may give erroneous or, at best, incomplete information."

"What are you suggesting?"

"We are prepared to offer financial assistance so you can consider our research before you publish. We'll provide whatever you need – laboratories, basic scientists, epidemiologists. An entire research facility, if you wish."

"I don't understand why you're so interested in helping me when my work has the potential to cause damage to one of your products."

Dr. Klimpf shook his head and frowned. "As I've already explained, the bottom line of our company is not profits. If one of our drugs is causing harm, we want to know about it. We're responsible people, Dr. Hartley, not a gang of cruel miscreants."

Alex felt like he was an eight-year-old schoolboy being admonished by a teacher.

Dr. Klimpf continued. "I don't want to dwell on the negative aspects of this. Let's look again at the positive side of things. There are several projects we have in the planning stages that would be perfect for you. We view this opportunity to work with you as the beginning of a mutually beneficial venture."

He put his palms together and sat back, staring at Alex.

Alex returned the stare. It would be easy for him to accept Dr. Klimpf's offer and reap the rewards, but he thought about Ingrid. What about her? "I appreciate the opportunity you are presenting, but I'd like to take some time to think about it."

"What is there to think about?"

Klimpf had him on the defensive, and Alex reminded himself to stay calm. "I need time to think. I'm not going to make any commitment today."

He stood and extended his hand to Dr. Klimpf.

Klimpf was angry. Several moments of awkward silence passed. He stood and walked to the window. He turned to face Alex, spread his feet, and crossed his arms. He looked exasperated, almost defeated. "Now, Dr. Hartley." He gestured for Alex to sit back down.

There was no way Alex was backing down, and he remained standing.

"As you know, every doctor who prescribes drugs must make an assessment of the benefits and risks it presents. Every time with each and every patient. Isn't that right?"

Alex nodded.

"There are benefits to a drug, and there are risks to a drug. The good doctor takes this information and decides whether or not to prescribe a drug to his patient. Correct?"

Alex nodded again, wondered where Dr. Klimpf was going.

"Benefit-versus-risk judgments are not limited to practicing physicians. Researchers and drug companies must also make them. If a drug killed ten patients but saved one life, most people would say that the risk to the ten who died outweighs the benefit of the drug to the one patient who lived."

This was strange, thought Alex. Klimpf was lecturing him as if he were a new medical student.

"Take DES as an example. It was used on millions of women in the fifties to save their pregnancies. Even if it did cause the harm you say it did, isn't life to those who were born without being harmed a greater total benefit than the occasional problem that your research suggests?"

Alex said, "I see your point, Dr. Klimpf. For a doctor to make a benefit-risk assessment, it is necessary to know what the risks are. You seem to be suggesting that if there is a benefit, doctors should ignore potential risks. That doesn't sound scientific to me."

"You are being difficult." Klimpf's face reddened.

"I am trying to understand your position."

Klimpf persisted. "We both know that if your article is published, irreparable damage may be done to Orex. We cannot stand by and tolerate such potential damage to our reputation. Let me paint you a picture. Let's look at your personal benefit-risk assessment. The benefits include those I've outlined to you already, but suffice it to say that with our help, you could achieve a worldwide scientific reputation. If you go ahead with this and it turns out your research is flawed, I can only offer you my condolences. You and your colleague's career will be ruined. You will be publicly accused of incompetence, malpractice, and worse."

Numbed by the implications of the man's words, Alex gathered his papers. Looking at Klimpf, he said, "I think we're through here," and walked from the room.

He drove from Ann Arbor in a blur – slowing, accelerating, and slowing again in the heavy traffic on the Edsel Ford Expressway. Dr. Klimpf had pushed all his buttons. His threat was clear. Alex was so distracted that he missed the exit that led to Ingrid's apartment.

~ ~ ~

From where she stood at her bedroom window, Ingrid saw Alex park on the street, and she watched as he started for the front door. She quickly went into the bathroom, ran a brush through her hair, and touched up her lipstick. Her pulse quickened as she realized he was coming to see her. She opened the door as soon as he knocked, and she immediately sensed something was wrong. The look on his face told her this visit was not going to be pleasant.

He greeted her perfunctorily and stepped past her, uninvited, into the small living room. He threw his jacket on the couch, loosened his tie, and slumped into the armchair, staring at the floor.

Ingrid waited and then said, "You went to Orex, didn't you?"

"Yes." His voice was low and tinged with fury. "I met with them."

"Tell me about it," she said softly.

She sat on the arm of the chair and placed her hand on his shoulder. Alex flinched at her touch. She awkwardly withdrew her hand and then slid off the chair. Sitting on the floor, facing him, she tucked her legs under her.

"Talk to me, Alex."

He described the entire encounter, leaving nothing out. When he finished, Ingrid sat quietly for a few moments. Then she stood and paced the floor.

"Those bastards. They're trying to buy us off. It's unbelievable."

Alex shrugged. "It's difficult for me to understand how something so simple can get so complicated."

Ingrid stopped pacing and looked at him. "It's not complicated if you do the right thing."

"It is complicated. Dr. Olmstead is also against this being published. He's my boss."

She surprised him by moving close to him. She smelled good, a faint aroma of soap. She gently touched his face and looked him straight in the eye. "We've got to see this through, Alex."

"I admire your ability to see things so clearly, but I don't think it's that simple."

Ingrid blushed. "The only difference between you and me is that I know the source of my strength. You don't."

I don't understand." Alex was confused. And her closeness clouded his thinking.

"It's simple. Science is knowledge. Science is truth. Truth is absolute. Either something's right or it's wrong."

"Yes, I understand. You're good for me. I need your logic and strength right now."

She bent over, kissed him lightly on the lips, and squeezed his hand. "You'd better go."

Damn. What was happening here? His body reacted to that sweet kiss in a way that shocked him. He took a deep breath and composed himself. Then he stood. "When will I see you again?"

"Soon. I'll call you."

CHAPTER 18

October 1985

Alex turned to look at the bedside clock and discovered that the night was only half over. He was wide awake.

How would he get back to sleep? He recited the alphabet backward as his mother had told him to do when he was a little boy. It usually worked, but not this time. An hour went by, and he was still wide awake. Must have been that kiss that Ingrid gave him. He couldn't stop thinking about it and the way his body had reacted.

He propped himself up on one elbow and turned again to look at the clock. Less than a minute had gone by. He swung his legs over the side of the bed, sat up, closed his eyes, and took several deep breaths, another calming method. That didn't work either. He still couldn't get his mind off the kiss.

Even though it was October, Detroit was in the middle of a warmer-than-usual Indian summer. It was one of those muggy nights. His air conditioner was going full blast, but it gave no relief to his clammy and sweaty body. Everything going on right now was so complicated, and her kiss had compounded the situation.

Opening his eyes, he stared at the clock again and watched the slow sweep of the second hand for a whole minute. This interplay of the research study, Dr. Olmstead, Rachel, and Ingrid was consuming him, draining his energy. What was the right thing to do? He was torn between doing what was best for him and his future and what was best for others. Was this a real issue, or was he being melodramatic? He longed for earlier times, simpler times, when others had made decisions for him, good or bad.

He thought about what Ingrid had said about how the two of them were so different, that she knew the source of her strength and he didn't. Thinking about it, he concluded that she was wrong. They both believed in the pursuit of truth. He should have told her so when she'd brought it up, but the kiss had short-circuited his brain.

He closed his eyes again and allowed his thoughts to drift back to his childhood. He thought about an important lesson he'd learned from his grandfather.

~ ~ ~

"Grandpa, I caught a fish, but it's stuck on something."

The older man reached over and took the fishing line from the young boy. He tugged gently until the snagged hook released from the weeds below the water.

Alex laughed loudly as the line broke the surface of the water. The worm was gone. "That must have been a really big fish, Grandpa."

The old man smiled at the pleasure of the seven-year-old. "It sure was. He gobbled up the whole worm. Bring that line in. I'll reload, and we'll go after him again."

Alex reeled the line in as he'd been taught, and he watched carefully as the old man took another earthworm from the rusted coffee tin and looped it through the hook.

His grandfather said, "We'll put the worm through the hook three times. That dang fish won't get away from us this time." He peered down at Alex and grinned broadly. Handing the line to him, he gestured to the water.

Alex slowly lowered the freshly baited hook while they sat side by side, knees touching. He patiently worked the fishing line up and down.

"You know what I think?" Alex asked. He looked up at his grandfather and grinned.

"What's that?"

"I don't think a fish took our worm. I think the line got caught on something down there."

"Why do you say that? It was a fish. Why else would the worm be gone? It was probably about this big." His grandfather held his hands about three feet apart and, his eyes twinkling, looked down over the top of his glasses to study Alex's reaction.

"Well, I think if it was a fish, he'd try to get this worm, too."

"Maybe he's swimming around down there, trying to figure out how to get it off the hook without getting caught."

His grandfather grinned at him. He sat silently for a few minutes, bobbing his line up and down, reflecting on the conversation. "Why do grown-ups always tell kids what they think they want to hear?"

His grandfather cleared his throat, bent down, and looked directly in his eyes. "It's questions like that that make me love you so much." He leaned over and gave him a giant bear hug. "You are some smart kind of kid."

"Grandpa, tell me why nobody tells kids the truth. Not only do they not tell us the truth, but they also don't like it when we tell them the truth."

His grandfather studied his face and paused a few minutes before he spoke. "Do you know what a little white lie is?"

Alex shook his head. The old man continued. "A little white lie is something you tell somebody when the truth will hurt their feelings. What's most important is that with the little white lie, nobody gets hurt."

"You mean like telling me a fish was on the line?"

His grandfather laughed heartily. "Exactly. It's part of being nice to other people. People will get angry or upset if you go around telling them the truth all the time."

Alex sat and thought. "How do you know?"

The old man studied the boy's face. "How do I know what?"

"When to tell a lie or tell the truth."

"Alex, that's an excellent question. Many people don't know the difference between the two and spend their whole lives telling lies when telling the truth would do best for everyone. What I do is try to figure out what's more important, whether or not it'll hurt the other person's feelings if I tell them the truth."

"Why?"

"Why what?" Much as he loved the kid, it often wasn't easy to answer his questions.

"Why are their feelings more important than the truth?"

"Getting along with other people is really important. If you tell the truth all the time, your friends will become your enemies." He hesitated. "Sometimes it's really hard to know what to do. There's an old saying, 'The truth hurts.' Why hurt somebody when it doesn't matter?"

"Like when you tell Grandma she looks nice when she wears that ugly hat?"

The old man laughed and hugged him. "Now, get on with your fishing. That big old fish is waiting for you down there."

That time so long ago was as clear to Alex today as if it had just occurred.

~ ~ ~

The next morning, Alex placed a call to Dr. Klimpf. Klimpf was not in his office, so Alex left a message with his secretary.

"I can't agree with your request. I thank you for your generous offer, but I can't go along with it."

He had no idea the chain of events this decision would set in motion.

CHAPTER 19

November 1985

Dr. Klimpf's message to the group was short and straightforward. "Plan A didn't work. Hartley won't withdraw the paper. Time to move on to plan B." He looked each member of the group in the eye. "I can't emphasize enough how important this is for Orex. Each of you also has a stake in the outcome." He looked directly at Ed Herold. "Are you set up?"

Herold nodded. He'd done his homework and was ready. This was going to be easy. "I'm taking care of the first item tonight."

"Has anyone talked to the mother yet?"

Herold replied, "That's also in place. Contact's been made, and it looks good."

Klimpf nodded at Dr. Pittsburgh. "Have you spoken to the senator yet?"

"I have an appointment for next Monday."

Klimpf nodded. "That's good." He turned to Dr. Ratner. "And you?"

Ratner replied, "I'm working on it. It'll be ready on time."

Dr. Olmstead nodded in agreement.

~ ~ ~

That evening, Ed Herold waited until Alex left Ingrid's apartment and then followed him home. Hartley sure picked some fine-looking broads, Herold thought. Once he'd seen that Alex was home, he drove to Detroit City Hospital and walked through the emergency room entrance as if he owned the place. No one challenged him. He smiled and set out to work his magic. He didn't even need the key he'd been given to Alex's small cubicle.

What he was looking for was in plain sight. The pile of materials was on the floor right next to the desk. He combed through the documents and found the sheet of paper he needed. He pulled a similar sheet from his pocket and compared the names on the two papers. They were precisely the same. He couldn't afford to make a mistake here. Better safe than sorry. He removed the document, carefully placed the new sheet into the remaining materials, and then put them back exactly as he'd found them.

~ ~ ~

Rachel and her father arranged to meet with Ted Wallace to tell him what Dr. Olmstead wanted him to do.

Ted listened and then shrugged. "He's been my best friend my whole life. I'm not sure I can do what you're asking me to do, even if you think it's best for him."

Dr. Olmstead looked directly at Ted. "I appreciate your concern. You being his best friend is exactly the point. That's why we're having this conversation. We're trying to save him from himself."

Ted hesitated, and Rachel jumped in. "Ted, you know that we both care for Alex and that anything that hurts him hurts us."

Ted shrugged again. "I wouldn't want him to be hurt, and I certainly wouldn't want to do anything that might hurt him."

Dr. Olmstead looked at his daughter and nodded.

Rachel continued. "You know that Alex is mesmerized by her. He couldn't spell 'science' if she were in the same room with him. She's leading him down a pathway into ridicule. You've seen the way he behaves around her, lapping at her feet like a puppy begging for a treat."

Ted thought for a moment and then turned to Dr. Olmstead. "What exactly is it that you want me to do?"

Fifteen minutes later, the plan was in place.

CHAPTER 20

Thaddeus "Pops" Wentworth, the Senate Appropriations Committee chairman, leaned back in his extra-large leather chair and took a deep inhalation of his cigar. Wentworth enjoyed both the prestige and the power of the position, which gave him control over the federal government's entire budget.

He looked at Dr. Pittsburgh, seated across the massive desk from him. "This is a great cigar, Arnold. Where did you get them?" He gestured toward the box on the desk.

Dr. Pittsburgh leaned forward. "They came from Cuba. I've done some work with a few Cuban scientists over the years, and they bring me a couple of boxes every time they come up here."

"Get me all you can."

"Consider it done!" Pittsburgh nodded. "I'll have more sent to you right away."

Wentworth took another deep inhalation and exhaled. Perfect circles of smoke rose above his head. "So, tell me why you're here."

"I've had a major breakthrough in my research. I wanted to make sure you're the first to know all about it."

"What's it about? I don't need any fucking scientific details. Just tell me what and why I need to know about it. I hope it's different than the last bullshit you put me through."

Dr. Pittsburgh felt trickles of sweat under his arms. For the past fifteen years, his research had been funded entirely by the federal government. The major thrust of his research had been the relationship between viruses and cancer. Back then, he had personally convinced Wentworth that viruses were the cause of all cancers in one form or another. The federal government had spent millions of dollars on research in many laboratories across the country to prove the relationship. Thanks to Wentworth's backing, Dr. Pittsburgh had been one of the primary beneficiaries of this largesse.

Still, the quest had, in large part, proved fruitless, and the government was now in the process of shutting down funding of virus-cancer research laboratories across America. Thanks to Wentworth, Dr. Pittsburgh's budget was still intact. When he'd met with the small group in Ann Arbor, Klimpf had briefed him on what he needed to do. When he'd received the call that plan B was necessary, he'd already made the appointment to meet with Wentworth in Washington.

"Because of your funding, a whole new era of scientific research has begun, and my lab has made an astounding discovery."

"You've been saying that since before I funded you the first time. Stop beating around the bush and get to it."

"Have you heard what is going on in San Francisco?"

"If you're talking about the homosexuals, yes."

"I've discovered why they are dying. Because of their abnormal sex acts, they are spreading a virus around that is killing them."

Wentworth shook his head. "Viruses again? I thought that we were through with viruses."

"It's a specific virus, and it appears to be limited to homosexuals. I discovered the virus and have named it HIV."

"Spare me the details, Dr. Pittsburgh, and take a moment and think like a politician. Why in the fuck would I want to do something that would only benefit homosexuals? Imagine what my opponent in the next election would say. 'Don't vote for Wentworth, because the only thing he's done is save the lives of thousands of queers running around California, screwing other queers.' Hell, the voters in my state would tar and feather me unless you can tell me right now why I should even listen to you any further about this crap."

"I understand your concerns. But you can be a hero. You can sell the concept that your efforts have prevented this terrible disease from spreading to normal people. Your voters will be alive because of your efforts." Dr. Pittsburgh paused. "Hell, I'd even move to Massachusetts and vote for you if you said that."

Wentworth sat back and laughed. "Goddamn, boy, you are good. You ought to run my next fucking campaign."

Dr. Pittsburgh hesitated for a moment. "There is one other thing. Do you remember Oskar Klimpf?"

Wentworth nodded. "We're good friends. Is this about Orex?"

Dr. Pittsburgh nodded. "It's about Orex, one of their drugs. A research study out of Detroit, similar to mine, is going to be published soon. Makes an Orex drug look bad, real bad. Klimpf called me when he heard about my study. He says that if the Detroit study is published first, Orex will lose millions. He wants to delay the publication of that study until after mine comes out. He suggested to me that if anyone could get that done, it would be you."

Wentworth picked up his pen, "Give me the goddamn details." One hand washes the other, he thought. This will cost Orex a bundle for his next campaign.

~ ~ ~

Dr. Petersmark hesitated for a moment and thought about the call he'd received from Senator Wentworth. Thanks to the senator, the *American Scientific Journal* received a substantial grant from the federal government every year. He sure as hell was not going to do anything to jeopardize that funding source. He picked up the phone and called Dr. Klimpf.

"Oskar, I thought I'd let you know what I'm going to do. I'll set Dr. Pittsburgh's paper up for immediate publication, and I'll delay publishing the Detroit paper for a couple of months, until March. That will give you some lead time to come up with a strategy for dealing with it."

"Try to delay it as long as you can. Do not publish the goddamn paper before March." Klimpf hung up abruptly.

Two weeks later, Dr. Petersmark placed calls to both Drs. Klimpf and Pittsburgh. The message was the same for both: "The publication date for Dr. Pittsburgh's study is fast-tracked for publication in December 1985, and publication of the Detroit study is set back until March 1986."

CHAPTER 21

October 2018

Katie placed her weekly call to Sylvia. "Anything new you want to talk about? Anything we haven't covered yet?"

Sylvia said, "I have been thinking, maybe too much, about when this all started, when I told Dr. Pittsburgh I couldn't validate the study. You already know how he started to abuse me sexually that day. I remember now what it was like after that happened. I couldn't stop shaking as I left his office. Luckily, a restroom was around the corner, and I ran in, making it in time before I vomited into the sink. I wiped my face with a cold towel and looked in the mirror. The shame and humiliation I was feeling could be seen in my eyes. What had I done to make Dr. Pittsburgh think it was okay to force himself on me like that? He was my mentor, my only confidant. We worked beautifully together, and we were both so excited that our research was on the brink of something huge. Somehow I must have encouraged him without meaning to. My instinct told me then that I should apologize to him. Then, more than ever before, I wished I had someone in my life to talk to about this – a mom, a sister, a best friend – someone who could tell me what I had done wrong to encourage his abusive behavior."

"I can only imagine how terrible it was for you. Tell me more about your early life."

"I have been a loner my entire life. I was forced into the foster care system at the age of three after my homeless birth mother died from a drug overdose. My birth father was unknown. I never knew true unconditional love, the kind that a child receives from its parents. I never had the love and attention from the same person for longer than a year or two, as I was bumped from one family to the next, never knowing if I would be welcomed or considered a burden. I grew up this way, feeling that I was unlovable but not understanding why. I always felt like the ugly stepsister. My foster parents blamed me for anything that went wrong in the various homes where

I was sent. At every place, it was always the same. If somebody broke something, it was my fault. When there wasn't enough money for expenses, it was my fault.

"Bouncing around the foster care system provided me with the basic needs – food, clothing, shelter, and safety – but bonding and a sense of being loved were always absent. I learned to be quiet and complacent, as rocking the boat still ended badly for me. I quietly watched as my siblings received new shoes and clothes for the start of each school year and I received hand-me-downs.

"The holidays were incredibly difficult. The presents would be piled high around the Christmas tree, all for my temporary siblings, and I would be content with a single gift, purchased from Goodwill, someone else's castaway. The train sets, sleds, and barbies would all be pushed aside when the relatives arrived with even more gifts. But none were for me, as I wasn't considered family. Pulling inward and protecting my heart from breaking due to the constant disappointments became my shield. I would hug myself at night and gently rock back and forth to imagine what it would be like if somebody loved me, falling asleep to the whispers in my head of a special somebody telling me how wonderful and loved I was, giving me some feeling of self-worth.

"So, I learned early on to depend only on myself. My goal was to age out of the system and begin my real life, where I was in control of my future. With that goal planted in my whole being, I read every book in the school library and took classes that forced me to study long hours, propelling me into a solitary life. Education was my best friend. Excelling in my classes got me a scholarship to Rutgers University, where I could lose myself in the crowds of goal-oriented students. At Rutgers, I discovered that I loved research – no surprise since I had spent my formative years reading rather than engaging in friendships and the normal teen boy-girl activities. When I graduated from Rutgers and was given the opportunity to receive my doctorate under the guidance of the famous Dr. Arnold Pittsburgh, I silently thanked the foster care system for making me into the loner I had become."

"Wow. You inspire me. What a great story."

Sylvia paused. "Going back over all this with you is like a therapy session."

Katie laughed. "Maybe I should become a shrink. But this was also good for me as it helps me to understand you so much better. It gives me a lot to think about when I'm preparing for trial. You've given me a lot to work with."

CHAPTER 22

November 7, 1985

Alex Hartley, MD
Dept. of Internal Medicine
Detroit City Hospital
Detroit, Michigan 48201

Dear Dr. Hartley,

As you know, your submission to the American Scientific Journal has been undergoing the process of peer review. I am pleased to announce that your work has been accepted for publication and will appear in the March 1986 issue.

Thank you for sharing your manuscript with the American Scientific Journal. I look forward to seeing it in print.

Jay Petersmark, MD
Editor

Alex read the letter three times and then folded it and put it away carefully in its envelope. When he reached the ward, he stopped at the nursing station and took it out to reread it, trying to absorb the realization of their success. He called Ingrid.

"Ingrid. We've done it."

"Done what?"

"It's been accepted. It's going to be in the March issue of the *American Scientific Journal*. Let me read the letter to you."

She listened while he read. "Alex, that's great news! We should celebrate this momentous occasion. But why do you think it's going to take that long to get it in print? This is November. Five more months to publish it? They've had it since summer."

"That's probably how long it takes. We need to celebrate. How about tomorrow night? I'll make reservations at the London Chop House."

"Wow! I've heard about that place. It's pretty expensive."

"Who cares! This is certainly worth celebrating. How many times in our lives will we have something like this happen?"

"Okay. But we'll split the bill."

"No way, Ingrid. This is going to be on me."

Alex knew that the "Chopper," was famous for reaping lavish treatment on celebrities and rudely treating all other patrons. Members of the attending staff at the hospital talked about it all the time, and he looked forward to his first experience. It was the place to see and be seen, the happening place in downtown Detroit.

When they arrived, they were seated in a distant corner of the restaurant, far away from the dance floor and Tables One and Two, the two best tables in the house reserved for the rich and famous. On the way to their table, Alex spotted Lee Iacocca, the innovator of the Ford Mustang and now the CEO of Chrysler at Table One and the mayor of Detroit at Table Two. Just being in the same room with these luminaries made Alex feel important. This was pretty special, and the best was yet to come. When they received the accolades for their research, he thought, they would be welcome at Table One, for sure.

Alex attempted to order a bottle of wine, and the sommelier gave him a sad smile and offered help. "Trust me to bring you and the lovely lady a beautiful wine."

When the bottle was presented and the wine poured, Alex raised his glass to toast Ingrid. He mispronounced the name of the French Bordeaux, which came with a price tag that would have fed the two of them for a week.

They both laughed at his mistake, and Ingrid said, "That's probably how the Russians say it."

"French is not my second language," he replied as she tried to stifle a chuckle. "Let's see if I can do better with the menu. Do you mind if I order for both of us?" He looked at the menu. Holy crap, he thought, look at these prices. This was going to cost him half his paycheck this month.

Once the hard part was over, Alex relaxed and focused on Ingrid. She was stunning in a strapless black cocktail dress that did nothing to hide her shapely body. Being with her, he thought, was worth whatever the cost of the meal was.

He smiled at her. "You look fabulous."

Ingrid blushed. "Thank you."

During dinner, they enjoyed getting to know each other better, sharing stories of their childhood and college experiences. She was so easy to be around. The night was happening too fast, and dinner was over before they knew it. The wine was gone, and not wanting the evening to end, Alex ordered two glasses of cognac. He could tell that Ingrid was enjoying the evening as much as he was. She was so different from other women. Not only was she super smart and beautiful, but she was also sweet and fascinating. He wanted to get to know her better, so he began to think about how he could make the evening last longer.

"Would you like to dance?"

"Oh, yes, I'd love to dance!"

They walked onto the crowded dance floor, and it was clear that they had no choice but to hold each other close. She seemed to melt in his arms. It felt so right. Their bodies meshed together, and Alex felt the stirring of an erection. She gently pressed her body closer. He couldn't imagine anything better than this.

They laughed when they realized that the music had stopped and they were alone on the dance floor. Regretfully they returned to their table.

Alex needed to use the restroom, so he excused himself. As he made his way through the standup crowd at the bar, he was stunned to see Rachel blocking his path, standing there and glaring at him.

"I see you and your friend are enjoying each other." She was glassy-eyed and slurring her words. "Are you going to fuck her tonight?"

Others at the bar stopped chatting. It was ominously quiet. What should he do? He reached out to her, and she shoved him in the chest with both of her hands.

"Don't you dare touch me. Keep your fucking hands off me."

The bar crowd gasped. They waited in delicious anticipation for the confrontation. Disappointing them, Alex turned and walked away, returning to the table.

"Ingrid. Let's go."

"Is there something wrong?"

"No. Nothing's wrong. I just realized how late it is, and I have to get up early tomorrow."

He paid the bill and steered Ingrid away from the bar.

As they drove away from the restaurant, Ingrid leaned over and kissed him on the cheek.

"This was really nice. I enjoyed the evening and getting to know you better."

"Me, too. I wish it didn't have to end."

She reached over and took his hand. "We can have a nightcap at my place."

She had not seen or heard the exchange that had taken place at the bar, Alex thought. That would have ruined the evening for both of them. He squeezed her hand. "That'd be nice."

They rode the rest of the way to her apartment in silence – and he regretted having told her he had to get up early the next day. He parked in the street in front of her building. They walked into the foyer, and she pressed the button for the elevator.

Alex looked at her and smiled. "I have a confession to make."

"Oh? What?" She held his arm as they waited for the elevator.

"I don't have to get up early."

She put her arms around him, stood on her tiptoes, and kissed him longingly on the lips. She smiled. "I was hoping you'd say that."

~ ~ ~

It took him a minute for him to remember where he was. Why was his right arm so numb? He raised his head and looked around. He realized his arms were encircling Ingrid, with his right pinned under her. They were lying together on the floor in the middle of her living room. He slowly recalled how they had gotten there and smiled.

In their mutual eagerness, they hadn't made it to the bedroom, nor had they completely undressed. They'd made love on the floor and had fallen asleep in each other's arms. He gently extracted himself from her and carried her, still half-asleep, into the bedroom, and tucked her into her bed. He went into the living room, dressed, gathered her clothing, and placed it on her bedroom chair. Kissing her gently, he turned and left the apartment.

~ ~ ~

As Alex drove home, he was unaware of the car that followed him. The car driver stayed at a careful distance and remained in front of his apartment until he turned the lights in his apartment off and went back to sleep.

~ ~ ~

Alex slept for a couple more hours, got up, and went straight to the hospital. Awesome night! He was full of energy and ready for anything. He was still high from the alcohol and Ingrid. He thought about the evening and hummed while he went over a patient's chart at the nursing station.

"Pretty chipper for so early in the morning. You must have won the lottery." The head nurse smiled at him.

Alex grinned back. "I feel like I won the lottery."

As he walked away from the nursing station, he heard her chuckling to the other nurses. "He must have gotten laid last night." They laughed raucously, and he felt his ears redden. He had gotten laid. He smiled to himself. She ought to try it some time, the old battle-ax.

As he walked along the corridor to a patient's room, he could picture Ingrid in his mind's eye. His senses still tingled with pleasure as he remembered the scent of her hair and the touch of her skin. He was captivated by this vibrant, sensuous, sexy, tough, brainy woman. Best of all, he knew she could be a friend, a colleague, as well as someone he could share his private thoughts with. He thought about Rachel. Some friend she had turned out to be.

~ ~ ~

Ingrid sat up in bed, and her first thought was: Where is Alex?

She looked at the clock and was surprised at how late it was. She had better hurry, or she would be late for work. But first, she wanted to take a few minutes to savor the evening – the touching and tasting of each other, his smell. Her emotions were like diamonds in a vault. She'd never before experienced the passion that he brought out in her, and she felt special, as if she were a daffodil basking in the warm sunlight of an early summer morning. She wondered what he was doing right now and realized how much she craved his attention. She hoped that the phone would ring and he would tell her he was coming bright back to continue where they'd left off. She laughed at herself for thinking something so silly as this.

She reluctantly got out of bed and walked into the kitchen. Alex was gone, but maybe he'd left a note. She looked around, found nothing, and felt a stab of disappointment. But there was joy in knowing that they had accomplished something magical together on so many levels: scientifically, emotionally, physically, and sexually. However, their research's coming publication paled in comparison to the feelings that he had stirred within her. She flushed crimson as she thought about it happening again.

On her drive to the hospital, the radio played a Barry Manilow song.

When will our eyes meet?
When can I touch you?
When will this strong yearning end?
And when will I hold you again?

~ ~ ~

These words mirrored what she was feeling. Her heart swelled with passion. She had to call her mom and tell her about her wonderful man, Alex. It would make her mom so happy.

CHAPTER 23

Late November 1985

The thought of Alex and Ingrid together infuriated Rachel. What was he thinking? What was he feeling? His fucking mixed messages were driving her crazy. She drove from her apartment building and headed toward downtown Detroit. She entered eastbound I-94 at Wyoming, and traffic was stop and go.

Was she losing her touch? It was usually not difficult to convince guys to see life her way. She could wrap guys around her little finger and get them to dance to whatever tune she wanted. She sang along with the radio.

I said something wrong,
now I long for yesterday.
Yesterday, love was such an easy game to play,
Now I need a place to hide away.
Oh, I believe in yesterday.

This music was too damn sad. She snapped the radio off, hit the accelerator, and sped up another ten miles an hour. She left the expressway at the Grand River exit and continued downtown on Woodward Avenue. She drove to the hospital, found a parking spot on the street right at the front door, jumped out of her car, and barged into the reception area. She ordered the receptionist to page Ted.

What the hell is taking so long? She paced back and forth and muttered to herself. Finally, she leaned against the wall, her arms folded across her chest, and tapped her foot while she checked her watch every few seconds. The sight of Alex and Ingrid together at the Chop House had driven her wild. She was beside herself with anger. It was obvious that Alex was smitten with Ingrid, and she feared losing him. Her imagination fueled her rage as she kept thinking about them walking in a park, holding hands, laughing, kissing, lying in bed and snuggling, or worse yet – having sex. These unwanted pictures popped into her head, and each time, her anger ratcheted to a new level of intensity. She couldn't stand it any longer. She needed to take action.

Rachel looked at Ted coolly as he approached, and she said without greeting, "Are you ready to get this done? If you care for him, we need to take care of this problem. We both know what's happening and what she's trying to do to him. It's time to stop her before it's too late. He needs our help because he can't do it himself."

Ted eyed her warily. Rachel was, to his thinking, a pit bull in heels, hardly the kind of person who helped others. How could she be trusted? "What do you suggest that's different from what we talked about with your father?"

"You do realize what's at stake, don't you?"

Ted reflected back on their meeting with Dr. Olmstead. It wasn't just Rachel who had concerns. Dr. Olmstead's concerns were also legitimate. Before he could say anything, Rachel interrupted his thoughts.

"Do you understand statistics?" She leaned forward and got right in his face.

Ted smirked. "Not really. I know that two plus two equals four." Lighten up the condescending bitch a little.

Rachel's eyes glared with anger. "Well, she makes two plus two equal six."

Whatever the fuck did that mean? He understood now why Rachel was so angry. She was jealous. He decided to play this out. "How so?"

Rachel huffed. "You don't know what the fuck I'm talking about. You'll just have to trust me. What Ingrid did was manipulate the data to draw conclusions that are nonsense. Unless we help Alex, he's in deep trouble because of the fraud she's committed to justify the results."

Don't talk down to me and get the fuck out of my face, Ted thought. He stepped back and said, "I've thought about this a lot since our meeting. You may know statistics, but you don't know Alex. I've known him a lot longer than you have and know him a lot better than you do. There's no way he'll back off if he thinks he's doing the right thing."

"What makes you say that?"

Ted leaned forward. "The first time I met him was when my family moved from Ludington to Detroit in the middle of the school year. I was in the fifth grade. There was a snowstorm on my first day. As I walked into the school, I slipped and fell in front of a bunch of kids, face down on the ground. They all stood there and laughed. You can imagine how I felt. All of a sudden, this kid pushed his way through the crowd and bent over to ask me if he could help. He pulled me to my feet and handed me his lunch. I'd ruined mine when I'd fallen on top of it. That was Alex. He's been my best friend ever since."

Rachel raised her upper lip. "Very touching. What the fuck does that have to do with what we're talking about?"

What an asshole, Ted thought. "I'm letting you know the kind of person you're dealing with."

Rachel smirked. "You may have known him longer than I have, but I know how he thinks better than you do. All he's thinking about is that blonde slut and what she can do for him." She hesitated. "And to him."

Ted eyed her for a moment and then smiled. "You've really got it bad for him, don't you?"

Rachel reddened. She looked at her nails. "Believe me, that slut is going down. Big time. If you're such a good friend of Alex, you'll try to save him from going down with her."

"I could care less about your little love triangle, but you already know I'll do what I can to help him." Ted grinned. Fucking bitch.

Rachel glared at him for a moment. "If you think that's why I brought you into this, then you're as dumb as they are." She walked away without looking back.

Ted watched her until she turned the corner and was out of sight. The clicking of her stilettos on the marble floor faded into silence. Alex had had a lot of girlfriends over the years, but Rachel was the worst.

In truth, Ted was frightened about what might happen to Alex. No one could ever understand how much Alex meant to him or the lengths he would go to protect him. It wasn't comfortable standing by and watching him go through all this without doing something to prevent him from destroying everything he had worked so hard to achieve. He understood what was at stake, better than anyone else could imagine. But the others had their plan, and he had his.

CHAPTER 24

Katie placed the weekly call to Sylvia. "Hi. Anything new?" Sylvia said, "I've tried to write a lot, make notes for myself so that I won't forget things that happened so long ago. Like I said last time, this is like going to therapy sessions."

"So, what do you have for me today?"

Sylvia paused. "I've thought a lot about the weeks after the abuse started. Everything was falling in place for Dr. Pittsburgh. He became an instant celebrity. Six weeks had passed by since that first meeting with Dr. Pittsburgh, and he had not mentioned anything about the ominous discrepancy in the research results. I'd carefully re-checked my work. There was no question that my assessment was accurate. My efforts to validate the original findings had simply failed to confirm the results. In the meantime, Dr. Pittsburgh had appeared on national television several times to trumpet his 'discovery.' It was probably more often than that if the constant chatter about his research in the lab was any indicator. My co-workers would not stop talking about it, and I was getting sick and tired of hearing about how brilliant Dr. Pittsburgh was.

"Meanwhile, his name was becoming a household word nationally. For the most part, others did not realize that I was listed as the co-author of the paper. A few reporters contacted me to give interviews, but I referred them to Dr. Pittsburgh instead. I felt I was better off not saying anything to anyone because he had me scared as hell about saying the wrong thing, making a mistake. As he said, I was better off keeping my damn mouth shut.

"During this time, Dr. Pittsburgh called me into his office many times, and he didn't have research on his mind. He would say, 'Be a good girl and earn your place in the program. And always remember – to get ahead, you have to give head.' He'd laugh each time he said it as if his crude attempt at humor might justify what he was doing to me. Or make me feel better in some way. It didn't. I didn't know which was worse, the actual sex or the self-loathing I took away each time. I resolved to block it from my mind and pretend that it didn't happen.

"It really was no different than when I was in foster care. I remembered the days when my siblings would make me miss the bus by locking me in the bathroom and I would have to walk to school in the pouring rain. I would finally arrive late for class, drenched from head to toe, clutching my notebooks to my chest to protect my precious papers from getting wet. I would be so agitated that I would lash out at anyone who would look at me as if I were a feral teen, with my crooked teeth and stringy hair, not a response that would be embraced by the popular kids. But they were my only family, and I always forgave them for their meanness. Somehow I always assumed that I probably deserved it."

Katie had taken notes. "No one deserves what you've gone through. Don't believe that for a minute. I've made arrangements for you to see a psychiatrist who specializes in treating victims of rape. He may be able to help you put this all in perspective. I'll have Leslie call you and give you the details as you'll need to fly to his office in Nashville to meet with him."

CHAPTER 25

Time passed quickly for Alex after receiving word that the paper was scheduled for publication in March 1986. Fortunately, his responsibilities at the hospital kept him busy, as did the time he spent with Ingrid and Rachel. His balancing act, juggling time spent with the two women, was a dynamic that changed from day to day. Rachel wanted his undivided attention, and Ingrid was simply grateful for whatever time he gave her. Rachel constantly harangued him about withdrawing the paper before it was published, and Ingrid restored his faith in "doing the right thing," as she put it. A gradual shift in Alex's affection toward Ingrid was the result.

~ ~ ~

Alex was sitting with Ted in the hospital cafeteria, catching up on their lives. He took a good look at Ted's face. "You look tired."

"My ass is dragging."

"Hot date last night?" Alex asked jokingly.

Ted shook his head. "I worked a double shift yesterday. Usually, they don't bother me, but I've been exhausted lately."

Alex leaned across the table and said quietly, "I think I'm in love."

Ted sat back. "This is about the tenth time you've said that since I've known you." He wasn't smiling.

"I'm serious. I think this is the real thing this time."

"That's what you said about Rachel a couple of months ago. Who is it this time?" As if he didn't know.

"Ingrid." Alex couldn't keep the smile from his face when he said her name.

Ted averted his eyes and gripped his coffee cup. He took a long swallow before he responded. "Sorry, Alex. I don't see the two of you together."

"Why not? She's absolutely perfect for me."

"There's more to life than getting laid, my friend. There's a whole lot more." Careful. Don't push too hard.

"Jeez, Ted. Give me some credit, will you? We've got a whole lot more going on than getting laid. She makes me feel good about myself. She's smart, kind, and respectful of others. And most importantly, we can talk about anything."

Ted shook his head. "Sorry, I disagree. You're thinking with your dick again, my friend. She's a stuck-up bitch, and I think she's major trouble for you, the way she struts around here, wiggling her ass and tossing her blond hair around as if she owns the damned place."

Alex was pissed. He stood and said, "Some friend you are. Even in college, you would do everything in your power to break up any relationship I was in. Now I find myself serious about this woman, and here you are once again, telling me she's no good for me. Can't you just for once try and get to know her before you decide whether she's right for me? I think she's perfect. Besides, when did I ever ask you to be the gatekeeper of my heart?"

Ted watched Alex walk away. You don't know the half of it, amigo.

~ ~ ~

"Are you sure?"

The lab technician nervously wiped his hand on his sleeve. "I ran it through twice. When I saw the results of the first test, I did it over."

Ted looked at the lab report. He couldn't believe it. He didn't want to believe it. He now understood why he'd been feeling lousy for the past month. Antibiotics didn't resolve his fever and other symptoms. The lab results indicated that his white blood cell count was low – extremely low.

The lab tech ushered Ted by the arm to a corner of the lab and said in a conspiratorial tone, "These results look like the patients in Dr. Hartley's study."

Ted looked at him, scowling. "What's that supposed to mean?"

The lab tech grinned. "Are you gay? It's okay. Your secret is safe with me." He placed his closed fist over his heart.

Goddammit. This guy could blab his mouth all over the hospital. Ted hesitated. "No, I'm not."

The lab tech squeezed Ted's hand and gave him a friendly smile. "There but for the grace of God go I. If you'd like, some night, we could have dinner together and talk about it."

Ted recoiled from the man's touch. Panicking, he turned and walked away. Fuck. He'd spent his entire life pretending to be something he wasn't, and now some dumb fucking lab technician knew the truth. This complicated matters for him. His whole fucking life was at stake. He'd been different as far back as he could remember, and he'd worked so hard to keep others from knowing. Now people would be able to guess about, to learn, his sexual orientation by looking at some dumb fucking lab report. It wasn't fair.

Thinking back to the meeting with Rachel and Dr. Olmstead, he realized they were right about who was responsible for this mess. The more he thought about it, the angrier he became. Pacing back and forth in the hallway outside the lab, he decided to do whatever it took to rectify the situation. It was all a matter of timing.

He muttered as he strode away, "I'll get that fucking bitch if it's the last thing on earth I do."

CHAPTER 26

February 1986

Ted knew he had to keep cool when speaking with Alex. He didn't want to tip his hand about what was in store for his friend. "What are you going to do when Rachel finally finds out about Ingrid?" He asked the question casually as he and Alex left the conference room after a weekly journal meeting.

Alex shrugged. "I tell Rachel nothing is going on with Ingrid and me. All Rachel knows is that she exists and we worked on the research together. I tell her it's purely platonic, nothing physical at all."

Ted laughed. "And I'm the fucking tooth fairy. Do you expect her to believe that?"

"You don't think she could believe I can have a platonic relationship with a beautiful woman?"

Ted laughed louder. "Some people could. Rachel doesn't happen to be one of them. And I'm another."

Alex stopped walking and thought about what Ted said. "I'm kind of proud of how pure she and I have been around each other. She's pretty damned serious about most things. But I've also been with her when she lets her hair down, so to speak." He laughed.

Ted stared at him. "Rachel seems like the jealous type to me. When she finds out what is really going on between you and Ingrid, she's going to go ballistic." He paused. "By the way, is Rachel as good in bed as everybody says?"

Alex frowned. What Rachel and he did together was their business and no one else's. The same with Ingrid. "Rumors. I don't listen to them, and you shouldn't, either. People say a lot of nasty things about those who are smarter or more attractive than they are. I suspect Rachel doesn't give most guys the time of day. I suspect that Ingrid doesn't, either."

"It's called denial, Alex. You're in denial. I bet that Rachel has slept with half the attending staff, single or married."

Ted was trying to irritate him, and he didn't like it. "That's not fair, Ted. What do the lawyers call it? Hearsay? I'm surprised that you'd say those kinds of things about someone else. Especially someone you don't even know. What's gotten into you?"

Ted shrugged. "Where there's smoke, there's fire. If the shoe fits, wear it. Pick a cliché. They all apply here."

Alex was upset with Ted, with what he was saying. "I still can't understand why you are so jealous of me and my relationships." He started to walk away. "I've got to get back to the ward."

~ ~ ~

Rachel and her friend Allison were seated at the bar of the Traffic Jam, Detroit's most popular downtown hangout. Rachel leaned forward. "It isn't any ordinary relationship, Allison. Alex and I are close in every way you can imagine. We have something extraordinary going on."

Allison lit another cigarette. "How does he feel about you? What does he say?"

"He's very quiet. He doesn't say much, but I can tell he likes me a lot. He compliments me, says nice things about me. I'm not used to that with men I've dated in the past."

"Somehow I can't picture you settling down with one guy."

Rachel pouted. "Why do you say that? I've always been a one-man woman."

Allison laughed. "Oh, right. For about three weeks, until you meet someone else."

"Well, I'm very picky, and I don't sleep with all of them."

"Most of them, but what does that have to do with it? We're talking about your Dr. Hartley here. When do I get to meet this hunk?"

"You'll have to wait a while." Rachel laughed. "I'm keeping him all to myself for the time being. Besides, he's busy right now on an important project, doesn't even have time for me. I intend to change all that soon. He doesn't know it yet, but pretty soon I'll have him all to myself, any time I want."

"I don't like that look on your face. What are you up to?"

"I can't tell you, but it's going to be soon."

"Sometimes you scare me, Rachel."

146

For a moment, Rachel thought about seeing Alex with Ingrid at the Chop House, what was in store for Alex, and her role in bringing it about. "He reminds me of a little boy, so sweet and innocent. There's a lot he doesn't understand about people and the way the real world operates. He thinks everybody is good, which, I suppose, is to my advantage. As you know, I can be a real bitch at times."

"Oh, really?" Allison grinned. "I didn't know that."

"It's not that I want to be a bitch. It comes with my career situation. Working for my dad and Dr. Ratner is challenging. To them, I'm 'the girl' – the girl to bring them coffee, clean up their lunch mess, and do their research for them. It doesn't matter to them that I graduated from the University of Michigan at the top of my class. Every day, I have to prove to them that I am not a 'complete disposable' and have significant value and contribute to their profession. But Daddy and my boss will never admit that I am anything more than a secretary."

A short, bald, middle-aged drunk bellied up to the bar and leaned close to her. "Well, let me say that with legs like yours, you must be a great secretary. I'll buy you a drink if you promise to wrap those legs around me later. I'm guessing they could wrap around me twice."

"Fuck off. Mind your own damn business!" Rachel took a drag on her cigarette and blew the smoke in his face. She turned and looked at Allison. "Now, what were we talking about?"

"You said something about being a real bitch at times."

The two of them laughed hard.

"**H**ere comes the celebrity." The ward clerk winked at Alex as he walked into the nursing station.

"What's this all about?"

She nodded at the table. A copy of the March 1986 the *American Scientific Journal* lay open to the article.

"It came yesterday after you left. You're famous, Dr. Hartley. Can I have your autograph? Please." Another wink, a smile.

"Sure, any time for you! As long as it's not on a blank check." He returned her smile and sat down to look at the published paper. Damn, it felt good. Finally seeing it in print made him feel proud and accomplished, and what a relief to know they had achieved the goal.

"He's going to be difficult to put up with now," the charge nurse said to the small group who had gathered around him.

"He probably won't talk to us anymore," said another.

"Who's this Ingrid chick?" said a third nurse, looking over Alex's shoulder at the article. "We didn't know you had a life outside of this ward. When did you find time to do this?"

Alex relished the good-natured teasing after taking all the crap from Rachel, and he realized he couldn't wait to tell Ingrid about these special moments.

~ ~ ~

After their paper finally appeared in print, the initial flurry of publicity and media interest died quickly. Things were back to normal within a week. Alex's relationship with Rachel was in shambles, but he and Ingrid were getting to know each other better, much better. He'd spent two nights at her apartment recently and looked forward to more of the same.

Alex and Ted were having their morning coffee in the cafeteria before rounds started. Alex noticed again how awful Ted looked. He'd lost a lot of weight, and his eyes were sunken. This had gone on for a long time. "What is it, Ted? You don't seem yourself lately. Are you feeling alright?"

Ted shifted uncomfortably in his seat and gazed at the table as he said, "Let's not talk about me. Alex, I think there's going to be major trouble headed your way."

"Trouble? What kind of trouble?"

"Things are being said about your research."

"My research? What do you mean? What have you heard?"

"The rumor is that the two of you falsified your data to fit the conclusions."

Alex felt like Ted had slapped him in the face. He felt his face redden. "That's bullshit. Where did you hear this?"

"Alex, I knew this was going to be trouble for you. I knew it."

"That doesn't answer my question, Ted. Where did you hear this?"

"I'm not sure you want to know."

"Know what? Of course I want to know! What kind of stupid game is this?"

Ted avoided eye contact. "I heard it from someone who said they heard it from Rachel." He fidgeted with his coffee cup and kept his eyes lowered.

"Rachel? Tell me what you heard."

"Rachel is telling others that her boss, Dr. Ratner, has evaluated your work and found that some of the data was made up simply to justify the findings."

Alex was horrified. "Ted, look at me. You know I would never do such a thing."

Ted slowly looked up at him. He hesitated before speaking. "I know that, Alex. But don't forget that you're not the only one involved in the research."

"What is that supposed to mean?"

"Don't be naive."

"Are you accusing Ingrid of doing something wrong?"

"I'm not accusing anyone. I'm telling you what I've heard."

"Do you believe this crap?"

Ted shrugged. "Honestly, I don't know what to believe. I wouldn't put it past Ingrid to be creative with the data to make herself look good. I think she's capable of anything that would further her career."

Alex shook his head. "You don't know anything about her."

"I'm not making this up. This is serious, Alex."

"It's a bunch of crap, and you know it."

"For your sake, I hope you're right."

Alex stood and pointed at Ted. "You should check your facts before you make accusations. Rachel is playing dirty because she's jealous of Ingrid." He turned and walked out of the cafeteria.

Later that morning, he received a phone call.

"Hello." He cradled the phone on his shoulder and continued writing in a patient's chart. He needed to work every minute because the hospital had admitted ten new patients the evening before. There was a lot to do.

"Is this Dr. Hartley?"

"Yes. What can I do for you?"

"I'm calling for your reaction to the news. What do you have to say?"

"News? Who is this?"

"David Shea, *Free Press*. What's your reaction?"

"My reaction to what?"

"I'm talking about the accusations against you."

"I don't know what in the hell you're talking about." Alex rolled his eyes at the ward clerk, who was sitting nearby with a puzzled look on her face.

"You better sit down if you're standing." Shea paused. "There was an editorial written by Dr. Robert Ratner, a local doctor, in this month's issue of the *AMA Journal* that accuses you of fraud. He claims that the medical data in your work was falsified. I tried to reach you yesterday for your reaction but couldn't locate you, so I wrote my article without your reaction. It's on the front page today. What do you have to say?"

"It's bullshit."

The ward clerk flinched as Alex angrily hung up the phone. He slammed the patient's chart shut and then went downstairs to the hospital lobby and bought a copy of the *Free Press*. There it was, right on the front page. The heading of the editorial screamed out at him as a sinking sensation arose in his gut.

Study Is Removed as Local Scientist Sounds Alarm. Alternative Cause of AIDS Discredited

A report published in the renowned American Scientific Journal was removed the week after it first appeared when its authors could not verify a database of medical records underlying the basis for the research. The study produced an astounding result and attempted to discredit Dr. Arnold Pittsburgh's brilliant discovery that AIDS is caused by HIV. The removed research claimed, instead, that the illness was caused in gay males by maternal use of estrogen during pregnancies. A third-year internal medicine resident and an epidemiologist, both previously unpublished, led the study. They depended on a questionable database of patient medical records.

Questions arose about both irregularities in the data and the provenance of the dataset used in the analysis. The data came from unverified medical records gathered by both authors. Critics were quick to point out anomalies in the research, including implausible findings that should have been detected during the peer-review process. The authors of the study declined to comment. An independent source has provided the medical records of one patient used in the study that indicates information at odds with claims made in the study.

Dr. Robert Ratner, a highly respected Detroit scientist and co-author of the widely used Textbook of Pharmacology, said, "The misuse of data can be tempting for researchers, but it must be understood where the data came from, its authenticity, and its quality if published research is to be deemed acceptable. The validity of the study is of no scientific value."

Though the removed article made no mention of one of its findings, an earlier draft version suggested a relationship between the moral degradation of homosexuality and the ingestion of DES by women that now must be reconsidered in light of the documented unscrupulous manipulation of data.

The removal of the article also raises troubling questions about the state of scientific research as the AIDS epidemic spreads. Many papers are being rushed to journals with little or no peer review. Critics fear long-held standards of even the most discerning journals are eroding as they face pressure to rapidly assess and disseminate new scientific reports.

Alex shuddered as he read. He felt clammy, his hands shook, and his gut retched. He wanted to throw up. He sat with his head in his hands. Removed? What the hell was this all about? What a shit-storm this had turned into. He went to a phone, called Ingrid, and told her what Dr. Ratner had done.

At first, she thought he was joking.

"It's no joke, Ingrid." He read the entire article to her over the phone.

"This can't be happening. There must be some mistake, Alex."

"I know. There has to be some explanation."

"Can we get together and talk about it later today?"

"I'm not free until late afternoon. I'll meet you in the cafeteria at about four o'clock."

What a bunch of bullshit. Alex threw the newspaper into the trash receptacle and left. He thought about calling Shea back and telling him what a piece of shit he was.

~ ~ ~

The rest of the day at the hospital was chaotic. Media people were everywhere, clamoring for comments from Alex. The crew of a local TV station, rebuffed in its efforts to speak with him, apparently started to conduct a live interview with a patient after telling him about the study results. Finally, security personnel removed all the media from the hospital.

Alex met Ingrid in the cafeteria. "This is a frigging nightmare."

She shook her head. "We didn't expect anything like this."

"It's the damn media. They'll do anything for a story."

Ingrid looked around, leaned toward Alex, and said softly, "That *Free Press* guy sure did a number on us."

Alex nodded. "He never even tried to speak to us, to get our point of view. I've tried to reach Dr. Ratner, but he wouldn't accept my call."

"From now on, we refuse to talk to them. They are all a bunch of liars and will publish anything that will sell newspapers."

"I agree."

The clamor continued the next few days. When Alex thought things had quieted down, another reporter would call and start hassling him for an interview. He refused all requests, but public interest in the study snowballed. The story in the *Free Press* was picked up by the wire services, and it made national headlines by the end of the week.

CHAPTER 28

March 1986

Rachel waited in the hallway outside of Ingrid's office until she was confident she was alone. Then she knocked on the door and walked in without waiting for a response. Ingrid sat at her desk. A copy of the *American Scientific Journal* lay in front of her. Her face was tear-streaked, her eyes red and swollen.

"May I help you?"

Rachel looked for a place to sit. Journals and books were piled on every available chair. She remained standing with her arms folded across her chest. "We need to talk."

"Who are you?"

"You know damned well who I am. Don't get cute with me."

Ingrid pushed her chair back and stood. "Tell me who you are and what you want or leave."

Rachel stared at Ingrid. A very long silence fell.

"You don't know who I am? Let me tell you. I'm Alex Hartley's fiancé. I'm here to tell you to stay the fuck away from him, if you know what's good for you."

"Alex doesn't have a fiancé."

"He sure as hell does. You're looking at her."

Ingrid hesitated. "He's never said anything to me about you."

"Why should he? He probably figures you'll stop screwing him if you found out."

"You'd better leave right now ... or I'll call security."

Rachel took a step closer. "I'm not leaving until I'm finished saying what I came here to say. You listen to me good, Missy. I've got a great thing going with him, and I'm not going to let a slut like you ruin it."

Ingrid reached for the phone. Rachel stepped forward and put her hand on top of Ingrid's. "Understand this. I'm not leaving until you promise to get the fuck out of his life." She dug her fingernails into the flesh of Ingrid's hand and smiled as Ingrid flinched from the pain.

"You're hurting me."

Rachel increased the pressure. She felt her fingernails bury deeper. With her other hand, she reached into her purse and extracted a folded piece of paper. "I'll hurt you a lot worse if you don't stay away from him. This is my phone number. Call me if you want further details about how your boyfriend is cheating on you."

She released Ingrid's hand, slowly walked to the door, turned back, and glared at her for a moment as she left.

Her next move was to call Alex.

~ ~ ~

Rachel called Alex and started right in on him. "You should have known something like this was going to happen."

"How can you say that? This is so much bullshit." He frowned at her arrogance.

"I'm surprised that it isn't worse."

"What do you mean?"

"From what I've heard –"

"You work for Dr. Ratner. You knew this was going to happen before my research was published, before it came out. Didn't you? How could you do this to me?"

"I tried to warn you."

Alex raised his voice. "You never said anything like this. You knew about this all along."

Rachel said quietly, "I knew Dr. Ratner was going to do something, and I gave you plenty of warning. You've got to think about what's happening and who's really responsible."

Alex was pissed. "What's that supposed to mean?"

"Put the blame where it belongs. Ingrid's the one who screwed up, not you."

"No one did anything wrong."

"Talk all you want, Alex. This is a problem that's not going to go away. There are only a couple of options. Either you did this together or one of you falsified the results. If it wasn't you, then it had to be her."

Alex shook his head. "No way. She'd never do something like that. She wouldn't. The results weren't falsified. Ratner and the article in the *Free Press* got it wrong."

"Think about it, Alex. How much do you know about her?" Rachel paused. "The people I've talked to say she's a bitch. They say she'll do anything to get ahead, to make herself look good. She's nothing but a whore. The sooner you realize that, the better it will be for you."

"That's nonsense! You're way out of line!"

Rachel stayed calm. "Think about what's at stake. Your career, reputation, everything you've worked so hard to achieve, it's all going right down the drain. You're a fine person, Alex. A lot of people admire and respect you. You need to expose her for what she is. It makes no sense for you to go down with her. If she has the chance, she'll blame it all on you. You can bet on that. I know you've got something going with her. Don't forget that I saw the two of you at the Chop House. She was climbing all over you. But remember, it's not worth destroying your career over a piece of ass. I think you need to start thinking clearly about what's actually happening here, Alex."

It was true, Alex thought, that he was smitten by Ingrid, but it was difficult for him to even think about her doing what Rachel was suggesting. He needed more information from Rachel first.

"What are you suggesting?"

Rachel outlined her plan. He listened without comment. Damn. She really did have a plan, but it was bullshit. He needed to speak with Ingrid and get the truth.

~ ~ ~

Ingrid and Alex sat in the coffee shop and looked nervously at each other. Ingrid's eyes were red from crying. He placed a copy of the *American Scientific Journal* open to their article on the table between them.

Rachel's phone call had shaken Alex badly. It was difficult to even think it possible that Ingrid was capable of doing what Rachel had suggested. On the other hand, Alex knew that he'd done nothing wrong. He'd expected that the study would cause controversy, but nothing like this. Was there any truth to the accusations? He felt a cold fury as he thought about the terrible dilemma they were in.

"Ingrid. I need to ask – is there any reason to think we did something wrong?"

"Alex, we checked the data very carefully. You know that we did." Her cool stare surprised him.

"Ingrid ..." He hesitated, couldn't bear the thought of asking her if she'd cheated, so he remained quiet.

Ingrid continued to glare back at him. She was an emotional wreck and had been stung by Rachel's diatribe, the accusations against them and their research. More importantly, she didn't understand the man seated opposite her. Was Rachel his fiancé? If so, he'd not only betrayed her but Rachel as well. She realized she did not know Alex at all. How could he have done this? How could he lie and make love to her when he had an emotional commitment to another woman? His fiancé, for God's sake! She couldn't bear the thought, but the truth was the truth. It was as simple as that. She despised liars and cheats and was surprised at the intensity of the hatred she felt towards Alex. Now this goddamn cheating liar was sitting right in front of her and implying that she was the one who had cheated on the research. She was mad as hell.

Ingrid stood and said, "You think I'm lying. I can see it on your face. Before you accuse me, you better look in the mirror. Don't forget one thing. You were the one who provided all the information for the study. All I did was crunch the numbers. I didn't change a damn thing."

She started to walk away from the table. Hesitating, she stopped and turned to face him. Her face was crimson. "I've heard all I need to know about you from your fiancé, Rachel. How dare you call me a liar. You're the fucking cheating liar. How could you do this to me?" She stepped forward and slapped him hard across the face. Then she turned and walked away without looking back.

~ ~ ~

Fiancé? Where had she gotten that idea? Alex sat and rubbed his face where she'd hit him. He was frozen in his chair, unable to move after hearing her accusations. He was

158

confused, didn't know what to think or believe. Rachel said that Ingrid was going to try to blame him. What was this fiancé thing all about? He tried to sort out the day's events in his mind as he heard his name being paged. How could so much crap happen in a single day?

He picked up the nearest phone and listened. The message was short and direct, and the hospital operator conveyed it with mechanic-like efficiency. "Dr. Olmstead will see you in the conference room of the hospital administrator ... now."

He walked over to the administration wing of the hospital, feeling as if he were moving through time and space into a bad dream. He knocked, entered the room, and looked around at those present. The administrator and Dr. Olmstead were the only people he recognized. He had no idea who the other three men were. The expressions on all their faces frightened him. He sat down in the proffered chair.

The administrator, Elwood Jones, a short, bespectacled man, said, "We are here to inform you, Dr. Hartley, that your privileges at the hospital are suspended."

"Suspended? Is this a joke? Are you kidding me?"

"This is no laughing matter. Given the serious nature of the charges against you, the hospital board believes that the situation requires immediate action. You have the right to appeal this board's decision, but your privileges will remain suspended while any appeal you might make is pending."

He gestured toward the three strangers in the room. "These men are from the Michigan Medical Disciplinary Board, and they have also suspended your license to practice medicine. We all sincerely regret having to take these actions, but you leave us no choice. You will, of course, be paid during your suspension, pending any final decision that may be made."

The group nodded as one, and Jones gestured for Alex to leave the room.

He walked away from the meeting in a daze. What had just happened? His senses, perceptions, thoughts, emotions, feelings – all seemed unreal. Numb beyond belief, he went to the doctors' lounge and sat down on the bench in front of his locker. What more could go wrong? How much more could he take? He felt betrayed and humiliated.

"Dr. Hartley, I'm sorry, but I have to ask you to leave."

He looked up to see the security guard in his neatly pressed blue uniform, staring down at him. "Sam. What did you say?"

"My instructions are to ask you to leave the hospital. I would appreciate it if you didn't give me any trouble. I'm just doing my job."

Alex stood and nodded. He felt tears well up in his eyes as he walked out of the room. Several young residents stopped talking and looked at him as he passed by them. Every shred of his dignity had been stripped away. He went into the nearest bathroom, locked himself inside one of the stalls, and wept. He couldn't remember the last time he'd cried. Never in his life had he felt such shame.

CHAPTER 29

November 2018

Sylvia called Katie.

"What's new?" Katie asked.

"There is something I thought about this week, and I don't know why I didn't mention it to you before now. I guess I just forgot about it."

"Well, what happened to you was a long time ago. I'm surprised that you remember as much as you do. What's the new thing?"

"It's ironic, but I did have some contact with Detroit in the past. Do you know the name Ingrid Kubilus?"

Katie thought for a moment. The name sounded familiar, but she didn't remember why. "No, I don't."

"How about Alex Hartley?"

"I know Dr. Hartley very well. He's an expert witness in many of our firm's pharmaceutical cases, including yours. He and my senior partner are best friends. Why do you ask? How do you know his name?"

"Remember, in my initial interview with you, I mentioned a study that came out about the same time as Dr. Pittsburgh's that showed that endocrine disruption was a more significant factor in AIDS than a virus?"

"Yes, I do remember."

"Dr. Hartley and Dr. Kubilus published a research paper in March 1986 that suggested an entirely different cause of AIDS than HIV. Do you know anything about that?"

"Yes. Now that you mention it, I do remember the name Ingrid Kubilus. She was the co-author of the paper with Dr. Hartley, but tell me what you know about it."

"It was sometime around the end of March 1986. Every morning for years, I've had coffee to jumpstart my day. Back then, I was finishing my morning fix, and an article in the *New York Times* caught my attention. The article's caption was 'Detroit Scientists Fraudulently Claim That Pregnancy Drug Causes AIDS and Homosexuality.' My first thought was that

Dr. Pittsburgh would be pissed off that some other scientist was getting attention about the cause of AIDS. I read the article, and it was short on details. The reporter appeared to be more intent on ridiculing the scientists than actually reporting the research findings' newsworthiness. The article suggested the research was done fraudulently, but I knew better, and I had proof that it wasn't."

"Let me stop you right there for a moment. What kind of proof?"

"I'll get to that, but let me finish what I want to tell you. I knew I had to get my hands on this research because the study's premise fascinated me. The authors of the study, Dr. Hartley and Dr. Ingrid Kubilus, found that the males had near-total destruction of T-cell lymphocytes, leading to fatal cancers or intractable cases of pneumonia. I was familiar with DES because I had kept up with the literature on maternal use during pregnancy and the development of a rare form of vaginal cancer in some female offspring.

"When I arrived at the lab that morning, I went online to PubMed, the national government database of medical and scientific journal articles. I found and printed out the Hartley-Kubilus study. After reading it, I was impressed with the quality and thoroughness of the work. If, as the news article suggested, the study had been done fraudulently, there was nothing in the research itself that gave the slightest indication that anything was amiss. I knew better because I knew why the charge was being made. I called the Detroit City Hospital switchboard and was connected to the Poison Center. I asked to speak with either Dr. Hartley or Dr. Kubilus. I talked to Dr. Kubilus. I had questions for her that she might not want to answer, but the answers were important to me in dealing with Dr. Pittsburgh, and they might help her, too. I remember the conversation like it was yesterday."

~ ~ ~

The phone rang twice before Ingrid picked up. "Hello."

"Doctor Kubilus, my name is Sylvia Anderson, and I'm calling from New York. I need a few minutes to explain why I'm calling, but I can assure you that it's crucial."

"Are you a reporter? If you are, I don't want to speak with you."

"No. I'm a scientist. I'm the co-author of the research published by Dr. Arnold Pittsburgh that claims HIV causes AIDS. You may have read about our research. It's been in the news lately."

"I've seen Dr. Pittsburgh on television, talking about the study. I didn't pay enough attention to know there was a co-author since Dr. Pittsburgh received all the press. What do you want from me?"

"I have your published research paper right in front of me. I've gone through it in detail a couple of times. It's very impressive, and I'd like to talk with you about it."

There was a pause at the other end of the line. Finally, Ingrid said, "How do I know you are who you say you are?"

Damn. "Let me put it differently. I think it's important that we talk because I know I can help you."

"Help me? Why would you want to help me? For all I know, you could be a reporter."

"I understand your concern. Will you agree to meet with me in person so I can prove to you who I am?"

"I'm going to hang up now unless you can give me one good reason why I should talk to you any further. Or why we should meet."

Sylvia needed to convince her that she was legitimate. "One good reason is Dr. Pittsburgh."

"Dr. Pittsburgh?"

"Yes. He and a drug company are behind everything that's happening to you right now. He wants to discredit your study to make him look better, and the drug company wants to avoid lawsuits."

"How would you know about what they've done? Or what I'm going through?"

"There are two reasons why I can help you. The first is that I came across a letter Dr. Pittsburgh left on his desk. He had a deal with a drug company, Orex Laboratories, to sabotage your study. They arranged to have Dr. Pittsburgh's study published before yours so that his work would already be in print by the time your work was published. They also arranged a claim that your study was done fraudulently. If your study was discredited, it would save Orex from having to pay out millions of dollars in lawsuits.

"Pretty much the same thing is happening to me. Dr. Pittsburgh published his research before I completed our validation studies. When I did complete the studies, I found that I couldn't validate the original results. Now he is threatening to accuse me of faking the research results he published if I expose the truth. The same thing you're going through right now. We need to meet in person so I can show you what I'm talking about. Can you meet with me?"

"I don't know who I can trust at the moment."

"I want to earn your trust. I'll fax you the letter. Read it, and you'll see I am telling you the truth. Please think it over. What would you have to lose by meeting with me if I am telling the truth?"

Ingrid was quiet for a moment. "Fax me the letter, and I'll give it some serious thought. Why don't you call me tonight, and I'll give you an answer?"

~ ~ ~

"We ended the call after Ingrid gave me her office fax and home phone numbers. I immediately faxed her the letter. I knew that she'd realize that I could be a help to her. What she didn't realize was how much help she could be to me, too.

"That evening, I called three times, but there was no answer. Finally, I gave up. I knew that she was distrustful of me, but I truly felt that she would know I was telling the truth once she read the letter. I didn't blame her. I probably wouldn't have trusted me, either. That letter was what she needed to prove her innocence."

CHAPTER 30

March 1986

I ngrid retrieved the letter from the fax machine and read it. This Sylvia Anderson was right. Everything was there in black and white. For the first time since her world had started falling apart, she had a feeling of hope. She made a Xerox copy of the letter and put it in the research file she kept at her office. She packed her briefcase, including the faxed letter, walked over to the medical library, and located the Pittsburgh study in the December 1985 issue of the *American Scientific Journal*. She read it twice.

This was unbelievable. There was no mention of any validation efforts in the paper. Why would the journal remove their study but publish a piece of crap like this? She checked her watch, and it was getting late. She hoped that she hadn't already missed the woman's call.

~ ~ ~

The intruder entered after dark. A sweeping glance around the small apartment provided all the needed information for what was to be done. The setting couldn't be more perfect.

A few minutes later, Ingrid entered the dimly lit foyer and started up the stairs. She avoided the elevator whenever possible, hoping that climbing the few flights would give her some exercise, which was otherwise sorely lacking from her schedule. With her demanding workload, there was no time for visits to the gym. She reached the third floor's landing and stopped to rest, putting her heavy leather bag down. It was eerily quiet. No TV sets blared – no loud music. The silence unnerved her. She picked up her bag and walked up the last flight of stairs to her apartment.

The climb did nothing to relieve a sense of impending doom that had grown more foreboding all day. She felt helpless, trapped by everything going on. She sighed deeply as she stood in front of her apartment door, turned the key, and entered the pitch-black room. The darkness did nothing to lift her spirits as the door clicked shut behind her. She searched for the overhead light switch, slid the deadbolt in place, and fastened the chain. She leaned against the door and reflected on all that had happened. Everything had gone so wrong. She thought about the phone call with Sylvia Anderson. Could she be trusted? Ingrid had never felt so defeated and confused. She took the faxed letter from her briefcase and reread it. Then she placed the letter on the bedside table and hoped that the woman would call so they could discuss this letter in detail.

The intruder watched through the slats of the closet door.

Ingrid picked up the bedside phone and dialed the number Rachel had given her. There was no answer, so she left a subdued but firm message on the answering machine. "Your threats don't scare me. I don't care what you want or what you think is going on with Alex and me." She slammed the phone down on the receiver hard enough to startle the intruder.

She walked to the bedroom window, opened it halfway, and took a deep breath of fresh air. Off in the distance, she heard the raspy voice of Ernie Harwell float through the air – a Detroit Tigers spring training night baseball game was in progress in Lakeland, Florida, transmitted to thousands of radios tuned to the venerable announcer. Detroit was a hard-working town filled with hard-working people. Baseball in this city did what it could to distract working men and women, but it offered no solace to Ingrid as she tried to shrug off the gloom that enveloped her.

She began to undress, a deliberate, orderly process. She placed her dress aside, removed her half-slip, and folded it neatly before putting it in a drawer. She unhooked her bra and shrugged it off her shoulders, stepped out of her underwear, and dropped both items in the hamper.

She went into the bathroom, stepped into the shower, and welcomed the warmth of the spray on her body, hoping it would wash away her sorrow. That woman Rachel sure had a lot of nerve barging into her office and threatening her. Hell, what she'd done to her hand could be considered assault. She did not linger in the shower lest she miss the expected phone call from New York. She turned the water off, wrapped her body in one towel, her hair in another, and walked back into the bedroom. She toweled herself dry and briefly examined her body in the full-length mirror. Carelessly she dropped the towel to the floor and turned her attention to her hair.

Why was her world falling apart like this? Everything had been going perfectly until today. Now the research paper was being trashed. The bitch Rachel had destroyed the relationship she and Alex had been building together. "This is more than I can take," she sobbed loudly, and then she threw herself across the bed and stifled her sobs in a pillow.

~ ~ ~

This was going to be easy. The intruder emerged from the closet, stepped silently alongside the bed, and dropped across her back. Pinning her head against the pillow to muffle her screams, the intruder jabbed the needle into the soft flesh of her right hip.

~ ~ ~

Ingrid felt the sting of the needle and the burning sensation of the chemical as it slowly spread into the surrounding muscle tissue. She was paralyzed with fright. She couldn't move. The weight of the person on top of her and the chemical's deadly effect rendered her helpless. In seconds, she was paralyzed. As the lack of oxygen to her brain brought merciful unconsciousness, her last thought of concern for her mother went unfinished, vanishing in a flash.

~ ~ ~

Heart pounding, pulse racing, Ingrid's killer rose slowly, stood, and looked around. Think! Think! Finish the job.

The syringe and needle were returned to the protective case and placed carefully in an inside coat pocket with one gloved hand. At the same time, a note was removed from another pocket and carefully placed beside the telephone. The killer picked up the faxed letter that Ingrid had left on the bedside table, read it, and put it in the same coat pocket. Finding Ingrid's razor in the bathroom, the killer returned to the bedroom and gazed briefly at the body lying peacefully on the bed. The telephone rang, startling the killer. It rang ten times and stopped. A moment later, the phone rang another ten times. The killer froze in place, waiting until it stopped.

Almost done, and with shaking hands, the rest of the plan was carried out meticulously. With a renewed sense of anger, the killer stood over Ingrid's body and smiled. Serves her right. The bitch had it coming. On an impulse, the killer took the suicide note placed on the bedside table and returned it to the coat pocket. The killer switched the bedside lamp off and left the dark apartment.

~ ~ ~

Ed Herold had parked at the end of the block, where he had a good view of Ingrid's apartment's windows. When the lights went out in her apartment, he checked his watch. It was almost an hour later than he'd expected, later than her usual routine. He'd wait another hour. He understood that it might take a while for her to fall asleep, given everything that had happened today. He opened his thermos and poured himself another cup of coffee. He was a patient man. He sipped his coffee and waited. When the time was up, he checked everything once again to make sure he had what he needed. He got out of his car, locked the door, and walked to her building. He knew his way around because he was thorough in everything he did, never left anything to chance. He'd been inside her apartment twice already on previous occasions while she'd been at work.

CHAPTER 31

March 1986

The knocking on his apartment door startled Alex, and he slowly rose off the couch and stepped carefully to avoid the pizza box and empty whiskey bottle at his feet. Who the hell could be knocking at his door? The rain beat incessantly against the windows of the apartment while, in the distance, a roll of thunder peaked to a crescendo. A couple of knocks in succession, a little louder and more insistent, made him hasten his shaky steps. He was still a little drunk, he realized. He opened the door and found himself face to face with an older woman sobbing into her handkerchief.

What the hell? Who was this? Why did she look familiar? He stared at her.

She asked, "Alex Hartley?"

"Yes. I'm Alex. Who are you, and what do you want?"

"I'm Ingrid's mother. Oh, Alex, she's gone. My baby girl is gone. Someone killed her." Her knees sagged, and she burst into tears.

Killed? Dead? Ingrid dead? The woman was Ingrid's mother? That's why she looked familiar. He wrapped his arms around her and held her while he tried to register the words in his mind. "I'm so sorry. Please come in and sit down." He cleared a space on the couch and sat next to her. He held her hands, and they sat silently for a few minutes until she composed herself.

"She didn't answer her phone or return my phone calls, so I went to her apartment to see if she was ill. She was lying on her bed, and she was dead. I'll never forget how she looked. It was horrible. Blood all over. I called the police. They told me she'd been dead for more than two days. Your address was in Ingrid's address book, and I wanted to make sure you knew. Last week, Ingrid told me that she was in love with you and the two of you were going through a difficult time at work."

Alex took several slow, deep breaths and hoped his breath didn't smell too much like alcohol. He tried to process the

169

news that Ingrid was dead. She loved him? Who would want to kill her? Why?

He asked, "What did the police say? Did someone break into her apartment?"

"There was no sign of a break-in, and the police are saying it's a suicide. But I know my daughter, and there is no way that she would kill herself! It doesn't make any sense. None of this does." She continued to sob uncontrollably.

Alex was numb, his emotions frozen. Tears would not come. He didn't know why. He wasn't holding back, but there was nothing there, a void. "Why do the police think she committed suicide?"

Ingrid's mother could barely speak through her tears and sobs. "Someone slashed her wrists and tried to make it look like she killed herself. She bled to death. My baby bled to death. She wasn't capable of doing such a thing, but I could tell that Detective Murphy, the policeman in charge, didn't believe me. Someone killed her and made it look like death by suicide. She was murdered, Alex. Murdered!"

Jesus. Who would do such a thing to Ingrid? It was too much for him to think about. She was dead. The reality of her death was finally dawning on him. "She was a wonderful person," he said, an awkward attempt to console her mother. His mind wasn't capable of dealing with the specifics, as the shock of the news and the lingering effects of last night's whiskey made any attempt to think logically impossible.

"She was all I had in the world." There were more tears and sobs. Alex didn't understand. Had Ingrid done this because of what he'd said to her?

Her mother continued. "Sooner or later, I'll prove to them she didn't kill herself. Whoever did this is not going to get away with it."

He nodded. What harm was there in placating a mother's memory? Wasn't it too early to make judgments about anything? The more he thought about it, the more he understood that her mother couldn't bear to face the unthinkable, that her child could willingly take her own life.

When she left, he grabbed a bottle of vodka from the freezer and sat on the couch. He took a large swallow right from the bottle and closed his eyes. He welcomed the heat of the booze as it reached his stomach. He took another large swallow and felt the effects reach his brain. He embraced the coming numbness, anything to take away the pain from the horrible reality of it all.

He kept drinking. His thinking got ugly fast and haunted him. Ingrid had good reason to be despondent. She was at fault for the fiasco with the research. Everything that had happened to the two of them was her fault. Rachel, Ted, Dr. Olmstead, Dr. Ratner – they were all right. But why was this realization not making him feel better? He hated thinking like this.

Outside, the pounding rain matched his mood. He chugged from the bottle. Ingrid was dead. Then it dawned on him. He was vindicated. Should he feel guilty for even thinking about it this way? Vindication is just a word, and he couldn't make the connection between the word in his mind and the sinking sensation in his heart. He was drunk, and he knew these were drunk thoughts. But it was so simple! All he had to do was pick up the phone and call Dr. Olmstead, and he'd be immediately reinstated. That was all he had to do. But it was more complicated than that. Something wasn't right. Something didn't fit. Lovely, beautiful, and sexy Ingrid killing herself? No. Not possible. It made no sense.

He drank until he passed out. He woke up in the middle of the night, still clutching the nearly empty bottle of vodka. His shirt and the couch were soaked with spilled booze. He was going to do something, but he couldn't remember what the fuck it was. He finished the last of the bottle and fell back asleep.

~ ~ ~

Detroit Police Detective Sergeant Joshua Murphy came by Alex's apartment early the next morning. Murphy was a tough guy with a lousy bedside manner. He would make a terrible doctor. He stared at Alex. "I'm having a hard time putting square pegs into round holes, doc, and I need you to help me out here."

"What can I do for you?"

"I understand that the two of you were close."

171

Alex hesitated. "That's true. We worked on a project together, and our relationship was developing into something more than a friendship."

"Her mother says she was in love with you." Murphy looked directly at him, his eyes unblinking. Sweat dripped from Alex's underarms. Murphy read from a notepad that was dwarfed by his huge hands and then looked at him again. "When was the last time you saw her?"

Alex paused. "I saw her at the hospital. Probably the day before she died." A tear welled up. He added, "A lot happened that day."

"What did you two talk about?" Murphy licked the point of his pencil and jotted a note as he spoke.

Alex thought back to that terrible day of the argument, the last time he had seen Ingrid alive, and the last words they had said to each other. He fought to hold back the tears as he said, "I don't remember. It was a bad day for both of us. We were both very upset."

"Where were you that evening? Can anyone verify what you did or where you were?"

Alex looked at Murphy. "Why? Is there something wrong? Is there something I should know about?"

"I ask the questions, and you answer them. What exactly did you talk about with Ingrid, and what did you do that evening?"

"She was horribly upset about the accusations being made against our research."

"So, it sounds like you think she killed herself."

Alex swallowed as he fought to hold back more tears. "I didn't say that. I don't know. She didn't seem the type to kill herself."

Murphy wrote on his notepad. "Anything else I should know about?"

"Not that I can think of."

"You haven't answered my question as to where you were that night."

"I'm not sure what day that was. I was thrown out of the hospital, and my medical license was suspended the same day

I last saw her. I've been in this apartment getting drunk ever since."

"Call me if you remember anything. Anything at all that would help us make sense of this death." Murphy handed him a card.

After he left, Alex stood at the doorway, relieved that he was gone. The detective's intimidating manner made him feel guilty, as if he'd done something wrong. He went back to his drinking.

~ ~ ~

Rachel was at her desk in the hospital when Dr. Ratner came out of his office and walked to her side. He leaned over and whispered, "That Ingrid girl killed herself."

"What?"

"She's dead. Her mother found her body in her apartment. I just spoke with the medical examiner, and he told me she slit her wrists and bled to death." He stared down at her. "You're smiling. I guess the two of you weren't friends, but you should at least act like you feel bad."

She shook her head. "Not a chance. When will Dr. Hartley be reinstated?"

Ratner looked around, leaned over again, and whispered, "Don't say things like that. Others might hear you. I don't think Hartley will be back."

Rachel started as though he'd slapped her face. "Why not? She killed herself. That proves Alex did nothing wrong."

"Appearances, my dear. Appearances. And keep your voice down."

Rachel thought about the suicide note. "What the fuck is that supposed to mean?"

"These things take time, a long time. It may never happen. Don't get your hopes up. Getting your boyfriend reinstated was never part of the plan."

Ratner stood up, walked back into his office, and closed the door.

Rachel sat and stared at the closed door for a long time. Fuck. Fuck. Fuck. This wasn't the way it was supposed to happen.

~ ~ ~

In Ann Arbor, forty miles away, Ed Herold sat across the desk from Dr. Klimpf. Herold smiled and said, "You're not going to believe this, but someone did the job for us. Either that or the girl really did kill herself."

Klimpf puffed on his cigar. "It's always good to have a real pro around to handle things when problems come up." He gestured to the small bar in a corner of the large office. "Fix us a couple of drinks, and we'll celebrate."

Herold stood and did what he was told. He came back with the drinks. "One thing is funny, though. There was no suicide note. I looked all over the damn place and couldn't find it."

CHAPTER 32

March 1986

A week later, Murphy sat with his supervisor, Detective Sergeant Rob Kistner, in a Greek Town coffee shop.

Kistner said, "Murphy, it occurred to me you're probably the only black guy on the entire Detroit police force with an Irish last name." He grinned at the huge man sitting opposite him in the booth. "So, what you got, you dumb Mick?"

Murphy shook his head. "Not much. The autopsy is clean except for scratches on the back of her left hand. No witnesses. Neighbors heard nothing." He shifted his weight and continued. "Strange, though. No fingerprints anywhere in the apartment. Everything wiped clean. That bothers me." He took a bite of the donut in front of him and handed the autopsy report to Kistner.

Kistner scanned the report. It began with the usual preliminaries, the time and place, and indicated that Detective Murphy and the mortuary technician had been present. A specimen of blood had been drawn for a routine toxicology screen. The language of the report was terse:

The body is that of a well-developed, well-nourished 25-year-old female. Rigor mortis, fully developed when the body was examined, was present in all muscle groups. The body smells of ethanol, leading the examiner to conclude that the deceased was intoxicated at the time of death. The fingernails are of medium length, clean, and unbroken. Other than as described below, the remainder of the skin surface is intact, without blemishes or scars. The natural head hair is of shoulder length and blonde. There are three deep scratch marks on the dorsum of the left hand, which appear to have been inflicted several hours prior to death. The left wrist has two extensive lacerations, one of which penetrated the radial artery such as to cause massive hemorrhage. There are no other external injuries. There are no defensive injuries to the hands or arms.

A detailed description of Ingrid's organs, including the brain, lungs, heart, liver, spleen, kidneys, stomach, and intestines, followed. Then came the conclusion:

There is no evidence of natural disease that could have caused or contributed to the death. The extensive wrist lacerations and severance of the radial artery, the lack of defensive injuries, and the strong odor of ethanol lead the examiner to conclude that a self-inflicted wound, complicated by alcohol intoxication, was the probable cause of death. The final diagnosis awaits pending toxicology results.

Murphy waited until Kistner looked up. "Her mother bothers me, too. Nice lady. Says there's no chance that her daughter would ever kill herself." He shifted his weight again. "Not much to go on. There's really not much we can do with this."

Kistner thought back to the scene at Ingrid's apartment. She'd been sprawled nude across the bed. "Damn shame. Fine-looking broad." He shrugged. "Did you see those tits? Write up the report. Close it out as a suicide. We got plenty of other things to do."

Murphy glared at his boss. "Please show some respect for the dead." He paused. "I think we should wait. Something else might turn up."

Kistner shook his head. "We got nearly a hundred murders a month going down in this fucking city, and you're worried about some broad who slit her wrists? No parent is ever going to want to believe that one of their kids could kill themselves. We're closing this. Write it up and close it."

~ ~ ~

Two days later, the office of the medical examiner sent the toxicology report of Ingrid's body fluids to the homicide department via interdepartmental mail.

Lisa Harvey was excited about her new job. It was temporary, to be sure, but it was a beginning. At eight o'clock that morning, she'd been in bed when she'd gotten the call to come to work. She knew that she'd be filling in for the secretary in the homicide department when the woman went on maternity leave, but she'd thought it would be next month. That's what they'd told her, anyway. Some things couldn't be predicted for certain. She'd been so excited when she'd learned she had been chosen for the temporary replacement job. The interviewer had told her they were interested in her because she was single and the mother of two children. The new mayor had promised he'd create more jobs for poor people, and she was poor, no doubt about that. It was a way out of the hell of poverty for her. She knew she lacked the basic skills required for this job, but she would try as hard as she could.

The phone rang as the interdepartmental mail was placed on her desk. "Hi, Mom." Lisa cradled the phone on her shoulder and removed the toxicology report from the envelope. She reached for the department stamp and placed the imprint on the face sheet of the report, just as she had been told to do. "It's a great job. I love it. They say I'm doing terrific. Hold on a second." All she had to do was file each piece of mail, or was she supposed to do something else with it first? She couldn't remember what she'd been told, and her supervisor was on coffee break. She looked around the office, but no one else was available to ask. She stood and walked over to the file cabinet, placed the report in Ingrid's file, and returned to her desk.

She picked the phone up. "I'm back. They got me filing and everything ..."

CHAPTER 33

June 1986

"The asshole comes in every day by ten." The bartender's toothless grin contrasted sharply with his bulk. He watched as Alex seated himself at the far end of the bar, where the room was poorly lit by an overhead fluorescent lamp that needed replacement. The darkness suited Alex just fine.

"Looks a little young to me," murmured one of the patrons.

"Never says nothing. Sits there all fucking day and drinks."

Alex knew they were talking about him. He couldn't care less. He held up two fingers and gestured at the bottle of cheap bourbon behind the bar. The walk to the bar from his apartment had shaken him to his core. One of the streetwalkers on the corner of Cass and Willis had been standing with her back to him as he'd approached. Goddamn, it's Ingrid, he'd thought. When she turned and saw him approaching, she said, "Fuck off." Alex felt his heart thump against his chest wall. It wasn't her. The disappointment was more than he could bear.

He'd found that the only way he could reduce the pain in his heart over Ingrid's death and his suspension was to stay drunk. Like a recurring nightmare, he'd wake each morning with an inconsolable sense of loss, the stab of intensity that she was gone and never going to come back. It was a reality that he couldn't face. Each passing day became a mirror image of the day before, a variation of a major theme: get drunk, stay drunk, and try not to think about anything else.

~ ~ ~

It took several moments for Alex to focus on his surroundings. He opened his eyes and looked around. He knew he was in bed, but he couldn't remember how he'd gotten there. He was holding one of his shoes tightly to his chest, as if he were holding Ingrid in his arms. A wave of

179

nausea swept through his body as he stood and staggered into the bathroom.

An old man looked back at him from the mirror above the sink. He barely recognized himself. Reddened by the ravages of alcohol, his eyes revealed the briefest glimpse of the fear and sadness that the events of the recent past had brought. He tried without success to recall what he'd done the previous evening. Maybe a drink will make me feel better, he thought as he splashed cold water on his face. He returned to the bedroom, where he put on the shoes and grabbed his jacket, and then he headed for the bar for some hair of the dog.

"You sure look a fuck of a lot better than yesterday," said one of the regulars, an old guy, as Alex sat down next to him. Hell, from what Alex had seen in the mirror this morning, he could have been the same age as this old guy.

"What do you mean?"

"Don't remember, eh?" The old man cackled and coughed at the same time, a thick, hacking sound from deep within his chest.

Alex said nothing. Sipping his drink, he tried to ignore what the old guy was saying.

"We never seen you mad before. Drunk plenty of times but never mad. Yelling and carrying on. We figured you was sick in the head." The old man coughed again.

Alex turned and looked at the man. "What was I yelling about?"

"About some drug company. You kept carrying on about some drug company. Made no sense to me or to any of us. Sure gave us a good laugh, though."

Alex sat silently, thinking. What had he done to himself? He was mortified over the loss of control of his life. He knew about blackouts from his medical training. Most of the derelicts that he'd treated at the hospital had suffered from them. How low did he need to get before he started doing something about his life and facing his problems? He stood, left the shots of bourbon on the bar, and walked out.

The phone was ringing when he walked into his apartment. For the past two months, he'd preferred to be alone, not engaging in conversation with anyone. Now he picked it up, eager to speak to anyone.

"Dr. Hartley, my name is Dr. John-Gunnar Fordland. I've tried calling you a number of times. I'm glad to have finally reached you. You don't know me and probably have never heard of me, but it's extremely important that we talk."

"I can hardly hear you. Where are you calling from?"

"Norway. I am a medical doctor in Norway, and I was the scientist who peer-reviewed your research for the *American Scientific Journal*."

Alex paused. "If you're going to say something bad about my research, I don't want to hear it. I don't feel comfortable talking to you. There's a lot that's happened –"

"That's exactly why we need to talk. I know about the accusations that have been made against you, and I'm convinced they are wrong. I want to help you."

"What makes you say that?"

"Your study results fit perfectly with everything else that is known about the effects of DES."

"I looked for earlier research and didn't find any."

"That's precisely my point. Orex has known for years that DES could cause problems."

"I'm not sure what you're saying and how it relates to my study."

"I'm saying that Orex conducted research similar to yours in animals and reached the same conclusions you did – a long time ago."

"How do you know? What makes you so sure that animal studies were done?"

"I did those studies."

"You did the studies? Seriously?"

"Early in my career, I performed research sponsored by Orex. My results were identical to yours, except I used animals."

"Why wasn't this published?"

"I thought it should have been. However, Orex disagreed with me. The terms of my research contract with Orex prevented me from publishing without their approval. That was a bitter experience. Since then, I've never done any research for anyone whose contract contained those kinds of restrictions."

Alex was skeptical. "Why are you telling me all this? Why would you want to help me?"

"Because, Dr. Hartley, you need someone on your side. More importantly, the issue is a lot bigger than the two of us. The health and well-being of a great many people are at stake."

"But if you are prevented from publishing your results, what can you do?"

"I've repeated the studies I did for them. This time, my university funded the research. The results were identical to my original research."

"I'm still not sure how all this helps me."

"That's why I have been trying to contact you. There is a lawyer in your city that I highly recommend you meet with. His name is Bob Riley."

"A lawyer? Why would I want to talk to a lawyer?"

"In my judgment, he needs your help, and you need his. He's suing Orex for the deaths of two of the men in your study. He came across my name in their internal documents and tracked me down after reading my research. I've agreed to be an expert witness in his case. Apparently, I can talk about my research in a courtroom, whether it's been published or not. I expect that he'd want the same from you."

Alex laughed. "I don't think he'd want any help from me. No one has said anything positive about my work. They say it was done fraudulently. Thanks for taking the time to track me down, but I don't think I need your help. It wouldn't do me any good."

"Please think about it. If you give me your address, I'll send you some interesting reading."

~ ~ ~

Within the week, a package arrived. It consisted of a series of research studies on DES. Alex read the materials carefully. Each was a variation on a common theme. DES had been administered in various dosages to pregnant rats, rabbits, and mice. Virtually all of the offspring of these animals developed cancers of various organs: skin, bladder, testes, liver, lungs, and brain. None of this work had been published. Orex had paid scientists to conduct the research and concealed the results when the studies had not come out the way they would have liked. The more Alex read, the more emotionally distraught he became. Could Orex actually conceal research like this, knowing that DES was being taken by pregnant women? How could they do such a thing?

He fell asleep on his couch with the research papers on his lap. He awoke in the middle of the night, crawled into bed, and tried to go back to sleep. He couldn't get comfortable and tossed and turned. Half asleep, half awake, all kinds of thoughts raced through his mind. He was a DES molecule, hurtling randomly through the bloodstream of some poor animal locked in a wire cage. He bounced from side to side against the walls of major arteries as he catapulted into various organs. He lodged momentarily inside the liver, where he attached briefly to the cells lining a bile duct. He turned and watched as these cells changed shape into a mass of cancer cells, which began feeding on surrounding normal cells. As the tumor grew, Alex broke away to continue his haphazard journey, dispersing a cascade of growing tumors wherever he alit.

He awoke again, looked at the bedside clock, and was dismayed to find that he'd been in bed less than forty-five minutes. Maybe a drink of water would help, he thought. He got up and drank greedily from the kitchen tap. He sat in the dark and began to think about what might have precipitated this strange nightmare.

Dr. Fordland and his research had given Alex an entirely new perspective on what he was going through. He closed his eyes and thought about Ingrid. From somewhere deep inside, a sob shook his body. Tears began to flow, and within moments, he was crying uncontrollably, his emotions a mixture of profound sadness and rage. "I'll get those bastards if it's the last thing I do," he promised himself. He looked at his watch. It was too late to call Riley. Either too late or too early. But he was going to follow Dr. Fordland's advice.

CHAPTER 34

July 1986

Two days later, Alex sat in a conference room in a downtown Detroit law office with Bob Riley and Gary Newton. He was surprised to see his friend Gary. Alex and Gary had been medical school classmates and first-year internal medical residents together at Detroit City Hospital. Gary had decided he wasn't cut out for the practice of medicine, so he'd dropped out of the residency program and gone to law school. He had doubled up on classes, finished the three-year program in two years, and recently been hired by Bob Riley.

"Here's the deal," Bob Riley said to Alex. "You need our help, and we need yours. We'll ask for a hearing with the medical board that suspended you. Dr. Fordland is coming to town soon to give a deposition in our cases against Orex, and we can also use him as an expert witness to testify in your favor. Once we get you reinstated, you can become an expert witness for us in those cases as well. One hand washes the other."

Alex smiled. "I like that. It's a deal."

"Tell us about yourself, Alex. What do you do when you're not practicing medicine?" Riley sat back and eyed Alex critically. He thought that the young man looked like he'd been run over by a steamroller.

Alex smiled ruefully. "Not much. I had a lot of interests as a kid but no time to pursue them. The last twelve years have been pretty much medicine 'round the clock."

Riley nodded and looked over at Newton. "We know all about that, don't we, Gary?"

Gary smiled back. "We sure do. Years of single-purpose toil leaves a huge void in the lives of young doctors. Most people don't understand the terrible sacrifices they make." He looked over at Alex. "It cost me my marriage with Bob's daughter."

Riley looked at Alex. "So, let's get busy. Be assured that we are going to do whatever is necessary to get your license back."

Riley assigned Newton the task of working up Alex's case, and Gary took Alex into his office. Alex told Gary the entire story, and Gary took copious notes. He interrupted Alex only when a particular point needed clarification.

When Alex finished, he said, "What I do know now is that I'm not going to walk away from all my education and training. No way am I going to give up everything I worked so long and hard for. Medicine is my life. So, I really need your help."

Riley walked back into the room. "I've set up a hearing date with the licensing board for early September. That's when Dr. Fordland will be in town after testifying to Congress. He wants to help you, and he's good, the best witness I've seen in my twenty years of practice."

CHAPTER 35

Late August 1986

Alex was sound asleep when the nurse called. "Dr. Wallace is dying. He is asking to see you. He needs to tell you something important. He's in Room 408."

Less than an hour later, he walked into Ted's room at the hospital. He barely recognized the shrunken shell of the man lying in bed. He remembered that Ted hadn't been feeling well the last time he'd seen him, five months earlier, but that was a far cry from the shriveled corpse-like figure now in front of him. He sat down at Ted's bedside and reached for his hand.

"Ted. It's Alex. I'm here." He squeezed Ted's hand gently.

Ted opened his eyes and turned his head toward him. "Alex. You came. I'm so grateful you came. I want to say goodbye."

Ted had been in Alex's life for what seemed like forever. The two of them had been like brothers ever since they were grade school kids. Alex sat there, at a loss for words as to what he could say that would comfort Ted. The rote, oft-repeated words that all physicians use to soothe dying patients escaped him. But Ted was more than a patient to him, and Alex's mind was a total blank. He sat quietly at Ted's side and held his hand.

A few minutes went by. Ted struggled to speak. "I have something important to tell you."

Alex moved closer. "Shush, Ted. You don't have to say anything to me. I'm here for you, dear friend." Tears streamed down his cheeks.

Ted took several raspy breaths. The rattle in his chest told Alex that his lungs were filled with fluid. "I've always loved you, Alex. I need you to know that ... I did a terrible thing." Two more raspy breaths. "I killed her. I killed Ingrid ... I hated what she'd done to you."

Alex heard the words, but his brain refused to process their meaning. He sat motionless, unable to move or respond.

187

A surge of anger welled up from somewhere deep inside him, and his tears flowed freely.

"You killed Ingrid?" he mumbled.

Ted nodded and closed his eyes. He took a deep breath. "There's more. Rachel was in on it. She planned the whole thing. I hate that bitch like I've never hated anyone. I left a suicide note in Ingrid's bedroom with Rachel's fingerprints all over it. Then I took it back."

Ted opened his eyes, nodded at Alex, took one last raspy breath, and died. Alex sat at his bedside and held his hand until a nurse came and ushered him to the visitors' lounge. She returned minutes later with a cup of coffee for him, and she waited quietly for a moment before handing him a sealed envelope.

She said, "You made him happy for being here with him. He asked that I give you this."

Alex waited until after she'd left the room before he opened the envelope. Inside were two single sheets of folded paper. He removed the first.

It was a copy of a typewritten letter on Orex Laboratories, Inc. stationery. It was dated November 17, 1985, and sent from the Orex president, Dr. Oskar Klimpf, to Dr. Arnold Pittsburgh, chairman of the Department of Biochemistry at Filmore University. He read the short message.

Dear Arnold,

This letter is being faxed to you to follow up on our conversation this morning. We will meet in Ann Arbor tomorrow. Edward Herold, our security consultant, will brief us on the actions that need to be taken to thwart the potential damage to you and Orex Labs if the Hartley research goes unchallenged. I was excited to hear that you are under consideration for a Nobel Prize. Mr. Herold will describe your role and handle any details for you that are necessary to secure the desired outcome. Dr. Ratner and Dr. Olmstead are also on board with the plan and will be present tomorrow. My secretary has made arrangements for your transportation in our private plane this evening, and you will be picked up at the airport. Hotel

arrangements have already been made, and you will return home in our plane at the end of our business. I look forward to seeing you again,

Gratefully,
Oskar

cc: Drs. Olmstead and Ratner

Alex removed the second sheet of paper. His name was typed in capital letters at the top. There was a message below, also typewritten;

Dear Alex;

I'm sorry about everything. I can't live any longer with this terrible burden of guilt.

Ingrid

Alex thought about the last thing Ted had said before he'd died. If Rachel had prepared this note, her fingerprints were all over it. He carefully folded both notes and put them back in the envelope.

CHAPTER 36

November 2018

Leslie and Katie, together with two law clerks, met in the conference room to go over Sylvia's file.

Katie said, "Leslie, do you have classes this Friday? I'd like you to go with me to New York to review the employment records that Filmore University has of both Dr. Pittsburgh and our client. I've also asked that the employment records be produced for the charming gal who replaced Sylvia as Pittsburgh's concubine."

Leslie shook her head. "Damn, you're breaking my heart. I can't go. I've got two exams next week, and lectures in both classes are Friday. I can't miss them." She paused. "But I've got some good news for you. I went into the storage area and pulled out Dr. Hartley's file from the time he was the firm's client. I found an interesting document that is going to make you pee your pants."

Katie laughed. "Leslie, you have such a way with words. You're going to make a great lawyer." She looked over at the two law clerks. "In my law school days, we called that a metaphor."

The clerks glanced at each other and rolled their eyes.

Leslie said, "Katie, are you sure you can remember back that far? Were they really using big words like that back then? Way back in 2013?"

They all laughed. Leslie slid a document across the table toward Katie. "Speaking of old times, feast your eyes on this."

Katie picked up the single sheet of paper. It was a copy of a letter dated November 17, 1985, sent from Dr. Oskar Klimpf, the CEO of Orex Laboratories, Inc., to Dr. Pittsburgh. She looked up at Leslie. "This was in Alex's file? This was right here in the office?"

Leslie grinned. "You got that right, girl."

"Why would we have this? What's it all about?"

Leslie shook her head. "I'm not saying anything. You're meeting with Dr. Hartley this week, so I'll let him tell you. But

I can promise you this – you'll pee your pants again when he tells you."

CHAPTER 37

September 1986

Gary and Alex settled into a routine in preparation for his hearing. They met in Gary's office at eight o'clock each morning, and Alex would bring coffee from the Starbucks in the lobby of the office building.

On their third meeting, Gary said, "Everything is falling into place. The Orex-Pittsburgh letter is terrific, and yesterday we finally got the complete autopsy report on Ingrid from the medical examiner. There's something in it you need to know." He opened the accordion file on his desk, removed a piece of paper, and handed it to Alex. "It's the toxicology report on Ingrid. It confirms what Ted told you. The detectives must have missed it when they concluded that she committed suicide. She died from a massive injection of digitalis. As you know, that would be instantly fatal. Your friend was murdered, Alex. This is solid proof she didn't kill herself."

Gary was right, Alex thought. It was solid proof. But Ingrid was still dead. Nothing could ever change that, but the information would help provide some much-needed closure for her mother. He said, "I've got to let her mother know about this."

Gary nodded.

~ ~ ~

Alex called Ingrid's mother from Gary's office and asked if he could stop by her house to talk. She was excited to hear from him and warm in her response when he arrived that evening. They sat in the living room and engaged in some polite chitchat for a few moments.

Alex stopped and looked at her. She was so beautiful, just as Ingrid would have been had she lived to her mother's age. His heart ached. "I have something to tell you. Actually, something to show you."

"What is it?"

"I have a hearing scheduled in a couple of days to have my medical license restored. The lawyers representing me are wonderful, and one of the things they did in preparation was order the autopsy report on Ingrid. It came yesterday and shows that Ingrid did not kill herself. As you suspected, she was murdered. Your instincts were right all along. She was injected with a huge dose of digitalis, a heart medicine that is a terrible poison in high doses."

Alex thought it was best not to mention the suicide note that Ted had left for him.

"Oh, Alex." She approached him, and they hugged and cried together for a few moments. "I miss her so much. Who would do this to her? Who would want to kill my baby?"

Alex couldn't bear to tell her the truth, or at least what he thought was the truth – that it was about jealousy. Ted had murdered her daughter because he was jealous of her, and Rachel had planned her murder for the same reason. "Some powerful people had a plan to frame Ingrid and me for publishing a fraudulent paper. Tragically, Ingrid's death was part of the plan. If it appeared that she killed herself, it would look like she was admitting that she'd falsified the results of our study.

"You know now that Ingrid didn't kill herself, and she didn't do anything wrong. I sincerely hope that brings you some comfort." He hugged her again.

"Alex, I'm so grateful you let me know. I just knew she didn't kill herself." She paused. "I'm glad you're here. I've been meaning to call you because I think I might have found something that may help you. When cleaning out Ingrid's apartment, I found a complete set of original research documents of your study in the bedroom closet. I knew that one of the claims they made against the two of you was that you falsified a letter from one of the mothers in the study, who supposedly claimed she never told you she took the drug during pregnancy. I found her records among the documents and got on the phone and called the woman. She told me that she never said anything like that. She explicitly said that she remembers taking the drug ... and she has a baby book to back that up. I have her phone number if you want to speak with her. She wants to help you if she can."

Those bastards, Alex thought. Every damn one of them bears the responsibility for Ingrid's death. Every one. Orex, Dr. Olmstead, and Dr. Ratner. Ted included. Rachel included.

On his way home, Alex stopped by Detroit Police headquarters and asked to speak with Detective Murphy. Murphy came out to the front desk. "I don't have much time. What is it that you want to talk about?"

"I think you need to rethink your finding that Ingrid committed suicide." Alex showed the detective Ingrid's toxicology report and the suicide note. He told him about Ted's deathbed confession. "Ted told me that Rachel Olmstead planned the murder. She typed the suicide letter, and he made sure that her fingerprints were all over it. I handled the letter at its edges and put it in a secure envelope."

"I'll look into this right away."

Alex added, "A massive dose of digitalis that could kill someone like this must have been obtained by a medical person. Ted Wallace and Rachel Olmstead both had the opportunity at Detroit City Hospital. There may be a paper trail if either of them got the drug from the pharmacy there."

Murphy shook Alex's hand. "This is helpful. I'll be in touch."

CHAPTER 38

Early September 1986

The day after Ted's funeral, Alex met with Bob and Gary at their offices so Bob could explain what was going to happen at the hearing.

"Alex, I want you to know that the hearing is closed to the public because the medical licensing board doesn't like to air their dirty laundry in the open. But it's important to be aware that the hearing is conducted just like a trial. Results are kept under lock and key. We have the burden of proving that you should get your license restored, and Gary and I are going to do exactly that ... and more.

"I'll be at Dr. Olmstead's office tomorrow morning, and we'll have a heart-to-heart chat."

CHAPTER 39

The Next Day,
September 1986

Bob Riley looked across the conference table at both Dr. Olmstead and Dr. Ratner, who were seated side by side.

His chat with Dr. Olmstead was meant to be private between the two of them, but given the circumstances, Bob had no objection to the other man's presence. He was surprised that there was no lawyer present and decided that there was no sense in being coy about why he was there.

"Gentlemen, I'm here to request that both of you support Dr. Hartley's petition to restore his medical license and his privileges as a staff member at Detroit City Hospital."

Dr. Ratner replied, "That's preposterous. Do you know what he did?"

Bob ignored the question. Instead, he retrieved from his briefcase Dr. Klimpf's letter to Dr. Pittsburgh. He slid it across the table.

"Both of you need to read that letter before we continue this discussion."

Dr. Olmstead looked up. "Where did you get this?"

Hardball time, Bob thought. "It doesn't matter where I got it. What does matter is where this letter will go next if you don't agree to do what Dr. Hartley needs done."

Dr. Ratner's face turned red. "That's bribery!"

Bob looked hard at both men for a moment. "That's not my name on the letter. But it's both of yours. Let me ask hypothetically what you think the medical licensing board, not to mention the local newspapers, will do if they receive this letter?"

Dr. Olmstead leaned toward him. "Can Dr. Ratner and I talk privately for a minute?"

Bob shook his head. "The time for talk is over. I'm not leaving this room, and I suggest that it's in both of your best interests to stay as well." He extracted another three documents from his briefcase and slid copies across the table.

"These must be signed before I leave this room. It was created for Dr. Olmstead's signature because I didn't know you were going to be here, Dr. Ratner. You can sign at the bottom of the documents below Dr. Olmstead's name."

Dr. Olmstead shrugged. "What is it that you want? What does this say?"

"There are several items. First, you are requesting that the licensing board restore Dr. Hartley's medical license. Second, you will affirm that Dr. Hartley has completed his internal medicine residency and should be board-certified in that specialty. When all this crap happened, Dr. Hartley was two months shy of completing his three-year residency, so he deserves some allowance and consideration for that. Next, you will both prepare and send a letter to the editor of the *American Scientific Journal* requesting that Dr. Hartley's research paper be re-published. The three of us will prepare a short statement reflecting the reasons for its re-publication based on a 'misunderstanding' at the time the paper was retracted.

"Finally, Dr. Olmstead, you promised Dr. Hartley a staff position in your department after he completed his residency in internal medicine, including training leading to his board-certification in toxicology. Your signature on this document will acknowledge that both those promises will be kept."

The two doctors looked at each other for a long moment.

Dr. Ratner asked, "What happens if we don't sign?"

Bob's response was immediate. "Dr. Ratner, you are asking the wrong question. You should be asking what happens to you if you do sign." He paused. "The answer to that question is nothing. Nothing will happen to either of you. I must tell you that that was Dr. Hartley's request. I disagree with him, but he insists on it. If I had my way, I would do whatever it takes to get you both thrown out of medicine. But he's my client, and I must honor his request."

Ten minutes later, Bob was on his way back to his office with copies of the agreement in his briefcase – signed by both doctors. There would be cause for celebration at dinner.

~ ~ ~

Three days later, Bob ushered Alex and Gary into the office of the medical disciplinary board in Lansing, Michigan. They sat across a long conference table from the three members of the board. Bob handed over a series of documents, with copies for each board member. The first was the document co-signed by Dr. Olmstead and Dr. Ratner.

One of the board members asked, "Wasn't Dr. Ratner the one who made the complaint against Dr. Hartley in the first place?"

"Yes." Bob handed over copies of the next document, the Klimpf–Pittsburgh letter. The sentence containing Olmstead's and Ratner's names was redacted.

All three members of the board raised their eyebrows as they read. One looked up. "Is there more?"

"Yes." Bob handed over copies of the toxicology report on Ingrid and the fake suicide note. "We received word this morning that the suicide note contains numerous fingerprints of the person who planned the murder, and charges against that person are in process."

A board member asked, "Who would that be?"

"Rachel Olmstead. Dr. Olmstead's daughter."

"Anything else?"

"Yes. Dr. Hartley is here to answer any questions or concerns you may have. I also have another witness waiting in the hallway if necessary. Dr. Fordland is an internationally recognized scientist who served as the peer reviewer of Dr. Hartley's research article that led to this whole mess. He was the one who successfully petitioned the *American Scientific Journal* to apologize and republish the research with an explanation. I respectfully suggest that there is enough evidence before you now to fully restore Dr. Hartley's medical license."

The three men rose as one. "We'll be back in a few minutes."

Ten minutes later, Alex's medical license was fully restored, and his suspension at Detroit City Hospital lifted. A week later, Alex received a certificate in the mail that proclaimed his completion of the internal medicine residency, and he became eligible to write the board examination to obtain certification in that specialty.

CHAPTER 40

December 2018

Katie flew to New York that morning, hopeful that her third attempt to take Dr. Pittsburgh's deposition would work out. She was wrong. Luxton called her on her cell phone at noon and told her that it was necessary once again to cancel the scheduled two o'clock deposition. Dr. Pittsburgh was at a meeting in Paris. Katie didn't get the sense that Luxton was playing games with her, but it still pissed her off. She had a lot of work to do back in Detroit to prepare for trial, and she didn't need to waste a day doing nothing.

She shared her thoughts with Luxton. He listened to her bitching and said, "Just like the last two times, I'll pay your airfare and expenses. All I can say is that I'm sorry."

Katie made sure to take advantage of the situation. Sylvia met her for dinner at Eleven Madison Park, the most expensive restaurant in Manhattan. Katie also ordered one of the most expensive bottles of wine the restaurant had to offer. Luxton had to pay some kind of price for his failure to produce his client. When Katie got the bill, she winced, and after careful consideration, she added a thirty percent tip. She didn't even like the wine, but Sylvia sure did. She gratefully drank her share.

During dinner, Katie said, "Sylvia, I'm pissed that I still didn't get to take Dr. Pittsburgh's deposition, but in getting ready for it, one of the experts on your case gave me a very interesting document." Katie handed her a copy of the faxed Dr. Klimpf letter.

Sylvia read the letter and flashed a huge smile at Katie. "I don't know how you got this, but I've seen this before. In fact, I first saw it on Dr. Pittsburgh's desk and borrowed it for a few minutes and made several copies. Remember how I told you earlier how I faxed a letter to Dr. Kubilus in Detroit years ago, just after her research study was retracted in the *American Scientific Journal*? This is that letter. I never heard back from her, and I've always wondered what happened. I was certain she would be thrilled to have received it. I've got a copy of this letter somewhere in my files at home, and I'm surprised I didn't give it to you already. I thought I told you about all this."

"Dr. Hartley was a co-author of that paper, and he is an expert witness in your case."

"Really? I can't wait to meet him."

"He's my law partner's best friend, a really great guy."

"Wonderful. We should have a lot to talk about."

"You will. We start trial on June 28. That's a Monday. I called the clerk's office this morning, and they advised me that the date is firm. I'll come into town the day before and call you when I arrive."

CHAPTER 41

September 1986

Rachel was sound asleep. At first, she thought she was having a nightmare as the sound of beating grew louder and louder. As she awoke, she realized it was someone pounding on her front door. She threw a robe over her nightgown, went to the door and looked through the peephole.

A tall black man was standing in front of the door. A white man, about half the size of the black man, stood behind him. She opened the door.

"Rachel Olmstead? Are you Rachel Olmstead?"

She stammered, "Yes, yes."

"You're under arrest for the murder of Ingrid Kubilus." Detective Murphy recited the Miranda warnings from memory and asked Rachel if she understood.

She nodded.

He said, "You have to answer verbally. Do you understand?"

She nodded again, "Yes."

"We are taking you in." He gestured to the other man. "Detective Garner will accompany you into your bedroom while you choose clothes to wear. You will then take those clothes into your bathroom and put them on while Detective Garner waits outside the door. Do you understand?"

Rachel nodded. She was numb.

When she finished dressing, Detective Garner handcuffed her with her hands behind her back. She was permitted a phone call three hours later, after she'd been photographed, fingerprinted, and processed. She called her father at the hospital.

"Daddy. I've been arrested. They think I murdered Ingrid. You know that's not true, I –"

Dr. Olmstead cut her off. "Stop talking right now. Don't say another word. Don't talk to anybody. I'll get a lawyer out to see you as soon as I can."

Rachel spent the rest of that day and night in jail. A lawyer, Devon Williams, finally arrived late the next afternoon.

Rachel thought Williams was an asshole. He sat there and lectured her like she was twelve years old.

"Rachel, listen to me. They have a suicide note with your fingerprints on it. They say you were the one who prepared it. The pharmacy at Detroit City Hospital has a voucher signed by you on the day of the woman's death for a huge amount of digitalis, the drug that killed her. They have reliable witnesses who can verify these documents. Unless you tell me how this happened, and make sure it's the whole truth, there's not much I'll be able to do for you. As it stands now, you're in deep trouble."

At first, she tried to blame Ted for everything. "It was his idea. He was deathly jealous of Ingrid, and he wanted her dead."

The lawyer sat and listened until she finished. He asked, "Is that everything?"

She nodded.

"Rachel. You're going to have to do better than that. You can bullshit me all you want, but I am telling you now, that story will not stand up in court. Just tell me the truth."

She thought about the Klimpf-Pittsburgh letter she'd seen on Dr. Ratner's desk. "A drug company, Orex, planned it all. Ingrid and Alex Hartley published some research that made the company's drug look bad. The company responded and did everything it could to make the study look bad. They hired a private investigator, who snooped around and doctored some of the original research documents to make it look like the study was done fraudulently."

She stopped and thought for a long moment. If she told the real story, her father and Dr. Ratner would also be implicated. A surge of mixed emotions ran through her body, and she kept on going. "The company asked Dr. Ratner, my boss, to look at the doctored research, and he concluded that the work had been done fraudulently. He didn't know the materials had been altered by the private investigator. They didn't stop there. The private investigator knew everything about Ingrid and had followed her for weeks. He murdered her and made it look like a suicide. I guess that he probably came around my desk and found some stationery with my fingerprints on it to use as the suicide note so the company could blame me if their plan fell apart. They also tried to frame Alex Hartley."

She added lamely, "I'm innocent. I did nothing wrong."

Devon Williams also knew about the Klimpf-Pittsburgh letter. When Dr. Olmstead had hired him to represent his daughter, his instructions had been clear. Dr. Olmstead and Dr. Ratner were to be kept out of it. The big, fat retainer fee had been given to him with that stipulation. He'd try and negotiate some kind of plea deal that would limit the focus to Rachel and Ted Wallace, the dead guy.

~ ~ ~

Rachel was shocked by her arrest. Her reaction started the moment the police walked into her apartment and cuffed her hands behind her back. Her feelings and thoughts were numbed by a vague, dream-like sensation of unreality. Except it was no dream, she thought, as the perception disappeared after the visit from the lawyer. The lawyer's matter-of-fact determination that she was going to prison for her role in killing Ingrid took her several hours to process. Ted Wallace murdered Ingrid, so why was she being charged? The lawyer's words and demeanor conveyed his recommendation that it was best that she plead guilty in the hopes of minimizing the length of her prison sentence.

Rachel fought the feeling of hopelessness that Devon Williams's visit had brought.

If she was being charged, why wasn't Dr. Ratner, or her father, or that Herold guy who worked for Orex, or Dr. Klimpf? Or Dr. Pittsburgh? They had all been at the same meeting in Ann Arbor that she'd attended. They'd all agreed on Plan B. The only reason she'd been at the meeting was that her father and Dr. Ratner had wanted her there. If Williams was already giving up on her this soon, maybe she needed another lawyer. She'd seen enough TV shows and movies to know that everyone charged with a crime pleaded not guilty at first.

~ ~ ~

Two mornings later, Rachel and Williams stood in front of Judge Cornelius Bailey, the judge who would hear how Rachel would plead. As the judge described to her what was going on, Rachel looked down at her feet. Never in her life had she experienced such shame. She wore a jail-issued, too-large orange jumpsuit, and her hands were cuffed in front of her. Two uniformed deputies stood behind her. The courtroom was full of people: witnesses, defendants, lawyers, and reporters.

The judge asked, "How do you plead?"

"Not guilty, Judge," replied Rachel,

The judge had a perplexed look on his face. "This is a bit of a surprise. I'd like to meet with counsel for both sides in my chambers."

Moments later, the young assistant prosecuting attorney and Devon Williams were sitting side by side in front of the judge's desk.

The judge looked at Williams. "You said she was going to plead guilty. What's changed?"

Williams squirmed. "Judge, I don't honestly know. For some reason, she changed her mind. I'm as surprised as you."

"Let's go back into the courtroom. I want to ask her a few questions." Judge Bailey stood and led the way out of his office.

The two deputies brought Rachel back to the front of the courtroom, where she stood facing the judge.

"Ms. Olmstead, I had a brief conversation in my chambers with your attorney and the prosecutor in your case. I want to make sure you understand what is going on here. You have indicated that you want to plead not guilty. Is that right?"

Rachel nodded. "Yes, Judge, not guilty. And I'd like to say something, if that is all right."

The judge nodded. "Of course. Go ahead."

Rachel turned and looked at Williams while she spoke. "Judge, I need a different attorney. He's tried hard to make me plead guilty for something I haven't done. I didn't hire him and never met him before he came to the jail and told me I was guilty and that you'd be easy on me if I did plead guilty. I don't think he knows anything about the situation, and he's never asked me one question about it."

The judge looked at Williams. "Is what she's saying true, counsel?"

Williams's face was beet red. "I invoke lawyer-client privilege, Your Honor. I don't think it's proper to tell the court what conversations I've had with my client."

Judge Bailey shook his head. "That's nonsense, and you know it. Your client, if that's what she is, has just made statements in open court that I'm asking you about. Are they true? Did you speak to her about the charge against her? Did you ask her any questions?"

Williams looked down at his feet and said nothing.

"I asked you some questions. You will answer them right now, or I will hold you in contempt of court."

Rachel said, "Judge, I can answer whatever questions you have. I can tell you exactly what happened except for one thing. I do not understand why I am being charged with a crime."

Judge Bailey held his hand up. "Hold on, Ms. Olmstead. Don't say one more word. I will allow you to hire another lawyer. If you can't afford a lawyer, I will appoint one from the public defenders' office to represent you. Is that satisfactory?"

Rachel nodded. "Yes, Judge. That's what I want, a different lawyer."

"I will accept your not-guilty plea and arrange for you to either contact another lawyer or obtain help from the public defenders' office." He looked at the two deputies. "You may take her back, but make arrangements for her to speak with someone."

He turned and looked at Williams. "Counsel, I'm fining you five hundred dollars for your disappointing performance this morning. You must pay it to my clerk before you leave the courtroom or go to jail until you do. But. I need to have you answer one question before you do anything else. Who hired you to represent this young woman?"

Williams shook his head. "Judge, I'm not at liberty to say."

The judge barked, "One thousand dollars! Tell me, counsel."

Williams stood silently.

The judge said, "Two thousand dollars and two nights in jail. Bailiff, take him away."

The court bailiff placed handcuffs on the lawyer and led him away.

The courtroom was buzzing. The reporters were having a field day.

~ ~ ~

A young lawyer from the public defenders' office filed an appearance on behalf of Rachel that afternoon. Her name was Molly Bailey, the judge's niece. There would be no conflict of interest because the arraignment was over and a new judge would be assigned for trial.

Molly met with Rachel at the jail, and Rachel eagerly told her the entire story and described her role.

"I did two things. I went to this Ann Arbor meeting, where a plan was discussed to discredit the research of Dr. Kubilus and Dr. Hartley. Months later, after the research was published, Dr. Ratner had me type a suicide note. He dictated it to me, and I typed it exactly as he told me. I handed it to him and have never seen it since." With Ted Wallace now dead, she thought, there was absolutely no one who could refute her about the note. She added, "I have a couple of documents at home about the meeting in Ann Arbor."

Molly said, "I'll ask for a bail hearing, and I am certain it will be granted. When you get home, the first thing you do is to bring me those documents."

The following week, Rachel sat with Molly in the lawyer's office. They talked for several hours.

Molly said, "You've given me some ammunition to negotiate what will hopefully be a good deal for you. To do that, your father has to be brought into the discussion. As far as I'm concerned, both he and Dr. Ratner are in this up to their necks. Also, everything you've told me brings the drug company, Mr. Herold, and Dr. Klimpf into the mix. This makes your involvement minimal. Any deal we make will have to implicate all of them. What do you think?"

Rachel thought for a moment. "Given that it was my father who made arrangements for the lawyer who tried to make me plead guilty, I say screw him. All my life, he's treated me like a piece of crap simply because I was a girl. The same goes for Dr. Ratner. Bring them all in. Go for it."

CHAPTER 42

June 2019

From a lawyer's perspective, Katie thought, one of the quirks of handling high-profile lawsuits was that the surrounding publicity would result in many phone calls to the firm from others who claimed to have had similar experiences. The frequency of such calls was dictated by the type of emotion that any given event generated. She'd recently represented a man who'd been found guilty by a jury more than a year ago. It had happened in a rural Michigan town, with him allegedly murdering his wife, and the hate calls and threats that had come into the office during the trial had put the entire office staff on edge. Gary Newton had hired a temporary security guard, who'd sat in the firm's lobby in case someone showed up to make trouble, even though the small town where the case was being tried was ninety miles away from Detroit.

The emotions of callers generated by the publicity in Sylvia's case in New York was different and more wide-ranging: from angry outbursts by men who felt that sexual abuse was a God-given right to sad, weeping women who had borne years of abuse by men who controlled their lives at home, the workplace, church, school, or elsewhere. The Me Too movement was also in full swing across the nation, and calls came from everywhere in the country.

The Newton and Hornsby law firm had a full-time business to run, and the numerous calls were interrupting the necessary daily activities of everyone in the office. At a weekly office meeting, Leslie came up with a solution that was eagerly accepted by both Gary and Katie. A hotline was set up specifically to take the influx of calls. Callers were directed to leave a recorded message as to why they needed to speak with a lawyer. Leslie volunteered to screen the hotline messages at the end of each day and make note of any deemed worthy of follow-up.

"Lucky me," she said to Katie. "I get to sit and listen to boring law professors all day at school and then come here and listen to stories so sad I need a new box of Kleenex every day just to dry my tears."

Katie grimaced. "Remember, it was your idea, but I can only imagine how difficult it is for you. I told Gary we should hire more lawyers to do what you are doing, and he said he'd think about it. Our trial starts next week, so maybe the calls will let up as soon as we get to New York."

"Really, I didn't come in here to complain. I can handle it. But I think you should listen to a call that came in today." She set the recorder on Katie's desk and pressed play.

Katie listened to the voicemail. The woman was crying hysterically, and Katie strained to understand the message.

The caller said, "I'm watching the news on TV, and I can't believe that someone is finally doing something to put a stop to his abuse. This monster needs to be put away for the rest of his life. He ruined my life with his abuse and manipulative behavior, and I want to help you destroy him. My name is Jayme Pittsburgh, and this despicable man is my father."

Leslie switched the recorder off. "I called and spoke with her for a while and told her you would call as soon as you could."

Katie was stunned. She said, "I don't know whether to laugh or cry. The implications of this are enormous."

Leslie smiled. "I got my crying out of the way when I talked with her. You've got Dr. Pittsburgh nailed now, Katie. Monsters always leave a trail, and eventually their victims come out of the woodwork to tell the truth. I read up about this before I came in to see you just now. Sexual abuse doesn't always start in the workplace. It can start at home, where a young family member is easy prey. The abuser rewards the victim with special attention and affection, making them feel loved and protected. In return, he has total control over the victim and does whatever he wants to satisfy his sexual perversions. Victims usually try to minimize their abuse and blame themselves. They are ashamed and live in a state of distrust and guilt until they can face their abuser and make him accountable for his deviant behavior."

214

Leslie took a deep breath and continued. "I printed out two of the articles on this subject for you to read before you call her."

CHAPTER 43

December 1986

The lead story on the front page of the *Detroit Free Press* featured the picture of Molly Bailey hand in hand with Rachel Olmstead, standing on the stairs outside the Wayne County Circuit Court.

Alex sat at breakfast and was fascinated by the article. He knew he'd have to call Ingrid's mom and tell her what happened.

David Brings Down Goliaths

Robert Olmstead, M.D., Richard Ratner, M.D., Edward Herold, and Oskar Klimpf, M.D., appeared at a sentencing hearing yesterday morning in Wayne County Circuit Court (State v. Olmstead, et al.) after pleading guilty to charges in the death of Dr. Ingrid Kubilus earlier this year. All four defendants pleaded no contest. The corporate defendant, Orex Laboratories, also pleaded no contest and agreed to pay one million dollars court costs and fines. The four individual defendants each received two years of probation and are required to perform one hundred hours of community service. Another defendant, Rachel Olmstead, had all charges dismissed against her. Drs. Olmstead and Ratner are both prominent local physicians and were required to surrender their medical licenses as a condition of the plea agreement. Both will be eligible for reinstatement after five years.

Public defender Molly Bailey, a first-year lawyer, received high praise from the sentencing judge for her dogged pursuit of justice on behalf of her client, Rachel Olmstead. The judge described her actions as "David bringing down Goliaths." Bailey is the niece of prominent Circuit Judge Cornelius Bailey, who told the Free Press that he was "proud of his niece and knows that she will have a long and successful career as a lawyer."

CHAPTER 44

June 2019

It was the first day of trial. Katie woke very early, made a half-pot of coffee, and spent a couple of hours reviewing her notes and opening statement. Around daybreak, she heard the neighbors' movements behind the wall that separated their apartments. The smell of frying bacon reminded her that she was hungry. She had missed several meals and honestly couldn't remember the last time she'd eaten. When in trial mode, this happened to her frequently.

She and Leslie had rented the apartment for two months, and they both loved its ambiance. The apartment building was located at 10th Avenue and 45th Street West, an area previously known as Hell's Kitchen. It was expensive, but compared to the cost of staying in a hotel, it was a bargain. Yesterday they'd made a practice run on the subway down to the courthouse and figured they had to leave by eight o'clock this morning to be in place at nine.

Katie sat over her coffee and thought about her client. Sylvia was finally going to have the opportunity to do something about her predicament. These events in her past had taken over her life and prevented her from moving forward. She'd told Katie over the phone that part of her wanted to run and hide but the other part was ready for battle. Her main concern was not to make a fool of herself on the witness stand. Katie didn't mention to her that that was her main concern as a lawyer, too. Katie loved trying cases, but acting like an idiot in front of a jury was number one on her list of things to avoid.

Katie didn't mention the contact she'd had with Dr. Pittsburgh's daughter the previous week. The daughter had agreed to meet and talk to Katie at some time during the trial, but no commitment had been made, either by her or Katie, as to whether she would appear as a witness.

Katie was ambivalent about the trial starting. She loved New York. Part of her was ready for battle, but the other part wanted to spend her days exploring the city with Leslie. They were together in this fascinating, vibrant city and going to trial in a courtroom before a judge she'd never seen or met.

A clerk at the courthouse explained the court procedure to Leslie. A judge would be selected by the court administrator this morning when they signed in. The criteria for assignment was simple. Any judge not in a trial on any given day was drawn by lot and assigned to a case scheduled for trial on that date. In most of Katie's cases during her six years of law practice, she'd known what judge she would have well in advance of a trial because assignments were made randomly the day a case was filed.

It was always helpful to know in advance who the judge was on any given case because judges were unique. No two were the same in terms of temperament, judicial philosophy, or political leanings. A neutral, unbiased judge was a rarity, as most were either staunchly liberal or conservative. In large civil cases, the political leanings of a judge frequently made the difference between success or failure. It was a crapshoot, and the thought that the judge they might get in Sylvia's case might hurt her chances of success increased Katie's level of anxiety.

No matter who the judge turned out to be, Katie needed to present Sylvia's case to a jury in a straightforward manner, without apologies or concessions. The jury needed to hear and understand Sylvia's explanation for why she submitted sexually to Pittsburgh for so long and then waited years before taking action. Katie had hired a psychiatrist to evaluate Sylvia and come to New York and tell the jury why she and a lot of other women were coming out of the woodwork to reclaim their long-lost dignity after years of silence about their sexual abuse. Katie was also going to present Alex Hartley and Dr. Fordland as witnesses to explain the science. Over the past few weeks, Newton, Leslie, and Katie had discussed this approach from every conceivable perspective and had settled on the best way to present these issues to the jury.

About an hour before they were to leave for court, Leslie stumbled out of her bedroom.

"Who's making bacon? Smells good. I'm starving."

"Our neighbors. Go next door and see if they'll make some for us." They both laughed. They had shopped at a nearby store yesterday afternoon and decided that yogurt was going to be their breakfast. Their refrigerator was well stocked with vegetables and fruit. They sat in the cozy kitchen and ate their yogurt while they discussed the plan for the day. The aroma of bacon stirred their senses.

When it came time, they headed downtown on the subway to the court stop. Katie checked in with the court administrator's office and sat in the back of a courtroom with Leslie and Sylvia, while Lamar Luxton and his defense team sat several rows in front of them. He had three other lawyers and two paralegals with him. The courtroom was full of lawyers and their clients, waiting patiently until a judge was assigned to their case.

About mid-morning, the clerk called their case, and Katie went forward to her desk, where she was joined by Luxton. The clerk handed each of them a slip of paper with the judge's name and the number of the courtroom. Luxton took one look at it, sneered, and walked away. The clerk smiled at Katie and whispered, "You're going to like Charley." She winked at Katie as she gave her directions to the courtroom of the Honorable Charles Thomas.

They took the elevator to the eighth floor and walked into the courtroom of Judge Thomas, who was already seated on the bench. He greeted everyone warmly. Thomas was an older black man, a bit on the heavy side, with a broad face that radiated warmth and friendliness. The assignment clerk was right. Katie liked him immediately.

Leslie tugged on Katie's sleeve and whispered, "He reminds me of Santa Claus."

Katie nodded. She also pictured in her mind's eye the judge dressed up like Santa, sitting in a department store at Christmas.

Judge Thomas said, "I'd like to meet with the attorneys in my conference room. Follow me, please." He stood and looked over at Leslie. "Are you an attorney?"

"No, Your Honor," she said. "I'm a third-year law school student and the paralegal for Ms. Hornsby on the case."

"You can come into my chambers with the lawyers."

Katie was not surprised by the judge's obvious interest in Leslie. She was stunning in appearance and reeked of a sensuality that captivated most men. The judge was apparently no exception.

The judge walked back to his chambers with Leslie, Katie, and Luxton and his team of three lawyers trailing behind.

When all were seated, the judge looked at Katie and smiled. "You must be the attorney for the plaintiff, because your opponent" – he nodded at Luxton – "wouldn't be caught dead representing an injured person. Against his religion, I guess." He giggled.

Luxton maintained a straight face, so Katie did as well. She said, "Judge, I'm Katie Hornsby, and I represent Sylvia Anderson, the plaintiff. My paralegal is Leslie Gibbons."

The judge smiled. "I see from the file that you're from Detroit. Welcome to New York. Leslie, I wanted you to come into chambers because every experience you can have as a law student will help make you a better lawyer. And the world can certainly use more great female lawyers."

Leslie smiled back at him. "Thank you, Your Honor."

"Ms. Hornsby, why don't you tell me about your case ... and when we're in my chambers, all of you call me Charley. When the robe is off, I'm Charley. When it's on, I'm Judge Thomas."

Katie gave the short version of Sylvia's case, and the judge nodded at Luxton. "Go ahead, Lamar, and tell me about your defense."

Luxton cleared his throat. "This is a classic 'he said, she said' case, Your Honor."

"Lamar, call me Charley."

Luxton stopped and looked at the judge for a moment. "Charley. My position is that the statute of limitations bars this cause of action against both defendants. The acts of sex the plaintiff complains about occurred, if at all, more than thirty years ago. There is no proof whatsoever that Dr. Pittsburgh, one of the most esteemed scientists in the world, forced her into even a single act of sex. I'm asking you to dismiss the case on that basis because the law is quite clear that the plaintiff would have had to file her case within three years of the alleged sexual abuse." He paused. "And I'm asking for costs to be imposed against the plaintiff."

The judge looked at Katie. "What do you have to say about that, Katie?"

She removed a prepared written response from her briefcase and read from the document. "Section 208 of the civil practice law and rules, as amended by chapter 485 of the laws of 1986, is amended to read as follows: if a person entitled to commence an action is under a disability because of infancy or insanity at the time the cause of action accrues, and the time otherwise limited for commencing the action is three years or more and expires no later than three years after the disability ceases, or the person under the disability dies, the time within which the action must be commenced shall be extended to three years after the disability ceases or the person under the disability dies, whichever event first occurs."

She looked up at the judge. "Our proofs will show that the plaintiff is disabled because of a mental state that was caused by the sexual abuse of Dr. Pittsburgh. She has post-traumatic stress disorder, commonly known as PTSD, which meets the threshold definition of insanity within the meaning of the newly amended law arising from rampant incidents of sexual abuse reported as a result of the Me Too crisis in our country. My position is that the issue of whether she has that disability is a question of fact for the jury to decide at trial."

Judge Thomas said, "I am assuming you will provide expert testimony from a board-certified psychiatrist to that effect, as the new law requires."

"Yes, Your Honor."

"Charley."

"Yes, Charley."

The judge said, "Lamar, I will take your motion to dismiss on that basis under advisement until we hear Katie's expert on this subject. Anything else? What is the status of discovery? Do you both have what you need from the other side?"

Luxton and Katie exchanged glances. Katie said, "Judge, I've come to New York three times to take Dr. Pittsburgh's testimony, and all three times, he's been a no-show. Other than that important exception, discovery is complete for both sides."

The standard rule in civil cases throughout the United States was that discovery of the other side's case was important to potentially avoid the need for trial. If everyone had the same set of facts in hand, settlement of a case was highly probable and would thus relieve the court of spending time in trial. Courts were flooded with lawsuits of all types, and anything that lightened a judge's docket was good.

Unlike previous civil cases Katie had tried, the element of surprise was a big part of her plans for Dr. Pittsburgh, so the lack of his deposition testimony didn't bother her as much as she let on. She could use Luxton's failure to produce his client as leverage during the trial whenever she needed some latitude in the scope of her questioning or when calling a witness that wasn't disclosed before trial. The role of the biggest surprise, Dr. Pittsburgh's daughter, remained to be determined, and she had other surprises in mind as well.

Luxton cleared his throat again. "Both sides have what they need other than the defendant's testimony."

The judge looked at Katie and smiled. "Is that so, Katie?"

She nodded, "Yes, Your – excuse me, Charley. Both sides have agreed that I'll be given wide latitude in questioning Dr. Pittsburgh."

The judge rubbed his hands together. "Any other motions or issues before we start jury selection?"

"Yes," Katie said. "One of the main reasons I agree with defense counsel is because he made it clear that the defendant, Dr. Pittsburgh, will appear at trial, even though he's dodged three separate dates for deposition." She paused and took a breath. "So, my motion is for Your Honor – Charley – to order that Dr. Pittsburgh appear during trial. I will need him to testify, and if he decides not to show, it will hurt my client's case."

The judge looked at Luxton. "Lamar, do you have any problem with Katie's request?"

"Judge, he's an extremely busy man."

"Answer my question, Lamar. You're not reneging on your agreement with Katie, are you? I asked you if you had a problem with her request."

"If she agrees to let me know in advance what day she needs him here, I have no problem with her request."

Judge Thomas looked at Katie. "Can you let Lamar know when you want his client here?"

"I will let him know two days before I call him to the stand."

The judge looked at Luxton, "Is that good, Lamar?"

"That's good by me, Charley."

Judge Thomas looked at Katie and smiled. "I'm a die-hard Yankee fan, but Jackie Robinson and Rogers Hornsby have been my favorite ballplayers ever since I was a kid. I'm curious. Are you a relative?"

Katie laughed. "Of Jackie Robinson or Rogers Hornsby?"

Charley laughed hard. "Well, I guess I asked the question wrong. Are you related to Hornsby?"

"No, but my grandfather was named after him. I have a baseball signed by Rogers Hornsby on my office desk. My grandfather caught a home-run ball and stayed after a game so that he could get his autograph. He was with the Cubs then, but he did play for the New York Giants in 1927."

The judge smiled. "You do know your baseball."

Katie smiled back at him. "I can't help myself when baseball is the subject, but since you started this, I have to tell a joke. What do you call forty millionaires sitting around watching the World Series?"

Judge Thomas guffawed. "I've heard this one. The New York Yankees."

"I've got a bunch more baseball jokes, but I'll spare you both right now."

The judge smiled. "This is all good, but the fun's over for now. Let's go into the courtroom and select a jury." He stood and started putting on his robe. "Katie and Leslie, Lamar already knows how I conduct jury selection, so I'll tell you before we go in. Basically, you do what you want, ask a juror whatever you want, everything except argue your case. You start arguing your case, I shut you down. Got it?"

225

Katie nodded. "I got it, Charley."

"Other than that, take as long as you want. Ask whatever questions you want. A lot of judges now do all the questioning during voir dire. I don't think that's a good idea. How is a lawyer supposed to pick a jury if you can't find out anything about individual jurors?"

They went back into the courtroom. Leslie whispered to Katie, "I really like the judge. It's refreshing to know he will help advance a woman's career."

Katie smiled at her. "And he really likes you, too. No big surprise there. Get Sylvia."

Leslie brought Sylvia into the courtroom. The three of them sat together and waited while a panel of sixty prospective jurors filed into the room and took seats in the gallery.

Surprisingly, there was a disproportionate number of young men in the group, probably around twenty. The entire group was a mixture of Whites, Blacks, Latinos, and a few Asians. Judge Thomas's booming voice silenced the murmurs in the courtroom as he walked in and sat down.

"Good morning, ladies and gents. I'm Judge Thomas. We're going to select a jury from among you folks and get this trial underway as soon as we can. The clerk is going to call sixteen names. If your name is called, come on up and have a seat in the jury box. My bailiff will show you what seat to take."

He nodded to the clerk, who spun a cylinder on her desk that contained each potential juror's name on a small card. She selected one and called out a name, and then she waited until that person was seated before she moved on to the next. In less than five minutes, sixteen people were seated in the jury box. Twelve men, at least eight of them younger than Katie, were in the panel. There were also four women; two were young, and the other two were around Sylvia's age. Hell, Katie thought, she could stand up right now and tell the judge she was satisfied with the jury.

The judge looked at the panel and spoke. He had a mellow, baritone voice. "Ladies and gentlemen, we are going to start the process of voir dire. Each lawyer will be asking you some questions. Make sure that you understand what the question is before you answer." He turned and looked at Katie. "Ms. Hornsby. Please introduce yourself and your client and proceed with your questions."

Katie needed to pinch herself. Was she dreaming? A jury selection process like this was a trial lawyer's dream. The opportunity was so unexpected that she hardly knew where to begin. In almost every case she'd tried so far in her short career, the judge had asked all the questions.

She stood and looked at the jury. "My name is Katie Hornsby, and I am the lawyer for Sylvia Anderson, the plaintiff in this action." She gestured for Sylvia to stand. Sylvia stood for a long moment and sat down. "Seated next to Sylvia is my paralegal associate, Leslie Gibbons." Leslie stood, nodded at the jury, and sat down.

"I'll ask the entire panel a few questions before I start on my questions for each of you. First, do any of you know Sylvia, Leslie, or me?"

The group shook their heads in unison.

"There are two defendants in this case. One is Filmore University. I would guess you all have probably heard of it because it is a prominent university right here in Manhattan, so let me ask a more specific question. Do any of you have any specific affiliation with Filmore University, either as a student or employee or through any other kind of relationship?"

Four of the jurors raised their hands. Katie walked closer and gestured to a young woman in the back row who had raised her hand. She was pretty and well dressed. "What is your name and connection to Filmore?"

"My name is Shelley Myers. I graduated from Filmore last year. I have a degree in botany."

Katie thought, Well, here we go. It didn't take too long to get down to the basics. "I should also mention the name of the other defendant, Dr. Arnold Pittsburgh." She looked at the young woman. "Do you know Dr. Pittsburgh?"

"Yes, I do. I took a two-semester class from him, a course called Experimental Biochemistry."

"When was that?"

"Last year."

"Ms. Myers, the purpose for my asking you and the other prospective jurors questions is to find out if there are any potential reasons, either for or against anyone involved in this case, that would prevent you from being fair and impartial in reaching a decision. Given that you know Dr. Pittsburgh, could you be fair to Sylvia Anderson after hearing and seeing evidence that he harmed my client in the way she claims?"

Myers bit her lip. "I think it would depend on what the evidence shows, but I really liked Dr. Pittsburgh. He was a good teacher, and I learned a lot from him. I'd have a hard time thinking he'd done something wrong. It would be uncomfortable for me to decide against him."

Katie moved closer to her. "Let me see if I can rephrase my question to help you clarify your answer. Picture the scales of justice in your mind. At the beginning of this trial, these scales are supposed to be even on both sides." She held her hands in front of her, each at the same level. "Would your feelings right now about Dr. Pittsburgh tend to tip his side of the scales in his favor in any way?" She lowered her left hand down a bit lower than the right.

Myers thought for a moment. "I think it would."

Katie looked over at the judge. "May we approach the bench, Your Honor?"

He responded. "No need, Ms. Hornsby." He looked at the young woman. "Ms. Myers, you are excused. Make sure to stop by the clerk's office on your way out of the building to pick up your check. Thank you for being here this morning." He looked over at his clerk. "Draw another name, please."

A pleasant-looking older man took the empty seat when his name was called.

Katie continued her questioning by following up with the others who raised their hands about Filmore University. Each had taken courses at the school, but none of them had heard about or knew Dr. Pittsburgh.

Katie moved a little further away from the jury box. "Does anyone else on the panel know Dr. Pittsburgh or know anything about his work?"

Everyone shook their heads. Katie looked at the court reporter. "The record should reflect that the entire panel has indicated that they don't know Dr. Pittsburgh or the nature of his work."

Her next series of questions was important, so she had to be careful about how she approached the topic. She stepped closer to the jury box. "Is there anyone on this panel who is familiar with what is called the Me Too movement? If so, please raise your hand."

All sixteen of the prospective jurors' hands went into the air.

"Does anyone on the panel have strong feelings, one way or the other, about women who make Me Too claims?"

Fourteen hands went up. She looked at Judge Thomas. "May we approach, Your Honor?"

"Come on up, counsel."

When in place, Katie said, "Judge, all but two of the potential jurors have indicated they have strong feelings about Me Too. I think it's really important to find out what these strong feelings are without influencing the other potential jurors. I request that each juror be questioned out of the presence of the others in your chambers to avoid this problem."

The judge looked at Luxton. "What's your position?"

Luxton smiled. "Judge, you and I are both New Yorkers, and we know that all New Yorkers have strong opinions about everything."

The judge said, "That's a good point." He looked at Katie. "Ms. Hornsby, I'll give you latitude in your questioning, but we would be here for a week if we start questioning jurors individually. I am denying your request."

"Thank you, Your Honor." Crap. Every statement made by a potential juror would be heard by everyone in the room. Katie returned to her spot in front of the jury box. She had to be careful about what questions she asked. "Let's start with the first row." She gestured to a young black man who was seated the closest to the judge's bench. "You raised your hand when I asked about Me Too and having strong feelings. What is your name?"

"Rob, Rob Ward."

"Mr. Ward, what kind of work do you do?"

"I'm an actor. And a waiter."

"Mr. Ward, you heard me earlier ask Ms. Myers about tipping the scales of justice in one direction or another because she knew a defendant in this case." She held both hands in front of her at the same height again. "Sitting here right now, before you've heard any evidence in this case, would the strong opinion you have about Me Too cause the balance to tip one way or the other?" She moved her hands up and down.

He smiled pleasantly at Katie. "If what you're asking is whether or not I can be fair and impartial, my answer is yes."

"Thank you, Mr. Ward. That was going to be my next question, but you beat me to the punch." She smiled back at him, took a step away, and looked around the jury box at the rest of the panel.

"Mr. Ward made my job easier." Most of the panel smiled at her comment. "Let me ask the rest of you. Please raise your hand if you know you cannot be fair and impartial without hearing the evidence."

Three hands went up.

She moved closer. "I'll direct this question to the three of you who raised your hand. Without telling us what direction your strong feelings take on the Me Too issue, is there a specific reason that has caused these strong feelings?" She nodded to the first of the three, another young man.

He answered, "Yes. There is a reason. Do you want me to tell you what that reason is?"

He avoided eye contact with Katie, and she had a bad feeling about this guy. This was exactly why she'd wanted to voir dire each juror privately.

Leslie wrote on her legal pad and slid it over for Katie to see. The note said, "Get rid of him."

"First, tell me your name and what you do for a living?"

"My name is Stanley Pechok. Like the guy before me, I'm an actor ... and a waiter."

Several of the others in the jury box chuckled. Katie smiled. Was everyone in the Big Apple waiting on tables until they got a role in a play?

"Mr. Pechok, are the strong feelings you have about Me Two positive or negative?"

He answered quickly, "Negative, very negative."

"And is it your belief that these negative feelings would prevent you from being fair and impartial if you were to sit on this jury."

He nodded. "No question about it. Yes."

Katie looked at Judge Thomas, who nodded and said, "You are excused, Mr. Pechok. Stop at the clerk's office and pick up your check." He looked at his clerk. "Pick another name."

For a moment, Katie thought the guy who'd replaced Pechok was his clone. She directed her attention back to the other two who had indicated strong feelings about Me-Tooism. The two men, one black, one white, were seated next to each other in the back row of the jury box.

"You both have heard the questions I asked. Are the feelings each of you have about the Me Too situation such that you would be unable to be fair and impartial?"

One man shook his head, and the other nodded. She directed her attention to the black man who'd nodded.

"Your feelings are such that it would prevent you from being fair and impartial if asked to sit on this jury?"

"Yes."

Judge Thomas said, "You are excused, sir. Please see the clerk downstairs on your way out and pick up your jury duty check. Thank you for being here today."

The man nodded and stood. He smiled and said, "Thank you, Judge. I was waiting to tell the lawyer that I am also an actor and a waiter."

Everyone in the room laughed as the man left the courtroom.

Another person was selected and sat down in the vacant seat.

Katie turned to the remaining potential juror who had indicated strong feelings. "You indicated by a shake of your head that you believe you can be a fair and impartial juror even though you have strong feelings about Me Too, right?"

"That's right."

"What is your name and what is your occupation?"

"My name is Steve Wheeler, and I am an accountant for a Wall Street bank."

She needed to get rid of this guy. He was a pretty boy. He also avoided looking at her. Her vibes about him were screaming, "No!" She didn't think he was being truthful. Gary Newton had always said that she should always follow her gut reaction. If Judge Thomas wouldn't dismiss this guy for cause, she could use one of her peremptory challenges and get rid of him. She could save the peremptory for someone else if she could get him to admit that he'd already made up his mind. But one way or the other, he was gone.

Leslie slid her legal pad over again. She'd written a simple "No" on it.

"Mr. Wheeler, have you had a personal situation involving Me Too that resulted in your strong feelings?"

"Yes, I once dated a girl who told all my friends that I sexually assaulted her. We never, in fact, had sex. It was a humiliating experience."

"I'm sorry to hear that you went through such a terrible experience. If the defendant in this lawsuit claimed the same thing that you did about not having sex, do you think you would be predisposed to believe him?"

"I think I can be fair and impartial. I would believe whoever was most believable."

So much for a challenge for cause. She would use one of her peremptory challenges to get rid of this guy. He wanted to sit on the jury too badly.

"Thanks, Mr. Wheeler." She looked for a moment at the two replacement jurors. "I'll ask the new replacements on the panel if you have any strong feelings about Me Too that would prevent you from being fair and impartial?"

Both said no. She liked both of them, an older gentleman and a middle-aged lady. She had decided that she wanted older jurors, because they'd be more likely to have conservative views on how men should treat women. People her age and younger were a heck of a lot more casual with regard to sex than older people and, as a rule, far more lenient about the concept of consent. Young people today went to parties expecting to get trashed and have sex, consent being implied for simply being at the party. In her younger days, she'd managed to avoid these kinds of parties, but she'd heard a lot of stories. Consent was a big issue in this case, and she needed jurors who understood the concept of boundaries. She knew her thinking was old-fashioned, but it was also the source of the rage she felt toward Dr. Pittsburgh. All the more so after hearing from his daughter. She decided to move on to a different topic – working women. "Members of the jury panel, is there anyone who holds a belief that a woman's place is in the home and that women should not work outside the home?"

To her great surprise, a middle-aged woman raised her hand.

Katie took a step in her direction. "Ma'am, what is your name?"

"I am Stella Adams, Mrs. Stella Adams. I'm a homemaker."

"Your answer to my question implies that you have reservations about women who work outside the home. Is that right?"

"You bet I do. I believe a woman's place is in the home. That's in the Bible."

Katie was dumbstruck. If she had been trying this case in a state somewhere in the Midwest, she might have expected this answer. She sure as hell didn't expect to hear it in New York.

"Mrs. Adams, if the evidence were to show that my client, Sylvia Anderson, is a single person who has dedicated her life to conducting scientific research for the benefit of all mankind, would having that knowledge tend to tip the scales against her because she was not a stay-at-home homemaker?"

Mrs. Adams thought for a moment. "I think it might."

Katie looked at Judge Thomas. "Your Honor ..."

He leaned toward the jury box. "You are excused, Mrs. Adams. Thank you for your service. Please stop by the clerk's office and get your check."

Mrs. Adams stood. "Thank you, Judge." She turned and walked out of the courtroom.

In past trials, Katie had tended to rush through jury selection and not pay much attention to who was on her juries. The events this morning so far had taught her how important it was to be less nonchalant about the process. Everyone who'd been dismissed would have torpedoed her case in a heartbeat.

It took two more days to finish jury selection. By the time they were through, only four of the original sixty potential jurors were left waiting in the courtroom. They finally had a jury of twelve, with two more designated as alternates. Katie was reasonably satisfied with the makeup of the jury. The two young women in the front row, seated next to each other, made her uncomfortable, but other than that, she was good. She would have used peremptory challenges to get rid of them, but the four people who had not yet been called looked to her like they all might be trouble.

That evening, Sylvia, Leslie, and Katie went to dinner at an Italian restaurant on Second St., close to Sylvia's apartment. They went over Sylvia's testimony since she was going to be the first to testify. Katie laid out the sequences of questions while she and Leslie enjoyed one of the best meals they'd had in their lives.

Sylvia smiled. "I told you this place was great." Both Leslie and Katie nodded in agreement.

Katie said, "The opportunities that this city provides foodies like us make it tempting to find any reason to return to the Big Apple."

After dinner, Leslie and Katie took a cab back to their place. Leslie said, "I am wishing right now that I was born Italian. That was so good. Can we eat there every night?"

CHAPTER 45

Usually, when Katie was in trial, she thought, felt, breathed, and dreamed only about what was going on in the courtroom. Her overnight focus kept her on her toes and prepared for any issue the defense might present in the courtroom. Instead, she woke this morning from a dream about Italian food exactly like last evening's meal. It was a pleasant distraction, but she reeked of garlic. She smiled to herself as if she didn't know if it was from the previous night's meal or the meal she'd consumed in her dream. Brushing her teeth an extra five minutes didn't make it go away.

When she and Leslie arrived at the courtroom, they sat down at the counsel table with Sylvia, and Leslie said, "We all smell like that restaurant last night. I'm craving Italian food. When is lunch?"

Sylvia and Katie laughed. They were all on the same page when it came to last night's dinner, and their chatter about food helped to ease the tension they were all feeling as the jury was seated and the trial was to begin.

The judge said, "Ready to give your opening statement, Ms. Hornsby?"

Katie nodded. "Yes, Your Honor."

She stood, walked to a spot a polite distance away from the jury box, and took a deep breath. She didn't want to share the reminder of last evening's meal with the jurors.

"Members of the jury, this case is about sex. But it's also not about sex. Let me explain this conundrum for you. In late 1985, a series of events began that rocked the scientific world such that thousands upon thousands of lives have been affected ever since.

"First, let me tell you a little about Sylvia. She was placed into the foster care system at the age of three after her homeless birth mother died from a drug overdose. Her birth father was unknown. When she testifies, Sylvia will describe how the effects of foster care helped shape her life. Sylvia excelled in school and on the softball field. When she graduated from high school, she was the valedictorian and class president of her class of 560 graduates. She received a two-minute standing ovation to her speech at the graduation ceremony, and the guest speaker for the evening told the audience it was the best speech he'd ever heard.

"Sylvia was also the star pitcher on the school softball team, and her record over three seasons was forty-five wins and one loss. The combination of academic and athletic excellence won her a scholarship to Rutgers, where she continued her winning ways in softball, pitching Rutgers to a conference championship three years in a row. At Rutgers, she also discovered a passion for science and, in particular, the field of biochemistry. She finished a four-year degree in three years and, as in high school, graduated as the valedictorian of her class. This bright, talented young woman was accepted, one of three candidates out of hundreds who applied, into the graduate program in biochemistry right here at Filmore University, which, as we all know, is one of the best academic institutions in the world. Sylvia wanted to obtain a doctorate in biochemistry, and she knew that it would take at least four years for her to complete the required training and another year or more to write a thesis before she could receive the coveted PhD.

"At that time, the biochemistry department at Filmore was headed by Dr. Arnold Pittsburgh, a research scientist of considerable reputation who had spent years conducting research on the causes of various cancers, with the ultimate goal of developing a biochemical cure for these dreaded diseases. Dr. Pittsburgh was impressed in every way with Sylvia, and shortly after she began her doctoral studies, he undertook the role of serving as both her boss and mentor. By the end of her second year under Dr. Pittsburgh's tutelage, she had conducted research and written five scientific papers that were published in major scientific journals. You may not know this, but most doctoral students never publish any research while in training. By the middle of her third year in the department, Sylvia's research had resulted in seven additional published articles. You will hear evidence that one of her major accomplishments actually resulted in Dr. Pittsburgh receiving the Nobel Prize in biochemistry in the early 1990s, and by the end of this trial, you may find yourself wondering why he was chosen for that award.

"Now, I'm going to stop right there because I want Sylvia to tell you the rest of her story when she is on the witness stand, about what happened to destroy her dreams and aspirations. Suffice it to say that her professional life, in effect, ended in the middle of that third year. As part of that story, you will hear from a world-class scientist who will describe an alarming relationship between well-funded academic programs and the pharmaceutical industry, who work together to tarnish the reputations and careers of fine scientists who get in the way of their profiteering schemes. You will be presented evidence that will show why that factor is important here.

"Added to that, in Sylvia's situation, Dr. Pittsburgh subjected her to his sexual whims and desires as though she were his personal slave. At the end of the trial, I will have the opportunity to speak with you again, and I will ask you to assess the amount of damage that Sylvia has suffered and to place a monetary value on something that should never have happened."

Katie turned to the judge. "Your Honor, that completes my opening statement."

Judge Thomas gestured toward Luxton. "Your turn, Mr. Luxton."

Luxton stood. "I have a motion, Your Honor."

"Save it until after your opening. I don't want the jury to sit around and wait while we deal with technical issues. There's nothing that can't wait until after I send them home."

Luxton buttoned his suit coat and walked close to the jury box.

"Ladies and gentlemen of the jury, my name is Lamar Luxton, and I represent both Filmore University and Dr. Pittsburgh. As you all know, there are always two sides to every story, and although my sister counsel has been vague about what this case is about, I will not be. This lawsuit is a sham being played on one of the most distinguished scientists in the world. Apparently, something Dr. Pittsburgh said or did to this young woman upset her badly enough to level these scurrilous charges against him. You will hear, perhaps from Ms. Anderson herself, that Dr. Pittsburgh was a stern taskmaster and that he demanded that everyone around him perform up to his standards of excellence. You will find out that for the first years of her graduate studies, the plaintiff did meet Dr. Pittsburgh's standards, going well beyond what most of his graduate students over the years had done. As the plaintiff's counsel has already told you, Dr. Pittsburgh received a Nobel Prize because of the quality of work done in his research laboratory. Quite frankly, Dr. Pittsburgh was, and is, perplexed by the sudden change of heart in the plaintiff's work effort and devotion to the principles of science, as well as the scurrilous charges she is claiming against him.

"According to the plaintiff, this is a case about sex. But it's really about sex that never happened. You will hear testimony from a psychiatrist who will tell you why young women make unsubstantiated claims against famous men of substantial means. All over the country, similar false claims are being made, all resulting from the media's overreaction to the alleged acts of one or two men in Hollywood, where, apparently, such conduct is normal. At the close of trial, I will be asking you to render a verdict of no cause for action in favor of Dr. Pittsburgh and Filmore University."

Luxton turned toward the bench. "That completes the defendants' opening statement, Your Honor."

Judge Thomas looked over at Katie. "Can you be ready with your first witness after lunch?"

She stood. "Yes, Your Honor."

~ ~ ~

During the lunch hour, Katie took Sylvia through her testimony one more time before her appearance on the stand.

"What happens if I start crying?"

"Don't worry. If you cry, you cry. The jurors will understand why you are crying. Your story is a sad one, and when they hear it, some of them may cry as well."

They returned to the courtroom and waited for the judge and jury to be seated. Leslie had arranged for a video projector

238

and large screen to be present. She set it up and made sure it was working properly while they waited for court to resume.

Katie held Sylvia's hand and squeezed it before she walked to the witness stand to be sworn in by the judge's clerk. Katie took a position at the far end of the jury box so it would be easier for Sylvia to make eye contact with the jurors from time to time when answering questions. Looking over at the defense table, Katie noticed Dr. Pittsburgh glaring at her. She glared right back. Fuck you, asshole, she thought. Returning her attention to Sylvia, she gave her a confident smile. Her trial experience had taught her how important it was to relax her clients and witnesses immediately once they had settled into the witness chair.

"Would you tell the jury your name for the record?"

"Yes. I am Sylvia Anderson."

"What do you do for a living?"

"I work as a research biochemist for a private laboratory in New Jersey."

"Please tell the court and jury briefly about how and where you grew up as a child."

"I've been told my mother died of a drug overdose when I was three. I have no memory of her. I also have no idea who my father is or where he might be. He has never been part of my life. I spent my childhood moving from one foster home to another in the Harrisburg, Pennsylvania, area. In total, I lived in twelve foster homes, never longer than eighteen months in any single home."

"Do you have any brothers or sisters?"

"None that I am aware of."

"Please tell the jury about your educational background."

Sylvia hesitated and looked down at her hands. Finally, she said, "After I graduated from high school in —"

Katie took two or three steps toward her. "Sylvia, I'm sorry to interrupt, but you'll have to speak up a bit. Would you start over with your answer?"

Sylvia looked up at Katie, and her eyes filled with tears. "I'll try to talk louder. This is so difficult for me to talk about."

Leslie grabbed a box of tissues from their table and walked it over to Sylvia, who took one and dabbed her eyes.

"Let's continue, Sylvia. If you speak loud enough for me to hear, then the jury will be able to hear you. You were starting to tell us about your educational background. Please go on."

"After I graduated from high school, I went to Rutgers, where I received a degree in chemistry and natural sciences. I graduated summa cum laude there and was admitted to the doctoral program at Filmore, where my plan was to obtain a PhD in biochemistry. I completed most of the requirements, but ..." She stopped and struggled to compose herself.

Judge Thomas leaned toward her and said, "Do you need to take a break?"

She shook her head. "No, Your Honor. I need to keep going. I'll settle down. I'm sorry."

Katie needed to slow Sylvia down a bit. "Please go back to your high school years. Did you have any special activities that you participated in or honors that you received?"

"Yes. I was the pitcher on our school softball team. I pitched every game the team played for three years. We won all the games but one. Also, we were state champions those three years."

"Did you receive any academic awards?"

"Yes. I was a National Merit Scholar and the valedictorian of my class. I gave a speech at graduation that the guest speaker told me was the best one he'd ever heard. He was a professor at Rutgers, and he took it upon himself to see that I received a fully paid tuition scholarship there. I graduated summa cum laude from Rutgers in three years rather than four. I also pitched Rutgers to three conference championships. My coach told me that if there was such a thing as a professional softball league for women, I would be a star in the league. I chose an academic career instead at Filmore, as I mentioned before."

She squared her shoulders and took a deep breath. "In the middle of my third year in the doctoral program, a couple of things happened, and I requested a leave of absence. I took a couple of weeks off and then went back to work. At that point, everything had changed. From then on, I struggled to complete the doctoral requirements. The last requirement was to write a thesis and then present it to a panel of PhDs who would determine whether or not the quality of my thesis and presentation met acceptable standards to award me a PhD. I started writing my thesis, but ... I was never able to finish. I've tried several times, but I can't do it."

"You've told the jury that 'a couple of things happened' in the middle of your third year in the graduate program that stopped your progress toward becoming a doctor in the field of biochemistry. What was it that happened, Sylvia?"

Katie knew she would never forget the look on Sylvia's face at that moment, like a wounded animal waiting for a hunter to finish her off. Her lips trembled, and she balled up the tissue in her hands. Her rate of breathing speeded up, and she was moving to the edge of control. Leslie poured her a cup of water from the pitcher on the table and walked it up to her. Sylvia's hands shook as she tried to take a drink, spilling some of the water down the front of her blouse.

"We'll take our morning break now." Judge Thomas stood and addressed the jury. "Fifteen minutes."

The bailiff stood and bellowed, "All rise."

The jurors rose and filed out of the courtroom. Several of them looked over at Sylvia with expressions of concern.

Katie gestured for Sylvia to follow her out of the courtroom and gave her a hug when they reached the hallway. Sylvia was a wreck: her hands shook, and mascara had run down her face. Katie took her into the restroom, where she washed her face and reapplied her makeup.

Katie hugged her again. "You're going to get through this, okay? Just like we practiced. When you feel like you're losing it, stop talking and take a couple of deep breaths."

"My mistake was looking at him. I could tell by the look in his eyes that he was threatening me, daring me to continue with my story."

Katie shook her head. "Sylvia, don't look at him. Focus on the jurors and try to establish eye contact with them. When Luxton starts to question you, don't let him rattle you. Don't argue with him. Listen to his questions and look at the jurors while you answer. Got it?"

She nodded. "Got it."

Leslie and Katie both hugged her. "Now, let's go back in and kick ass, squeeze balls, and take names." Gary Newton had said this once during a trial when Katie was second seat. She loved the expression, and it was now a part of her vocabulary. "We're going to take him down, right? You got this, girl!"

Sylvia laughed.

When court resumed, Katie asked her the question again. "What are the things that happened in the middle of your third year in the graduate program that stopped your progress toward becoming a doctor?"

"At the time, there were a number of gay men in the San Francisco area who were dying from a rare form of cancer, Kaposi's sarcoma, and I suggested to Dr. Pittsburgh that it would be interesting to look at what was happening from a biochemistry point of view. He agreed and had me draw up a research protocol that might give us some information about the cause of these deaths. Our lab had already done a considerable amount of work on viruses, and we had both the equipment and technical skills to put something together quickly. I called a colleague in San Francisco and arranged for him to send me tissue samples from a number of the young men who had died.

"When I started working on the research protocol, I found that there was a strange virus present in the tissues that I'd never seen before. I went to the literature and discovered that no one else had, either. I isolated the virus and used it for a series of studies on rats and mice, as I was looking for clues about what had happened to these men in San Francisco. Several weeks later, I reported to Dr. Pittsburgh that the virus appeared to be toxic to T-cell lymphocytes in laboratory animals. T-cell lymphocytes are a part of the immune system that functions to destroy bacteria and cancer cells.

"The T-cells are made mainly by the thymus gland, which is positioned above the breastbone. The thymus gland is one of the endocrine glands in the body that is present in children through the late teenage years, when it slowly starts to turn into fatty tissue. All of us, at any given time, have cancer cells circulating in our body, and T-cell lymphocytes kill those cancer cells. If something interrupts or eliminates the T-cell lymphocytes, cancer cells can continue to grow until full-blown cancers occur. Likewise with bacteria. T-cell lymphocytes kill bacteria. No T-cells, the bacteria flourish and can cause fatal infections."

Katie watched the jury as Sylvia spoke. They were listening to her every word. She interrupted. "Let me ask. Can you clarify what T-cells are?"

Sylvia looked at Katie with a puzzled expression. She continued. "We didn't know back then, but we do know now that it is a specific subset of T-cells that do these things. This subset is now called CD-4. The initial study suggested that this virus was killing off the T-cells. When I showed the results to Dr. Pittsburgh, he became very excited, and he decided that we should look further into this by doing more research." She stopped and took a deep breath.

"A basic scientific rule is to make sure you verify the results you see from one study by doing another study exactly like you did the first one. This process is called validation and is the standard requirement of all scientific studies before you start making any claims about the original study. I don't want to imply that this is a simple process. Each study takes a month or more to complete, and everything that was done in the original study must be repeated exactly the way the first study was done." She stopped and looked at the jury. "Do you understand?"

The two alternate jurors appeared to be sleeping. The rest of the jury nodded their heads.

Katie interjected, "Please continue with your explanation, Sylvia." She was doing great so far, but Katie knew that the rest of this story was going to be extremely hard on her.

"I didn't know it at the time, but Dr. Pittsburgh had submitted the results of the original testing to a journal before I finished the validation study. Even before the research was accepted for publication, he called a press conference and announced he had discovered a new virus. He called the virus 'HIV' and claimed that it was what was killing the gay men in California. HIV is an acronym for 'human immunodeficiency virus.' He called the disease AIDS, for the scientific name 'acquired immunodeficiency syndrome.' By the time I finished the validation study, the research had already been accepted for publication. When I first saw the published paper, I was chagrined to see that I was listed as the co-author. Upon finishing the validation study, I was mortified to discover that the results of the follow-up study were different from the original study. The validation study was inconclusive about the relationship between the virus and the destruction of T-cell lymphocytes, so I repeated the study a third time. This second attempt to verify the original result was also negative."

Katie asked, "Sylvia, what is the significance of your negative follow-up studies with regard to your claim that Dr. Pittsburgh sexually abused you?"

"When I reported the negative results to Dr. Pittsburgh, all the trouble began. He became angry, threatened me, and told me that if I said anything about these negative studies, he would claim that I altered the original findings and committed scientific fraud. Before I could leave his office, he–"

Katie moved several steps closer to her. "Sylvia, let me interrupt. Can you summarize why this particular study, the HIV-AIDS study, is so important for us to understand in the context of why you brought this lawsuit against Dr. Pittsburgh?"

"Yes. Quite simply, the results of the original research could not be validated by my attempts to do so. Dr. Pittsburgh knew that the original results weren't validated, but he submitted the original research for publication anyway. He wanted to be the first scientist to claim that he'd discovered the cause of what was killing these gay men. The fact that he received the Nobel Prize for the research shows how important it was for him to be the first person to show what caused the gay men to die. But the original research should never have been published. When I told Dr. Pittsburgh that the original results could not be verified, he became angry and started threatening and abusing me to keep me quiet. This is the connection between the publication of this study and his abusing me."

Katie looked at the jury as she asked the next question. "Can you describe this important connection?"

Sylvia moaned and closed her eyes. She shook her head. "I don't know if I can tell what happened. It's all still a nightmare."

Judge Thomas leaned toward her. "You can tell us what happened. That's why the jury is here, to hear your story. Take a deep breath and take your time."

Katie loved Judge Thomas. This was the kindest thing she'd ever seen or heard in a courtroom – and from a judge, no less.

Sylvia gathered herself, took a deep breath, and continued. "After I told him about the failed attempts to verify the results of the original study, he rushed at me as I was leaving his office. He grabbed me forcefully, so hard that it hurt. He told me that he owned me and I was to do anything and everything he said. He forced me down to my knees and made me give him oral sex. I did what he told me to do because I felt I had no choice."

Several of the jurors gasped.

Sylvia started to cry, and Judge Thomas was on his feet. "We'll give her a few minutes and take our break now." He stood, walked off the bench, and was out of the room before the bailiff said, "All rise."

Katie was proud of Sylvia. She had faced the challenge and done, so far, what she needed to do. She still needed to finish the story and then face cross-examination. It wasn't going to be easy, but she had the tough part out of the way. Katie made a mental note to tell the judge how grateful she was that he'd been so kind to Sylvia today.

When court resumed, Katie said to Sylvia, "What happened after that day?"

"It was like I became his sex slave. He made me do anything and everything he could think of. It went on for more than two years. I continued to work in the lab, but I lost my energy. I started to lose weight, more than twenty pounds in two years, and I felt like there was no one I could talk to about my predicament, about what was happening or what he was doing to me. I had started to write my thesis by the time this all began, but I couldn't muster up the energy to follow through on it. He'd call me day or night and tell me what he wanted me to do to him. He'd show up at my apartment in the middle of the night. He'd call me into his office in the middle of the day and lock the door. I was totally helpless. To keep the peace, I did everything he demanded. This happened regularly for more than two years until a younger woman in the lab became his go-to choice for sex. Even after that, whenever she wasn't available to him, he'd call me in or come to my apartment at night."

"Why did you continue to submit to him like this?"

"He constantly threatened me. He told me that if I ever tried to tell anyone about the fact that the original study hadn't been validated, he'd put the blame on me and tell everyone that I was the one who failed to do the right thing. He also said that he'd see that I would never get my PhD."

"Please continue."

"One morning, I'd had enough. I went into the lab on that day and quit – five years of my life down the drain. I went home and stayed in my bed for days, not eating, not sleeping, not thinking. Finally, I pulled myself together and started applying for research jobs. Getting hired was difficult, as I had the education but not the credentials. When I was offered a job at Create Inc. in New Jersey, I took it, and I have been there ever since."

"One more question for you, Sylvia. What is your annual salary at Create?"

"I make eighty-five thousand dollars a year. When I first started with them, it was forty-five thousand dollars. I have received a raise every three years."

"You are aware that a biochemist with a PhD degree and your experience would receive a much higher salary than yours?"

"Yes. At Create, there are several PhD biochemists who have been there as long as I have, and their salaries are $235,000. I work alongside them, and I do the same things they do."

"Thank you, Sylvia. That completes the direct examination, Your Honor."

Luxton was on his feet. "May I proceed, Your Honor?"

Judge Thomas nodded. "Go ahead."

Luxton approached Sylvia, turned, and looked at the jury. "I heard you say that there was no one you could talk to about what you claim happened, right?"

"Yes, that's right."

"You also said that you didn't talk to anyone about what you claim Dr. Pittsburgh was doing to you, right?"

"Yes."

"So there is no person, associate, friend, or relative who can corroborate what you've told this jury, right?"

"Yes, that's right."

"From the way you described the research leading up to the conclusion that HIV causes AIDS, one would think that you were the one who made this astounding discovery. Is that so?"

"I don't think I said anything that would give anyone that impression."

Luxton walked back to his table and picked up a piece of paper. "I have the transcript of your earlier testimony today. Let me read a statement: 'When I started working on the research protocol, I found that there was a strange virus present in the tissues that I'd never seen before. I went to the literature and discovered that no one else had, either. I isolated the virus and used it for a series of studies on rats and mice as I was looking for clues about what happened to the men in San Francisco.'"

Luxton stopped and looked at Sylvia. "Did you make that statement this morning?"

"I did say that this morning."

"You found a strange virus present in the tissues of those homosexual men that you'd never seen before, right?"

"Yes."

"And you searched the scientific literature and discovered that no one else had seen the virus before, either, right?"

"Yes."

"Then you isolated the virus and used it for a series of studies on rats and mice, right?"

"Yes."

"To make it perfectly clear, you claim you tested a virus that neither you nor any other scientist in the world had ever seen before in your animal research studies, right?"

"Yes, that's right."

"And Dr. Pittsburgh listed you as the co-author of the study in which it was claimed that a new virus called HIV was discovered, right?"

"Yes, but without my knowledge."

"And this was the study that won a Nobel Prize for Dr. Pittsburgh?"

"Yes, that's right."

Luxton moved two steps closer to Sylvia. He was tall, around six-four, and he was close enough to her that she had to look up at him. Sylvia shifted her shoulders toward the jury and looked in their direction. It was a good move, and he backed off.

"Isn't it true that because you are the co-author of the study, you were asked on many occasions to speak at medical and scientific meetings, right?"

"Yes, I was asked, but I never said yes."

"One thing you didn't mention during your testimony with your lawyer is how long ago these alleged sex acts took place. At what time period do you claim they occurred?"

Katie jumped to her feet. "I object, Your Honor. The speech counsel gave is argumentative."

The judge nodded. "I agree. Mr. Luxton, you don't have to give a speech. You are free, of course, to ask proper questions. Please do so when you restate your question ... properly."

"Ms. Anderson, how long ago did these alleged acts take place?"

Sylvia hesitated. "Nineteen eighty-five to nineteen eighty-seven."

Luxton turned toward the jury with a huge smile on his face, as if he'd won the lottery. "Nineteen eighty-five? Thirty-three years ago?"

Several of the jurors squirmed at Luxton's theatrics. They didn't buy into his act. Katie made a note to bring his phony ploy to their attention later, at an appropriate time.

Leslie made a note on her legal pad. "This guy is a real asshole."

Sylvia smiled at the jury and then at Luxton. "You're very good at math, Mr. Luxton. And quick, too."

Katie winced. She didn't want Sylvia to get too sarcastic with Luxton. It could backfire on her. But the jury liked it, and Katie noticed that every one of the jurors smiled.

Luxton pressed on without missing a beat. "Thank you, Ms. Anderson, but my math skills are not at issue here. What is at issue is why you waited so long to file this lawsuit."

Katie stood. "Objection, Your Honor. That's not a question, and it's argumentative."

Judge Thomas shook his head at Luxton. "Objection sustained. You know better than to argue with witnesses, counsel. I want it to stop right now."

"Thank you, Your Honor." Luxton turned back to Sylvia. "Thirty-three years is a long time ago. Memories fade with time. How can you be so certain about events that happened that far back in your past?"

Even though it was another argumentative question, Katie decided to pass on making another objection. She and Sylvia had discussed the approach to answering this question for two hours yesterday. Katie knew Sylvia could handle it without her running interference.

Sylvia cast a quick glance toward Katie before she spoke. "The first day Dr. Pittsburgh forced me to have sex, I thought someday that someone might ask me this question. If that ever happened, I knew that I had to protect myself because it was his word against mine. Without proof, no one would ever believe me. I didn't think about this question for just one or two seconds. I thought about it all night that first night because I couldn't get to sleep, and then for two weeks after that because I still couldn't sleep. It was such a terrifying experience."

Luxton was a seasoned, polished lawyer who had probably tried cases before Katie was born. She could visualize the gears in his brain working overtime as he worked out the details for his next question. Because Dr. Pittsburgh was "too busy" to waste his time for a deposition, he had not been deposed, a standard practice in most cases. Luxton had had a junior lawyer take Sylvia's deposition, and he'd done a terrible job. As a result, at this point, Luxton had no idea what Sylvia might say or how she might respond.

The cardinal rule for any lawyer conducting a cross-examination is to never ask a witness a question to which the lawyer doesn't already know the answer. He made his decision. He was a pro.

"Thank you, Ms. Anderson. That concludes my cross-examination, Your Honor."

Katie couldn't get to her feet fast enough.

She placed herself squarely in front of the jury box. "Sylvia, you mentioned to Mr. Luxton about the need to protect yourself if someone might ask you about this in the future. How can you be so certain about events that happened so long ago, specifically the sex acts that Dr. Pittsburgh forced you to engage in?"

Luxton stood. "Objection. Your Honor. This question is beyond the scope of redirect examination. I asked no questions about what she may have done to verify her alleged accusations. She indicated that she'd done something, but I didn't ask her what it was. I assumed that if she had some kind of proof, her lawyer would have admitted it into evidence during her direct examination."

Judge Thomas looked over at Katie. He had a somber expression on his face. "What's your response, Ms. Hornsby?"

What in the hell could she say now? Like Luxton, she had gears in her brain, too, but right now, they were frozen in place. She opened her mouth to speak but didn't know what to say. Maybe her brain could figure it out if she started talking.

"Judge. Defense counsel did, in fact, broach the subject of how my client could be so certain about being sexually abused by Dr. Pittsburgh. In doing so, he raised the issue for the first time about what, other than her own say-so, caused her to remember the details of the events that occurred so long ago. By failing to ask the logical follow-up question, he planted a seed that if left unanswered, would allow the jury to conclude that she has no support for her claims other than her word.

The purpose of redirect examination is to clarify and explain an issue raised for the first time during cross-examination. I am now entitled to have my client clarify the issue raised by Mr. Luxton."

The judge stood. "Let's take a short break. Court will adjourn for fifteen minutes."

Katie used the short break to call Gary Newton on her cell phone. She quickly filled him in on the situation. His response made her heart sink.

"Why didn't you introduce the evidence during her direct examination? Katie, I think you might be in trouble." The line went silent for a long moment. "You've still got the hair expert, right? The guy who identified all the pubic hairs as Pittsburgh's?"

"Yes. I do."

"Well, make sure that the judge knows that you have an expert who can verify the evidence. I think the judge is concerned about committing reversible error if he allows her to testify about the calendars. If he thinks the evidence is still going to be admitted through another witness, his concern about being reversed goes away. I think that's the way you have to go, Katie. Good luck. Call me tonight and let me know what happened."

Leslie walked up to her. "The judge wants to see us in chambers. Now."

Katie and Leslie walked through the courtroom to the door of the judge's chambers. Leslie had the box of Hallmark calendars. When Katie looked at her for an explanation, Leslie said, "The judge wanted to see the proof we have."

Judge Thomas gestured to Leslie to bring the box of documents directly to him. She placed it on the table, and the judge indicated that she should sit next to him. Katie sat down next to her while Luxton and his two associates sat across from them.

The judge looked at Leslie. "Leslie, tell me what's in the box."

Katie was amazed. Leslie looked at her, and Katie nodded for her to answer the judge's question.

Leslie removed one of the Hallmark calendars from the box. "Judge, Sylvia pasted a pubic hair from Dr. Pittsburgh in one of these calendars every time he molested her. There are twenty-four calendars in this box, and a total of 442 public hairs taped into them, one for each date that he raped her. I know 'cause I counted them myself."

Luxton reacted. "Judge, this is improper. This young lady is only a paralegal, and she's acting like she's a witness."

Judge Thomas looked coolly over at Luxton. "Lamar, this is all off the record and informal. If you have a problem with this, let me know, and I'll call the court reporter in, and you can put your objections on the record. If you are insinuating that I don't know the difference between a witness and a non-witness, I suggest that if you do make a record, you phrase your objection very carefully."

He turned and looked at Leslie. "Mr. Luxton does raise an interesting question, Leslie. You said you are in your third year of law school?"

Leslie smiled. She had a killer smile.

Katie had watched many different men react to that smile over the past few years, and she noticed that Judge Thomas's reaction was no exception. She jumped in. "Leslie is going to join our law firm next year after she graduates and passes the bar exam."

"Well, Leslie, you're going to be in good hands."

Katie noticed that the judge had been having a hard time keeping his eyes off Leslie ever since the trial had started. The men on the jury had watched every move she'd made as well.

The judge stood. "Let's return to the courtroom. I'll put my ruling on the record."

When court resumed, Judge Thomas took his seat with a somber expression on his face. "I am going to permit the question. Ask the witness the question again, counsel."

Katie hadn't breathed since the moment Judge Thomas had walked back into the courtroom. After his ruling, she took a deep breath, stood, and walked to the far end of the jury box.

"Sylvia, why are you so certain about events that happened so long ago, specifically about the sex acts that Dr. Pittsburgh forced you into?"

Luxton stood. "I renew my objection, Your Honor."

"Objection overruled," replied the judge. To Sylvia, he said, "You may answer the question."

"First, let me say that by training, I am a research scientist and, as such, it is my habit to make a record of everything I do in the laboratory. Early in my training, I found that this habit also served me well in my personal life. As an example, I can tell you that I have exercised at least three hundred days every year since my early twenties, and I know this because, every day I work out, I write it down in my notebook. So, to answer your question about Dr. Pittsburgh, I methodically kept track of every time he forced me to have sex over more than two years. However, I didn't write about it each time it happened. Instead, I took one of Dr. Pittsburgh's pubic hairs that I found on my body or my clothing after each encounter and taped it to that date on a Hallmark calendar. I have twenty-six of these calendars. Dr. Pittsburgh forced me into various sex acts fifteen to twenty times each month, 442 times altogether."

Several of the jurors gasped. Katie waited a moment and walked back to her counsel table. She took the box with the twenty-six calendars and carried them to Sylvia. "Let the record reflect that I have handed the witness twenty-six Hallmark calendars that have been marked Group Exhibit One for identification. Sylvia, will you tell the court and jury what Group Exhibit One is?"

"Yes, the exhibit contains the twenty-six calendars I talked about. On those calendars are 442 pubic hairs, each one taped to the exact day that Dr. Pittsburgh forced me to have sex with him."

"I move that Group Exhibit One be admitted, Your Honor."

The judge looked at Luxton. "Any objections?"

Luxton stood. "May we approach the bench, Your Honor?"

Judge Thomas waved the attorneys up. "Go ahead, Mr. Luxton. Tell me what your objection is."

"Judge. First of all, I move to strike the testimony of the plaintiff in describing this exhibit on the basis that it is unduly

253

prejudicial to my clients and likely to trigger the improper passion of the jury."

"Denied. What else do you have?"

"I object to the admission of this exhibit on the same grounds. Your Honor, it is clearly prejudicial and will improperly influence the jury. We all heard the jurors who gasped when this subject first came up. I submit that those gasps are proof that the jury will be unduly inflamed by the presence of this exhibit during their deliberations. Furthermore, the exhibit is merely cumulative to the testimony of the plaintiff."

"Denied. The exhibit is admitted. Anything else?"

Luxton shook his head. "No, Your Honor."

Judge Thomas looked over at the jury. "Group Exhibit One is admitted. Please continue, Ms. Hornsby."

Katie turned to Sylvia. "During Mr. Luxton's questioning, he asked you about answers you gave him that 'one would think that you were the one who made this astounding discovery,' referring both to the discovery that HIV causes AIDS and to the discovery of HIV. Please tell the court and jury why you make no such claim, even though you are listed as a co-author on the research that was published."

Sylvia nodded. "It was, and is, standard practice in all areas of scientific research to designate the 'leader' of a research team as the principal author of any and all research. It was Dr. Pittsburgh's laboratory. He was the boss, and I was a mere doctoral student. I would never expect credit when working on a project like we're talking about here. That would be presumptuous and totally inappropriate, and I made no such claim then, nor do I make that claim today. I was shocked when I realized that I was listed as a co-author. I did not participate in the writing of the article, nor was I aware that it had been submitted. As I mentioned earlier, I was in the middle of attempting to validate the original findings when I found out that Dr. Pittsburgh had published the paper."

Katie checked her notes. "Thanks, Sylvia. Your Honor, that completes my redirect examination."

Luxton stood. "Judge, I have nothing further."

"Then we'll take a short break."

As the judge and jury left the room, Katie looked at Leslie. "You rock, girl. I think the judge likes you."

Leslie smiled. "I know he does."

CHAPTER 46

After the short break, Katie planned on calling Dr. Pittsburgh as an adverse witness during Sylvia's case. Given that she had been successful in getting the calendars into evidence, thanks to Leslie and her enchanting smile, and coupled with the jurors' reactions, she decided that she had enough proof of Dr. Pittsburgh's culpability. She didn't see the need to put him on the stand now. When, and if, Luxton put Dr. Pittsburgh on the stand in his defense, she would have the opportunity to reinforce a few details on his cross-examination. The decision to pass on his testimony at this time was also a matter of timing. An expensive, out-of-town expert witness was waiting in the hallway and would provide testimony on the damage that Dr. Pittsburgh's culpability had caused. If she called Dr. Pittsburgh to testify at this moment, the waiting expert would add another five thousand dollars to his bill because he'd have to stay in New York until the next day.

Before Katie did anything else, though, she hugged Sylvia when she came off the stand. "You were fabulous."

"I was so nervous."

"It's good that the jury saw your raw nerves on display. Nothing wrong with that, but it was your testimony that dazzled me. We accomplished everything we set out to do and more. I loved the preamble to your discussion of the calendars. It was absolutely perfect."

And it was perfect. Katie wasn't blowing smoke.

Judge Thomas asked, "Do you have another witness, counsel?"

"Yes. Your Honor, the plaintiff calls Dr. John-Gunnar Fordland."

Dr. Fordland had been sitting in the back of the courtroom. He walked up and was sworn in by the clerk, and then he seated himself in the witness chair. He was a nice-looking man with an unruly mop of blond hair that kept falling over his eyes. He spoke impeccable English with a distinct foreign accent that lent an aura of credibility to his words.

Katie approached him. "Will you tell the jury your name and what you do for a living?"

"Yes. My name is Dr. John-Gunnar Fordland, and I am a professor of medicine and research at the University of Bergen in Norway."

"Have you, at any time in your career, done research on the drug DES?"

Yes, I have done a number of studies over the years on DES as it pertains to what happens to offspring when the drug is given to pregnant organisms."

"When you use the term 'pregnant organisms,' what does that mean?"

"Excuse me, excuse me. I'm sorry. I should have used different words. I use that term to include animal studies. I have studied the effect on offspring when pregnant animals, such as the rat, mouse, rabbit, and dog, are given DES. Those are the pregnant organisms. I have also studied the same effect in humans."

"How many studies have you done and over what time period?"

"All told, I have conducted fifty-two studies on DES effects, but only forty-two of these studies have been published."

"Why is that?"

"The first ten studies I did were for Orex Laboratories, the maker of DES, and were not published because I was under contract with Orex. The terms of my contract gave them control over what studies were published and they chose not to allow the studies to be published."

"Why is the fact that Orex did not permit your ten studies to be published important, Dr. Fordland?"

"It is important because it delayed information for other scientists to know that DES was causing major problems in the offspring of many human beings for at least ten years."

Katie looked over at the jury and asked, "Dr. Fordland, the matters at issue in this case include testimony that Dr. Arnold Pittsburgh sexually assaulted Sylvia Anderson for over two years to keep her quiet about his failure to validate the findings of his study published in December 1985. Also that Drs. Pittsburgh and Orex Labs arranged to have his research published before another study, the Detroit study, that revealed DES given to pregnant women caused AIDS in the male offspring of those pregnancies. The Detroit study was submitted for publication months before Dr. Pittsburgh's. Can you tell the jury why these facts are important in the context of understanding the haste to publish Dr. Pittsburgh's paper before the Detroit research paper?"

Dr. Fordland nodded. "Yes. My contention is that AIDS is not caused by HIV, a virus, but by endocrine disruption. The Detroit study you describe was one of the first to demonstrate that endocrine disruption occurs in humans. In the early to mid-1980s, there was widespread public concern about a disease that was killing gay men in the San Francisco area and fear that the cause of whatever was doing this might spread to the city population. There was a rush by scientists worldwide to try to identify the cause of this problem. In December 1985, Dr. Pittsburgh published what I call his preliminary findings, which claimed that a virus, HIV, was causing the disease he named AIDS. It must be noted that because Dr. Pittsburgh's study was the first one published on the issue of what was causing AIDS, he received the Nobel Prize. In March 1986, the Detroit study was published in the *American Scientific Journal*, and it described the impact of maternal DES on male offspring who died as a result of this disease process that was being reported in the gay male population in San Francisco. In other words, over a fairly short period of time, these two studies presented research that implicated two completely different causes for the deaths occurring in gay men.

"The protocol used in the March 1986 study duplicated another study published in 1971 that demonstrated a significant impact on the female offspring of mothers who took DES during their pregnancy. Taking the March 1986 study, which was done on males, together with the 1971 study, done on females, they demonstrate that both female and male offspring have suffered endocrine disruption by their mothers' exposure to the coal-tar derivative DES. I use the term 'endocrine disruption' because the ovaries in women and the testes in men are endocrine glands whose normal functions were disrupted by the drug DES. I should also include another endocrine gland, the thymus gland, in this discussion. DES damages the T-cells formed by the thymus gland, and the lack of T-cells in both female and male offspring results in the inability to destroy cancer cells and other foreign invaders, such as viruses or bacteria in the body.

"The significance of arranging for Dr. Pittsburgh's study to be published first was further reinforced when, within a few short months after the research on male offspring was published, the Detroit scientists who published the study were falsely accused of scientific fraud because the drug company, Orex, wanted to avoid substantial litigation if it became accepted that DES was a major cause of AIDS. As a result, the simple explanation that HIV was the cause of human AIDS became the prevailing scientific opinion."

Katie asked, "What conclusions have you reached as a result of your training, experience, and research as to the cause of AIDS?

"My contention is that AIDS is not caused by HIV, a virus, but by endocrine disruption."

Dr. Fordland described his findings about the effects of DES on fetuses and the role of the drug in AIDS. He concluded by saying, "HIV, I submit, is an opportunistic virus that infects tissues that are made susceptible after being damaged by in-utero exposure to endocrine disruptors of a profoundly wide type. In other words, HIV is a cofactor but not the cause of AIDS."

Katie looked at the jury. "Please tell the court and jury why you say endocrine disruption causes AIDS. Can you explain?"

"Yes. Animal studies, in-vitro tests, and early human studies show that chemicals cause many adverse effects. The chemical industry says, 'Those are bad studies. Show me the human evidence.' The human evidence takes years and requires that people get sick. We should not have to use the public as guinea pigs. Strong, reliable, and reproducible evidence documents the presence of low concentrations of endocrine disruptors in human tissues and fluids, as well as in environmental samples. Many studies indicate that samples collected from humans and the environment typically contain hundreds of contaminants."

Judge Thomas leaned forward. "Counsel, approach the bench."

Katie had a bad feeling about what was on the judge's mind. She and Luxton went to the sidebar.

Judge Thomas looked at her. "You already know what I am going to ask. What does Dr. Fordland's testimony have to do with the issues in this lawsuit?" He looked at Luxton. "And I'm surprised you haven't objected."

Luxton nodded. "I was going to move to strike Dr. Fordland's entire testimony when he was through, Your Honor."

Katie said, "I have one question remaining for Dr. Fordland that will tie everything together, Your Honor."

The judge looked at Luxton. "What is your position, Mr. Luxton?"

"Your Honor, I move that the entirety of Dr. Fordland's testimony be stricken from the record now as being totally irrelevant to the claims in this lawsuit. Furthermore, to permit this to continue will further inflame the jury over an issue that doesn't matter and has no bearing on this case."

The judge looked back at Katie and held up one finger. "I'll give you one more question, and I'm letting you know right now that I am considering striking the testimony unless the good doctor can, as you say, tie everything together."

Katie walked slowly away from the bench. She was in a quandary. She hesitated as she tried to frame a question in her mind that would pass muster with the judge.

After a moment, she asked, "Dr. Fordland, what relevance does the publishing of Dr. Pittsburgh's research before the Detroit research have on the issue of Dr. Pittsburgh sexually abusing Sylvia?"

"Dr. Pittsburgh sexually abused her to keep her mouth shut about the inadequacies of his study, and he also threatened her with the loss of her potential PhD if she revealed that her follow-up studies failed to confirm his findings. Had she been able to convince him to wait until the validation studies were completed, his research might still have made him famous because he identified the virus known as HIV for the first time in history, but in all likelihood, he might not have received a Nobel Prize. Instead, by bumping the Detroit research aside and getting Dr. Pittsburgh's study published first, the real question of the role of endocrine disruption in AIDS, and many other diseases, was sidetracked and never answered for years and years."

"Thank you, Dr. Fordland. That completes the examination, Your Honor."

Judge Thomas said, "Mr. Luxton, any questions before I rule on your motion?"

"Yes, Your Honor." Luxton stood and walked toward Dr. Fordland. "What about human studies. Can you cite one human study in support of your claims?"

Fordland smiled at Luxton and then turned to the jury. "I am so happy that you asked me that question. One of my colleagues, a highly esteemed epidemiologist, tells me that epidemiology is like a bikini bathing suit. What it reveals is interesting, but what it covers up is critical."

Everyone in the courtroom laughed.

Dr. Fordland continued. "But to further answer your question, sir, the Detroit DES study we've been talking about is a classic retrospective epidemiological study of humans. I mentioned that earlier, as well as the DES study on female offspring."

"That completes my cross-examination, Your Honor, and once again, I renew my motion to strike Dr. Fordland's testimony."

Judge Thomas said, "I am taking the motion under advisement. I will issue an order before the end of the case." He turned and looked at Katie. "Do you have another witness, counsel?"

CHAPTER 47

Katie stood. "Your Honor. Plaintiff calls Dr. Alex Hartley." Alex walked to the front of the courtroom, and the clerk administered the oath. He settled himself into the witness chair. Given the judge's concern about the issue of endocrine disruption, she needed to have Alex's testimony be short and sweet, not engage in a lengthy explanation of something the judge might toss out as having no relevance to Sylvia's case.

"Dr. Hartley, will you tell the jury about your professional training and experience?"

Alex said, "I am board certified in internal medicine and medical toxicology. I am a professor of medicine at the Detroit Medical College, and I am the founder and director of the poison center at Detroit City Hospital. All told, I have published sixty-two scientific studies in peer-reviewed journals."

"I want to focus very specifically on a study that you and Dr. Ingrid Kubilus performed in the mid-1980s. Can you briefly describe that study?"

"Yes, we performed a retrospective epidemiological study on six patients who came through Detroit City Hospital with a condition now known generically as AIDS. Our study revealed that each of the men had been exposed to the drug DES by virtue of their mothers taking the drug during the respective pregnancies of each man."

"Was this study published?"

"Yes, it was submitted for publication in October 1985 and published in the *American Scientific Journal* in March 1986."

"Before the study was submitted for publication, were you under any pressure to not publish it?"

"Yes. Two clinical professors at the hospital where I was working, together with officials at Orex Labs, the maker of DES, exerted continuous pressure on my colleague and me to not publish our research findings. I subsequently found out that Dr. Pittsburgh was part of that effort as well."

"Why did it take more than six months to have your paper published after it was submitted?"

"Orex and Dr. Pittsburgh arranged to have his study published first, several months before ours, even though our paper was submitted a couple of months earlier than his. Both studies had looked at the potential causes of what is known as AIDS. Dr. Pittsburgh's study implicated HIV, and our study implicated the drug DES. Orex, the maker of DES, wanted to avoid lawsuits that would follow if our paper was published."

"Once your research was published in March 1986, were there any additional efforts to challenge your results?"

"Yes, my colleague and I were accused of committing fraud. I temporarily lost my license to practice medicine, and my colleague, Dr. Ingrid Kubilus, was murdered. Our research was removed from the scientific literature."

"Your colleague was murdered?"

"Yes. On the same day my license was suspended, Dr. Kubilus was murdered in her apartment. It was made to look like death by suicide apparently to create the impression that she felt guilty about committing the alleged fraud. But when toxicology studies were done, it was found that she had been injected with a huge dose of digitalis that resulted in her immediate death. The actual murderer died in 1986, but the woman who planned the death was charged, and she turned around and testified that the murder was part of a plan created by Orex, Dr. Pittsburgh, and two Detroit physicians, Dr. Ratner and Dr. Olmstead, to destroy the credibility of our study."

"Did you have your medical license restored?"

"Yes, all of the information about the false accusations was presented at a hearing, and I was immediately reinstated. I should mention that the drug company, Orex, and all of the individuals involved in this, except for Dr. Pittsburgh, were charged and pleaded no contest to the murder of Dr. Kubilus. Drs. Olmstead and Ratner had their medical licenses suspended for five years as a result."

"The bottom line, however, is that your research was delayed so that Dr. Pittsburgh's research could be published first?"

"Yes, that's correct."

"I have no further questions, Your Honor."

Luxton stood. "I have no questions, Your Honor, and I renew my motion to strike as applicable to the testimony of both Dr. Fordland and Dr. Hartley."

Judge Thomas said, "As I indicated previously, I have taken the motion under advisement. Any more witnesses, Ms. Hornsby?"

"Yes, Your Honor. He is waiting outside."

Before she went to get the witness, Leslie grabbed Katie's sleeve and whispered, "Honey, you got a pleasant surprise in store for you. Wait until you meet this dude."

CHAPTER 48

Katie found Dr. Judd Ashton sitting on a bench outside the courtroom. She shook his hand. "Great to meet you. Are you all set?"

"I'm ready." He stood. "Let's go."

Katie felt a little shiver down her spine when she shook his hand. She was shocked at the electricity he generated in her little charging station. They had never met in person, but she had spoken with him by phone the week before when she'd still been in Detroit, and he'd seemed pleasant. She certainly was not prepared for this hunk rocking a man bun. The female lawyer who'd recommended him to her couldn't say enough positive things about him, and now Katie understood why. She had sent Sylvia to Dr. Ashton for a thorough psychiatric examination. Sylvia had spent eight hours with him at his office in Nashville, and he'd billed Katie five thousand dollars for the time. Katie wondered what he'd charge her for two or three hours of a little game of one on one. She smiled at the thought. That was all the time she'd need to get him to let down his hair. As they walked together into the courtroom, she suppressed a grin at the juicy thought. No platters of Italian food in her dreams tonight; she had a new dream lover.

Katie nodded and grinned at Leslie in acknowledgment of her earlier comment about this hunk. "Your Honor, the plaintiff calls Dr. Judd Ashton."

Katie noted that the two young women jurors in seats one and two both sat a little taller in their seats and fussed with their hair as they watched him take the stand after being sworn in by the judge's clerk. Apparently, there was enough electricity in the air to charge their batteries as well. Katie smiled to herself. Leslie had the judge and male jurors mesmerized, and now Dr. Judd would handle the ladies on the jury.

"Would you state your name and tell the court and jury your occupation?"

"Yes. My name is Judd Ashton, and I am a psychiatrist. My office is in Nashville, Tennessee."

"Dr. Ashton, would you tell us, please, about your educational and professional background?"

"I am a graduate of both undergraduate and medical school at Vanderbilt University. I took an internship, two years of residency in emergency medicine, and four years of psychiatry residency training at Massachusetts City Hospital in Boston. After I completed my training, I moved back to Nashville and opened a private practice. I am board certified in both emergency medicine and psychiatry. I currently teach at Vanderbilt's medical school, where I run the sophomore course in diagnostic psychiatry and the local rape crisis center. I also spend two afternoons a week in the emergency room at our university hospital. I have written four books in the field of psychiatry, including two on the psychiatric effects of sexual assault."

"Have you testified previously as an expert witness in the field of sexual assault or rape?"

"Yes. Approximately thirty times since I started in private practice."

"Dr. Ashton, let me turn your attention to Sylvia Anderson. At my request, have you evaluated her with regard to any impact that the sexual contact by Dr. Arnold Pittsburgh may have had on her?"

"Yes. May I explain?"

"Please do so."

"My staff and I spent eight hours with Sylvia. The first two hours were spent administering standard psychological testing, and then I interviewed her thoroughly for six hours."

"Do you have an opinion, based on your evaluation and professional background and training, as to whether or not Sylvia has suffered any trauma with regard to the sexual encounters with Dr. Pittsburgh?"

"Yes. It is my considered opinion that Sylvia suffers from a profound post-traumatic stress disorder that is permanent and will persist for the rest of her life."

"What is the basis for your opinion?"

"There are two distinct issues with regard to Sylvia." He looked over at the jury. "I am certain you have noticed that she has an elegant persona about her that is quite endearing. She is beautiful, well dressed, and very meticulous about what she says and does. However, underneath all those positive attributes is a terribly frightened woman who learned early on in her life that she must, without question, be perfect, nice, kind, and obedient in all respects so that others will not reject her or cast her off. Sylvia's specific situation started early, as she was passed on from one foster home to another. A little girl wanting and needing love and continuously being rejected in her life situations becomes ripe fodder, so to speak, for the Dr. Pittsburghs of the world. Some authoritative men have an inherent instinct for predation of such little girls and women, who can be bent or shaped in any direction the powerful man wants. The little girl, in Sylvia's case, submitted to the demands of the predator time after time after time because she needed to protect herself from her greatest fear, fear of rejection. A literal mental freezing began at the very first moment Sylvia was sexually abused by Dr. Pittsburgh. When the twenty-six months of sexual abuse stopped because Dr. Pittsburgh had found a younger prey, the feared rejection happened. The mental freezing was already permanently embedded in her mind."

Katie moved a little closer to him – but not close enough, she thought. "Doctor Judd, let me interrupt you for a moment. Can you describe what you mean by 'mental freezing'?"

"Yes. There are certain intimate facts that Sylvia has permitted me to talk about. First, she was a virgin when Dr. Pittsburgh assaulted her. Second, the 442 sex assaults perpetrated on her by Dr. Pittsburgh are the only sexual contacts she has had in her entire life. Any chance at a fulfilling, loving life, including sex with a loving partner, was forever taken away by Dr. Pittsburgh's assaults. They were assaults not only on her body but also, more importantly, on the very essence of her emotional and moral well-being. As such, this instantly created a 'mental freezing,' a state of chronic depression that manifests itself in frequent suicidal ideation. I use the word 'freezing' to characterize the sudden

279

onset of this at the very first assault by Dr. Pittsburgh. Her emotions right now continue to be frozen in time."

"Can you describe the depth of Sylvia's reaction to the sexual assaults?"

"Yes. This reaction in Sylvia to the sustained sexual abuse by Dr. Pittsburgh is, in effect, a moral injury. Moral injury is a transgression of conscience. It is what happens when a person's deeply held values, beliefs, or ways of being in the world are continuously violated. It can be found everywhere. On the battlefield, it is called post-traumatic stress disorder, or PTSD, but PTSD can occur in civilian life as well: behind closed doors of churches and temples; in hospitals, bars, brothels, prisons, and unemployment lines; at borders and in detention centers; on school playgrounds and social media; and even in the unsuspecting house or office next door. This is because, wherever human beings are, moral injuries can be inflicted by others.

"With moral injuries, memories don't trigger fear. Instead, they beget shame, guilt, rage, disgust, emptiness, and despair. With PTSD seen on the battlefield, a primary concern is physical safety in kill-or-be-killed situations. With moral injury, it is existential safety – or trust. A moral injury makes people question themselves, others, life, or their God. It makes them question their ability to do right or be good. A moral injury diminishes one's character, ideals, ambitions, and attachments. It leaves people feeling contaminated in their being or that something they once held dear has been sullied. 'Unworthy,' 'beyond redemption,' 'gone forever,' and 'emotionally dead' are how Sylvia and many other rape victims have described the experience. Many PTSD veterans of combat express exactly the same emotional responses.

"The byproduct of Sylvia's moral injury, the emotional damage, was her walking away from her nearly completed goal of obtaining a PhD and, instead, settling for a job that clearly is below her intellectual capabilities for the last thirty-three years."

Katie was transfixed. Wow, she hadn't expected what she'd just heard from Dr. Judd. Everything he'd said made absolute sense, but most of it had never occurred to her before. She and Sylvia had talked generically about a moral injury, but Dr. Judd had taken the concept to a depth greater than she could have imagined. She was stunned into momentary silence.

After an awkward pause, she gathered herself and asked, "Dr. Judd, do you have an opinion on whether or not Sylvia suffers from a disability that would have prevented her over the years from taking action against Dr. Pittsburgh for what he'd done to her?" This was an important question that she and Dr. Judd had discussed at length over the phone. This needed to be addressed because the possibility of Judge Thomas dismissing the case due to the statute of limitations issue was still an open question.

"Yes. I do have an opinion."

"What is your opinion as regards the mental status of Sylvia that may have prevented her for years from instituting a lawsuit against Dr. Pittsburgh?"

"It is my opinion that Sylvia had a disability from the moral injury I described earlier, which prevented her from thinking about a lawsuit from the very first moment that Dr. Pittsburgh began his sexual abuse of her. Let me give an example of how post-traumatic stress disorder or moral injury causes a loss of reasoning power and meets the definition of disability. There are many military veterans who return home from combat who have PTSD. It is virtually impossible to get most of these veterans to talk about, or even think about, what they have witnessed on the battlefield. What happened to Sylvia is exactly the same as those veterans. They become frozen in time as a direct result of whatever experience they went through. People who know a veteran think that the veteran simply doesn't like to talk about what he experienced in combat, but it is more complex than that. He can't talk about it not because he doesn't want to but because his mind is frozen in time because of the loss of reasoning power, the moral injury, about events he experienced. This is also applicable to Sylvia. I wasn't here for her testimony, but I would bet that she had great difficulty here in this courtroom talking about what happened with Dr. Pittsburgh. Her mind cannot let her relive the experiences. She is disabled because of the moral injury inflicted on her by Dr. Pittsburgh."

She waited until the jury could process the significance of his response. "Dr. Ashton, have your opinions that you expressed today been reached with reasonable psychiatric certainty?"

"Yes. I might add that an additional basis for my opinions is my treatment of several hundred rape victims at the rape crisis clinic I founded in Nashville. I want to mention one other major factor that I neglected to say earlier. Sylvia, in the real sense of the word, also suffers from what is commonly referred to as the Stockholm syndrome, a condition in which a victim develops an alternate reality by becoming favorably disposed toward the attacker or abuser. Patty Hearst is the most famous example of this phenomenon. She was kidnapped by a vigilante group at the edge of the political world back in the 1970s, and shortly after her capture, she began to identify so closely with the group that she actively participated in their criminal acts, including the robbing of a bank. As a supplement to my previous explanations, I would add this phenomenon as an additional factor in understanding what Sylvia has gone through. We see this quite frequently in rape victims when there have been consistent multiple rapes by the same perpetrator."

"Thank you, Dr. Judd. That's all I have, Your Honor."

The judge looked at Luxton. "Cross-examination?"

"Yes, Your Honor." Luxton moved quickly to the edge of the jury box. He turned and looked at Dr. Ashton.

"Doctor, you are being paid for your appearance here today, correct?"

Dr. Ashton said, "That is right."

"Tell the jury how much you are being paid for spending this half-day with us."

"My fee for today's appearance is ten thousand dollars."

"And did you work on this matter before today? I believe you testified that you spent nearly a day with the plaintiff?"

"Yes, I did."

"And how much did you charge for that day?"

"Five thousand dollars."

"Do you charge an initial retainer fee?"

"Yes. I require an initial retainer of twenty-five thousand dollars when I am hired for litigation purposes. The charges for meeting with Sylvia and the court appearance today are deducted from that amount. If I do nothing else on this matter, I will refund ten thousand dollars to Ms. Hornsby."

"How many times have you testified in court?"

"As I mentioned earlier, this is the thirtieth time."

"Would you say that you averaged about fifteen thousand dollars in each of those cases?"

"I don't have the exact amount for each case, but that's a fair statement."

"So, it would be reasonable to suggest that you have received approximately four hundred and fifty thousand dollars providing testimony for rape victims?"

"That's a reasonable estimate."

Luxton turned to the judge. "I have nothing more, Your Honor."

"Ms. Hornsby, any redirect examination?"

Katie stood. This was going to be good. "I have one question for you, Dr. Ashton. What do you do with all the money you earn testifying for rape victims?"

"I donate every single penny to our rape crisis center."

"Thank you, Dr. Ashton." She looked at Judge Thomas. "May Dr. Ashton be excused? He has a flight out of LaGuardia at six o'clock."

Judge Thomas leaned forward. "The witness is excused. Thank you, doctor. Travel safely."

Katie waited until Dr. Ashton left the courtroom. Then she said, "Your Honor, the plaintiff rests."

The judge nodded at Luxton. "Will you be ready to begin your case tomorrow morning?"

"Yes, Judge."

Judge Thomas looked over at the jury. "We'll break for the day and resume at nine o'clock tomorrow morning."

Leslie and Katie chatted with Sylvia and Dr. Ashton outside the courtroom for a few minutes. Katie begged off having dinner with Sylvia and Leslie as she needed alone time for the preparation of the defense witnesses that were coming up.

Dr. Ashton was headed to the airport, but if he had been sticking around for the night, it would have been simply good manners to make herself available to dine with him. Him, her, no Sylvia or Leslie. Who needs food when a yummy man bun is available? A girl can dream, can't she? She couldn't keep a smile off her face at the thought.

CHAPTER 49

The next morning, Judge Thomas came into the courtroom and sat down. The jury was already in place. "Good morning, everyone." He looked at Luxton. "Ready, Mr. Luxton?"

"Your Honor, the defense calls Dr. Arnold Pittsburgh."

Katie's initial thought as she watched Dr. Pittsburgh shuffle to the witness stand was that this was a scene right out of central casting. The doctor's messy hair looked like it had been sprayed in place. His blue plaid shirt, corduroy pants, green bow-tie, and brown sports jacket with leather elbow guards couldn't have been more of a caricature of "absent-minded professor" if he'd actually set out to achieve it. She guessed he was about eighty years old.

He sat in the witness chair after being sworn in by the clerk.

Luxton set himself up in front of the jury box and began his questions. "Good morning, Professor. Please tell the court and jury your name and your occupation."

Before he responded, Dr. Pittsburgh removed a pair of bifocals from his shirt pocket, put them on, and looked over at the jury.

"My name is Arnold Pittsburgh. I am a professor of biochemistry at Filmore University."

"How long have you been a professor at Filmore?"

"I started at Filmore as an assistant professor in 1979 and became a full professor in 1982."

Luxton led Dr. Pittsburgh through fifteen minutes of his detailed history of achievements: receiving a Nobel Prize, acceptance by his peers internationally, speaking engagements all over the world, and 150 published studies.

Luxton said, "Dr. Pittsburgh, you have mentioned that your 150 published studies were peer-reviewed. Will you please tell the court and jury what it means to have research peer-reviewed?"

"Yes. Before a piece of scientific research is published in a reputable medical or scientific journal, the editor of the journal sends copies of the article to independent scientific experts in the same field of research. Those experts review and evaluate the research for accuracy, adherence to scientific principles, and whether or not the research advances the knowledge of the particular area of science in question. The last requirement is, perhaps, the most important because there is always a great deal of research that merely replicates research that has been previously published. If all that duplicative research were published, there would literally be hundreds, if not thousands, of articles that merely reiterate the original findings, and these articles would swamp journals and scientists with loads and loads of information that is not useful because the information does not advance the knowledge of the particular area of science."

"Would this 'useful information' requirement also include research that tends to refute or reject scientific knowledge that has already been published?"

"Yes, of course."

"Ms. Anderson has testified that she performed additional studies regarding your published paper on HIV and AIDS that rejected the findings you reported. Is that correct?"

Dr. Pittsburgh looked at the jury and nodded. "Yes, I am aware of that claim by her."

"To your knowledge, has Ms. Anderson published the research she claims refutes your original findings regarding HIV and AIDS?"

"No, she has not."

"Has she submitted her research to any peer-reviewed medical or scientific journal in an attempt to get her alleged findings published?"

"I am unaware of any effort by her to do so. I should point out that as the author of the original research, if such a submission had been made by her, I would surely have received a copy of the research from the publication editor prior to publication to afford me the opportunity to respond to the submission when, and if, the research was going to be published. That is standard practice throughout all areas of science. Because I have never received such information, I assume that she has never submitted her research to any journal for publication."

Luxton once again looked at the jury and asked, "Ms. Anderson claims that she gave you her research studies that refuted your claims in the HIV-AIDS paper shortly after your research was published, right?"

"She does claim that, but she never gave me any research that refuted my original findings."

Luxton then changed the focus of his direct examination. "Dr. Pittsburgh, let's talk about you and Sylvia Anderson. Did there come a time when you struck up a romantic relationship with her?"

"Yes. Sometime in the first or second year of her doctoral training, she and I established a very nice relationship. During our time together, we enjoyed each other's company greatly, or at least, I thought we did. But judging by her complaints against me now, apparently not." He looked at the jury and shook his head. "Our relationship had a rocky start and a rockier ending, but the time we had together, in my opinion, was worth all the suffering she's put me through since."

"Did you ever abuse Sylvia sexually?"

"No, I did not. Never. To be sure, we had sex, a lot of sex. But abuse her? Never."

"You say you and she had a lot of sex. Where did this take place?"

"We had spontaneous sex. I am considerably older than her, and she made me feel young again. She would walk into my office, lock the door, and we'd have sex. I was flattered by the attention she gave me. She was, and is, a beautiful woman."

"In the middle of her third year in her training with you, she quit. Do you know why?"

"No, I never understood why she left. But unfortunately, it happens too frequently in the field of biochemistry. Doctoral students face all kinds of pressures, and we lose too many of them simply because they can't handle the pressure. If I had to guess, I would say that is why Sylvia quit when she did. In fact, when she left, I went into a state of depression because we were so close in our relationship and she ended it without any explanation. One way or another, I made it through that rough period. I missed her. But sexually abuse her? No way."

Katie was alarmed at her own reaction to his testimony. He was believable. She suspected that most of the jurors felt the same as she did. She and Sylvia were going to have a heart-to-heart talk when this was over. But right now, she had to gather her thoughts and focus on her cross-examination of him. She had expected to confront an arrogant asshole, but instead, Dr. Pittsburgh was a nice and gentle old man. What the fuck was she going to do?

Luxton continued. "Dr. Pittsburgh, did Sylvia Anderson ever complain to you about the publication of the research reporting the discovery of HIV and its relationship to the disease we now know as AIDS?"

"Yes, she did. She was upset that she did not receive the accolades that I was receiving after the research was published. I received the highest honor a scientist can get, the Nobel Prize, in 1992. She claimed that as a co-author, she deserved the same kind of recognition I was getting. In my opinion, she was jealous of me for getting all of the attention."

Luxton turned and smiled at the jury. "That's all the questions I have, Dr. Pittsburgh."

Judge Thomas nodded at Katie. "Ms. Hornsby. You may begin your cross-examination."

Katie stood. "Thank you, Your Honor." She walked up close to the witness. "Dr. Pittsburgh, I'm Katie Hornsby, and I have some questions for you about your relationship with Sylvia. First of all, who is Megan Griffeth?"

Dr. Pittsburgh reacted as though she had slapped his face. "Ms. Griffeth, now Dr. Griffeth, was one of my doctoral students." His face reddened.

"You've spoken openly about all the sexual activity you had with Sylvia. Isn't it true that you started the same type of sexual activity with Megan Griffeth before Sylvia left your training program?"

"I don't remember."

"What is it that you don't remember, the sex with Ms. Griffeth or the date it started?"

"I'm not sure what you're getting at."

"Let me ask this a different way. Have you, at some point in your illustrious career, had sex with Megan Griffeth?"

Katie had seen pure hatred in the eyes of witnesses before, but never anything like the expression Dr. Pittsburgh sent toward her. She now understood the meaning of the phrase "if looks could kill."

Dr. Pittsburgh looked past her, toward Luxton. "Do I have to answer that? I don't know what this has to do with this case."

Judge Thomas said, "Doctor, answer the question."

Dr. Pittsburgh glared at Katie. "Yes."

She took another step forward. "Are you saying, yes, you had sex with Megan Griffeth?"

"Yes."

"More than once?"

Dr. Pittsburgh looked up at Judge Thomas. "My relationship with Dr. Griffeth has nothing to do with this lawsuit, Judge."

Judge Thomas leaned toward him. "Answer counsel's questions. I'll let you know if I think she's invading your privacy."

Dr. Pittsburgh turned and glared at her again. "More than once."

"You testified earlier that you went into a state of depression when Sylvia left your program. Was having sex with Dr. Griffeth part of the therapy for your recovery from that state?"

Luxton stood. "Objection, Your Honor. Counsel is badgering the witness."

"I'll withdraw the question." Katie had made the point, and the jury had heard it. "When did this relationship with Dr. Griffeth begin? Before she became a doctor?"

"I already told you that I don't remember."

Luxton stood. "Your Honor, I object. Counsel is still badgering Dr. Pittsburgh."

Judge Thomas looked over at Katie. "Ms. Hornsby, I agree. Move on to a different topic."

"Your Honor, I have a few more questions that touch on this area. I need a little leeway."

Judge Thomas nodded. "I'll permit more questions, but you'll do so at your own peril. If you go too far, I'll stop you."

"Thank you, Your Honor." She went back to her table and picked up an exhibit. "Dr. Pittsburgh, have any of your doctoral students ever complained to school authorities that you were sexually harassing them?"

"No, of course not."

Katie nodded at Leslie, walked up to the witness stand, and turned toward the jury. Leslie moved to the projector.

Katie held up the document and looked it over briefly. "Who is Holly Ridgefield?"

"Ms. Ridgefield was in my doctoral program, but she had a nervous breakdown. She didn't last a year."

"She filed a sexual harassment complaint against you before she left your program, right?"

"I'm aware of that. It's my understanding that a committee looked into her complaint and found that it was without merit."

"While Holly Ridgefield was in your program, did you ever have sex with her?"

"I don't remember."

"You don't remember? Does that mean you might have had sex with her but you can't remember?"

Luxton stood. "Objection, Your Honor. Dr. Pittsburgh has already answered the question."

Judge Thomas shook his head. "I'll allow the question. Objection denied."

Dr. Pittsburgh looked at the judge. "What was the question?"

"Let me rephrase it, Your Honor. Dr. Pittsburgh, with regard to your statement that you cannot remember, did you mean to tell this jury that you might have had sex with Holly Ridgefield but that you don't remember whether you did or not?"

"Yes."

Katie nodded toward Leslie, who turned on the projector light. A copy of the exhibit Katie held in her hand appeared on the large screen. The jury could read right along with the doctor while she questioned him.

"Let me see if I can refresh your memory, Dr. Pittsburgh. I am going to read a statement from the complaint filed against you by Holly Ridgefield in January 2006."

Katie read from the document. "Dr. Pittsburgh had a Christmas party for his staff at a local restaurant on December 18, 2005. After the party, he drove me home, and we sat in his car in front of my apartment building and talked for a few minutes. He became aggressive and forced my head down onto his lap, where he had exposed himself. He forced me to perform oral sex on him. I was crying and tried to get out of the car, but he wouldn't let me out until I promised I'd never tell anyone about this."

Katie looked at Dr. Pittsburgh. "Does hearing that statement refresh your memory with regard to whether or not you had sex with Holly Ridgefield?"

"Yes, it does. I remember that incident well. She begged me to have sex with her."

"Your Honor, I offer Exhibit Twelve into evidence. For the record, it is a certified copy of the complaint Holly Ridgefield filed against Dr. Pittsburgh."

Luxton rose to his feet. "Objection, Your Honor. The document is rank hearsay and should not be admitted on the basis that it is apparently being offered to prove the truth of the matter described. Also, it is irrelevant and prejudicial."

Judge Thomas leaned toward Katie. "What do you have to say about Mr. Luxton's hearsay objection?"

Katie had anticipated this objection because Luxton was right. Her attempt to use the document to prove the truth of Ms. Ridgefield's complaint against Dr. Pittsburgh without more at this moment was hearsay. For that reason, it was not admissible on that basis, but it opened the door for her to get the document into evidence with another witness who, in fact, was on standby out in the hallway. "Your Honor, I request that the court permit me to mark this document for identification purposes only at this time, and I withdraw my request for admission into evidence."

Judge Thomas smiled at her. He knew what she was doing. "Exhibit Twelve is marked for identification only."

"Thank you, Your Honor." Katie turned her attention once again to Dr. Pittsburgh. "Let's talk about your claim that Sylvia was jealous of your fame for the research she did in your program. That's a mere supposition on your part, correct?"

"No, it's not a supposition. It is true that she frequently complained about not getting attention for her work. She made it clear to me that I was treating her unfairly."

"You claim that you and Sylvia 'had sex, a lot of sex.' Did all this complaining you say she made about not receiving any credit or attention for the research come before, during, or after each time you had sex with her?"

Dr. Pittsburgh started to speak, but then he stopped. He sat for a long moment.

Katie stepped closer toward him. "Can you answer that question, Dr. Pittsburgh?"

"I don't remember."

"In your earlier testimony, you said, quote, 'We had spontaneous sex. I am considerably older than her, and she made me feel young again. She would walk into my office, lock the door, and we'd have sex. I was flattered by the attention she gave me.' End quote. Do you remember saying that?"

"Yes, it's true."

"Doctor, I'm having a difficult time understanding why, on the one hand, you contend there was frequent voluntary sex and that you were flattered by the attention Sylvia gave you and, on the other hand, you claim she made it clear to you that you were treating her unfairly. Do you see the contradiction here? Can you explain why she would lock the door behind her and have sex with you right in your office while, at the same time, complaining about being treated unfairly by you?"

"She did. That's all I can say."

"Did Sylvia ever complain to you about your sexual affair with Megan Griffeth?"

"I don't remember."

"Did Sylvia ever tell you that she was jealous of Megan Griffeth?"

"I don't remember. She probably did."

Katie looked at Judge Thomas. "Your Honor, I move to strike the 'probably did' portion of Dr. Pittsburgh's answer and request that you advise the jury that his answer in that regard be disregarded. The basis for my motion is that that portion of his answer is one hundred percent at odds with the first part of his answer when he said that he doesn't remember."

Luxton said, "Objection, Your Honor. His answer is what it is. This is cross-examination. If Ms. Hornsby wants to clarify what he means, she can ask him to do so."

Judge Thomas said, "Objection sustained. You can ask the doctor to clarify his response if you wish, Ms. Hornsby."

"Thank you, Your Honor. Dr. Pittsburgh, what is the basis in fact, if any, for your statement that Sylvia probably did complain to you that she was jealous of Megan Griffeth?"

"I really can't say at the moment."

"To further clarify your testimony, you said earlier that you didn't remember whether or not you started having sex with Megan Griffeth while Sylvia was still working in your research lab. Have you suddenly remembered, fifteen minutes later, that you did start having sex with Megan Griffeth at the same time you were having sex with Sylvia?"

"No. I don't think so."

"Did Dr. Griffeth ever complain to you about your having sex with Sylvia?"

"No. I don't remember."

"Is your answer no or that you don't remember?"

"I don't understand your question."

"Let's move on to a different subject. Is it your position that the research paper on HIV and AIDS you published in 1985 had been validated by your research laboratory at the time you submitted it for publication?"

"At the time I submitted the paper, it was my professional opinion that the work was valid."

"Dr. Pittsburgh, I respectfully suggest to you that you have not answered my question. My question limited itself to the existence of validation studies done in your laboratory prior to the time of submission. Can you please answer this question?"

"Validation can occur in a variety of ways. I was satisfied that my research had been validated at the time of submission. It probably would not have been accepted for publication if it hadn't been validated."

"You knew at the time of submission of your paper for publication that Sylvia was still working on validating your research by performing a study identical to the one that you submitted, right?"

"She was checking the results of our study, as I recall."

"Her validation attempts were done under your direction and supervision as the head of your laboratory, yes?"

"It's true that I am responsible for any research done in my laboratory. Both then and now."

"Do you remember the day when Sylvia came to your office and reported to you that she had not been able to verify your original results?"

"I have a vague recollection of that."

"Do you remember having sex with her for the first time on that day?"

"Vaguely, yes. As I recall, we had sex to celebrate the fact that my research had been accepted for publication."

"The basis for your search on HIV and AIDS is that AIDS is an infectious disease, right?"

"That's right. AIDS is an infectious disease. And it is caused by HIV. I received the Nobel Prize for that research."

"Would you have believed AIDS is infectious if you had known that not even one of the doctors and health-care workers who have treated the thousands of American AIDS patients since 1985 has been confirmed to have contracted AIDS from a patient?"

"Let me answer that question this way. It is true that a number of scientists in the world believe that to be the case, but there are several reported instances of health-care workers who have inadvertently stuck themselves with needles while obtaining blood specimens from AIDS patients and come down with AIDS."

"Even if that would not have changed your mind, would you still believe that a sexually transmitted virus was causing AIDS if you knew that none of the wives of more than fifteen thousand HIV-positive American hemophiliacs has contracted AIDS from their husbands?"

"Yes, I still would believe that HIV causes AIDS. To me, the virus is the cause of AIDS only when it is transmitted through the blood of an infected person."

"Or would you have believed that AIDS was contagious if you had known that after a marriage of fifteen years, neither the wife nor the six-year-old daughter of the late tennis star and AIDS patient Arthur Ashe developed AIDS or even became HIV-positive?"

"Yes, I would still believe that HIV causes AIDS because it is highly probable that neither the wife nor child was exposed to Mr. Ashe's blood."

"Or that the long-term lover of the movie star Rock Hudson had no AIDS symptoms years after Hudson died from AIDS in 1985?"

"Yes, I still believe that HIV causes AIDS and that there are some individuals who can be exposed to AIDS through sexual transmission of body fluid who, for one reason or another, do not develop the disease."

"Would you believe that AIDS was sexually transmitted if you had known that after a thirteen-year marriage and two children, the husband of the late AIDS patient Elizabeth Glaser is healthy and HIV-free?"

"Yes. Same answer."

"Is it true that the most common form of cancer seen in AIDS patients is Kaposi's sarcoma?"

"Yes, that is true."

"And it is true, is it not, that Kaposi's sarcoma was known to exist well prior to your discovery of HIV?"

"Yes, that is true."

"Would you have believed in an AIDS-causing virus if you had known that nobody has ever contracted Kaposi's sarcoma in the US from a blood donor with Kaposi's sarcoma?"

"I am unaware of anything like that. Are you saying that that is true?"

"Dr. Pittsburgh, I will say respectfully to you that I am the one who gets to ask questions. Your function here as a witness is to answer this question. Do you have the question in mind, or would you like me to repeat it?"

"I know what the question is. Unless you can demonstrate your statement to be true, I will stick with my prior answers. I still believe that HIV causes AIDS."

"Isn't it true that more than ten percent of men who are diagnosed as having AIDS test negative for HIV?"

"Yes."

"Let's move on to another topic. Can you tell the court and jury what endocrine disruption is?" Katie walked over to an easel and wrote the words "ENDOCRINE DISRUPTION" on the board.

"Yes. Endocrine disruption is when a chemical, or mixture of chemicals, interferes with any aspect of hormone action."

"In 1971, it was shown that a chemical, a drug named DES, that was given to pregnant women in the 1950s caused vaginal cancer in some of the daughters of those pregnant women. That drug, DES, was the first known drug to cause endocrine disruption in humans, right?"

"I believe that is correct."

Luxton stood. "Your Honor, I object to this line of questioning. What does endocrine disruption have to do with anything in this case?"

Judge Thomas rubbed his chin. "Approach the bench, counsel."

Luxton and Katie walked up to the sidebar. Judge Thomas waited until the court reporter was seated and indicated she was ready. He said, "Ms. Hornsby, I'm inclined to agree with Mr. Luxton. We are right back to the same question I had earlier. What in the world does endocrine disruption have to do with this case?"

"Your Honor, I am reluctant to give a full response to your question because, in doing so, I would be prematurely disclosing an important area of cross-examination coming up. I can say this, however. Endocrine disruption as a concept is directly tied to the research that Sylvia and Dr. Pittsburgh were doing when she worked in his laboratory. The court permitted my questions and Dr. Fordland's answers during the plaintiff's case in chief. Once again, I need some leeway in how I approach this because it can be complicated, but I will do my best to simplify it. I also point out that Mr. Luxton made no objections to the questions as they were being asked. My additional position on that is that an objection not timely made is forever waived."

Judge Thomas thought for a moment. "I'll give you fifteen minutes. If you haven't convinced me by then, you'll have to go on to something else."

"Thank you, Judge."

Katie checked her notes and stepped away from the witness box. "Dr. Pittsburgh, was there any reason for you to submit your research to the *American Scientific Journal* so hastily before the validation study being conducted by Sylvia was completed?"

"No. As I said previously, I felt that the original study was self-validating. And I don't agree with your use of the word 'hastily.'"

"Do you know Oskar Klimpf?"

"Yes, but I don't understand why you are asking me about him."

"Dr. Oskar Klimpf was the longstanding medical director of Orex Labs, the drug company that was the maker of DES, right?"

Dr. Pittsburgh nodded.

"You have to answer aloud. Motions of the head can't be reported by the court reporter."

"Yes." Dr. Pittsburgh shuffled nervously.

"You are aware that a 1986 study conducted in Detroit revealed that some male offspring of DES mothers who took the drug while pregnant resulted in the same condition you called AIDS?"

"I don't remember the details, but there was a study done at the time that made that claim. There was a great amount of research going on at that time that was attempting to discover whatever was killing thousands of gay men in San Francisco. Society looked to the scientific community to quickly come up with both the cause and the cure of what is now known as AIDS."

"Was the Detroit study showing that DES caused AIDS published before or after your study was published?"

"My study was the first published study in the world that identified both the virus and its relationship to the cause of AIDS."

"A moment ago, you said you didn't understand why I was asking you about Dr. Oskar Klimpf. For the record, I am handing you proposed Exhibit Thirteen, and I ask you to take as much time as you need to read the exhibit because I will ask you some questions about it when you are done, okay?" Katie handed Dr. Pittsburgh the proposed exhibit and walked to the defense table, where she gave Mr. Luxton a copy. Leslie turned the projector on so the jury could read the document.

Dr. Pittsburgh read for a few moments and then looked up. "I've read the exhibit."

"For the record, Exhibit Thirteen is a copy of a letter written to you by Dr. Oskar Klimp, the medical director of Orex Labs, and it is dated November 28, 1985, right?"

"It appears to be. I don't remember ever seeing this letter."

"In fact, you responded to this letter on December 5, 1985, by writing back to Dr. Klimpf, right?"

"I don't remember."

"Dr. Pittsburgh, let's see if I can refresh your memory. Will you identify proposed Exhibit Fourteen for the court and jury?" Katie handed him a copy of the exhibit and gave Luxton a copy as well. The document was also projected on the screen by Leslie.

Dr. Pittsburgh's face turned red. "This exhibit appears to be a copy of a letter I wrote to Dr. Klimpf on December 5, 1985. May I ask where you obtained this letter from? It is marked 'Privileged and Confidential.'"

Katie ignored his question. "Dr. Pittsburgh, now that you've read your December 5, 1985, letter to Dr. Klimpf, does that refresh your memory about receiving his November 28, 1985, letter to you?"

"No, it doesn't."

"Well, let's first discuss Exhibit Fourteen, your letter to Dr. Klimpf of December 5, 1985. Do you remember sending that letter to him?"

Dr. Pittsburgh shook his head. "No."

"That is your signature on Exhibit Fourteen, isn't it?"

"It appears to be, but it is easy to forge someone's signature."

"Do you remember Ed Herold, a private investigator employed by Orex Labs, visiting with you in your office on November 30, 1985?"

"No, I don't remember."

"Do you remember a telephone conversation you had with Dr. Oskar Klimpf on November 26, 1985, about the research of Detroit Drs. Alex Hartley and Ingrid Kubilus that had been submitted to the *American Scientific Journal* for potential publication?"

"I don't remember."

"Your letter of December 5, 1985 to Dr. Klimpf discusses the meeting you had with Orex's private investigator, Ed Herold, in your office, right?"

"This letter describes such a meeting, but I have no memory whatsoever of such an event."

"Please examine proposed Exhibit Fifteen for a moment." Katie handed Dr. Pittsburgh and Luxton the proposed exhibit, and Leslie displayed it on the screen. Dr. Pittsburgh looked over the document and then nodded to Katie.

"Dr. Pittsburgh, proposed Exhibit Fifteen is a letter written to you by the editor of the *American Scientific Journal* dated December 15, 1985, right?"

"It appears to be, but I have no memory of receiving this letter."

"Exhibit Fifteen describes a conversation you had with Dr. Petersmark, the editor of the *American Scientific Journal*, on December 10, 1985, right?"

"That's what the letter says. I have no memory of such a conversation."

Katie looked at Judge Thomas. "Your Honor, can we approach the bench?"

The judge waved the lawyers up. Katie waited until the court reporter indicated she was ready.

"Your Honor, I have two witnesses who can verify the authenticity of Exhibits Thirteen through Fifteen. While Dr. Pittsburgh indicates he has no memory regarding any of these documents, I'd like to proceed by asking him questions about their contents. I am requesting that you permit me to continue questioning Dr. Pittsburgh now rather than interrupting his cross-examination and delaying the trial to bring these witnesses to the stand to authenticate them. I am prepared to proceed either way, but it is my preference to continue at this time with Dr. Pittsburgh."

Judge Thomas looked at Luxton. "What is your position?"

Luxton shrugged. "Judge, I think it would be patently unfair to Dr. Pittsburgh to be grilled about documents about which he has no memory. His lack of memory about these documents would be the same whether or not someone comes in and authenticates them."

Katie replied, "Except that, Your Honor, he would be responding to evidence that had already been verified for authenticity."

Judge Thomas looked at her. "Why is this so important? What do these letters have to do with the issues in this lawsuit?"

Katie paused to collect her thoughts. "Judge, these letters indicate quite clearly that the Detroit research paper was already submitted to the *American Scientific Journal* for publication but was shunted aside so that Dr. Pittsburgh's research would be published months before the Detroit study. In that way, Dr. Pittsburgh would be the first scientist in the world to identify the cause of AIDS rather than the authors of the Detroit study, and this would also benefit the drug company Orex Labs by minimizing potential lawsuits against the company from claims that DES caused AIDS."

"I understand what you're saying, Ms. Hornsby, but you haven't answered my question. What does all this have to do with the issues in this lawsuit?"

"Your Honor, the testimony to date makes it clear that Dr. Pittsburgh rushed his research by submitting it for publication before the plaintiff completed the validation study to verify the claim that HIV caused AIDS. The proofs demonstrate that Dr. Pittsburgh did two things to protect himself: he listed Sylvia Anderson as a co-author, even though she was unaware that the paper had been submitted for publication, and when she called his attention to the fact that the validation study failed to verify the results of the original study, he victimized her to keep her quiet by subjecting her to frequent sexual assaults and threats of blaming her for the deficiencies of the paper if the truth was made public. In a word, he browbeat her to keep her mouth shut. Thus, introduction of this evidence is relevant to show Dr. Pittsburgh's motive for doing what he did to the plaintiff."

Katie watched in agony while Judge Thomas thought about her response. He closed his eyes for a moment, opened them, and said, "Let's break for the day. I'm going to need time to think about this. I'll make my ruling when we start tomorrow morning, and I'll permit limited argument from both sides on this issue before I do. Both of you can submit a written brief as well. My concern is the limits of the admissibility of evidence that is marginally relevant to the issues in this lawsuit. Where should the line be drawn?"

Katie walked back to her table and sat down next to Sylvia while the judge excused the jury and left the courtroom. Sylvia looked at Katie. "What happened up there? Why do you look so worried?"

"I have a lot of homework to do tonight. I've got to convince the judge about admitting the evidence that shows that Dr. Pittsburgh helped manipulate the publishing dates of his research."

CHAPTER 50

Katie hardly slept that night, and the tug of sleepiness grabbed her as she took the subway downtown to the courthouse. Leslie had left for court an hour earlier as she needed to reset the projector so they could display evidence on the large screen. The equipment had been removed yesterday after court because another judge had needed to use the courtroom for a long hearing.

Katie closed her eyes to rest them and enjoyed the rhythm and sway of the train. A man seated next to her gently tapped her arm. "Do you get off here?"

She opened her eyes and jumped to her feet. "Thank you. I appreciate you waking me up. I probably would have slept all day if you hadn't."

The man grinned. "You were sound asleep. I could tell you're a lawyer, with the briefcase and all."

"Thanks again."

She rushed out of the subway tunnel and into the courthouse and took the elevator to the eighth floor. When she walked into the courtroom, Luxton was standing in front of the bench, talking to the judge, and Leslie and Sylvia were seated at their table.

Judge Thomas saw her and said, "Good morning, Ms. Hornsby. Join us up here, and we'll get started."

She gathered her notes and joined them at the sidebar. "Sorry I'm late, Your Honor. I'm a bit depressed this morning. I read about the Houston Astros' cheating thing."

Judge Thomas said, "Anyone who is a baseball fan is disappointed. I think the Red Sox started this a couple of years ago."

Luxton added, "I agree. The damn Red Sox will do anything to beat the Yankees."

Katie smiled. "There once was a pitcher so bad the crowd started singing, 'Take Him out of the Ball Game'! I think they should take Houston out of the ball game for a whole season. They've got to do something more to them than what they've done. A fine of five million dollars to the owner is a slap on the wrist."

Luxton laughed and nodded. "We do agree on something."

Judge Thomas looked at the two of them. "We're all on the same page when it comes to baseball. So, let's get back to why we are here. As I said yesterday, my concern is about the marginal relevance this big issue, this endocrine disruption business, has to the lawsuit. Ms. Hornsby, do you have any additional arguments to make before I rule?"

This was not good. The fact that the judge asked only her, not Luxton, to argue was an ominous sign that he was going to rule against her.

"Yes, Your Honor. The New York Court of Appeals in People v. Davis, 43 NY 2d 17, at 27 states that relevant evidence means 'evidence having any tendency to make the existence of any fact that is of consequence to the determination of the action more probable or less probable than it would be without the evidence.'

"The relevance in this case is the necessity for the jury to have not only all of the facts but the context in which they occurred so that they can understand why a prominent doctor like the defendant would do the things he did to my client, i.e., the facts of the consequences that he would likely experience if his alleged fraud was exposed by my client. The risk to Dr. Pittsburgh if he was exposed to charges of scientific fraud were so much greater than other scientists given the level of fame and recognition he enjoys. His threats to my client that if she exposed the truth, he would blame her makes the issue of endocrine disruption directly relevant to Dr. Pittsburgh's and my client's conduct. There is no danger that the evidence, if admitted, would prolong the trial to an unreasonable extent or confuse or mislead the jury. Indeed, I submit that the evidence is absolutely necessary to allow the jury to understand why a man of such importance would do such a thing to my client. That completes my argument, Your Honor."

Judge Thomas looked at Luxton. "Do you have anything to add?"

"No, Your Honor."

"I am going to permit the evidence to be introduced. Ms. Hornsby, please keep in mind, however, that this case is about sexual abuse and not what causes AIDS. I am concerned that the jury might be confused if you make this a full-blown trial on that issue." He gestured to the bailiff. "Bring the jury in and let's get started."

Katie finally took a deep breath. She looked at her hands. They were still shaking.

Dr. Pittsburgh returned to the witness stand, and the jurors settled in their seats. Judge Thomas said to the jurors, "At the time we finished yesterday, there was an issue on the admissibility of three exhibits, thirteen, fourteen, and fifteen. I have allowed them into evidence. Ms. Hornsby, continue with your examination of Dr. Pittsburgh."

"Thank you, Your Honor." she stood and walked close to the witness stand. She held up the three exhibits. "Dr. Pittsburgh, yesterday afternoon, we discussed three exhibits about which you said you had no memory. Have you reviewed these exhibits over the evening, and have they in any way refreshed your memory about the events that are depicted in them?"

"No."

"Let me ask you some specific questions about each of these exhibits." Leslie had placed the first exhibit in the projector, and a large image flashed on the screen. "Exhibit Thirteen is a short letter dated November 28, 1985, from Dr. Oskar Klimpf to you that states, 'Pursuant to our phone call on November 26, a private investigator, Edward Herold, will meet with you in your office next week to discuss certain arrangements that have been made to accommodate an early publication date of your HIV-AIDS research report. We both agreed that it was best to delay publication of the Detroit research by any necessary means.' I am slightly confused about the answer you gave because I asked two questions and you gave me one answer. First, did you review that exhibit last evening?"

"Yes. I looked it over."

"Did your 'looking it over' refresh your memory in any way about the events described in these three exhibits?"

"No, it did not."

Katie nodded at Leslie, and Leslie put the next exhibit on the screen. "Exhibit Fourteen is a letter from you to Dr. Oskar Klimpf dated December 5, 1985, and marked 'Privileged and Confidential.' That letter describes a meeting between you and Ed Herold, a private investigator sent to you by Dr. Klimpf, in which the two of you discussed a plan to expedite the publication of your HIV-AIDS research while seeking a delay of the Hartley-Kubilus research publication. The letter notes that both research projects had been submitted to the *American Scientific Journal* but the Detroit project had been submitted several months earlier than your research. Have I adequately described the substance of the first paragraph of this December 5, 1985, letter?"

"I think so, but I remember nothing about this."

"Forget the letter for a moment. Did you arrange to have your HIV-AIDS research published before the Detroit research?"

"I recall discussions with an editor at the *American Scientific Journal* about the need to publish my research as quickly as possible because it was so important to inform the medical profession about my findings right away."

"It was important for the medical profession to know about the potential causes of AIDS once that information had been discovered through scientific research?"

"Yes, and I was the first to do so."

"Being first has brought you worldwide accolades, right?"

"Yes, it has."

"Including a Nobel Prize?"

"Yes."

"Even though another scientific study was submitted before yours, one that clearly identified a cause of AIDS as something other than HIV, right?"

"I don't remember."

She nodded at Leslie again, and Leslie placed the next exhibit on the screen. "Exhibit Fifteen describes a conversation you had with Dr. Petersmark, the editor of the *American Scientific Journal*, on December 10, 1985, right?"

"That appears to be the case. But I have no memory of this."

"Exhibit Fifteen describes a phone conversation you had with Dr. Petersmark requesting an early publication date for your research. Does that refresh your memory?"

"No, it doesn't."

"Reference in Exhibit Fifteen is made to the 'Detroit study.' Isn't it true that the Detroit study also dealt with the same exact issue as yours, i.e., the cause of AIDS?"

"I don't recall."

"Let me see if I can trigger your recollection about the Detroit study. Would you concur with the idea that the Detroit research revealed that men with AIDS had mothers who took the drug DES during their pregnancies with these male babies and the Detroit paper cited DES as a statistically significant cause of AIDS?"

"I do remember that now. You are correct."

"Let me ask a hypothetical question. Do you suppose, if the Detroit study had been published first, before your study, that the international publicity you received in being the first to identify a cause of AIDS would have instead gone to the Detroit study?"

Luxton stood. "I object, Your Honor. The question calls for speculation about facts that never occurred."

Judge Thomas said, "Objection sustained."

"Dr. Pittsburgh, do you admit that you were prepared to claim that Ms. Anderson had committed scientific fraud if your published study was invalidated by the lack of validation in her follow-up studies coming right out of your laboratory?"

Luxton stood again. "I object, Your Honor. The question calls for speculation about facts that never occurred."

Judge Thomas said, "Objection sustained."

Katie was not surprised by the judge's rulings. At least the jury had heard the questions, and they would certainly think about them. She asked, "Orex Labs was the maker and seller of DES, right?"

"I think that is correct."

"Did Orex provide any funding to you or your research laboratory regarding your research on HIV and AIDS?"

"Not that I recall."

"Has Orex provided any funding to you or your research laboratory since the publication of your research on HIV and AIDS?"

"Not that I recall."

She walked back to her table and rooted through a large box of potential exhibits they'd brought with them today. She found what she was looking for and took the substantial package of research reprints up to the witness stand. "For the record, I have handed Group Exhibit Sixteen to Dr. Pittsburgh. Doctor, would you please look through the seventeen research reprints that make up the group exhibit to verify that they are reprints of research in which you are designated as the principal author?"

Dr. Pittsburgh scanned through the reprints. He said, "Yes. These are all reprints of research that has been done in my laboratory in which I am listed as the lead author."

Katie went to the easel, which held a large pad of paper. She turned the first page over and read from what she'd written on the next page. "Funding for this study was provided by Orex Laboratories, Inc." She turned and looked at Dr. Pittsburgh. "Dr. Pittsburgh, will you please look at the last page of each of the seventeen reprints and tell the jury whether or not the exact sentence written on the easel appears on each of the seventeen published research papers."

Dr. Pittsburgh took less than a minute to look through the documents again. "Yes, that language appears on the last page of each of these research reprints."

"Dr. Pittsburgh, these reprints have been placed in chronological order, earliest to latest. Will you please tell the jury the date of publication of the first reprint in the packet?"

"November 1987."

"Will you please tell the jury the date of publication of the last reprint in the packet?"

"January 1994."

"To the best of your knowledge, has Orex continued to fund any of your research since January 1994?"

"I can't say. I don't know."

"Let me switch to another topic. You have people with PhDs working on research in your laboratory at Filmore, right?"

"Yes."

"What is the average salary of a PhD working in your lab?"

"It depends on the number of years of work. The first year, starting salary is currently 125 thousand dollars. I have others who have been with me for ten or more years, and they are in the 250-thousand-dollar range."

She looked up at Judge Thomas. "Your Honor, that completes my cross-examination."

Luxton stood. "Your Honor, I have no additional questions for Dr. Pittsburgh. May he be excused?"

Katie was surprised. She had to think fast. "Your Honor, I have no objection to Dr. Pittsburgh being excused from the courtroom at this time, but I request that he be subject to recall as per my prior agreement with Mr. Luxton and the court's ruling on this issue."

Judge Thomas looked down at Dr. Pittsburgh. "Doctor, you are excused, subject to recall."

Luxton said, "Your Honor, the defense rests."

Katie was surprised that Luxton didn't have more evidence to offer. She'd expected a parade of scientists coming in to testify in support of Dr. Pittsburgh. Judge Thomas looked at her. "Do you have any rebuttal witnesses?"

"Yes, Your Honor. If this is a good time for a break, I can make a couple of phone calls. I didn't expect Mr. Luxton to rest his case this soon."

Judge Thomas said to the jury. "Ladies and gentlemen, we are going to take a lunch break now. It's only 11:30, but I'd like you to be back at two o'clock. That gives counsel some extra time to line up potential witnesses. So, please have a leisurely lunch."

CHAPTER 51

When court resumed, Katie put Sylvia back on the stand and handed her Exhibits Thirteen, Fourteen, and Fifteen.

"Sylvia, have you seen these documents before today? And if so, where have you seen them?"

"The first time I saw these exhibits, they were on Dr. Pittsburgh's desk."

"How was it that you saw these documents on his desk?"

"Dr. Pittsburgh was out of town. He called me at the laboratory and asked me to find an article that he said was probably on his desk. These letters, the three of them, were the only documents on his desk. I called him back from his desk phone, described the three letters to him, and asked if any of these were what he needed. He had me read the last of the three letters to him over the phone."

"Do you have a present memory of this phone conversation and these three letters?"

"Yes, I do. I remember it vividly because it was the first time I knew that Dr. Pittsburgh had already submitted the HIV-AIDS research for publication before I'd completed the validation study."

"Thank you, Sylvia. That's all I have, Your Honor."

Judge Thomas asked, "Mr. Luxton, any questions?"

Luxton stood. "Yes, Judge. Ms. Anderson, did you make copies of these letters?"

"Yes."

"Did Dr. Pittsburgh authorize you to make copies of these letters?"

"I don't remember. He might have, but I don't recall."

Luxton raised an eyebrow at the jury. "Your Honor, I'm through."

Judge Thomas looked over at Katie. "Do you have another witness ready to go?"

"Yes, Your Honor. I'll be right back." She walked out of the courtroom and nodded to a lady seated on a bench. "Ready?"

They walked back into the courtroom together, and Katie said, "Your Honor, the plaintiff calls Mrs. Ethel Greenspan."

Mrs. Greenspan walked to the witness stand and was sworn in by the clerk. She sat down.

"Will you tell the court and jury your name?"

"My name is Ethel Greenspan. Mrs. Ethel Greenspan."

"I understand that you are retired now, but in the past, were you an employee at Filmore University?"

"Yes. I was Dr. Pittsburgh's secretary from 1982 until 2006."

Katie held up the three exhibits. "Prior to coming here today, did you have the opportunity to review Exhibits Thirteen, Fourteen, and Fifteen?"

"Yes."

"Have you seen these exhibits previously?"

"Yes. I was in charge of all of Dr. Pittsburgh's mail, both incoming and outgoing. I remember these three letters very well because the research study they talk about was such a big deal at the time."

"Sylvia Anderson testified that she saw these letters on Dr. Pittsburgh's desk and made copies of them. Is there anything wrong with that?"

"No, not at all. Sylvia was an important part of the project, and she was entitled to any information about it that was available."

"Thank you for coming down here today, Mrs. Greenspan. That's all the questions I have."

Judge Thomas said, "Mr. Luxton?"

"Judge, I have no questions."

The judged turned to Katie. "Anything else, Ms. Hornsby?"

"Yes, Your Honor. The plaintiff recalls Dr. Fordland."

Dr. Fordland returned to the stand. Judge Thomas reminded him that he was still under oath.

"At my request, have you examined Exhibits Thirteen through Fifteen?"

"Yes, I have."

"Did those documents form part of the basis for the expert testimony you have given in this courtroom?"

"Yes, they did. However, I must say that the opinions I rendered were also arrived at by my personal interaction with the people at Orex Labs, the medical director of the *American Scientific Journal,* and Dr. Alex Hartley all back in that time frame. The exhibits you mentioned simply corroborate the basis for my testimony."

"Thank you, Dr. Fordland. That's all the questions I have."

Luxton stood. "I have no questions, Your Honor."

"I have more rebuttal witnesses, Your Honor."

Katie walked into the hallway and brought an attractive woman into the courtroom. The clerk administered the oath, and she seated herself on the witness stand.

"Will you please state your name?" asked Katie.

"Holly Ridgefield."

"Is it Dr. Ridgefield or Ms. Ridgefield?"

"Ms. Ridgefield."

"Have you, at any time, been a doctoral student in Dr. Arnold Pittsburgh's biochemistry department?"

"Yes."

"Let me show you what has been marked as plaintiff's Exhibit 12. Please review it for a moment for the purpose of answering the question of whether or not you are the person who prepared that document."

Ms. Ridgefield looked briefly at the document. "Yes. This is a complaint I prepared against Dr. Pittsburgh for sexually assaulting me while I was a doctoral student in his program."

Katie nodded at Leslie, who displayed the report on the large screen.

"What happened after you were sexually assaulted by Dr. Pittsburgh?"

Luxton was on his feet. "Objection. Prejudicial, immaterial, and irrelevant."

Judge Thomas looked at Katie. "Your response?"

"This exhibit and testimony are now being offered to show a pattern of behavior on the part of Dr. Pittsburgh with regard to his sexual abuse of young women working in his laboratory. As we have heard from the witness stand, Dr. Pittsburgh likes to say that all the women he's had sex with did it voluntarily.

In other words, his pattern of sexual abuse includes the habit of lying about it as well."

Judge Thomas thought for a long moment. "The objection is overruled. You might ask the question again, Ms. Hornsby."

"What happened after you were sexually assaulted by Dr. Pittsburgh?"

"I went into a deep depression and had to withdraw from the doctoral program."

"Did you ever have sex with Dr. Pittsburgh voluntarily?"

"No. Never."

"How many times did Dr. Pittsburgh sexually assault you?"

"It was over a one-year period of time. It seemed like every day, but it was probably only fifty times or so."

"Thank you for coming here today. I know it wasn't pleasant for you. Your Honor, at this time, I offer Exhibit Twelve into evidence."

"Exhibit Twelve is admitted. Any cross-examination, Mr. Luxton?"

"No, Your Honor."

Judge Thomas turned and looked kindly at the witness. "Ma'am, you may step down. You are free to go." He looked up. "Anything else, counsel?"

Luxton said, "No."

Katie took a deep breath. This was the biggest moment of the trial. "Yes, Your Honor. Plaintiff has one last rebuttal witness. I'll get her from the hallway."

Katie walked out of the courtroom and gestured to the woman waiting on the bench. They walked back into the courtroom together.

Katie announced the witness while she looked directly at Dr. Pittsburgh. "Plaintiff calls Jayme Pittsburgh."

Dr. Pittsburgh jolted like he'd been stabbed in the heart. He leaned over quickly towards Luxton and said in a voice loud enough to be heard throughout the courtroom, "You've got to stop this."

Luxton was on his feet. "May I have a few minutes to confer with my client, Your Honor?"

The judge said, "Certainly. We'll take a short break."

Fifteen minutes later, when court resumed, Dr. Pittsburgh was gone. Luxton stood. "Judge, can we approach the bench?"

The judge waved the two attorneys up.

Luxton whispered, "Your Honor, can we do this off the record?"

Judge Thomas looked at Katie. "Is that okay with you?"

Katie nodded. "As long as I can reserve my right to insist that everything that is going to be said will eventually be put on the record."

The judge nodded at Luxton. "With that understanding, go ahead. Let's hear what you have to say."

Your Honor, the witness that Ms. Hornsby just called is Dr. Pittsburgh's daughter, his estranged daughter. He hasn't seen her in more than twenty years. We don't think she should be permitted to testify. Who knows what goes on in family disputes? Who knows what she might say about her father? Ms. Hornsby has ambushed us, as we had no idea that the daughter would be called as a witness."

Judge Thomas looked at Katie. "Is that true? Was this witness on your witness list?"

Katie replied, "No, she wasn't listed, Your Honor. I didn't know she existed until she called me several days before trial started. But since then, I have had her allegations investigated thoroughly, and there is no question that what she will testify to is the truth. No question at all."

The judge looked at Katie. "What kind of allegations?"

Here goes, Katie thought. "Judge, Dr. Pittsburgh sexually abused his daughter for years. In fact, she was removed from the family home twice before she reached her teens as a result of his well-documented sexual assaults."

Luxton sneered. "And just how well documented are these scurrilous claims?"

Both Luxton and the judge looked at Katie.

Given the seriousness of the moment, Katie's emotions swayed between sadness, anger, and a hard-fought sense of vindication for Sylvia. She wanted to smile and cry at the same time. "Are photos good? I have twenty or so photos. If that's not enough, how about two probate court adjudications ordering Dr. Pittsburgh to stay away from his daughter, to keep his damn hands off her?"

Judge Thomas glared at Luxton. "I know now why you wanted to keep this off the record. Let's go into my chambers. Just the three of us." He stood and gestured for the two lawyers to follow him.

Once the three were seated, Judge Thomas said to Katie, "Let me see the photos and probate court documents."

Katie slid the large envelope across the table toward him. The judge gasped when he saw the photos. He was visibly upset. He took out his handkerchief and dabbed at his eyes. After he set the photos aside, he reviewed the two court adjudications. He looked over at Luxton. "Because we're off the record, I'll tell you that I could strangle your goddamn client to death with my bare hands. Did you know about this?" He gestured at the materials in front of him.

Luxton shook his head. "No, I didn't, Your Honor. I knew there were family problems, but I didn't know the details."

Judge Thomas took a deep breath. "You have problems now, Lamar. I think you ought to call your clients, both Pittsburgh and the university. Get approval to settle. If I let the jury see this stuff, they'll throw the book at the bastard and more than likely go a lot higher than twenty million dollars. How did he ever avoid going to prison?"

Katie said, "Judge, with all respect, my client is not interested in a settlement. Mr. Luxton told me at the beginning of trial that there would be no deals, and I'll stand by what he said. No deal."

The judge thought for a long moment. "Katie, I don't like the thought of putting his daughter through any more of what she's already experienced, particularly if all your client wants is revenge. That's not what the three of us sitting here stand for. Go back out and talk with your client and be sure to come back with a number that will end this case. Lamar and I will wait right here."

Katie walked out of the judge's chambers and returned to the courtroom. She sat down next to Sylvia, with Leslie on Sylvia's other side. She said in hushed tones, "This is what happened. The judge doesn't want to subject Pittsburgh's daughter to any more trauma than she's already had in her life. He wants me to get a number from you that will settle the case."

Sylvia whispered back, "You already know that I'm not here for money. I want that son of a bitch to suffer as much as he's made me and others suffer. I feel sorry for his daughter, but don't forget that she contacted you, wanting to help give this monster his due. She deserves that, as do all of the other women he's abused over the years."

Leslie leaned over. "Can I add my two cents worth? The judge is a kind-hearted old man. He doesn't want to see anyone hurt. But I think he's saying that more because of his level of comfort than the daughter's. Sylvia is right. The daughter came to us. She wants to tell her story, same as Sylvia. This is about woman power. We shouldn't not do what we came here for just because it'll make the judge uncomfortable or because he thinks it's going to be hard on the daughter. That's male chauvinism at its worst. Let her decide, not him. Look what Dr. Pittsburgh has already gotten away with. He probably avoided jail time because of who he was, how much money he had, or how many friends he had in high places. We all know that there's lots of men in prison, probably for life, for doing a hell of a lot less just because they weren't big shots."

Katie thought for a hard moment. Sylvia and Leslie were both right. This wasn't about making the judge comfortable – or letting him decide for the young woman what was best for her when he didn't even know how she felt or what she wanted, and it was the same for Sylvia. She was Katie's client, not Judge Thomas.

She stood. "Thanks, guys. I'll be back in a few minutes."

She walked back into the judge's chambers and sat in the remaining vacant chair.

"There is no number, Judge. My client wants to go to the jury on this."

The judge studied Katie's face. "Should I bring her in here and talk with her?"

"It wouldn't work, Judge."

"Well" – Judge Thomas stood – "We'll take a short break and then get started."

CHAPTER 52

Twenty minutes later, Katie stood and approached the witness.

"Please state your name and tell the jury what it is that you do for a living."

My name is Jayme Pittsburgh. I am a trained social worker, and I work in the family division of the probate court in Philadelphia."

"How old are you, Ms. Pittsburgh?"

"I will be fifty-four next Saturday."

"One of the defendants in this lawsuit is Dr. Arnold Pittsburgh. Are you related to him?"

"Yes. He is my biological father, but his parental rights were terminated when I was fifteen years old."

Will you tell the court and jury why his parental rights were terminated?

Do you want the short version or the long?"

"Let's start with the short version. If I need further information, I'll ask you additional questions, okay?"

"Okay. The short version is that his rights were terminated by a court because he sexually abused me, starting when I was eight years old and continuing until I was fifteen. He did the same thing to my sister, who was two years older."

"What does your sister do for a living?"

"She doesn't. She committed suicide when she was sixteen."

The courtroom became eerily silent. Katie looked over at the jury. Two of the women jurors were crying. Katie could feel the tears starting in her eyes. She took a deep breath.

"Your father has testified during this trial that he had several sexual relationships with his students that were entered into purely voluntarily by the women. Have you heard him make those kinds of claims before?"

"Yes. Several times in situations in court involving either my sister or me, he said that we were both eager to have sex with him, that we forced ourselves on him."

319

"Is that true?"

"No, absolutely not."

"Is it just your word against his, or can you prove what you say?"

"I gave you photos when we first met. Some of them show me tied up and gagged while he forced himself on me. Others show me with bruises and lacerations on my body because I fought him and begged him to stop."

"Katie walked up and handed Jayme two photographs. "Are these two photographs examples of what you just described?"

"Yes."

"Your Honor, I move the admission of Exhibits Sixteen and Seventeen."

Luxton stood. "No objection, Your Honor."

The judge said, "Admitted."

"Jayme, is your father in the courtroom?"

"No. He ran out of here as fast as he could when he saw me walk in."

"Thank you, Jayme. I have no more questions."

Judge Thomas said, "Any questions, Mr. Luxton?"

"No, Your Honor."

The judge looked at Jayme. "You may step down. Any more witnesses, Ms. Hornsby?"

"No, Your Honor."

"Mr. Luxton?"

'No, Your Honor."

"We'll go over jury instruction at eight o'clock tomorrow morning in my chambers, and I'll have the jury come in at ten o'clock for closing arguments. Mr. Luxton, I am denying your motion to strike the testimony of the two doctors on the basis that their testimony has relevance to the issues in this trial."

CHAPTER 53

Katie stayed up all night for two reasons: first, the sadness in her heart from the testimony of Pittsburgh's daughter wouldn't go away, and second, she really needed to refine her closing argument because what had previously seemed straightforward had become complicated because of the mixture of Me Too and endocrine disruption. If the jury was confused, she might even lose the case despite Jayme's appearance.

When Katie and Leslie arrived at the courtroom, they were surprised that it was packed with spectators. They were also surprised because Dr. Pittsburgh had returned. He looked beaten down, sad, defeated.

"Would you look at this, the asshole came back," Leslie whispered to Katie. "You just might become a national celebrity after today, girl. Now, put your big girl panties on and go up there and convince the jury to send a message to that monster so nothing like this happens again."

After the jurors were seated, Judge Thomas nodded at Katie. "Ready to give your closing?"

Katie stood. "Yes, Your Honor." She walked to the podium, turned, and faced the jury.

"Members of the jury. I am proud to stand up here on behalf of Sylvia Anderson and proud that she has selected me to present her story to you. We are approaching the finishing line, and Sylvia and I thank you for the attention you have given in carrying out your duty as jurors. Other than voting, sitting as a juror is the one function in our society that makes our country unique and the envy of other countries throughout the world. We are a nation of laws, and it is the system of trial by jury that gives meaning to these laws by allowing people like each of you to determine, on a case-by-case basis, what the facts are. Before you begin your deliberations, Judge Thomas will tell you what the law is, and you will then deliberate and determine what the facts are in the context of that law. In the truest sense of the words, you are judges of the facts, while Judge Thomas is the judge of the laws.

"I had a professor in law school who gave me the best definition of a trial from the viewpoint of the trial lawyer. He said three things were important for a lawyer. First, tell the jury what you're going to prove. Second, prove it, and third, tell them what you proved. We've gone through the first two parts together, and we are now at the third part, where I will tell you what I've proved. Let me begin.

"Everyone here today – the judge, the defense lawyers, the plaintiff, the defendant, me, and you as members of the jury – have witnessed an extraordinary historic moment play out in this courtroom. We have all been witness to the merger of two events, one involving mankind and the other involving womankind."

Katie stepped to the easel and printed both words in large block letters.

MANKIND   WOMANKIND

"In 1983, Sylvia Anderson, fresh out of being an all-A student, a star athlete, and number one in her graduating class at Rutgers, began doctoral studies in biochemistry under Dr. Arnold Pittsburgh at Filmore University, right here in New York. When faced with a challenge of his claim of victory for all mankind, Dr. Pittsburgh did to Sylvia what some men in power have always done: hurt the women closest to them who are the most responsible for their success in the first place."

She walked to the easel and struck a line through the word "womankind."

Several of the women jurors nodded.

"In this trial, the lid was blown off the machinations of Dr. Pittsburgh, and the tragic results to Sylvia have been put on full display for your assessment as you begin your deliberations. I will now ask for your patience in allowing me to take the time to review the evidence you've seen and heard in this courtroom that supports Sylvia's claim against Dr. Pittsburgh and Filmore University."

Katie took several steps closer to the jury and looked them in their eyes before she continued.

"When Sylvia first came to my office, seeking my help, the first words out of her mouth were, 'This is about sex and it's not about sex.' At first, I thought she might be playing a word game with me, but as I listened to her story, I began to appreciate her puzzling statement. I understood what she meant. In the proofs I've presented to you, I've intended to cover both aspects of this conundrum, this challenging riddle Sylvia presented to me when she first came into my office.

"I will tell you first why this is not about sex.

"This story began in 1985, in two places: New York, at Filmore University, and Detroit, at Detroit City Hospital. In that year, Sylvia was a third-year doctoral student, with the defendant Dr. Pittsburgh acting as her mentor and supervisor of her training. Under Dr. Pittsburgh's direction, Sylvia was conducting research in response to reports of an alarming number of deaths in gay men in the San Francisco Bay area that was reaching epidemic proportions. No one knew why this was happening, and researchers worldwide were working feverishly to find answers for the deaths. A race was on to determine who would be the first to come up with the answer. The history of epidemics has created heroes of epic proportions, men like Pasteur, Jenner, and Jonas Salk, for their contributions to understanding the processes of diseases that ravaged the population. The temptation to follow in the footsteps of these famous scientists was huge. Dr. Pittsburgh was on a mission to be the first to identify and cure this epidemic.

"In New York, Sylvia, under the guidance of Dr. Pittsburgh, performed a series of experiments on blood samples of several of these men, and one of these experiments provided some hope. That study indicated that a previously unknown virus might be the culprit. Sylvia reported the finding to Dr. Pittsburgh and then began the process of attempting to verify the first result by performing the same study again, but this time, she received different results. It is standard scientific practice that any scientific result must be verified by repeating it to confirm that the original result was true. Until that verification is done, the original study must be considered unverified.

Bleakley-Lange

"At the same time, in Detroit, Dr. Alex Hartley, a third-year medical resident, and Dr. Ingrid Kubilus, an epidemiologist, pursued an epidemiological study on patients in the Detroit hospital who were dying of the same deadly disease seen in the San Francisco men. Their results found that DES given to mothers during their pregnancies with these men was highly statistically significant, such that the drug could be said to be the cause of their deaths. These two Detroit doctors used the same methodology used in a classic 1971 study that revealed that the daughters of women who had taken DES during pregnancy were developing a rare form of vaginal cancer.

"The Detroit doctors submitted their research findings to the *American Scientific Journal*, the most prestigious medical journal in the world, in November 1985. Once the *American Scientific Journal* received that paper, all hell broke loose. The *American Scientific Journal* notified Orex, the maker of DES, and Orex began a strong effort to convince the Detroit doctors not to publish the research. They did this by using two Detroit doctors who had a longstanding relationship with Orex and who practiced at the same hospital as the researchers. When Orex was notified by the medical journal that the Detroit research was going to be published anyway, Dr. Pittsburgh, acting in concert with Orex, hastily submitted his unverified research in December 1985. This was done for two reasons. Number one was to keep the negative information about DES from becoming public. Number two was to give Dr. Pittsburgh the opportunity to claim that he was the first scientist in the world to identify the virus called HIV as the cause of the diseases that were killing the gay men in San Francisco. That effort included getting the *American Scientific Journal*'s agreement to delay publication of the Detroit research until March 1986 and immediately publish Dr. Pittsburgh's unverified research in December 1985.

"However, even before the Pittsburgh research was published, Dr. Pittsburgh, in his zeal to be the first, held a press conference announcing his results. He claimed that the new virus, HIV, was the cause of the deaths of the young men. He called this disease that killed the men AIDS. As a result, he became the immediate darling of the scientific world, while Orex continued its efforts to undermine the potential damage that the Detroit DES research would cause to their bottom line, i.e., corporate profits, when the damaging research implicating their drug as the cause of AIDS was published in March 1986.

"Orex had been sued by hundreds of young women as a result of the 1971 study I mentioned earlier. The drug company sought to prevent the families of young men dying of AIDS from suing them for the same reason as these young women. Orex had also enlisted the services of Dr. Ratner, a prominent researcher in Detroit, who wrote a scathing letter accusing Drs. Hartley and Kubilus of scientific fraud within days after the research was published in March 1986. The research was immediately removed from the scientific literature, and Dr. Hartley's medical license was suspended. The worst part of this terrible story is that Dr. Kubilus was murdered in a manner that made it appear to be death by suicide for the purpose of claiming that she killed herself over her guilt for committing fraud. Subsequent toxicology results revealed, however, that she had been murdered by injecting her with a fatal dose of the drug digitalis. This whole scenario is relevant and important in your deliberations because Sylvia had, in fact, discovered through her research that Dr. Pittsburgh's claim could not be verified. She repeated the original study and found different results. The importance of this detail is underscored by the fact that Dr. Pittsburgh received a Nobel Prize for his so-called research. This is the 'not about sex' part of this trial.

"Now I will tell you about the 'sex part' of Sylvia's complaint, which happened because of the 'not about sex' part.

"Shortly after Dr. Pittsburgh made his public announcement at the press conference, Sylvia

reported back to him that her attempts to validate the findings of the research had been unsuccessful. In other words, Dr. Pittsburgh's mission to achieve fame was in jeopardy if his own research laboratory couldn't confirm his reported findings. It is a basic principle of scientific research that original findings must be validated before they can be accepted as true by scientists.

"Dr. Pittsburgh thus began his campaign against Sylvia in a number of ways to keep her quiet about the negative studies. If she tried to disclose the subsequent negative study, he threatened to destroy her reputation by claiming that she was the one who had cheated on the original study. He also launched a terrible pattern of control over her, forcing her to submit to his sexual whims and desires to demean and destroy her sense of value and integrity. This use of his power to manipulate and abuse her further minimized the likelihood of her disclosure of the negative studies that failed to validate the original research. This pattern of intense sexual abuse continued for over two years. Sylvia, in a word, became a nervous wreck of a person.

"And sadly, as you have heard, Sylvia was not the only victim of Pittsburgh's pattern of sexual abuse of young girls and women.

"You have heard the expert testimony of Dr. Judd Ashton, who described the impact of this sexual abuse on Sylvia and how it has permanently destroyed her life ambitions and economic livelihood.

"It was Dr. Judd's opinion that Sylvia had a disability from the moral injury that prevented her from thinking about a lawsuit from the very first moment that Dr. Pittsburgh began his sexual abuse of her due to the PTSD described by Dr. Ashton similar to the emotional trauma suffered by soldiers on the battlefield. Dr. Judd also spoke of the Stockholm syndrome experienced by those who are held captive in one way or another, in which the victim begins to identify with the perpetrator, and he described how this was a mechanism at work with regard to Sylvia."

Katie paused and looked at the jury. "As you may recall, Dr. Judd is a board-certified psychiatrist who is the head of a rape crisis center and has treated rape victims ever since he started practicing psychiatry. He has written four books, two of which deal with issues with particular regard to the consequences for women who have been raped.

"Now, it is my responsibility to offer you a way to assess this terrible damage suffered by Sylvia. Unfortunately, you, as the jury, do not have a magic power to restore Sylvia to her status prior to the time Dr. Pittsburgh began sexually abusing her or to remove her PTSD. But the law and this lawsuit permit a way to assess and compensate that loss in terms of dollars. At the close of these arguments, Judge Thomas will read you the instructions you are to follow as you deliberate. One of those instructions addresses the issue of how long Sylvia will likely live based on statutory mortality tables. That date for a person of Sylvia's current age is eighty-one years of age. Sylvia is currently fifty-six years old and thus has a life expectancy of twenty-five more years. What this means is that Sylvia has suffered and will continue to suffer from the harm caused by Dr. Pittsburgh for a total of fifty-eight years. She was twenty-three years old when the rapes started in 1985. Dr. Pittsburgh is the only person Sylvia has ever experienced sex with, as she was a virgin at the time of the first sexual assault. One way of approaching this particular area of the damages suffered by Sylvia is to ask how much it would be worth to go through one year of adult life without experiencing a fulfilling personal and sexual relationship with someone. I respectfully suggest that one year of that terrible loss would be worth one hundred thousand dollars. Multiplying that figure by fifty-eight years is 5.8 million dollars.

"Now let's look at the economic damage caused by Dr. Pittsburgh. Sylvia's current salary as a non-doctoral research biochemist is eighty-five thousand dollars. You've heard testimony that the average salary of a PhD in Sylvia's field of biochemistry is 235 thousand dollars, i.e., 150 thousand dollars more a year than Sylvia's salary. Taking this figure from the present time to the age of sixty-five would mean nine years of future lost income, i.e., 1.35 million dollars. There is no precise way to evaluate the past economic loss experienced by Sylvia from this differential other than to say it was substantial and has gone on for thirty-one years. I say thirty-one years rather than thirty-three years because it would have been likely that Sylvia would have received her PhD two years after this sexual predation by Dr. Pittsburgh started. The law leaves it up to your sound judgment when considering all of the factors as reasonable measures of making Sylvia whole. Because the law does not permit it, there is one thing I ask you not to do, and that is to not punish Dr. Pittsburgh for the rapes he committed on Sylvia. Whatever verdict you render must be limited to solely compensating Sylvia for the harm caused by those sexual assaults.

"The court will also instruct you that because Dr. Pittsburgh was an employee of Filmore University, the university is responsible for all the damage caused by Dr. Pittsburgh due to a longstanding law called respondeat superior. Literally, the master is responsible for the acts of the servant.

"Finally, on Sylvia's behalf, I thank you for your time and attention to this gravely serious matter and wish you Godspeed in your deliberations. Mr. Luxton has the opportunity to speak with you now, and I will have some additional time after that to clear up any issues that may arise."

CHAPTER 54

Lamar Luxton stood, buttoned his suit jacket, and walked close to the jury box. He stood silently for a long moment and looked at each of the jurors.

"Ladies and gentlemen, this is my last opportunity to speak with you about this case. Yesterday, just yesterday, I was walking down the street in front of my office building, and I saw a young woman wearing a T-shirt sporting a cheeky 'Ban Men' slogan. Seeing that made me think about this trial and the dynamics of this era in the United States, when it has become fashionable to label men, all men, as sexual predators of helpless women.

"This trial is the story about a poor, helpless woman who has 'suffered' at the hands of an attractive, prosperous man. By her own admission, she engaged in acts of sex more than 442 times with that man, with nary a complaint while it was happening. It is only thirty-three years later that she finally comes forth, when it becomes part of the thing to do. That 'thing' is to blame the man for everything that has happened in the woman's life – everything. Such thinking turns a woman from being an active participant in sex acts between two consenting adults into a victim. Instead of recognizing that sexual activity between a man and a woman is a normal biological phenomenon, the act, in retrospect, becomes a vehicle for blaming one of the two persons involved, the man, because things didn't quite turn out the way that the other person, the woman, thought they would. The way it turned out in this case is that the man, Dr. Pittsburgh, stopped sexual activity with the plaintiff to begin a relationship with another woman. This lawsuit by the plaintiff is the equivalent of a stuck-out tongue pointed by a pouting girl at a playground playmate who walks away and starts to play with another.

"Let's look at the details of the plaintiff's claim in that context. First of all, the plaintiff is a beautiful woman, and it is highly likely that many more men than Dr. Pittsburgh were attracted to her by her looks. In other words, the plaintiff literally had the power of the 'pick of the litter' when it came to selecting a man she would become intimate with. She had that choice.

"Next, the status of the plaintiff as a world-famous scientist has been minimized in this trial. It must be remembered that she was designated as the co-author of the research paper that Dr. Pittsburgh presented to the scientific community. Dr. Pittsburgh did this to acknowledge and recognize the contribution the plaintiff made to the amazing discovery that the virus known as HIV causes AIDS. Does this sound like an act of a man exploiting this poor, helpless victim simply because she is a woman? By her own testimony, she acknowledged the opportunities she was given to speak at national and international scientific meetings.

"Next, you must ask yourselves why the plaintiff began collecting the pubic hairs and continued to do so over, she says, a two-year period of time. I submit that it is likely that she did so because she was smitten by positive feelings for Dr. Pittsburgh and did what so many others do when enthralled in a profound emotional relationship, that is, collecting scraps and bits of cherished mementos as a reminder of how special the relationship was. Instead, the plaintiff would rather have you believe that she kept these mementos as a means of guaranteeing proof that Dr. Pittsburgh was abusing her. There is another aspect of this that you should consider in your deliberations. The plaintiff said that Dr. Pittsburgh used her sexually as a backup when his new flame was unavailable after the initial two-year relationship was changed. Why does she not have pubic hairs for these subsequent occasions? I submit that it is reasonable for you to conclude that she, in fact, did keep those earlier specimens as mementos. Once the relationship, such as it was, was over, she stopped doing so because the treasured pubic hairs lost their romantic significance to her as a symbol of the ongoing relationship.

"Next, this sexual relationship between the plaintiff and Dr. Pittsburgh began in 1985, which, I know, sounds like a long time ago to most of you on the jury. I can tell you that it seems like yesterday to me, but the point I want to make is that 1985 wasn't in the Middle Ages, and women weren't second-class citizens. A woman, Geraldine Ferraro, ran for the office of vice president of the United States in 1984. Women had the right to vote for more than sixty years at that time. Roughly half of the college graduates in the country were women. The point I want to make is that women, including the plaintiff, were free to make choices as to how they lived their lives, and that included the choice of sexual partners.

"Next, I want to make clear that I am not suggesting in any way that there are no instances when a man abuses a woman for sexual purposes. The crime of rape was on the books then, as it is now. It is true that men get women drunk and take sexual advantage of them, just like it is true that some women go out and drink at bars so they can find a sex partner. That happened in 1985, and it happens now. But I submit that no woman has sex with a man more than 442 times because she has no control over the situation. There is no claim by the plaintiff that Dr. Pittsburgh used drugs or alcohol to eliminate her sense of control in these 440-plus situations. As I said earlier, this lawsuit is the literal sticking out of the tongue of a pouting woman whose sexual playmate has cast her aside for somebody else.

"Next, what in the world does endocrine disruption have to do with this case? I am sure you have asked this question to yourselves, as I have, as you listened to the evidence presented in this trial. This case is strictly about alleged sexual abuse that occurred more than thirty years ago and the claim that the abuse caused the plaintiff to become 'disabled' such that she couldn't recognize that she might have a cause of action against Dr. Pittsburgh. The role of endocrine disruption is a red herring and has nothing to do with the case before you. It is Ms. Hornby's figurative way of putting lipstick on a pig, to dress the pig up to make it look important.

"That leads to another issue, the so-called disability of the plaintiff, which caused her to wait thirty-three years to file this suit. I submit that the claim of disability is absolutely wiped out by the plaintiff's own admission that she kept the pubic hairs for future use to prove that she was being abused sexually. Such an intent from day one of when she claims the sexual abuse started and carried out over a two-year period of time indicates clearly that she did have an intent to do something, to prove at some point in time that Dr. Pittsburgh abused her. To follow the plaintiff's line of reasoning automatically leads to the logical conclusion that she had every intention of filing a lawsuit back in 1985 and 1986. I would expect that you might ask why the expert presented by the plaintiff, Dr. Judd, never addressed her keeping pubic hairs from the sex between her and Dr. Pittsburgh. I submit to you that a reasonable response is because keeping all these pubic hairs indicated that she had the intent to file suit at the first minute she taped the first pubic hair. Dr. Judd simply ignored these telling facts in constructing the opinions for which he was paid fifteen thousand dollars. It defies reality to say that she was unable to file suit until other women began to complain of Me Too situations thirty-three years later. In short, there is no merit whatsoever to the claim of the plaintiff.

"This concludes my remarks on behalf of Dr. Pittsburgh, and he and I both thank you for your attention. I respectfully request that you find for Dr. Pittsburgh and Filmore University by addressing the first two questions on the jury form in their favor.

"The first question is, 'Did the plaintiff have a disability at the time that the alleged sexual acts occurred such as to prevent her from instituting a cause of action at that time?' I request that you answer this as no on Dr. Pittsburgh's behalf.

"The second question is, 'Did the defendant sexually abuse the plaintiff in the course of their master-servant relationship?' I request that you also answer this as no on Dr. Pittsburgh's behalf and on behalf of Filmore University.

"Godspeed in your deliberations."

CHAPTER 55

Judge Thomas nodded at Katie. "Counsel, any rebuttal?"
Katie stood. "Yes, Your Honor."

She walked over in front of the jury and took a moment to establish eye contact with each of them.

"This is my final opportunity to address the issues raised by Mr. Luxton. He started with the statement about the 'dynamics of this era in the United States, when it has become fashionable to label men, all men, as sexual predators of helpless women.' Sylvia and I have made no contention that 'all men' are sexual predators preying on helpless women. And it is the facts of the situation presented to you as evidence in this case, rather than some sweeping, unfounded proclamation, that you must consider when rendering your verdict.

"Counsel for the defendants speaks disparagingly of the 442 times that Sylvia was subjected to sexual abuse at the hands of Dr. Pittsburgh and suggests to you that she had control over her own life such that she cannot be considered a victim. In doing so, Mr. Luxton forgot to tell you that the only evidence – the only evidence – before you on that critical issue is the testimony of Dr. Judd, who carefully described what is well known as Stockholm syndrome, and that Sylvia met all of the criteria of that syndrome. Keep in mind that Mr. Luxton brought no expert witness in to provide evidence that Sylvia did not suffer from Stockholm syndrome, and he could have done so if he could have found a psychiatrist somewhere who was not in agreement with Dr. Judd. In other words, Mr. Luxton's opinion is not part of the evidence you must consider.

"Mr. Luxton also mocks me because of the endocrine disruption that is such a huge part of this case. In the event that I have confused you, I must clarify for you why endocrine disruption is part of this lawsuit. Two fine expert witnesses, Dr. Fordland and Dr. Hartley, have testified that Dr. Pittsburgh's premature announcement of the HIV-AIDS relationship was to offset the impact of the Detroit DES study. Dr. Pittsburgh wanted to be the first in the world to explain what was happening to gay men in our society. He achieved that goal and won the Nobel Prize for that achievement. But at what cost? His study was published before the Hartley study, which showed DES to be the cause of AIDS. Dr. Pittsburgh became famous, and the two Detroit researchers were thrown under the bus; one was murdered, and the other had his medical license taken away when they were falsely accused of fraud.

"This coupling of the two events was the very reason Dr. Pittsburgh began subjecting Sylvia to sexual abuse; his purpose was to demean her as a scientist who had knowledge that if disclosed, would discredit his findings in the eyes of the wider scientific community. He browbeat Sylvia into submission, using her status as a woman to keep her quiet. The fact that Dr. Pittsburgh ultimately received the Nobel Prize for his research shows you quite clearly how great the stakes were regarding the need to sabotage the Detroit researchers' claim that endocrine disruption was the major factor in causing AIDS and not HIV.

"Dr. Judd, a nationally recognized expert in the problems of victims of rape, identified and discussed the elements in Sylvia's situation that are common to all such victims. The major feature in these master-servant situations is that the master is a bully, and bullies have the ability to recognize women who are predisposed to being bullied. Sylvia's background of being shunted from one foster home to another created the soil for the compliance demanded by a bully, i.e., exactly the type of compliance demanded of Sylvia by Dr. Pittsburgh to keep her mouth shut so that he could be the famous scientist who discovered the cause of AIDS. So, it is clear that endocrine disruption has played a major role in the facts supportive of Sylvia's claim.

"Mr. Luxton tells us that Sylvia is also an internationally famous scientist and Dr. Pittsburgh put her in that position. The reason she declined to participate in scientific conferences was that she was so terrified by Dr. Pittsburgh that she kept her mouth shut.

"Finally, there is no gain or seeking fifteen minutes of fame in stepping forward with accusations like Sylvia has made. Survivors of sexual abuse are dragged through the mud the minute they raise their voices. They are immediately met with suspicion, and their entire identity is picked apart in a cruel display of theatrical misogyny. Survivors who step forward for the violation against them are traumatized once again by society and the system for doing so. There is an incredible amount to lose by accusing another of sexual assault – that is exactly why many women, like Sylvia, never file a police report against their attackers. Statistics show that 95% of survivors of sexual assault do not report their attack, for a variety of complex and traumatic personal reasons. And that risk is only amplified the more notable and prominent the accused is.

"So, I submit to you that Sylvia is a hero for standing up for herself, as well as for all women who have been sexually traumatized, one way or another, by men in power. I have used a word several times during this trial to depict a confusing and difficult problem or question that was created for Sylvia by the events you have heard about in this trial. It is your task now as a jury to resolve this 'conundrum' for Sylvia.

"As a jury, you have no power to go back and restore Sylvia's life as it once was or award her the PhD she deserves to have. But you do have the power to compensate her for those losses by evaluating them in an award of money damages, as the law requires.

"One final item as a sad and terrible reminder. Think about how Dr. Pittsburgh insisted that the sex between him and Sylvia was mutual and that many times, she was the instigator. Sylvia testified otherwise, as did another doctoral student of Dr. Pittsburgh's and Dr. Pittsburgh's daughter, who was accused by Dr. Pittsburgh of being the sexual aggressor at fifteen years of age, the very same way he now suggests that Sylvia was. The same way that Jayme's sister was accused by her father before she took her own life by suicide at the age of sixteen. This is way more than a 'he said-she said' situation that very shortly will require your deliberation. I submit to you that it is a 'he said-they said' given the testimony of the women

335

who have appeared in this courtroom top testify about what Dr. Pittsburgh did to them. Perhaps the most important determination you will have to make is who to believe, Sylvia or Dr. Pittsburgh? I submit to you that the testimony of Dr. Pittsburgh's daughter, who was removed from her family home by authorities twice as a result of the same conduct by Dr. Pittsburgh, clinches the deal on this question in Sylvia's favor. Her sister, who committed suicide at sixteen years of age after years of sexual abuse by her father, is also a silent witness on this question as to who should be believed. The question of who to believe is left to your sound judgment as jurors.

"Once again, I thank you on Sylvia's behalf for your time, attention, and efforts as you perform your sacred duty as jurors."

CHAPTER 56

Judge Thomas spent the next thirty minutes reading the instructions the jurors were to follow during deliberations.

When he finished, he looked to his bailiff. "Bailiff, escort the jury to the jury room to begin their deliberations." The bailiff stood, walked to the jury box, and indicated that the jury should follow him.

When the last juror exited the courtroom, Judge Thomas said, "Counsel, I want to thank you for conducting such a fine trial in my courtroom. I will be in chambers, and I suggest that you stick around for the remainder of the day. In my experience, if the jurors have any questions, they usually ask them in the first two hours of deliberation."

Katie sat down next to Sylvia. She could see that she was emotionally distraught. She took her hand and squeezed it gently.

Sylvia said, "Katie, I can't thank you enough for everything you've done. I'm embarrassed to say this, but I'm still thinking about that huge amount of money you asked the jury to award me. As you know, it's never been about money for me. I just wanted my life back and to reveal Dr. Pittsburgh for the fraud he is. I'm worried that the jurors are going to think I'm a gold-digger just looking for money."

Katie thought for a moment. "What would you like to happen?"

"My honor. My dignity."

"Let me think about it for a minute. Do you mind if I talk with Mr. Luxton?"

"No. Go ahead."

Katie walked over to the defense table and whispered to Luxton, "Could we talk outside for a moment?"

They left the courtroom and sat on the bench in the hallway.

Katie said, "Lamar, we both know what happened here, and my guess is that the jury is on our side. But once the jury comes back with a verdict, only one of us walks away the winner, and the other is the loser. I'm going to suggest that you pay Sylvia five million dollars, that Filmore University give her the PhD she rightfully deserves, and that Dr. Pittsburgh resign immediately. I also suggest that Filmore hire her as a full professor in the Department of Biochemistry. We can wrap this up right now."

Luxton started laughing. "Let me talk to my clients, and I'll get right back to you."

He walked back into the courtroom, and Katie stayed on the bench to gather her thoughts before going back inside.

A distinguished-looking man with an amazing head of gray hair and a Van Dyke beard to match approached her. During her chat with Luxton, she'd noticed him standing a discrete distance away. She'd also seen him sitting in the back of the courtroom during trial over the past couple of days and had decided that he was one of the many newspaper reporters monitoring the trial.

"Ms. Hornsby, may I have a minute of your time?"

Katie shook her head. "Sorry, I don't have time for an interview just now."

"I am not a reporter. Permit me to introduce myself. I am Jesper Kurland. I'm here on behalf of the Karolinski Institute in Sweden, more specifically, the Nobel Assembly." He handed Katie an embossed business card.

Katie stood and shook hands with him. "I apologize, sir. I certainly have time for you. Reporters have been constantly pestering me for comments during the trial. I've turned them down so often I mumble, 'No comment,' in my sleep."

He smiled. "You have a sharp wit. Much like your performance during trial. I will be quick about what I have to say. The Nobel Assembly is the committee that determines winners of the Nobel Prize each year. Due to the publicity that newspaper and television news have given this trial, the committee has concerns about Dr. Pittsburgh with regard to his status as a previous winner of a Nobel Prize. The committee is very protective and sensitive to any conduct of Nobel Prize winners that may have a negative impact on the integrity of the award. They have sent me here to evaluate the nature of the charges against Dr. Pittsburgh. Given the disclosures made by his daughter and other witnesses, as well as your client, I am prepared to recommend that the committee consider taking the Nobel Prize away from him. After the jury reaches a verdict, I would very much appreciate an opportunity to have a confidential chat with your client."

I know that my client will be receptive to such a meeting, and I agree that we should wait until after the case is resolved."

They shook hands again, and Katie returned to the courtroom. She reported the substance of her brief meeting with Kurland to Sylvia and Leslie. Sylvia was ecstatic.

Twenty minutes later, Luxton waved Katie over to a corner of the courtroom. "This is what we can do. Pittsburgh will not resign. Filmore is good with the awarding of the PhD and the full professorship, annual salary of two hundred thousand dollars until retirement at age sixty-five. Those two things and three hundred thousand dollars. One other thing we insist on is a confidentiality agreement. No disclosures to anyone. "

Katie shook her head. "Let me talk to Sylvia, but I know she will reject your offer. The only reason I'll relay this to her is because it's my professional obligation to disclose all potential offers."

Katie took Sylvia out to the hallway and explained the offer.

Sylvia said, "I like everything except the confidentiality requirement. I also want him to surrender his Nobel Prize, give it back. It's important to me that the whole world knows what kind of person he is."

Katie nodded. "My reaction to your receiving the doctoral degree and a professorship says to the world that you were right and Dr. Pittsburgh was wrong even if there is a non-disclosure agreement. In my opinion, the three hundred thousand dollars is an insult. My hunch is that they will pay a lot more, and I would like to work on that amount. Given the interest of the Nobel Committee in taking some action against him, I would surmise that taking his Nobel Prize away would bring him some negative publicity."

Sylvia smiled. "I didn't think about that. You are right. Go back and make them sweat about the no-tell aspect. Maybe the Swedes will take his Nobel Prize away. That's what I really want, and the jury can't do that."

Katie went back to Luxton, and they huddled in the corner again. She said to him, "The confidentiality agreement is going to cost your clients three million dollars. Everything else is good. Come up with the money, and we have a deal."

"I'll be right back." Five minutes later, Luxton came back to her.

"We've got a deal. Three million dollars, the PhD, and the non-disclosure agreement. Right?"

"Right. Let's go tell the judge before the jury comes back."

Judge Thomas invited the two lawyers into his chambers. "You have settled?"

They both nodded, and Katie told him the details.

"That's perfect, Katie. I'm happy for your client, and I agree it's best for both sides to resolve this. I don't like confidentiality agreements, but in this case, it makes good sense. You'll both be interested to know that the jury has just sent out a note that they have reached a verdict. They will be disappointed to find out the case is settled, but I have a nice little speech ready for situations like this. They'll go away feeling satisfied that they carried out their duties as jurors."

~ ~ ~

Mr. Kurland took Sylvia, Katie, and Leslie to lunch after the jury was discharged and the judge had given his farewell to the trial participants. After they were seated, he repeated everything he'd told Katie outside the courtroom. "I assume, Ms. Anderson, that you would have no objections to my recommendation that his Nobel Prize be taken away?"

Sylvia smiled. "None whatsoever. If there is anything I can do to help make that happen, please let me know."

The look on Sylvia's face was the first genuine smile Katie'd seen since they'd first met.

Mr. Kurland leaned toward Sylvia. "I must inform you about one factor that is very important to the committee. If they decide to take the prize away from Dr. Pittsburgh, they do so in secrecy. They abhor publicity, and an action like this

340

would cause all kinds of negative publicity worldwide. Inasmuch as you are the nominal complainant in this situation, you must agree to, likewise, keep this matter secret. Dr. Pittsburgh's name would silently be removed from the list of Nobel Prize winners, and he would be informed that any future claim by him of being a Nobel Prize recipient would result in a default judgment against him for the amount of money he received in obtaining the prize, plus interest from the date of receipt. That, of course, would be a considerable amount of money."

The smile on Sylvia's face disappeared. "How would I know it has been taken away if it's done in secret? And what could the committee do to me if I tell anyone?"

Kurland smiled. "Those are two good questions. The committee will notify you in writing that action has been taken, and it has no legal recourse against you whatsoever if you decide to disclose the information."

CHAPTER 57

That evening, Sylvia, Leslie, and Katie celebrated at dinner with Alex Hartley at their favorite Italian restaurant. After too much Italian food and wine, Leslie and Katie left the party and took a cab to their apartment.

Leslie said, "You notice what I noticed?"

"I think so."

"I think our boy Alex is going to get laid tonight."

Katie laughed. "I was surprised they didn't do it right in front of us at the table. And I was wishing Dr. Judd was there to console me."

"He'd do more than console you, honey."

"In my dreams."

They both laughed hard.

Leslie looked at Katie and smiled. "I've got something important to tell you. While you were busy settling the case, the judge called me into his chambers. He wants me to clerk for him for a year when I pass the Michigan bar exam. He's been appointed by the president to the federal bench and will move to that court in two months.

Katie's eyes opened wide. "Are you kidding?"

Leslie shook her head. "No, I'm not. I told him I would."

Katie leaned over and hugged her best friend. "That is wonderful. I am so happy for you. I'll miss you terribly, but it is the best thing that could ever happen to a new lawyer."

EPILOGUE

Six weeks later, Sylvia received a letter from the Nobel Committee advising her that Dr. Pittsburgh's Nobel Prize had been taken away. She set the letter down in front of her on the table and thought for a few moments about everything that had happened in her life since the trial had ended. Rather than accept the teaching position at Filmore that the settlement called for, she'd received a better offer from another institution, which she'd immediately accepted.

She then read the announcement in the *Detroit Medical News* to Alex during breakfast at his apartment. "The Detroit College of Medicine is pleased to announce the appointment of Dr. Sylvia Anderson as full professor in the Department of Biochemistry. She will also serve as Assistant Director of the Detroit Poison Center under Dr. Alex Hartley."

She added, "I particularly like the 'under Dr. Alex Hartley' part. I liked it last night, and I know I'd like it again this morning." She grinned at Alex.

He looked at his watch. "We've got time. Plenty of time."

ABOUT THE AUTHORS

ABOUT THE AUTHORS

Tom Bleakley is a trial lawyer who specializes in cases against the pharmaceutical industry as well as pro bono cases involving constitutional issues and matter of public interest. He has an extensive background in medicine and pharmacology, a Ph.D. in developmental psychology and has represented many children with prescription-caused birth defects in his trial experiences against the drug industry. In addition to previous novels dealing with the dangers of prescription drugs, Tom has co-authored a two-volume textbook, "A Teaching Program in Psychiatry."

Marcia Lange was born and raised in a small Connecticut town, the middle child of five. Upon graduation from high school, she struck out for the big city to find her future. By accident or, as she says, desperate need, she began a career in financial services which she thought would be temporary and, to her surprise, retired after a highly successful 35 years. While climbing the ladder to success in a predominately male industry with a very thick glass ceiling, Marcia raised two sons and instilled in them the importance of hard work and dedication as a path to achieving success in life. This was the era of super moms, women who did it all and strived for perfection in every aspect of life. Her children were introduced to books as she read to them each evening beginning in infancy. Gift giving occasions always included a new book or two. Upon retiring, Marcia embarked on a journey to see the world. She needed to share her experiences with family and friends and began photographing and writing about her travels in a daily blog. She received many compliments on her writings as was told by many that her daily posts were anxiously awaited and enjoyed. Her love for reading and writing was enhanced by becoming a beta reader for a friend and a new journey, to do some writing of her own, resulted in her co-authoring **Conundrum**, her debut novel. Recently, she has developed a philanthropic passion for inspiring disadvantaged children to achieve greatness. Currently one can find her splitting her time between CT and FL writing, playing golf, cooking, and reading. Always reading!

ABSOLUTELY AMA⚡ING eBOOKS

AbsolutelyAmazingEbooks.com
or AA-eBooks.com